ARGUA

V. Keifs

Argua

First Edition: 2023

ISBN: 9781524318185
ISBN eBook: 9781524328177

© of the text:
   V. Keifs

© Layout, design and production of this edition: 2023 EBL

Dedicated to my beloved parents,
Vicente and Kaye, for being my reason to live.

To Celia, for blessing me
with true friendship and sisterhood.

To Mauricio, for being the kind of friend
who brings light to a dark day.

To the Jain family, for saving my life.
And to Gabriel, an angel true to his name.
Because in this life, love and gratitude should be shown.

شکریہ

Table of Contents

The Caucasian man entered the African village alone. As he watched one of the villagers approach him, walking half naked and barefoot, his instinct told him that this time there would be no resistance from the tribe. The African stood before him speaking his native tongue, which was unknown to the white man, who directly took his stick, and without saying a word to the African, drew a triangle on the earthen ground they were standing on. Then, the African showed the stranger the way to a distant hill of red stone. Once there, the man stopped and pointed the visitor to the top of a huge boulder.

"Is it there?" he asked aloud, knowing the African would not understand, but to his astonishment, the native answered with a simple yes.

"Is it because it is an albino?" asked the Caucasian.

"No, because of animals," said the African, starting to climb towards the summit.

Despite not understanding the answer, the traveler followed the other until he reached the top. Once there, to his astonishment, he saw a series of carvings of signs and triangles under his feet and on the walls of an agglomeration of rocks, which were shaped like a basket that left a large hole in what seemed to be a hill. As if that were not enough, to one side lay a lion, several cheetahs, and a cackle of hyenas, surrounding a cave.

"Here albino give luck, everyone want albino... Hunt albino, cut albino, sell, or keep albino, for luck... But animals defend magic child... We protect albino, but no one can protect us from animals."

The stranger grasped the stick in the middle and twisted it in his hands as if frustrated. Instantly, two sharp golden blades protruded from each end of the elaborately crafted stick, creating a double-edged weapon. Seeing this, the African quickly fled the scene, rushing down the rocky hill and alerting the village with his screams. The screams reached the ears of a small creature white as snow but with African features; the famous albino that the Caucasian man was looking for.

When the creature crawled out of the cave it was exposed to the dangers of the scorching sun and was completely blinded by the bright sunlight, its body covered in burns. But despite how weakened it looked, it seemed to be calm and relying on the protection of the ferocious animals that surrounded it.

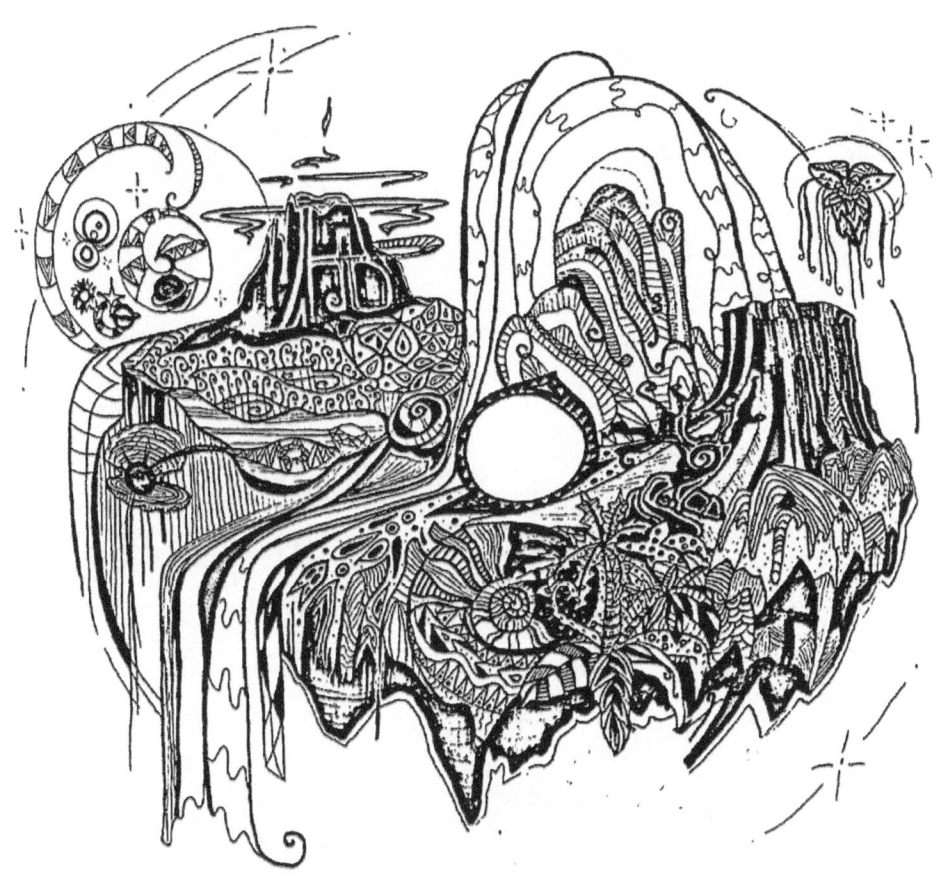

Chapter 1
Midnight Stories

"Grandma! Grandma!" the children could be heard shouting throughout the house.

"What's the matter, kids, what's all the fuss about?" the old woman asked from her rocking chair where she was reading a book by the fireplace.

"We've seen it, Grandma... We've seen it..." whispered the older of the two children, almost breathless.

The old woman, who had her back to them, was silent for a few moments as she slowly closed the book and looked into the fire, which seemed to have changed color and lessened in intensity, while the children waited anxiously for their grandmother to pay attention to them.

"What exactly did you see?"

The older one held her tongue when she noticed her grandmother's strange reaction, but the little boy plucked up the courage to speak by hiding behind his sister with only his head peeking out from under her arm.

"Argua, Grandma."

The old woman looked them straight in the eye.

"And... where did you see it, little ones?" she asked.

"At the lake. Old Bill warned us not to go there, but James ran away, and I had to go after him. We were playing by the lake, and then we saw something shining. James picked it up and it started to snow, Grandma!" Sasha exclaimed.

"Christmas!" shouted the little boy with a big grin on his face, as it was his favorite time of year.

"I was going to take it out of his hands, but Bill came yelling, so we ran home to show it to you. I think it's a magic stone, Grandma," said the girl.

"What an imagination you have, my little ones," replied the old woman, smiling and going on with her reading.

Sasha looked at her brother and nudged him, which made him move closer to their grandmother. He stood motionless behind the rocking chair where the old woman was sitting.

"Children, Grandma needs to rest. You have given me too much excitement today with your stories. You have a great imagination, just like your grandfather. He was always telling amazing stories."

James looked at Sasha not knowing what to do. She gestured with her hands, "Come on! What are you waiting for!", so the young boy walked over to stand in front of his grandmother and held out his hand.

"My Dear, I don't have any candy," the woman replied before looking up at him. She peered over the top of her reading glasses at a tiny turquoise gem on the little boy's palm.

"Ohhhhh," the old woman whispered as her eyes misted and lit up when she noticed the tiny stone.

"Take it, Grandma."

The woman brought her decrepit fingers close to the gem, but stopped short, as if the emotion of the moment had blocked her or something prevented her.

"Where did you say you found it?" the old woman asked.

"On the shore of the lake, Grandma," replied the little boy.

"Are you all right, Grandma?" asked her granddaughter.

The woman rose from her chair with great excitement, albeit slowly due to her age, and went straight to the bookshelf to grab a volume. She then opened the large book in question. It contained within it a huge, dried leaf from some kind of exotic plant. The old woman sat back down in her chair, took out the curious leaf and told the little boy to put the stone on it so that she would not have to touch the gem with her own hand. She seemed to be trembling a little from excitement.

James obeyed. He took the stone and put it in the center of the leaf, and for a few moments there was only silence while his grandmother looked carefully at the gem on the dried leaf for a while. The children watched in puzzlement, wondering if the poor woman had gone gaga, when suddenly the bract began to turn its tips towards the center, as if trying to wrap the jewel, but due to its dryness, it began to crack, and little flakes detached from it, falling from the palm of the old woman's hand.

"Run, children, bring a glass jar with water!"

The siblings reacted instantly, captivated by the excitement of the moment, and searched the house for an empty jam or jelly jar. They turned the kitchen upside down. Once they found one, they ran back to the sitting room where their startled grandmother was waiting anxiously.

"Here, Grandma!" she proffered.

"Water, children! Quickly!"

The little ones took the pitcher of water their grandmother used for daily rehydration, which was constantly refilled by the help to quench the lady's extreme thirst, especially during her long hours of reading in front of the fire in her private parlor. They poured the water into the empty jar, which the old lady held in her hands, until it was full, spilling the rest on the bluish Persian rug that practically covered the entire floor of the small study.

"Sorry, Grandma," Sasha apologized as she wet the floor.

"It is only water, my love. Now watch carefully." The old woman promptly put the crumpled leaf and the gem within it, along with the remaining pieces of leaf, inside the jar, which she immediately closed with the lid, and stood silently observing its interior practically without blinking. After a few moments, James impatiently inquired, "What are you looking at, Grandma?"

"Shhhhhh! Give it time," she said quietly. After a few seconds, the leaf began to hydrate and take shape with the loose pieces placed in the jar. It took on a lurid green color as the plant was brought back to life. After this, it began to rotate, slowly transforming itself into a soft silk wrapper, until the gem was completely sealed by the magical leaf. By the time it stopped moving, it was levitating in the water, right in the center of the jar, suspended between the surface and the glass bottom of the container. Then Grandma opened it and tried to reach inside to pull out what had formed inside, but the opening was too small, so she asked little James to pull it out for her.

The jewel had completely merged with the leaf, like a precious green stone, with a smooth texture and clear-cut appearance, as if it had been polished by a professional. The most curious thing is that after a while of being out of the water, it turned white, with the same brightness and luster of a pearl, although somewhat larger.

"That's it!" the old woman announced.

"That's it?" he inquired.

"Yes."

Grandma got up, picked up the precious object and went to the desk in the sitting room. There she took a pile of papers, put them on the table, and placed the beautiful stone on top of them. "A wonderful paperweight!" she announced.

"A paperweight?" the children repeated, perplexed.

Grandma laughed, looking at the dumb expression on the children's faces.

"All this for a paperweight?! I don't understand it at all... And the stories you were telling us? I thought they were true and that the stone came from those places you were telling us about, because it's magic! How did you know that would happen with the leaf? And why did you keep it in a book?" her granddaughter wanted to know.

"Shhh. Shhhhh! Enough with all these questions," the grandmother interrupted them as she sat down exhausted in the rocking chair. "You must never tell anyone about what happened. Do you understand?" demanded the old woman.

"But Grandma!" the little boy rejoined.

"You want answers. I understand. but to understand you must be ready." After saying this, the grandmother turned to them and, looking the little girl straight in the eye, asked, "Do you think you are ready?"

"Yes, Grandma, I am!" she exclaimed firmly.

"What I am about to explain to you can never leave this room. You must promise me on your brother's life."

Sasha looked at James and nodded her head.

"Well, make yourself comfortable! But first, bring your grandma a pitcher of water."

Sasha ran downstairs to the kitchen, where she hurriedly filled the pitcher. Because she wanted to get back to the sitting room as quickly as possible, she slopped the water all over the corridors of the mansion. That huge house could easily frighten a girl of her age, especially at that late hour, and the immensity of the building with its high ceilings made it colder. It was as big as it was dark, and any person simply wanting to go to the bathroom could easily get lost.

Sasha's every step created a small echo that resonated throughout the empty rooms of the mansion. Sometimes it took several seconds to hear the echo of her footstep, which gave the impression that there was another person at the other end of the hallway, hidden in the darkness. But the most terrifying area for the girl at that time of night was the great main staircase, not because of the sounds as she climbed it, but because of the energy that could be sensed in it; an energy sometimes as palpable as the prickling of the skin when immersed in icy water, which leaves it taut and the hairs standing on end for ages. Thus, if she had to go up it, Sasha made sure to do it in a hurry, holding her breath, so as to get to the second floor as soon as possible.

Once at the top, she would stop dead in her tracks and lean her back against the wall opposite her. She then looked to see if anyone or anything was following her, even though she knew that was impossible, seeing that it was all a figment of her imagination. But her fantasies and fears were uncontrollable. The panic they provoked in her could overwhelm her gullible self with the fear, or rather terror, of the dark, and she had to turn on the lights of the house, perfectly coordinating them with wherever she had to go, so as not to wander for a second in total darkness. After checking as usual that no one was following her, Sasha entered the room completely out of breath.

"You look like you've run a marathon, my dear," her grandmother remarked when she saw her arrive.

"I'm sorry, Grandma, it was too dark," Sasha confessed.

"Someday, little one, you will see that fear as something so insignificant that you won't even remember it. Walking down a hallway in the dark will be as easy as breathing."

The girl looked at her grandmother doubtfully. Clearly, neither her grandmother nor anyone else understood the suffering she went through daily; the inner fear she had to deal with twenty-four hours a day. She tried to control it in front of her family and guests. But it was a constant battle to strengthen her courage as she tried to overcome the daily agony of that horrible phobia which prevented her from enjoying a calm, normal life, and so altered her emotional state that it left her tormented to the point of sleepless nights. She used to go for days and even weeks without sleep, despite her young age. This was not the only phobia the poor girl had. She was also afraid of the water in the sea or lakes. She was afraid of their dark depths and of the unknown that lay in the abyss, since the worst of her fears was to be devoured by some sea creature or, worse still, to die by drowning. Poor Sasha felt completely misunderstood. So, she avoided talking about her fears and just tried to ignore them. But this only made her seem reticent, inhibited, and shy.

"You were going to tell me a story, remember?" the girl remarked after putting down the pitcher.

"Oh, yes... My memory is not what it used to be, dear."

Grandma took a big gulp of water, gazing at the fire and, without taking her eyes off the flames, she began to speak.

"A long, long time ago, long before you were born..."

"Where did the stone come from?" James interrupted her, excitedly. "What powers does it have? Why was it in the lake?"

"Don't be in such a hurry, little one, everything in its own time."

Grandma looked out of the circular window and saw through the glass a sky covered with gray clouds. "A storm is brewing," she thought. And after a brief silence, she continued her story with her eyes fixed on the window.

"There was a storm here when I was just a girl. A tremendous storm that made history worldwide, not just because of its magnitude, but because of the peculiarity of a mysterious hole that formed in its core, right over the lake where you were playing today.

"The storm was of such caliber that people in the area thought that the end of the world was coming. A more rational assumption was that the hole between the thick clouds covering our land presaged the arrival of a hurricane which, for the first time in history, would devastate the entire area. The truth is that it was something that had never been seen before. It was a kind of inverted tornado. I mean, the spiral of the cyclone, which forms its column, did not descend towards the earth, and affect the town. No, this one was different. Instead of making contact with the ground, it soared into infinity, out beyond the atmosphere and towards outer space, like a kind of tunnel or black hole. That helix of dark, gray, and white clouds, which covered the entire sky like a large Danish, spun around the enormous hole in the center that absorbed all the cloud within its reach. It expanded like a cotton blanket for miles and miles around until it reached the black hole at its epicenter, which the universe had created in some inexplicable way.

"It drifted over the town like a thick, heavy ceiling and the hole in it grew smaller and smaller, marking out the heart of the storm, which was right over what used to be the mansion's beautiful, verdant grassland. It was not until after the end of that natural disaster that the beautiful lake first appeared and replaced the lovely meadow that once stood on our land. It is still here with us nowadays as a reminder of what happened that day.

"The dimensions that the storm attained were such that from its center it spread out over the great house of Courdeil and its environs, reaching the distant villages and even the capital. The colossal downpour, which was accompanied by a terrible gale that emitted a roar like that of a gigantic raging beast, was of such immensity that, despite being good English folk who are accustomed to the daily rains of our beloved England, we ran to shelter in our houses, fearing that the sky would fall on us. Squalls of rain, hail and blizzards swept through the area like a bloodthirsty raging typhoon, lashing people with such aggression that it tore their clothes and almost broke their skin.

"The whole town and the surrounding area were completely deserted. The entire population had immediately taken cover out of a fear so great that even the most skeptical took to praying that day.

"Crops were wiped out. Property was devastated. The horrible experience of those who were not fortunate enough to make it to safety in time left their loved ones bruised and scarred for life. It was a miracle that humans were only injured as, despite having a greater sensitivity to danger than we do, numerous animals in the area were not so fortunate. Many pets that were tied up or caged outdoors were abandoned to their fate when their owners fled in search of shelter.

"There is no justification for such cruelty. Even though people were terrified and had little time to think or react that day, there is no excuse for what they did. They just ran for cover to save their own skins without thinking of anyone but themselves. This is the most primeval of human instincts which is triggered in extreme circumstances; that is when the true spirit that dwells in each of us shows itself.

"But, during the worst moment, when the chaos erupted most severely over our land, out of all that selfish and cowardly mob, a vintage car appeared, the only vehicle on the road. In spite of the aggressiveness of the squall and the poor visibility, which had evicted all forms of life from the streets, it moved through that hellish environment, wobbling around, weaving crazy esses along the village roads and freeways, dodging every obstacle that was thrown in its path as it tried to maintain a steady course towards our mansion.

"Few of the locals, who heard the honking of the horn amidst the sound of the blizzard and thunder, imagined that the reckless driver might be the young Squire of Courdeil, as he was called in the village. Your grandfather. And so, while the masses stayed hidden, Charles, as he was called by those who knew him, enjoyed the adrenaline rush of the moment, for such opportunities did not come his way every day. An adventurous, thrill-seeking soul like his could not let that unique moment pass him by, not even for the safety of the damsel he was courting at the time and who was riding shotgun inside his car at that very moment.

"For the lad, that moment was an opportunity to put the young girl to the test. In those days, it was difficult to gauge how avidly and fearlessly a woman might engage in novel experiences; especially if her behavior was deemed inappropriate for a lady and, thus, risked her becoming a victim of gossip. Girls always have been, and even today still are, raised differently from siblings. They were not raised to think for themselves without fitting the profile created for females within the patriarchal system in which we live. The accepted wisdom is that girls are burdened with the regret that they have a sell by date for beauty and marriage; procreation and family; and having to choose between family and career. But for Charles, women were much more than that. He liked to surround himself with the most intelligent and extraordinary women in the world, as, according to him, nobody learned more than from these creatures, since, despite having the whole world against them, they dominated both the feminine and the masculine sides equally, and that, in his view, made them the strongest beings in the universe.

"You see, your grandfather wanted to change the world. But even someone as passionate and wealthy as he was, after so many attempts to fight against the inequality and injustices of this planet and its societies, felt he was beginning to lose hope. In the long run, this demotivated him, and a few months later, led him to a melancholy, which culminated in a devastating acceptance stemming from his fear that he would not find a woman who did not have the stigma engraved on her skin of believing that her inevitable destiny, in the society in which she lived, was to 'fit in and please a man'. For this reason, trying to adapt to the circumstances, he stopped looking for that rebellious little jewel and started dating any girl, even though it was tremendously disheartening for him to see so much ingenuity and creativity thrown away because of the ridiculous expectations imposed on her by her own gender.

"His anti-establishment stance aroused envy among the other men in the area as his progressive, open-mindedness, by which he empathized with the opposite sex, made him irresistible in the eyes of any girl or woman, not to mention his being cushioned by an incredible fortune," the old woman commented.

"Grandma, the story..." begged the little boy, uninterested in the topic.

"Shut up, James, don't be stupid!" said Sasha, who understood the importance of what her grandmother was saying.

"Well, the couple in question were laughing inside that beautiful Bentley inherited from your great-grandfather, Charles' father, whom he almost never saw during his lifetime, because he was always abroad or far away. So, when the storm intensified, your grandfather didn't hesitate to accelerate, not caring that the automobile's paint was beginning to chip and peel off until the bodywork was exposed. The gentleman was indifferent to his inheritance. Fortunately, or unfortunately, he did not appreciate the value of material things. Instead, he knew how to enjoy everything that he had within his grasp, without limits, the way it was or as it was offered to him at the time, and he did not know his father well enough to respect what had once been his. She recollected that he could be distant; a stranger even; and that he was isolated from his family. But above all, he was the kind of person who did not think long or hard before launching into whatever had caught his fancy. He was characteristically impulsive, both in word and deed, with a tremendous drive for good, but, unfortunately, also for bad.

"But Charles, your grandfather, was all heart, with a soul charged with passion and devotion to his loved ones," said Grandma, cutting off the narration of the story as she clutched her chest in a grief provoked by the memory of the man she once loved.

The Mansion

Grandma grabbed the armrests of the armchair and exclaimed theatrically:

"Cour!!! Courdeil!!!!! For God's sake, Charles!!!!" she shouted. "That's what the girl said, between nervous laughs, as she clung on to the arm of your young grandfather and buried her face in his shoulder so as to avoid looking out of the car window. She was terrified to be out in the great storm.

"Your grandfather tried to calm the young woman by telling her that they were almost home as he drove the hail damaged car through the heavy rain. He barely made it in one piece to the large gates, beyond which lay the mansion's drive, which were chained and padlocked shut. With no one to open them, Charles had only one option left. 'Hold on tight and don't look straight ahead!'

he told her as he stomped on the gas and rammed the Bentley into the locked gates. When they didn't give way, he backed the Bentley up and rammed the gates again. He repeated this several times before he managed to break through the gates, leaving part of the car's skeleton exposed to the storm.

"Once inside the grounds, he skidded his way up the muddy drive and onto the sweep of gravel edged with lawn that surrounded the front of the mansion and brought the car to a halt just inches from the first step.

"Almost instantly, two maids rushed out of the front door with a wooden table over their heads, with a gap between them, and began calling: 'Miss! Miss! Come under the table, please! Hurry, Miss! We'll take you inside the house, where you'll be safe!'

"The girl, who accompanied your grandfather as his passenger, jumped out of the car and ran, covering her head with her arms which were protected by white opera gloves that reached almost to her shoulders and thus protected her skin, until she reached the safety of the plank. 'Take her inside, quick!' Charles commanded from inside the car as the wood of the table began to crack from the tremendous blows it was receiving from the sharp pieces of ice thrown down on it from that infernal sky.

"The maids obeyed their master and immediately returned for him, but Charles had noticed with concern an overturned carriage at the side of the house. 'What happened? What's that carriage doing there? Is my mother all right?' he asked them from inside the car as the storm cracked the windshield into a spider's web pattern.

"'Yes, sir, your mother is all right! We took the carriage out as a first resort to protect them, but the horse didn't hold out long in the storm, even with leather armor, and ran away, overturning the carriage,' said one of the maids with concern, because the horses were her responsibility as stable maid.

'Which horse was it and where is it now?' asked Charles.

"'It's Dumper, sir. He went into the forest, sir! I'm very sorry, but lucky, he will have been able to find shelter. He is a very strong horse, so he is most likely all right, but we won't know for sure until the storm has passed. Now, please sir, you must take cover. Please come before the table breaks on us. It is too dangerous to be out here, sir,' wailed one of the maids in distress.

"'Thank you for your concern! Tell my mother I'll be right back,' replied the young man as he released the handbrake. 'Go inside now. Quickly! That's an order!' Charles shouted to them.

"He drove what was left of the car, which now moved like a drunken snail, over the muddy grass in the direction of the forest that belonged to the manor of Courdeil. He hoped to find the animal safe and sound under one of the enormous canopies of the magnificent trees with which the forest abounded. Fortunately, the hail began to diminish, but a strange mist appeared out of nowhere and in a matter of moments everything was transformed.

"From the sky our lands must have looked like they were a watercolor, turning from faded green to a watery brown; a sad painting created by the droplets of the fine drizzle that was rinsing the ground. Meanwhile, the car kept lurching from point to point, leaving deep tire tracks in its wake. But Charles wasn't the only one making his way as best he could through the crazy landscape. Several animals appeared in front of him along the way, including a herd of deer whose bodies were peppered with wounds from the heavy hailstones. Disoriented by the lights of the vehicle and the poor visibility, the poor things were running frantically. Despite having slowed right down, the downpour was making it difficult to drive over the soggy terrain. Eventually, the Bentley, or rather what was left of it, crashed into a mossy stone wall.

"In the meantime, the maids and the rest of the servants who looked after the Courdeil family waited anxiously inside the mansion along with the girl the young master had brought with him. She was desperately looking for her beloved through the cracked and rain-streaked windows through which nothing could be seen. Charles's mother, who sat in solemn silence, watched her indifferently as she waited for her son. She had a chair next to a three-tiered fountain, which stood in the middle of the hall immediately behind the huge, weathered, wooden front door, which was decorated with irons studs that had rusted over time and were now an orange-brown color. The fountain was something to behold being fashioned out of artificial stones that imitated large turquoises and white shells that resembled magnolia leaves. Because of the unusual curvature in the shells' design, the water meandered aesthetically around the delicate edges and made a considerable impression on visitors as they entered the house.

"The young woman sat on the edge of the fountain, in the center of the high-ceilinged circular hall with its large dome, enjoying the hypnotic sound of the rain falling on the cupola above her and watching the rivers of water sliding down its glass panes. At the sides of the hall, there were arches that led into the adjoining rooms. The walls between these arcades were adorned with paintings of large-leaved mahogany trees decorated with flowers and fruits that gave them a most exquisite decorative touch. This was enhanced by the real vines which, emerging from small crevices that opened between the floor and the walls, climbed between them. On both sides of the hall, there were wooden benches with the varnish worn off by the passage of time and their copper tacks coated in verdigris. They had been placed there to allow the magical ambience of the room to be fully admired.

"Behind the fountain, the curve of the back wall was interrupted by a grand staircase which, after a few lower steps, was blocked by a wall which forced it to divide into two flights of stairs that curved away in opposite directions to arrive at different places on the second floor. The walls of this magnificent entrance hall blended perfectly with the fountain, the dome, the arches, the plants, both painted and real, and the spectacular staircase.

"This curious wall that bisected the staircase was adorned on each side with a stone engraved to simulate a marble pearl that rested on a tongue of stone that hung down the wall, which in turn was surrounded by shells sculpted in plaster with radial striations in the shape of webbed fingers. When viewed from afar it looked like a massive marine shell; seen up close the detail and expression of these human extremities seemed as real as looking at one's own fingers digging their nails into wet plaster.

"Now imagine this incredible architectural work of art in its entirety; from its glorious door, passing its fountain surrounded by arches and painted walls replete with authentic flora, to its unusual, curved staircases. The hall had clearly been designed to impress anyone who walked through the huge front door.

"Imagine how Charles's mother would have felt sitting there listening to the torrential rain. She surely appreciated that she was uniquely privileged despite the dark mood which had engulfed the room because of the remorselessly ferocious storm; a storm which was so brutally violent that the servants became overwhelmed by it and knew that it would be ingrained in their memories for as long as they lived. In years to come, though, they would discover a hitherto unknown pleasure: the joy having survived against the odds.

"There were so many people there that they could not all fit in the room, so some of them went up the stairs to make more space. When those people looked over the ornate railings, they discovered an extraordinary, new perspective as, even though the day was dull, the light combined with the magnificent designs to give the illusion that they were not indoors but outside. If one were to look at the outside of the mansion, one would appreciate the tricks used by the architect to let more light into the interior of the house. Due to the high ceilings, a second set of circular windows was placed above those of the first floor, and it was through these that people standing on the stairs could view the grounds.

"In this way, the building created the illusion that it had three floors instead of only two, as the exterior facade exhibited three rows of windows. The round windows of the central row were simple lights, subtly tinted with soft shades of bluish green," their grandmother told them.

"Grandma, the mansion you're talking about in your story, is it this house?" asked the little girl.

"Yes, dear, but everything I have described to you is practically forgotten now. The paint is worn, and the plants are dead. The façade and the round windows are hidden under the ivy and other plants that have covered the outside of the house. But let's get on with the story," Grandma suggested, and continued her narration using the different voices.

"'Where is Charles?' your great-grandmother asked.

"'The young master didn't want to come in and went in search of his horse,' one of the maids answered. 'Do you want us to go and look for him?'

"'No, no. Stay here and bring some tea to... Excuse me, dear, what's your name?' Charles's mother asked, looking uncertainly at the young woman her son had brought home.

"'Sara, ma'am. My name is Sara,' replied the girl with a curtsey, trying to conceal her excitement as she introduced herself to the mistress of Courdeil.

"'All right, Sara, sit down and have a nice, hot cup of tea. And I'll have a cup too, please,' the lady instructed the maids. Then, noticing that both the poor girls were soaked through, continued, 'Ah, you had better go and change your clothes first or you'll catch your deaths of cold.'

"'Yes, ma'am. Thank you, ma'am,' the two maids replied before scurrying away.

"'Don't worry about my son, really. Everything will be fine,' she told Sara reassuringly. 'I trust him completely. He's impulsive, but he has my intuition and his father's instincts; I'm sure he'll be alright. As soon as the storm abates, he'll be back, and if not, we'll go look for him. I would know how to find my son even if he were a needle in a haystack,' your great-grandmother explained with a mischievous smile as she closed one eye and peered with the other as if looking through an imaginary magnifying glass, to reassure those present by her confidence and composure.

"So, while the maids were getting changed, other servants fetched sandwiches and a tea tray set for two.

"'No. This isn't right. Prepare tea and sandwiches for everyone and serve it on the big table,' my mother-in-law ordered them.

"'But, ma'am, you have a guest,' one of her maids objected.

"'I'm sure Sara will be more than delighted to have tea at the same table as the servants and the stable maids on a day as exceptional as this. Besides, in this house, whoever works for me not only respects the house and its routines but is also part of the family. That's what living together is all about. And here we know everything about everyone, don't we?' remarked your great-grandmother, looking at Betty, the maid who had brought the tea. Betty responded with a subtle wink at Sara as she picked the tray up again with an elegant delicacy.

"'In this house we are a family, a real one, Miss Sara,' said Betty, addressing the guest, who was perplexed by the maid's boldness.

"'Excuse me, Betty. It was Betty, wasn't it? What did you mean by a real family?'

"The maid stopped gracefully and, giving a gentle toss of her head, turned to the young woman.

"'From woman to woman, sometimes a heart and mind can be more attached than blood ties. I think you get my drift since you and Charles seem to be very close, in spite of your, um... differences.

"Sara was quite taken aback hearing the maid mention the master of the house by his first name and, on top of that, address her with such confidence, for she was of the upper-class and a guest.

"'Ma'am, I vehemently believe that you should curb your maid's attitude, or she may end up hoodwinking you, or worse, finishing up with your son in her bed. It would not be the first time that a servant girl has used a bastard child as a way to get set up for life,' Miss Sara said, visibly shaken.

"But we must return to Charles. By now the fog had thickened in the forest so that not even the car's headlights were able to penetrate it but, despite the lack of visibility, Charles was vainly trying to start-up the Bentley after the collision. Although the hail had mercifully stopped, the sky was still weeping its torrents, and the thick, black clouds made it seem like midnight. Undeterred, your grandfather got out of the car and started walking blindly through the dense fog, which seemed to thin the deeper he went into the forest. Confounded by this, Charles looked at the sky through the treetops and discovered a curious nucleus set in the center of that stormy spiral, a hole surrounded by a cluster of pink clouds that spread with the slight movement of the helix. And as he watched, the spiral started changing color, going from white to gray and then to almost black, like a giant worm coiling up on itself and covering the whole sky.

"'Damn it!' Charles shouted when he stumbled and hit his forehead against one of the trees. 'Brrrrfffffff. Hhihhhhhhhh,' whinnied the horse in response to the sound of his master's voice. 'Dumper!' Charles cried in astonishment as he rubbed his forehead which still smarted from the blow.

"Then he noticed that the fog had almost dispersed in that patch of woodland, which allowed him to look round, and see the horse, its leather armor lacerated by the storm, no more than five feet away from him. But something didn't add up. As he drew closer to the animal, he noticed that there seemed to be a line between where he was and the place where Dumper was standing. Something strange was going on, but he couldn't figure out what. So, trusting his instincts, he walked slowly through the rain toward the steed. But when he stretched out his arm towards the horse, he was astonished to discover that it seemed to have passed through a curtain of water, the other side of which was free of rain. He boldly strode forward into the area where the wily Dumper awaited him, which was completely dry.

"Turning all the way around, he observed in amazement that the outer fringes of the grove were encircled by a wall of droplets which separated it from the rest of the woods. 'It is just as if the strange spiral above me is creating different rotating microclimates as it changes color,' he mused.

"Suddenly, something knocked into his back, propelling him through the rain curtain, which soaked him again.

"'Dumper, my friend,' Charles crooned as he stroked the horse and removed the leather armor which, being saturated, seemed to weigh a ton. But when he tried to get on the animal's back, he discovered that his feet had sunk deep into the ground. 'Whoa, boy, hold still,' he said soothingly to Dumper as he tried to free himself from the sticky mud and remove it from his shoes, but the weight of the water and the remains of mud on his clothes prevented him from moving with any agility.

"At last, after a long time struggling against the loam and covered from head to foot with dirt, Charles had an idea. Clinging on to the harness, he gave Dumper a slap on the haunches, which made him bolt, pulling your grandfather out of the ground like a carrot. As the animal galloped away, Charles struggled to keep his balance, but when eventually the mount slowed, he was able to bring him under control.

Looking up at the sky, he discovered that the hole he had seen earlier had grown much larger and deeper, revealing a pink funnel in its interior, which curiously narrowed as it rose into the firmament.

"'Come on, my friend, let's see what the hell this marvel up there is.' Advancing at a slow pace because of the muddy ground, they headed towards the center of that bizarre hub. Suddenly, something cold brushed their faces. Out of the corner of his eye Charles glimpsed something silky white floating through the air. It took him a moment or two to realize what it was. 'Snow. My friend, it's snow! Isn't it fascinating? But how is it possible?' he laughed awestruck that it could be snowing in the middle of June, as he held out his hand to catch the thickly falling flakes.

"By now, chilled to the bone, they had arrived at the epicenter of the storm. It sat right over the vast grassy clearing which lay in a hollow in the middle of the woods. Charles had known it his whole life and Bill kept his tools in a shed there. But what had that very morning been a meadow, was now an enormous ice shelf. The immense amount of rain and hail that had fallen had first flooded it and then the plummeting temperatures had frozen it. He earnestly hoped that Bill hadn't been in his shed and wondered what he would make of it when he saw it the way it was now.

"'I don't know which I prefer,' he quipped sarcastically, to evade the disquiet that was beginning to bubble up in him.

The Servants

"Far from the ice, the huge door of the mansion burst open and a blast of wind laden with rain flooded the entire entrance.

'Charles?!' Miss Sara shouted.

"But it wasn't Charles. It was a gigantic, thickset, colored man, soaked and smeared with mud from head to toe, who blocked the doorway with his massive frame.

'Bill!' exclaimed Betty, the sassy and sensuous maid, who was petite and pretty.

'Go to him, my dear,' said her mistress. Betty gratefully ran to give Bill a hug.

'I'm fine, my precious,' he reassured her, treating her with the utmost gentleness.

'Bill, go and change, please, and then join us for tea,' your great-grandmother ordered him, and then added, 'You must be freezing.'

"'Ma'am, if I told you what I just saw, you wouldn't believe me, and I know you would want to set out right now to see it for yourself,' he replied. His voice was deep and gruff, but also warm.

"'How can the lady go out in this weather? Are you crazy?' demanded the young guest in rebuke.

"'Oh, no, my dear young lady,' your great-grandmother replied with a smile. 'This gentleman is the person I would trust most with my life.'

"'But, Mrs. de Courdeil, though I understand that living here alone may make you feel the need for a family to protect you, a woman in your position surely has a duty to maintain the distinction between rank and service. It is my opinion that your staff are far too over familiar and are overstepping the bounds of decorum. If I may be candid, you should not tolerate that kind of behavior, least of all, public displays of affection between staff, such as we have just witnessed, when they are supposed to be working,' Sara, who was horrified, rebuked. 'From the lack of wedding rings on their fingers, it is evident that they are not even married!' she continued before turning to Betty and Bill. 'I suggest that if you wish to continue in your employment, you should restrain yourselves, and show more respect for the lady of the house, her son and her guests,' Sara counseled.

"'If I could, I would marry Betty in the blink of an eye,' the big man exclaimed. 'I'm sorry to have bothered you, miss,' he apologized with his head bowed. 'But if you'll excuse me, I'll go and change now.'

"'If you really love and respect her, you should propose to her and put an engagement ring on her finger and not leave it at mere lip service,' replied Sara getting up from the table.

"'Goodness gracious, Bill, haven't you noticed?' Betty said shyly, leaning her head with a sweet smile on the man's huge shoulder.

"'You can't notice what you can't see, my love. When a beautiful flower appears before you, you only appreciate its beauty, not its roots.'

"Betty, on hearing those sweet words, looked at Bill with moist eyes, and gave him a delicate kiss on the cheek.

"'Oh, for God's sake, you're so deluded. Why do you let yourself be fooled by empty words that are carried away by the wind? Have a bit of dignity and control yourself instead of flaunting yourself like a hussy in front of everyone. Have a little self-respect, can't you, and try to behave more like a lady,' scolded the indignant guest.

"'Aren't you cold, Bill?' his mistress asked, changing the subject.

"'No, ma'am, but I think I'd better go and change, I wouldn't want to spoil your carpet,' he apologized.

"'Oh, don't worry about the carpet. It can be cleaned or even replaced, but moments like that are priceless, you know. Now, please sit next to this wonderful young lady who is sheltering with us on this most inhospitable day. The poor dear is worried about Charles,' explained your great-grandmother.

"So, Bill took a seat next to Sara, but his body was so large that when he sat down it rubbed against the young lady's, wetting her with his huge forearm. And if that wasn't enough of an outrage for the young lady, when he tried to fit his legs under the table, he ended up spilling tea all over Sara's dress.

"'Mrs. de Courdeil, I don't think this attitude, which encourages your servants to sit at the same table as you, enjoying tea and cake in the company of your guests, is at all appropriate. They should be working; that is their place in a grand house like this,' Sara complained.

"'Excuse me, my dear, I may be getting old, but I'm not senile yet. The attitude I adopt in my own home is surely for me to decide, is it not? Your generation seems to hold very conservative ideas,' she observed.

"'Oh, no, madam, you are far from elderly, but by not keeping your distance from your servants, you lose their respect. Familiarity breeds contempt in my experience. Worse still, you could lose the respect of the other eminent families. You must know that the repute of a family like yours, which is recognized far and wide, can be lost through the slightest whiff of scandal, damaging centuries of good reputation,' she corrected.

"'You are right, Sara. What I do with my life in my own house is everyone's business as is my inherited fortune or my position in this house. Clearly, what I do or don't do is of great interest to society,' replied Mrs. de Courdeil firmly.

"'Yes, madam, that's why when I met Charley, detecting his good heart, and seeing the great interest he had in me, I thought I could help him to adapt to the social mores and become as refined as his ancestry demands. In fact, I can help you both. You would benefit from abiding by the accepted rules of behavior, which would require a few small changes in the running of the house. I assure you that society will speak well of you, not just to your face, but also behind your back,' the young woman argued enthusiastically, trying to somehow get closer to her beloved's mother and away from Bill's damp, muscular body.

"'You clearly misunderstood me when I said that what I do with my life and in my house is everyone's concern. My lifestyle is my own affair. I live by my own principles, not those imposed imperiously from on high, which the majority only adhere to out of fear and ignorance and for the sake of appearance. But I tell you, they will break those precious rules fast enough if they think they won't be found out. And they have the audacity to criticize me and the way I run my house and demean these good people. The hypocrites! The way they look at things shows not just deficient intellect but a lack of empathy, driven by fear of the unfamiliar or, more aptly, fear of difference. That is precisely why they need people like us in this house, who see beyond the machinations of the invisible string-pullers that try to run the world like a puppet show.'

"Miss Sara was stupefied and shocked at these words. She stared open-mouthed at Mrs. de Courdeil, who was just getting into her stride.

"'Apparently, in this ovine world, it is the person who has good intentions, is tolerant and considerate, even to those who are really unpleasant, who is considered the miscreant, and not those who impose their views on others, unwittingly spreading cruelty and injustice. They hide behind a mask of respectability but are filled with jealousy and hatred. Believing their own lies does not absolve them of their sins.

"'All minds, Sara, are at the mercy of preconceived and fixed ideas that restrict free-thinking and encourage compliance. But some of us have learnt how to rid ourselves of those chains and think and act for ourselves without harming anyone.

"The servants watched the young guest intensely as she endured the old lady's tirade. Sara, whose hands were trembling as she lifted her cup to her mouth, could barely swallow the tea she had been sipping.

"'The lack of self-control and secretly doing the very things one publicly denounces, is, as it always was, endemic. We live under a thick veil that clouds the vision of your dear society, so that all commune in a mutual benightedness. Everyone adulterates the truth, claiming that they alone are authentic, when it is all a deception. We all know with which foot each person limps, even though they deny it. The populace is manipulated from the cradle to the grave so that, even if they become aware of this farce, the status quo is so deeply ingrained as to be accepted as altogether normal.'

"Young Sara swallowed saliva as she set the teacup down on the table before interjecting.

"'I beg your pardon, Mrs. de Courdeil, I didn't mean to offend you. It may be that something as simple as a modification of your servants' attire would improve their attitude and put them in their place. While it is very gratifying to see two women employed as stable maids, it is clear that a man could do that work better. And, as for the way your maid Betty dresses, one could almost mistake her for a guest or even your son's fiancée.

Surely, dressing her more appropriately would benefit the smooth running of this house.'

"'Tell me, my dear, setting aside the nature of the work and adequate remuneration for their labor, which do you think is better? To have disgruntled servants or a contented staff? As you are my guest, I will explain for you why I employed these girls. I didn't select them for their strength, though they are both physically and mentally stronger than many men, but for their skill with the horses and their efficiency. So, if they want to dress in what is most comfortable for their duties, they are free to do so, since this not only enables them to do their job better, but also improves their quality of life. Happy people work better. And I see your distaste, but I don't see that it is any of my concern, and certainly none of yours, if they want to be together as a couple, because I believe everyone should have total freedom of expression to love whoever they please. It does no one else any harm,' your great-grandmother replied.

"Despite feeling extremely uncomfortable, Sara maintained her stance. 'Madam, I only know that things have always worked in a certain way and, up until now, it has worked well. Change may seem progressive, even amusing at first, but if something has always been done a certain way, it means that it is a successful method and that it will only deteriorate with change. Don't you see that in this house there is no authority? Without leadership there is chaos. Think of the prestige of your good name, I implore you!'

"'Did you hear that, Betty? Go at once and change into the uniform you should be wearing,' the lady of the house ordered the maid, who left in haste but without complaint. Bill turned and looked at Sara, his face filled with contempt.

"'If you plan to stay with Charley, as you so affectionately call him, you should know that he will let me, and Betty stay here in the mansion as long as we live. We will have children, in or out of wedlock, and they will come in all colors. I can't think of a better place to raise my children, but so far, we haven't been lucky in that way,' the big man said with a deep laugh, as if coming straight from his belly. 'I remember when Charles was little. His room always seemed so tidy. But it wasn't really; he had hidden his toys under the bed, and one day, there were so many under there that they started to tumble out. So, I asked him why he hid his toys under the bed instead of putting them away. And he answered me, "Because if you had seen them on the floor the way I enjoy them, you would force me to change it and I wouldn't want to play with them anymore."'

"Your great-grandmother's demonstration of her control over her servants merely confirmed Sara's worst fears when Betty reappeared, dressed as the boy society had tried to make her be for most of her life, until she arrived at the mansion.

"'Oh my God, Betty!' exclaimed the guest, horrified.

'Don't you think it's better to be honest about what always was and always will be?' Betty asked. 'We may be from very different worlds, but can't we live and let live, each in our own way? If we were friends, Miss Sara, I promise you, I could give you advice such that you could have any man you wanted, and him wrapped round your little finger too,' she added.

"'In this house not even the words of the Almighty have any value if they are not accompanied by good deeds, good manners and, above all, tolerance and respect. That's what really counts in this life. So, if you're going to stay under this roof, you need to know what's what. Bill, for example, likes to eat with his hands. Betty likes to dress like the woman she really is, even though she was born in a male body. Not even when dressed as a man, which clearly goes against her nature as a woman, can the femininity she exudes be concealed. And I have to say that she always wears her uniform impeccably. I have never seen a maid with such elegance and finesse. You see, in this house we tolerate, dear, we do not punish.'

"'Now, I don't allocate positions to my staff because of their sex; women in the kitchens and men on the grounds but place them where they can be exceptional at their jobs, which benefits both me and them. That is why everyone in this house dresses appropriately for the job they do. What difference does it make how they do their work as long as they do it well and do no harm to others? If I wanted to be looked after by strangers, I would go and live in a hotel. But I want this house to be my home, not just a place I stay. And for that to happen, I need to get to know each and every member of staff under my roof as the unique individuals they are. In return, they come to know me and my needs almost better than I do,' said Mrs. de Courdeil proudly.

"'This is intolerable,' said the young woman scandalized. 'Charles was only a child and so can have had nothing to do with any of this! It was quite improper for a woman to make an exhibition of herself as Betty did earlier, flirting with this man and showing inappropriate affection. But to raise children outside of the sacred bonds of marriage between a man and a woman! And then, it turns out that she isn't even a woman! Don't either of you have any dignity? Surely a colored man has it hard enough in our society without the added burden of such a scandal!' Sara protested indignantly.

"'Oh, yes, Miss Sara, but I just love to feel the food between my fingers and fill my mouth. The best part is that when you finish, you can still savor the food while you slowly suck your fingers clean. Food, miss, just like life, is perceived as having more aroma and flavor when it is made and eaten to one's taste, if you know what I mean.' Bill said, pulling out a piece of cake with his hands and licking his fingers as Sara stared dumbfounded at him.

"Betty, dressed in a black tuxedo, white shirt and black tie, very politely, made an effort to hide her face behind the silver tray she held in her white gloved hands, so as not to make Miss Sara blush any further.

'What were you coming to tell me, Bill?' Mrs. de Courdeil asked, seemingly indifferent to her guest's discomfort, as the robust man continued to suck his fingers. The servants burst out laughing at Sara's astonished face which was contorted with chagrin.

"'Mrs. de Courdeil, I am very sorry for the circumstances under which we have met, but if you will excuse me, I think I should leave. If you would be so kind as to call me a cab,' said the young lady, anxious to get out of there.

"'You want to leave so soon? You seemed so worried about my son. Don't you want to wait for your Charley anymore?' your astute great-grandmother asked.

"'I'm sure that, as you said, Charles will be fine. Anything is better than staying inside this madhouse,' the young woman replied.

"'As you wish, my dear. But you understand that there are no cabs today, although the rain seems to be easing. I could ask one of my maids to take you to the village by motorcycle if you wish. I'm sure it will be easier for you to find a ride from there to wherever it is that you are going. We can even lend you an umbrella.

"Mrs. de Courdeil and the servants watched with laughter as one of the girls bore Miss Sara away, sitting on the motorcycle like a lady, that is, sidesaddle, and struggling with the umbrella she was trying to use to shield her from the rain and the mud thrown up from the wheels as they struggled to grip the waterlogged ground.

"'Ma'am, I honestly believe that this young lady has been one of the best the master has brought home,' Bill said.

"'I don't know whether to laugh or cry at your sarcasm,' his mistress replied. 'Although I must admit, if it weren't for these little ladies that he's been bringing home lately, my day-to-day life would be a lot duller. Where do you think he finds them? He's certainly not looking for his mother in them. I don't know what will happen when I can no longer protect him from his stupidity,' she said.

"'Ma'am, knowing you, when you have passed away, your ghost will haunt this house and torment any poor girl your son chooses; and I'm sure that you will continue from the life beyond to entertain those of us who are still left,' he replied shrewdly.

"'You can be sure I will. By the way, what was it you were coming to tell me when you came to the house before tea?'she asked.

"'I want to show you something that will divert you even more than that young lady your son brought home, but you will need to wear your riding boots,' Bill said.

The Sign

"Meanwhile, Charles was riding towards the ice. He got off his horse and continued on foot, setting his course towards the core of the storm. When he reached the ice, he stepped cautiously on it, fearing that it might break under his weight. But at that exact moment, there was a deafening rumble that sounded as if the sky was splitting in two. The young man looked up and saw the center of the spiral slam shut. Then it began to open again, revealing a small hole through which torrential rain began to fall. Though this intrigued him, the cold was starting to chill him to the bone, and he was in two minds as to whether to continue or not.

"Suddenly, something astounding caught his attention. The snow which had been falling around him, inexplicably transformed into droplets of water which hung in the air almost as though time had stopped. Mouth agape and unable to believe his eyes, Charles reached out to try and touch them. Even his bemused horse attempted to lick them.

"Your grandfather was so amazed by what was happening that he quite forgot the cold that had seeped into his bones and stopped to enjoy the inexplicable phenomenon. Sliding across the ice, his body passed through the wall of droplets in front of him. And when he looked over his shoulder, he was fascinated to see the torso-shaped tunnel his passage had left in its wake.

"He scooped the water molecules into his hands, collecting and compressing them until they joined together to form a large sphere that floated in the air, apparently without being affected by gravity. Next, he tried molding the droplets into shapes with his hands, and even putting some in his mouth. When he spat the liquid out, it created tubes of water, which he watched entranced as they drifted along in midair. Beguiled by the slow movement of the huge bag of water, and by how it was getting ever larger as it incorporated all the drops in its path, he watched until it collided with the tree trunks at the edge of the ice and broke apart, forming small amorphous structures which scattered in slow motion, before stopping at some indeterminate point on their trajectory.

"The climatic aberration emitted a second enormous rumble from within its immensity; a rumble so loud that it shook the ice beneath Charles's feet and forced him to stop his game. He imagined that the sky was complaining, as though it was suffering from severe indigestion from having binged on so many clouds. As the rumbling intensified, the ice began to crack, and Charles thought it would be wisest to turn back. But as he glanced towards the core of the storm, which was the source of that monstrous, infernal sound that kept booming and echoing over the celestial vault, he stopped in his tracks. Gazing intently, he discerned a terrifying aperture, and a thousand questions began to cross his mind, including, 'Will this be my last day?'

"Petrified, he mentally reviewed his life up to that moment, asking himself whether he had any regrets or unfinished business, and whether he was ready to die. At the same time, he continued to stare unblinkingly at the sky that seemed to be preparing to engulf him along with the world around him. Presently, the dreadful noise began to diminish and transformed into a kind of hubbub that came from where the atmospheric spiral had formed. Then something tiny emerged from it and slowly descended through the channel of water that fell from the core. Believing his mind was playing tricks on him, Charles slapped his face to bring himself back to reality. Yet it became clear that it was no hallucination, but as real as life itself, despite the object's ability to defy the laws of physics. Even though the ice continued to fracture beneath him, he began to wend his way, carefully sliding his feet, towards the mysterious object which continued its slow descent. He strained his eyes trying to make out what it was until, although it made no sense at all, it became blindingly obvious. Looking back on that day, filled with all the strange events he had experienced, your grandfather abandoned logic and just accepted whatever he saw in front of him no matter how impossible it might seem. What he had taken to be an object was actually a person.

"Astonished by the situation in which he found himself, he felt helpless as he had no idea what to do. His first instinct was to call for help; but his cries, loud and desperate as they were, lost themselves as they crossed the emptiness of the frozen lake and entered the surrounding woods. Besides, there wasn't a soul around to hear him, let alone help him. In near despair, he was alarmed by the complexity and paradoxes of the problem. Then, without further thought, he left Dumper and ran as fast as he could until he slipped and slid across the ice towards the descending figure. The paralyzed raindrops formed globules as they ricocheted like particles of quicksilver off his head, hands, and torso, while he kept his gaze firmly fixed on the person, whose descent had become considerably faster than before.

"When the falling person was only a few feet from the surface of the lake, he began to plummet towards the ice, which clearly would not withstand the impact, and probably would end his life and that of Charles, who by now was directly under him. Giving a cry as the other person's body hit him, Charles crashed through the ice and, as the darkness closed in on him, he was enveloped in the frigid waters of the lake. He felt as if a blanket of sharp shards was piercing him to the very bone. For a few seconds Charles lost consciousness and his body, paralyzed by the impact, was slowly sinking into the black, glacially cold abyss of the lake.

"It may only have been the product of delirium; the effect of an intense dream in which things seem real or at least feasible. But what your grandfather experienced, while he stood with one foot in this life and the other in the hereafter, he adamantly believed was a guardian angel.

"'Wake up,' murmured a faint, almost inaudible whisper in his ears. 'Wake up! Wake up!' insisted the voice inside his head, repeatedly, until he opened his eyes in bewilderment. The sensation was strange. Even though he was under water, he could breathe. His eyes seemed to have adjusted to being under water so that he could see clearly, and he had an unimpeded view of the bottom of that shadowy lake. Not only could he perfectly see the grass he had so often run across as a child, but he could feel it too. He marveled that he had been standing there talking to Bill just the day before.

"Charles put his feet firmly on that now flooded meadow and looked for the hut where Bill kept his tools. Unexpectedly, a dreadful pain shot through his body like a sheet of needles, forcing him into a fetal position and hugging his chest tightly. He hadn't realized that time down there was limited, and hypothermia was beginning to take its toll on him. He was gradually losing his vision and having difficulty moving.

"But what of the person he had seen descending from the storm; the person who had fallen on him? Surely, he must be dead or, at best, unconscious. He set out, impulsively swimming along the bottom, twisting and turning, desperately searching for the body. The icy surface, which was like frosted glass, let little light penetrate to the depths, so he couldn't be sure, but he thought he saw the silhouette of someone in the distance. Nonetheless, he swam there without hesitation.

"When he got there, he grabbed whatever it was and launched himself as fast as he could towards the icy ceiling. He adjusted his course so as to make for the only possible escape route: the same hole through which they had fallen. As he approached the hole, he sensed an arm reaching into the cold water, and making a last effort to save himself, Charles stretched out his arm as far as he could. He felt a strong grip take hold of his arm and then he was being yanked out of the water, dragging the other being, the one that had fallen from the sky, with him to safety. Then he gave way to the darkness that was closing in on him."

The Unique Girl

Grandma stopped talking as she watched the last flickering of the tiny flames that were guttering out of the nearly burnt logs in the fireplace. Her hands were resting on the armrests of her rocking chair, and although she looked serene, it was like watching a calm river, flat on the surface, but full of strong currents beneath.

"Old Bill has a Bentley like the one you're talking about. Is it the same car? I'd like to hear more of the story, Grandma. That's if you aren't too tired, of course," Sasha gabled breathlessly, the words cascading out of her and rending the silence.

Despite looking as if he was asleep, James had been listening to his grandmother from start to finish. Although at times he had been half dozing, straining to keep his eyes open, even though they were stubbornly trying to close and drag him to the deepest part of Morpheus's limbo, he had managed to stay awake.

Grandma smiled softly as she watched the fire die as the last glow of the embers disappeared.

"Where were we?" she asked. "Ah, yes. The warmth of the fire in his room brought Charles back to consciousness. But when he awoke, he was unable to remember what had happened. He vaguely remembered the clopping of a horse's hooves mingled with blurry images of passing over muddy ground and a deep voice he thought might belong to Old Bill.

"'Good morning, my dear!' his mother greeted as she opened his bedroom curtains wide. This startled him.

"'Mom! What are you doing in my room? How long have you been here? Were you watching me?' he quizzed her in a daze.

"'My dear Charles, who do you think brought you to your room, eh?' your great-grandmother replied.

'You? Yes, yes, of course,' commented the young man, scratching his head in bewilderment.

"'How could I get you on a horse and into your room, my dear? Of course, you must still be affected by the blow. Bill and I found you unconscious in that exquisite lake that has formed over our old meadow. We got you on the horse, brought you home and, obviously, Bill carried you up to your room, but it was I who got you out of your wet clothes, although, I'm sure Betty would have been delighted to do it and it would probably have cost her much less effort than it did me.' Charles looked mystified. Surely, his mother must be teasing him. 'All right. I undressed you, but she dressed you and I think she even did your hair, so you need to thank her. And if it hadn't been for Bill, you might have become a permanent part of our new feature in the woods.'

"Charles began to remember what he had experienced when he crossed over a frozen lake that had never existed there before. But he thought he must be ill and that it had all been a figment of his delirium.

"'Are you going to tell me what you were doing there? Because the last we heard, you were going to go get Dumper and come straight back,' his mother prompted.

'I... I must have been delirious. If I told you, mother, what I imagined I saw, you would never believe me,' replied the young man, lost in thought.

'By the way, your dear, young Sara...'

'Who?' Charles interrupted his mother, while rubbing his temples with his fingers.

'The young lady who was with you in the car,' his mother said tetchily. 'She called to see how you were, but I see she is no longer of any importance to you, and I can understand why. I certainly would have lost interest in such a banal girl myself after this curious discovery,' said his mother, looking out the window. 'I think it proved a very interesting day for all of us.'

"Charles, rubbing his eyes, went to stand next to her. Though he heard her words, he could not grasp their meaning nor what she intended. Your great-grandmother leant against the window frame and calmly lit her pipe. When he glanced to see what she was looking at, his heart lurched and missed a beat. He couldn't stop staring at the beautiful figure walking the garden.

"You saved her life, my son. When Bill grabbed you and pulled you from the lake, you were holding her arm in an iron grip, and she came right out behind you. We had trouble prizing your fingers from her arm. And while you seem to have amnesia, she remembers absolutely everything and has been waiting almost a whole day to thank you.

"It was then, as Charles gazed into the distance, gawking at the light glinting off the ice, that he comprehended that everything he had seen the previous day had been real.

"'Who is she, mother? Because I swear, I saw her fall from the sky, as if that storm…' your grandfather hesitated, perplexed, and confused.

"'I think you're going to be very, very surprised when you meet her. She's not like other women, Charles, or even like any other people you know; she's truly special.' After saying this, she took the glass that had been left on the bedside table for when the young man awoke and poured some of the liquid over her hand. 'Watch this, Charles.' Then she poured some water against the window and, to her son's amazement, instead of falling towards the ground as demanded by gravity, the drops of water began to spiral around the glass in the direction of the young woman in the garden. Go to her and watch what happens to water around her. I think it is our duty to protect her. Do you understand, my dear?'

"Charles put his finger on the window to see if he could impede the liquid, but it was unstoppable. Then he remembered everything that had happened: the storm, the fall, the soft, sweet voice in his head. A shiver ran through his body. He realized that it must have been that young woman who awoke him in the depths of that frozen lake and gave him the power to survive underwater for the brief time necessary to rescue her. But how?

"'Go talk to her, Charles, but please be gentle. She's not like any-one you've ever met before. I think fate sent her to us for some purpose we don't yet understand.'

"Betty knocked at the half-open door. She wore a simple maid's uniform but with great elegance.

'How are you feeling, young sir? Do you need me to help you dress? I don't mean to intrude, but today is different and you have to make a good first impression, although I think you've already done that,' she said with a twinkle in her eye when she saw that the young master was restored to health.

"'Thank you, Betty, but I think it was possibly she who saved me,' the young man answered, observing the figure as she wandered in the garden.

'I'm glad you're alive, sir. The girl hasn't eaten anything since she got up, so I thought it wise to prepare a brunch for two. A cozy little meal and a moment of privacy between the two of you might help the young lady open up a little more to us. Well, to you, since, according to her, you saved her life. And she hasn't stopped asking how you are since you both arrived.'

"Charles grinned and ran to Betty to hug her with all his might.

'You're the best,' he blurted, giving the maid a kiss on the cheek. Despite the difference in their station in life, being much the same age, they related to each other almost as if they were brother and sister.

"Afterwards, while Charles was dressing, she advised him on how to deal with a sweet, sensitive woman, who was so different from the others. Knowing that the newcomer might be somewhat traumatized by what had happened, especially as she was now in an unfamiliar place, Betty gave the young master strategies on how to approach the mysterious girl without scaring her and gain her trust.

"Once ready, the master looked doubtfully at Betty, but she gave him a confident nod, so your grandfather tried to remain calm and not run down the stairs towards that extraordinary and intriguing girl who had fallen from the sky. The maid followed him down the stairs, watching his every step.

"When he reached the girl, she had her back to him and was kneeling on the grass. He stood and watched silently as the dew that rested on the small stems levitated around her because of the power she emanated.

"Charles tried to remain calm, but, to his amazement, the young woman sensing his presence, turned, ran towards him and flung her arms around him, tucking him into a tight embrace.

'Thank you,' she whispered in his ear.

"He immediately recognized her voice and knew that it was indeed she who had saved his life. Enthralled, he returned her embrace. They stood there holding each other.

"'I see that the young master is now with our special guest, ma'am. What should we do?' Bill inquired as he entered the room where, through the stained-glass window, Charles' mother was watching the young couple.

"'My dear Bill, I don't think we can do much more. Fate came knocking at our door and we opened it wide. Now, all we can do is wait, watch, and cross our fingers that everything goes well. Of course, we must prepare the estate for a new mistress. And we must make sure, Bill, that the secret never leaves this house. Today is the beginning of a new era. There will be hard days ahead and some big decisions will have to be taken. Whoever stays here will never be able to leave; those who are no longer right for service here must leave as soon as possible; there can be no exceptions.'

"Bill nodded in acknowledgement of his mistress's orders.

"'I will personally see to it that Miss Sara doesn't stick her nose where it's not wanted and that the servants don't say anything after I have selected those who will be staying. Will there be anything else, Ma'am?' the huge man asked.

"'Yes, Bill. One thing more. You have been a good friend and a loyal servant to this family, so I want you to have the Bentley. The house will bear the cost of repairing the vehicle,' offered your great-grandmother. 'Please accept it as a token of our deepest appreciation.'

'That is too generous, Ma'am' he mumbled.

"'My friend, you always wanted to be part of our society, didn't you? Well, accept this gift so that you can feel, even if only briefly, that you are as much a part of it as any one of us, which is, after all, what you are to us. You gave me back my life by letting me be part of yours, so let me repay you the debt of gratitude I owe you in my own coin. Besides, I'm sure Betty will be thrilled to have you take her for a spin in that beautiful car once it's fixed. I assure you every girl likes to feel the eyes of the world on her as a dashing, handsome gentleman drives her in his wonderful chariot to some special spot,' his mistress reassured without moving from the window.

"'I'm most grateful,' Bill said as he made his way to the door to set the plan in motion.

'By the way, Bill, what shall I tell the young lady?' asked your great-grandmother just before he reached the door.

'All in good time, ma'am. For now, it's better that she knows nothing and adapts to our way of life.'

"After this, the man went out, softly closing the door behind him. Mrs. de Courdeil smiled as she pensively studied the young folk in the garden and blew a jet of smoke from her pipe against the window.

The Dream

The grandfather clock gave its last reverberating dong. It was already midnight and the children had fallen fast asleep in front of the hot ashes in the hearth. So, grandma got up out of the rocking chair, taking with her the jar where the magical gem which little James had found on the shore of the lake, had been kept, and went to the window. She peered through the glass at the beautiful moon that looked larger than usual. It illuminated the woods with its intense white glow which was reflected perfectly on the little piece of the lake that could be seen from the stained-glass window. She sighed, closing her eyes as she gripped the jar tightly. Then she took one last look at the children, to check that they were still asleep, before looking through the stained-glass again, clutching the water-filled jar against her chest.

She lifted the jar so that the rays of the full moon, which was shining brightly, pierced the water with their luminescence. Immediately the water began to exhibit small flashes of fluorescent blue. Grandma's palms began to tremble. She tried to open the jar with her aged hands. When she was finally able to open it, it felt like an earthquake. She dipped her fingers into the liquid in the jar and moistened her face with them. Almost instantly, her skin began to whiten, leaving behind the spots and wrinkles that marked the aging of her complexion, and in a matter of seconds her face took on the appearance of an eighteen-year-old girl, with porcelain-like skin, large eyes, and full lips.

After several seconds staring dumbfounded at her reflection in the glass, she moistened her fingers again, but this time she placed them only between her eyebrows. As she pulled her hand away from her forehead, a mark, like a small indentation, which hadn't been there before, appeared.

Suddenly, she discerned a large silhouette at the edge of the woods. It was looking towards her window. Moments later it disappeared, as if it had felt the old woman's gaze upon it. She closed the jar, clutching it tightly to her chest. After drawing the curtains of the little room, she hid the jar behind some books on the huge bookshelf that filled one of the walls, picked up the gemstone that served as a paperweight and left the room visibly worried, slamming the door behind her.

Sasha opened her eyes and looked at her brother, who lay asleep beside her, curled up on the floor in front of the hearth. The rocking chair was empty and there was no trace of her grandmother. She noticed that the curtains were drawn, and the door closed.

"James! James, wake up!" she called softly as she shook him by the shoulder.

"What is it?" he mumbled, forcing his eyes open and trying to clear his head.

"Grandma is not here; I think she's gone."

James looked at the table and discovered that neither the water jar nor the stone were there.

"Did she go to bed?"

Sasha got up and looked out the window.

"James, look!" she exclaimed after pulling back the curtains, "See! There in the woods!"

The little boy jumped up and ran to see what his sister was so excited about. Looking out of the window, he saw what appeared to be a dark shape with glowing eyes staring directly at the window or, rather, at them. It was moving in the direction of the mansion; advancing very slowly, as felines do before they pounce on their prey, with a huge claw extended. It seemed to be preparing to attack. But at that very moment, a woman wearing a white cloak came out of nowhere and raised her arms towards the mysterious creature, which disappeared instantly. The woman remained motionless as if waiting for something, but all was still, and the fearsome monster did not reappear. Even so, the woman remained standing there, her back to the children, who continued to watch attentively from the window, until, suddenly, she removed her huge hood, turned her face towards the window, staring at the siblings, who, frightened, stumbled backwards falling one on top of the other. Sasha hurriedly crawled across the floor to the window, pulled the curtains shut, grabbed her brother by the hand and fled to her room, where they hid under the bed.

The children were terrified. They spent hours under the bed, clinging onto each other, and hardly daring to breathe. Finally, shortly before dawn, the darkness of the room and their exhaustion overwhelmed them, and they succumbed to sleep despite their determined efforts to remain alert. Sasha, with the horror of what she had witnessed still roiling in her head, imagined herself falling through the darkness. Her fall ended abruptly when she awoke on the back of what seemed to be an enormous bird. It seemed to be covered with precious stones, or rather, to be made of them. Its fine feathered wings were fashioned out of a beautiful, crystal fabric, so light and delicate that it was a wonder it didn't tear as it flew.

The girl was so entranced by what she saw that she almost fell off the fascinating bird as it ascended through a dense layer of pastel pink colored clouds. From above it looked like a soft rosy blanket, and she felt an intense warm light that wrapped around her like a mother's embrace.

With a graceful bank to the left, the formidable creature raised its right wing, which was then backlit by an immense star. Sasha noticed that a large spider's web of tiny, fiery, coral-colored lines that followed the animal's veins were now mapped out on the wing. Thanks to the intense glow from the setting sun, which pierced the magnificent plumage, she could see the delicate shimmers on the surface of the extremely slender, translucent layers of gemstones that comprised the wing. The sunbeams exposed its interior a thousand times better than when we shine a high-powered flashlight on our hand. Its exquisite skeleton and general physiognomy consisted of moonstone, jade, beryl, quartz, tourmaline, and other gems, all sculpted so finely that they were diaphanous, and thus, revealed the tiny, delicately colored arteries, which reminded Sasha of the lines one imagines in the interior of a diamond.

These thin layers of beautiful gems, which seemed to her to be woven as if they were silk, changed color according to the angle at which the light emitted by the sun's rays struck them. With each change of position, the range of colors emanating from the bird's body altered so that the whole ensemble had the same effect as a love potion on whoever looked at it, with all the confusion of emotions and the dazed feeling of wanting to surrender to the complete vulnerability its unusual beauty elicited.

Instantly, another creature emerged from the thick carpet of clouds over which she was flying. It was another beautiful bird, the twin of the one on which she rode, except that the feathers and stones were in different colors. On its back was her little brother, James, who was wearing the biggest smile Sasha had ever seen on his face. Ecstatic, he had his eyes closed and was clearly enjoying the ride in the warm breeze, as their mounts glided side by side towards the reddish sun. But below them a small stain began to darken the blanket of clouds. As it expanded, it darkened and dirtied the clouds like when ink is dropped in water. Then an apocalyptic figure leaped out in front of them.

Immediately, the birds opened their wings to their fullest extent until they were almost vertical, which unintentional-ly caused the children to fall from their backs. The children showed not the slightest sign of fright or, indeed, any reaction at all, because they were still under the spell of the beautiful birds on which they had so recently been riding. Therefore, bewitched, they fell into the void like two rag dolls, uselessly inert, and unable even to scream. Even though they were aware that they faced certain death, their bodies were completely relaxed as they passed through the cooling clouds. It was as though body and mind had been separated, and all they were left with were the daft grins that were still glued to their faces.

They only felt the gentle wind, which smoothed their clothes, ruffled their hair, and rocked their limbs, caressing them like the breath of the soft whisper of an angel. Surely, they were at the gates of the sweetest death anyone could wish for. The sense of comfort transported them back to when they were just babies and their mother used croon to soothe them before gently tucking them in. The memory was so attractive that, for a few seconds it diminished the sedative effect, and they shed a few tears for what they had forgotten and only recovered, when least expected, on the way to their deaths.

Sasha looked at her brother at the same instant he looked at her. Both had a relaxed smile and teary eyes as they continued their descent. Having regained a small part of their childhood that had become lost with the years, they felt at peace with themselves. But just when they had accepted their fate, having passed the clouds, a gigantic wave appeared, rushing towards them, carrying everything before it, cushioning their fall.

Though they took in everything, they were still unable to act, even when they started sinking, becoming submerged in the water until they were completely enveloped by it. They felt the coldness of the salty liquid slowly awakening them from the enchantment. They started to be able to move their fingers slightly, and bit by bit recover the use of their numb bodies. The girl stretched out her arm, and with great effort, tried to grasp her brother's hand, but the strong sea currents separated them, and they lost sight of each other in the ocean foam. Their bodies were twisting, turning, and spinning over themselves until, without warning, the sea cast them out onto a beach.

James began to cough up water. The unpleasant taste of salt and the stinging in his eyes had woken him up. Once conscious, he noticed that he was lying on very fine, white sand. He felt it on his face and could sink his fingers into it. He understood that the effect of the bird was finally over.

Sasha, on the other hand, had her eyes fixed straight ahead, on the immensity of the turquoise blue sea that emitted flashes of light from below its surface, as if there were phosphorescent creatures swimming there. Beyond the vastness of that crystal abyss, she registered a huge gray cloud that was gradually approaching the beach.

"Do you think it's coming from where we fell?" James asked.

Sasha looked at her brother, startled, as she hadn't realized he was standing next to her; she was still in shock after what had happened, and her mind was elsewhere.

"You made me jump, James," she accused. "Have you ever seen black lightning before?"

The boy turned his eyes towards the horizon, completely stunned by the question, but before he could answer, the ground on which they were standing began to soften and transform into quicksand from which it was impossible to escape.

"I'm scared, Sasha!" James exclaimed anxiously.

His sister took him in her arms and was trying to lift him up above her.

"James, I don't think any of this is real. I think it's just a dream. Think about it. When have you ever seen a bird like the ones we rode on? Maybe it's my dream and I'm just imagining that you are here with me," said the girl, hoping to calm him down.

"But it's you and me in it! I'm touching you and I'm feeling you! What if it's my dream, Sasha?!" James asked, his breathing ragged. He began hitting himself in the face to try and wake himself up.

"Listen to me, James!!! We can't escape from this sand, so I think what we should do is relax like we did in the fall. Look what happened before! There's no way this is real. Things like this don't happen when we are awake, so we must be in a dream. We just have to wake up."

Sasha hugged her brother tightly, trying not to show her fear, and to stay strong. "I don't know how to get out of here, James, but I do know that this has to be a dream, because nothing we've seen here exists in the real world. You do know all these things are impossible, don't you? So, if we can't get out of here, I think what we should do is just let go," she explained.

She was worried for her brother, since being smaller, the sand would cover his head sooner, and she didn't have much more strength left to lift him up. "Relax, James, I'm not going to let go of you" she reassured.

And she held him tightly, lifting him on top of her so that the little boy would have more time to breathe before being engulfed by the earth, but in doing so she only managed to make them sink more rapidly. The little boy's panicked screams echoed through the depths of the sandy earth, "Hold your breath and close your eyes, James!!!" was the last thing she shouted to her brother before they were squeezed into the darkness under the sand, leaving behind a deserted and silent coastline.

Chapter II
Watery Memories

"Sasha, Sasha! Wake up, Sasha!"

The light dazzled her as she opened her eyes.

"James?!" said the girl, delighted to see her brother alive. "You're all right! Ow!" she exclaimed as she banged her head against the boards of the bedstead as she tried to sit up, having completely forgotten they had fallen asleep under the bed. She hugged her brother as if she had lost him and just got him back. Thank goodness it was just a bad dream! she thought to herself.

"Sasha, look," James said, as he rolled over next to her and pointed to the bare feet of a youth.

The siblings looked at each other, holding their breath to keep from making a sound, but when they looked back at those feet, they had turned toward them. A hand grabbed the girl and dragged her out.

"Wake up, Sasha!" she heard someone call.

"Yes?" she answered in a daze.

"Always in the clouds. Come on, let's get to class," said a female voice, which she recognized as that of her best friend, Carol.

"I'm not sure what happened to me. I think I was remembering a dream that I thought I had erased from my memory. Very strange. I'm sorry, what were you saying?" the girl asked her friend, as they crossed the garden in the quadrangle of their boarding school, the buildings of which were built of large, sculpted stone.

"Hey, scumbag!" someone yelled.

"Sasha, look out!" shouted Carol.

Sasha, already a teenager, had half turned towards the sound, when straight away a book hit her full in the face with such force that she fell to the ground, smacking her head so hard that she was knocked out.

"Oh my God, Sasha, you're bleeding! Somebody go fetch Matron!" Carol cried in alarm.

"What happened? Ow, that hurts," Sasha complained as she opened her eyes in the infirmary.

"Relax, it is just a bump," her friend commented, passing her a hand mirror. Sasha looked horrified.

"Ha! Ha! Ha! Don't worry, it will only last a few days. A big nose gives a person character!" Carol joked, trying to play down the injury.

"Did you see who it was?" Sasha asked.

"No. Just some idiot. I have to go to class now. They only let me wait until you woke up. You have to stay lying down for a while. Matron's orders. And you get to miss the lesson, you lucky thing! Anyway, catch you later!" Carol laughed in amusement.

"OK, thanks, Carol," the invalid nodded, still feeling a little giddy.

"Oh! And I'll leave you the book that was thrown at you as a souvenir. Finders keepers, losers weepers. So, screw them! See you later, alligator!"

Sasha held the book in her hands as she lay on the cot in the large chamber, which once had been part of an ancient monastery, but which was now fitted out as the school's infirmary. As such, its walls were made of stone and paneled wood, with large, stained-glass windows that illuminated the room in a psychedelic way, the light creating kaleidoscopic shapes on the gothic walls. It reminded her of the way light and shadow played on the walls of the family mansion, which she had not been to since she was a little girl. For some strange reason she had been thinking about it for the first time in ages, moments before that book hit her in the face.

Geology. "As fast as they disappear with the waves, with a few drops they'll appear just as quickly," Sasha read, looking at the cover of the book that had been thrown at her. But when she opened the book to the first page, it was blank. So, she turned to the second page, but it was also blank. So, was the next one. She started flipping the pages, but they were all the same: completely empty. "No wonder they threw it at me, that's all it's good for," she said out loud in frustration. Then she threw the book against the wall, which it bounced off hitting her squarely on her sore nose. "Aaaahhhhhhhhhhhhhh!!! Damn it!!!" she exclaimed holding her nose tightly as she held her breath, but the pain wouldn't stop, and tears escaped and fell onto the open pages of the tome lying on her lap.

It was then that she noticed that her teardrops, which were splashing on the blank leaves, revealed strange, inky shapes that seemed to be floating to the surface of the page. "It can't be. It's not possible!" she muttered to herself. The young woman tried to stand up, with the aim of showing the book to someone else and prove that the blow to her head wasn't causing hallucinations, but she felt really dizzy.

"Matron! Matron," she called with difficulty. Matron immediately rushed to her aid and, after putting her back on the bed, took the book from her, closed it, and placed it on the nightstand. "A glass of water, please," Sasha begged. "I need to show you something." But as she was saying this, Sasha lost consciousness.

When she awoke, Sasha found herself lying on her bed in her room with Carol watching her from the foot of the bed.

"What a mess you've made of today, girl. I didn't know a person could pass out so often in one day. Not to mention the number of times we've frustrated your attempts to break your nose. The lengths some people will go to just to get out of going to class," her friend quipped, trying to hide her concern with humor.

"Very funny, Carol," Sasha replied, trying to remember how she had gotten to her room.

"But how are you feeling?" Carol asked, concerned that her friend still seemed to be disoriented.

"There's something I have to tell you," Sasha blurted, corroborating Carol's concern about latent after-effects, even though Matron had given her friend a clean bill of health. At that instant, all the lights in the boarding school went out, leaving Queen Victoria College, Windsor, in darkness.

"What's happening?" Sasha exclaimed in fright.

"Relax, it's probably just a power outage caused by the storm. We can use candles until the power comes back on. Do you remember where we left them? This room is a complete mess. We have got to start tidying this dump up. You leave your books and papers scattered everywhere. If you are not careful, they're going to start thinking you're a moron or else that you're one of those geniuses who live like a hermit in isolation, surrounded by mountains of trash.

Sasha looked out the window, watching the raindrops lash the glass and leave little rivulets.

"Tears," she uttered aloud.

"Seriously, you need to stop talking to yourself," Carol commented, scrabbling through the drawers in search of the candles.

"Where is the book?" asked Sasha as though she hadn't heard Carol.

"The one that hit you in the face? It was right next to you. You wouldn't let go of it even though you were asleep. I tried to take it from you to see whose it was, but you were grasping it so tightly that it was as if it were literally stuck to you."

At that moment, Sasha jumped out of bed and ran out of the room clutching the book in her hand.

"Sasha! Sasha!!!! Stop it! That blow to your head must have knocked a screw loose!"

But her friend had already reached the quadrangle and was standing in the pouring rain with the book open and her arms outstretched. She was soon drenched by the deluge. But with each drop of rain, to Sasha's elation, a series of lines began to emerge, branching out across the pages of the tome. Though completely soaked, she started to laugh exultantly.

"You've definitely lost it," said Carol, astonished by her friend's strange behavior.

"Like when the undertow of the tide washes away letters written on the sand of the seashore!!! As fast the waves make them disappear, the raindrops make them appear just as quickly!!! Don't you see, Carol, the pages of this book are white, empty, until they get soaked with water!!!!" Sasha called back, dancing in the rain and acting like a loony.

"What on earth are you saying?" replied her companion, observing her from the cloister that surrounded the quadrangle's garden.

"Ladies, this is a girls' boarding school, not a mental asylum," a voice declared in a stentorian tone. "You had better have a jolly good reason for this behavior," the teacher warned them indignantly.

"Please, miss! I think Sasha may still not be right after the blow to the head she suffered today."

The mistress looked at Sasha, who was laughing crazily, and, in response, gave a curt nod to Carol, "Then I suggest you take your friend back to her room before someone calls the porter."

Listen, if you're going to send her home, I think I maybe should go with her to make sure she's okay! Well, I guess she didn't hear me," Carol said, watching the teacher's retreating back with one eye while keeping the other on her deliriously euphoric friend.

"Hey, Carol! Take your weirdo girlfriend back to your room and play the fool there. Nobody can sleep with you idiots making a rumpus out there," a schoolgirl shouted down from one of the windows above, which drew a chorus of laughter from her classmates.

"Well, you brainiacs should have thought of that before you threw a book at her head, you losers!" Carol scolded them as she gave them the finger.

She then firmly, but kindly, took her friend by the arm and dragged her to the gallery that surrounded the cloister-like orchard, with its huge columns that supported the students' rooms above.

"Carol, look," said Sasha, showing her a blank page of the book.

""You've had one blow too many on your head, today, and it's addled your brains," her friend lamented, staring at the empty page, and wondering whether Sasha had completely lost her mind. Fixing her eyes on the empty page. "What do you expect me to say, Sasha?" she asked, dismayed. "The pages are blank."

"No, Carol! I mean, yes. But only until the water touches them. You're soaked from the rain, run your hand across the page and you'll see."

Carol touched her hair to better soak her hands before running them over the page of the book her friend was so effusively showing her. "Well?" she demanded when she didn't observe any changes on the paper.

"Wait, Carol. Be patient. I promise the writing will appear."

The girls waited for a long time, squinting at the pages in the poor light that reached the book, since the cloister was not well lit. The illumination merely consisted of a few low watt lamps in wall sconces, which provided emergency lighting in case of a power outage. They provided just enough light to get from one place to another without having to wander around in the dark for too long at unsociable hours. Perhaps it was one of the headmistress' tactics to encourage the girls to return to their rooms promptly when dusk fell; especially on dark days, like this one, when the storm prevented them from hearing the footsteps of the naughty girls who escaped at unseemly hours.

"Please, Sasha. We're soaking wet and you're acting like a nutcase, embarrassing us in front of the whole boarding school, which doesn't do us any good. "Don't they already ridicule us enough without your handing yourself to them on a silver platter? You know, I don't care what they think, but do you really need to prove them right? Because that's what you're doing, when you act crazy like this. I'm not asking you to become a boring pedant, like those assholes; just to act a bit more normally so that we won't always be the butt of their jokes. You get what I'm saying?" she said in an attempt to make her friend see reason.

"Carol, I swear that when the water touched these pages earlier, they filled with ink. I don't understand why it's not happening now," Sasha said as she looked through all the pages of the book, which were devoid of letters. "Do you think I made it up or imagined it? I know I really saw it, Carol. You believe me, don't you? Or do you think I'm hallucinating? Maybe I should go back to the infirmary. My God, maybe I've gone crazy!" she exclaimed in alarm.

"Shhh, calm down. I don't think you made it up, not at all. You know I'd stick my neck out for you, but I didn't see anything at all. I guess it's possible that it was so fleeting that I didn't have time to see it."

On hearing these words, Sasha looked at Carol with sisterly love. She was so good to her. Instead of detachedly telling her that she had lost her marbles, she reacted by supporting her, as she always did, with gentle, positive words, accepting her claim with courtesy and politeness.

"Carol, you are the best friend anyone could ever have. You know, you don't have to be so kind and lie to me. There's enough trust between us for you to tell me the truth. You didn't see anything on the pages of the book, and we both know that it's possible that there really wasn't ever anything, that it was a product of delirium caused by the bump on my head. Or maybe, I've lost my mind, which is only to be expected given that everyone already thinks I'm weird and crazy. Maybe they're right and it's finally happened. You know the saying, there's no smoke without fire," said Sasha.

"Ha, ha, ha, ha, ha! Did you hear that, girls? You can't get any dumber than that. Look at her, babbling about how ink came out of blank pages in her book. What a load of baloney! They are so pathetic that they need to dream up such inane fantasies. Please, you can't get any lower, you're pitiful," snapped Lara, one of the most irritating girls in the school, who had come down with her entourage to see what mischief she could make. Though

Lara was a class captain, she was also a bully, and Sasha was one of her favorite targets.

"You're right, Lara. I thought I saw something, but it was probably only a shadow or maybe a hallucination," answered Sasha embarrassed.

"Don't talk rubbish! If you said there was ink coming out of its pages, then there was ink coming out of its bloody pages," Carol retorted angrily.

"Carol, let it go. You know I must have imagined it as it isn't possible. You don't have to defend me," her companion apologized, sagging.

"But what are you saying, Sasha?! That's not true. If you say you've seen it, you've seen it. I believe you! Why don't you trust in yourself?!" her friend shouted at her, tremendously impassioned, annoyed that she had let the dastardly Lara screw her like that.

"Please, Carol. You're embarrassing yourself," said Sasha awkwardly.

"Wow, Carol, it looks like your girlfriend just left you," the repulsive leader of the clique commented mischievously.

"Don't be childish, Lara. You all know that Sasha is my friend, not my girlfriend. Or is it that you want her for yourself? You say it so often that it sounds like that's what you want. Wait, maybe it's me you want. Or both of us! Oh my God! Are you in love with us?!" Carol, who never let herself be crushed by anyone, taunted.

"Are you trying to confuse everyone with nonsense or what?" Lara, who sensed for the first time that she had a potential rival, replied quickly. She was careful to choose victims who lacked self-esteem and ensured their humiliation by always having her clique to back her up; girls who basked in her approval and who would never risk losing it by challenging her egocentric and dictatorial behavior. Lara was a very toxic person, and no one wanted to get on the wrong side of her.

"Me? Don't make me laugh, Lara. Clearly, you're the one trying to confuse everyone by making it look like we're the ones with the problem, when it's really you. Why else are you always after us? When did we ever bother you?"

Lara's entourage began to waver and doubt her leadership, and fell back a bit, leaving her somewhat exposed.

"What are you idiots doing? You're not going to believe her, are you?" Lara demanded, trying to intimidate them.

"I don't know, Lara... It's true that they are a bit odd, but they never bother anyone. And it's true, you are the one who always goes looking for them," answered one of her minions.

"Wow, Lara, your sidekicks seem to be losing faith in you," Carol pointed out. "Maybe it's time you turned over a new leaf and let them have a life of their own, or are you afraid that if you do, you'll be all alone?" she finished triumphantly.

The Book

"The only freaks here are you! It doesn't matter what you say about me. It's meaningless, because the only freaks in this place are you," she objected, fearing she'd already lost.

"At least we know how to have fun on our own, without the need to meddle in anyone else's life to entertain ourselves," Carol continued like a true vigilante, giving the girl a taste of her own medicine.

"You hit the nail on the head, Carol. She's not only bored but she really wants to hang out with us, because she's fed up with the sycophants that trail round after her, sucking up to her all day long and doing whatever she says with a simper. And, of course with an amoeba sized brain like hers, she's jealous of our ideas. Can you imagine how soporific her thoughts must be, that's if she ever gets any at all in that empty head of hers?" Sasha chimed in, emboldened by Lara's sudden vulnerability.

"It must be exasperating to remain in a retinue whose sole purpose is to faithfully follow a person with a brain the size of a gnat, who never proposes anything other than spite. She does nothing but carry on banal conversations that have but two topics: criticizing others and bragging about herself; and the second only happens when there's no one at hand to put down. How sad that the only way she can feel good about herself is by denigrating others," she continued surprising everyone there, as it was the first time the young woman had ever raised her voice in her own defense.

"It's natural that they are obsessed with us. They only chase us nonstop to see all the exciting things we get up to every day. After all, our life is a thousand times more interesting and fun than theirs will ever be," Sasha concluded, delivering the killer blow.

"Oh, boy! Maybe we'll become the coolest girls at the school," Carol conjectured, freaking out with pride and excitement. She and Sasha cracked up, euphoric at having surprisingly won their battle of wits against the hateful Lara.

"See! They are not normal? Who laughs like that?" Lara asked uselessly.

"Clearly, not you!" shouted Carol, bursting into laughter again. She was laughing harder than ever, while Sasha was rolling on the floor and laughing her head off at those impotent bullies.

At that moment, Sasha let go of the book. Inadvertently, her water-soaked hair touched the pages, completely soaking them. And in that instant, Carol saw the pages which had become wet changing from blank sheets to pages with small spots on them.

"Sasha, look!" she called.

Sasha picked up the book and Carol hugged her with great joy. "I told you so! See, Sasha, I didn't doubt you for a second," she confirmed, showing her loyalty, and helping her friend believe in herself for once, as she knew Sasha suffered from a tremendous lack of self-esteem, something Carol was trying to change.

"Look at them! Isn't that romantic?" the bully remarked insensitively.

"What? Are you, envious, Lara? You know, I don't like girls in that way, but if I did, there would be nothing wrong with it. Of course, if I did, I wouldn't look at you even if I was blind drunk and stoned out of my mind, so you can forget it, okay? You don't stand a chance with either of us. We're way out of your league, Lara. So why don't you take your little gang and go do something trite like paint your nails or play with make-up."

Then Carol helped her friend up off the floor. "We're leaving now, Larakins. I know you're dying to come, but it's a private party," said Carol looking the vanquished bully squarely in the eye.

But Sasha only had eyes for the book; despite playing along with her friend to make that jerk Lara rage, she was no longer paying attention to what was going on, since her mind was fixed on the magic of those pages. She wanted to get to the room as quickly as possible so that she could solve the mystery. She couldn't understand why the first time she wet it the ink showed, but then, when she repeated it with Carol, nothing happened. All these unanswered questions were going to keep her awake all night.

"Did you find the candles, Carol?" she asked. "Because we need light to see the book,"

"The only one I found must have fallen somewhere or I must have lost it when you ran out in the rain. But don't worry, the halls are full of them, so we'll just borrow one."

And with a leap, Carol grabbed a candle from one of the candlesticks along the halls. The flame went out with the movement. "Well, we can relight it with another candle when we get closer to the room. Although, it might be better if we go to the library, because our room is a mess," she remarked in the hope that her friend might start being tidier.

"But will it be open at this hour?" Sasha asked, not taking anything for granted.

"The way you've complicated things so far today, that shouldn't worry you. If we find it closed, we'll open it. What's the big problem?"

The girls headed for the library, Sasha with the book in hand, full of excitement and intrigued by what had happened. She had a hidden absorption; a feeling that she had somehow been waiting for this all her life. Carol, on the other hand, was in her element, delighted to push the limits of her boredom. She would use any excuse to break the rules, which she felt had been created by some tremendously lackluster person, whose principal form of entertainment was to annoy others by imposing absurd restrictions and pointless rules that impinged on their daily life. She was convinced that this person must feel great satisfaction when they created the regulations, which Carol considered superficial and stupid, to maintain the status quo by favoring certain classes, races, and sexes. Like a dictator, their aim was domination, and, irrespective of what anyone's own culture and customs might be, everyone had to be fitted into the same mold, thus, sustaining the rule-makers' futile society.

"I knew it," Sasha said dejectedly when she reached the library and found that the door was locked. "What do we do now?"

"Chill! I have the solution. I saw it in a movie, and it looked simple enough." Carol removed a bobby pin from her hair and began to move it around the inside of the lock.

"Are you sure that's going to work? The keyhole is a lot bigger than that pin; I get the impression that you're just moving it around inside without touching the lock mechanism," Sasha said.

"Hey, don't make me nervous. I need concentration for this. And keep your voice down."

Moments later Carol had had enough and kicked the door open with a thunderous bang, which reverberated throughout the hallways.

"What did you do that for?" Sasha asked perplexed.

"Keep your voice down, you fool, they'll hear us!" Carol replied with a laugh as she entered the room.

"How can you tell me to keep my voice down when I'm sure the whole school heard you breaking the door down. The headmistress is going to kill us!"

Carol ignored her and closed the door. Then she blocked it with a chair so they wouldn't get caught unawares. "See? If they try to get in, they won't be able to. And when we're done, we'll leave the door closed and they'll never know we were here. OK, when they see the broken lock, that'll be another story. But let's examine your book now, and please, Sasha, keep your voice down, or we're going to get caught."

Sasha couldn't help but laugh. You had to appreciate Carol's caliber, not just because she was the only person in life who went through everything in her own way without caring what anyone else thought of her, but because she was also quite witty, even in the tensest moments. Her sense of humor helped calm the situation, which encouraged anyone who might be nervous, and instantly banished anxiety with a good laugh.

The girls chose one of the more hidden aisles as the location for their investigation. They sat down at the desk that was closest to the window, and placed the candle in the middle of it, sticking it there with a few drops of its own wax. The rain, from the tremendous storm, which seemed to be getting heavier by the minute, beat a tattoo against the windowpanes beside them. The girls opened the book and studied the blank pages. They were as before

"Let's be smart and review the facts. What's the difference between the first time you saw the ink, the second time, when nothing appeared for me, and the third time, when we were in front of the girls and the traces were clearly visible?" Carol asked.

"The first time it was my tears that wet the pages. The second time I went down to the courtyard and let the water drops fall on the book, as I had deduced that the title was a riddle."

Carol listened to her friend, looked at the cover of the book and read the title aloud.

"Wow, aren't you clever, Sasha. I mean, I would have got it quickly too, since it's clear that the letters disappear with the waves and reappear again with a few drops of water, just as you said earlier. But it would never have occurred to me to check it out in the rain. It is most curious: the title of the book reveals the only way it can be read. But what kind of science is this, and whose book is it?"

"My God, Sasha, what if it's toxic? Who knows what chemicals were used to make it react like that to water? We were so intrigued we didn't stop to think. We could be poisoning ourselves unawares. Curiosity killed the cat! What if it was an evil plan of Lara's? No, she is not smart enough to create such an incredibly good plan." The girls laughed at the absurdity of the idea.

"Let's think. Who would throw such a precious, innovative volume like this at someone else?" Carol wondered aloud.

"Maybe someone who couldn't figure out the riddle. We should ask around or put up a poster to find out who had the book before and ask them where they found it," proposed Sasha naively.

"Do you really think that by putting a notice on the wall of this horrible place, where everyone hates us, you'll get a response from any of the girls we unfortunately have to live with? I can hear them now, 'Ah, yes, it was me who threw it in your face. Yes, of course, it makes perfect sense'," Carol replied, bringing Sasha to her senses.

"What if we put up a notice saying, 'Book found in the cloister with unrecognized handwriting. The owner of this volume is requested to collect it immediately from the library'. If I saw a picture of the book and learnt that it contained mystical letters, my curiosity to know what is written on its pages would definitely make me take the bait," said Sasha slyly.

"It sounds like a wicked plan to me. It's perfect! But we shouldn't we read it first?" Carol asked excitedly.

"Yes, of course, we should. But how do we make the ink reappear?" her friend wanted to know.

"Good question. Okay, let's review. The first time you were in the rain, the second time I soaked the book with water without anything showing up in it, and the third time you soaked the book yourself with soaked hair," Carol briefly recapped.

"It was rainwater each time, but the letters only appeared when I did it. That doesn't make sense," Sasha remarked.

"I don't know, maybe I should do one and then you the other. That way we could check your hypothesis."

Carol wrung out the water in her hair over the open book and waited to see what would happen. Nothing. Then she moved the water with her finger across the pages, but still nothing happened. "It's your turn, Sasha. Try your hand."

Sasha soaked her hands in her wet hair and placed her palm on the first page of the book, held it there for a few seconds and then lifted it up. Immediately, the two young women felt a shiver run down their spines. She slammed the book shut so quickly that it blew out the candle, leaving them in the dark of the library. The only light they had now was the lightning, which flashed across the window and briefly lit the aisle they had chosen to decipher that magical tome.

Busted

Just then, a fearsome sound swept through the dark corridors of the library and reached the ears of the girls: the library door was being opened. Both girls' hearts tightened as though gripped by a fist. They heard the chair, which Carol had so strategically left blocking the door, scraping over the floor. The noise lasted an interminable five seconds. Without a moment's hesitation, they immediately hid under the table they had chosen to decipher the riddle of the book and, feeling a rush of adrenaline, held each other's sweaty hands tightly. Suddenly, the table was aggressively pushed aside exposing the frightened girls to a fierce glare.

"What are you two doing here at this hour? And I hope you have a very good explanation as to why you broke the lock and blocked the door with a chair," the headmistress thundered.

"Headmistress, how lovely to see you! Your voice is like the sound of angels right now," Carol exclaimed, relieved.

"That's enough of your lip, missy. Your blarney won't get you out of this predicament, my girl. Lara, very responsibly, has kindly informed me of the outrageous behavior you both exhibited in the quadrangle. And if that was not bad enough, you then seriously damaged a door with the purpose of entering a room, which you both know full well to be out of bounds at this hour. What on earth were you thinking? These actions constitute very grave offences, and you are both suspended until we decide what to do with you," she said with great authority.

"Lara is nothing but a malignant, pedantic liar, who delights in trying to make other girls feel small so that she can feel better about herself. She's rotten inside, Miss. She's evil! Can't you see that?" Carol replied resentfully.

"She's not the only one who's seen you creating havoc, girl," the woman scolded her, trying to discipline the young woman. "Nor is she the one who broke into the library after hours."

"Come on, Headmistress, we only broke the lock because we were dying to study. We're only allowed to expand our knowledge in the library at certain times of the day. I don't know about you, but my mind is voracious, and so is Sasha's. We just wanted to read a few books together and this is the only place we can find them. So, we had to break down the door: it was an attempt to satiate our intellectual curiosity. It was either that or let the intellect die forever."

The principal glared at Carol over the top of her glasses, pointed at the two students, and announced, "I will personally take you back to your room and see to it that you stay there until breakfast time. Now, come along, chop, chop!"

The next day, when her last class of the afternoon ended, Sasha was surprised to see a chauffeur waiting for her with her things already packed in her trunk, ready to take her home. She didn't even have a chance to say goodbye to her friend, Carol.

Of course, the headmistress had deliberately organized it this way. She'd had the boarding school's maids pack her things while she was in class, and the porter bring them down to the entrance, so that everything would be ready for when she was collected after her last class. She had further arranged that the friends would be in separate classrooms for their last day, and, thus, would have no opportunity to play up or make a scene when they said goodbye to each other.

As soon as she was in the car, it started. Sasha looked out the back window trying to find Carol.

"Stop! Turn around immediately, please! I have to say goodbye to my friend! I said stop!" she pleaded desperately.

"I'm sorry, Miss, I have strict orders to take you directly home," the driver replied.

"Home?! I don't have a home!" Sasha wailed as she tried desperately to open the window, which the driver had blocked, to shout to her friend. Her attempts to make herself heard were futile. Trapped inside the vehicle, Sasha could only watch tearfully as her friend, who had gone out in search of her, disappeared from view as she was driven away from the boarding school.

***

After they had been going for about an hour, the scenery changed. There was nothing to be seen but dense woodland on both sides of the road; tree after tree, one after another, always the same monotonous view, which harmonized with the gentle rocking of the speeding car, causing Sasha to fall asleep with her head resting against the window. It was not until several hours later that the young woman awoke. Looking through the glass, she noted that the landscape had changed little. There were still trees, but of a different variety than before.

"Where are you taking me?" she asked the driver.

"To the Mansion of Courdeil, Miss."

Sasha was perplexed.

"I haven't been there since I was a child. Why there?" she asked intrigued.

"You'll have to ask your grandmother about that, miss. I'm just doing what I was told."

After passing through the midst of a lush and seemingly endless wood on a road that seemed to be in the middle of nowhere, the stone walls of the great mansion began to appear before them.

"Here we are, Miss."

Sasha watched the large gates at the entrance swing slowly open with a rusty groan, which gave the place an even gloomier air than she remembered. Then they entered a gravel drive lined with large sycamore trees that led them straight to the main door of the mansion.

"I had forgotten how impressive this place is," Sasha confessed as the car pulled into the gravel sweep in front of the house.

As soon as the car stopped, the chauffeur jumped out and opened the door for Sasha, giving her the freedom to breathe the refreshingly pure air that brought back so many memories. After getting out of the claustrophobic car, in which she had spent so many hours during her interminable trip, she noticed that the front door to the mansion was open. There she saw an old woman with long hair, who was dressed only in a white nightgown and standing barefoot on the cold stone of the steps, was waiting for her.

"Grandma?"

The old woman smiled and opened her arms, waiting longingly for her granddaughter to come to her.

"Come, my dear. Look how much you have grown! You are already quite the young lady."

Sasha approached her cautiously and hugged her timidly, as she was still bewildered by all that had happened. She found it very strange to see the affection of her grandmother, an old woman she had not seen since she was a child and who she barely remembered. In addition, her unexpected return to that place, had aroused a strange feeling that disturbed her very soul.

"I know you're wondering what you're doing here, but don't worry, everything in its own good time," her grandmother soothed.

"I guess I'll have to have the concussion treated and wait for them to decide what punishment they are going to give me for breaking the rules," the young woman replied.

"Don't worry, my dear, that's all taken care of. You won't have to go back to that horrible place ever again. Never again. Not that place or any other like it," said the old woman.

"But, Grandma, what are you saying?" her granddaughter asked, bewildered by the conversation. "At some point, I'll have to go back to boarding school. They've only sent me here until..."

"My dear, I have spoken to your headmistress and made some permanent changes, nothing for you to worry about," said the old woman, making it clear that she had pulled strings to get her out of school in the middle of the semester, something that was not permitted.

"But, Grandma, my friends!" exclaimed the frightened girl.

"What friends? Carol? It's no secret that she's your only friend, my dear, and that doesn't mean you're a misfit; it just makes you even more special, but you don't know that yet and that's why I won't let you go back to that place. Don't worry about Carol. I'm sure you'll see her again, because true friendship never disappears, even if a thousand years go by. And if it should be that you never meet again, for whatever reason, that's because she wasn't a real friend. Either that or she's dead."

Sasha looked at her grandmother in shock, wondering whether she was joking or if she had gone senile since she had last seen her.

"My dear, friendship and love go hand in hand. When they are genuine and pure of heart, they are meant to be, and therefore remain, no matter what happens. A true bond never disappears."

"Maybe your path is not the same as hers. No two people are the same, and to grow we have to follow our own path. When there is a fork in the road, both have to choose which route to take, and, often, the ways part. But when something is authentic, those paths will cross again without the time spent apart affecting their feelings."

"Now, I want you to go up to your room, take a bath and put on something comfortable. You won't need to wear that uniform anymore," said Grandma firmly.

Feeling desolate, Sasha headed for her old room. Every step she took brought back memories of that huge house. On the walls were paintings and photographs, which were half-covered by the climbing plants that created an indoor botanical garden, giving that extravagant and forlorn mansion a much wilder look. As she climbed the stairs, she ran her hand over the cold, white marble of the walls. But on the last step, she stopped with a shudder, and stood still. She was now in front of the door to her room, just as she had seen it in her vision the day before, when she didn't know whether it was a memory or just a dream. She wondered if her brother, James, would remember any of it, or had it just been the fruit of a madwoman's vivid fantasy?

She took a deep breath and opened the door. It was exactly the same as she remembered, except for a long green dress that seemed to be attached to some sort of bathing suit. The garment had been laid on the bed with a note beside it that read, "When you are ready, come take a swim." So, wanting to clear her head, she took off her school uniform and put on the stylish and innovative swimsuit. Then, she descended the magnificent stairs, a beautiful, translucent, green silk train trailing out behind her, delicately gliding down the white stone steps and over the quartz floor of the hall. The huge front door stood open, and she passed through it into the open air, where a warm breeze was blowing.

The lilac-colored clouds on the horizon, which looked as though they had been painted with soft brushstrokes, gave evidence to the proximity of a beautiful sunset. Enjoying the spectacle, the young woman walked barefoot across the lawn, which lay in front of the mansion. She could feel the coolness of the grass between her toes, which provoked a sense of freedom in her and spiritual peace.

Something seemed to be spurring her on and, thus, she reached the woods almost before she realized it. She was brimming with joy as she discovered her wild surroundings like a newborn fawn. She felt a quickening, as she experienced something she had never encountered, not even as an innocent child. Her five senses merged, and she was transported into a synesthetic trance.

Sasha walked through the woods as if it were part of her, sensing the moss, the damp earth, the bark of each tree, internalizing the energy of everything around her. The reddish light that pierced the leaves of the treetops illuminated her aura. She closed her eyes and let herself be swept away by the endless cloak of sensations that enveloped her soul. But at that moment she reached the edge of the woods and noticed the estate's large lake. It was even more beautiful than she remembered it, lying there like a mirror tinted by the rosy sky. The surrounding trees and hills were reflected on its calm, flat surface, which was bordered with small stones that sparkled like gems. It was an exceptionally idyllic and magical setting.

"I was here. I remember it. It was real!" Sasha stepped forward and slowly dipped her feet into its cool waters, trailing the silk of the opulent turquoise-green cloak attached to the swimsuit with every step. The pink sparkles of the water and the glints of rhinestones from the depths of the lake ran across the fabric. "This is where it snowed in the middle of summer," she thought. The young woman looked up at the sky and raised her hand trying to reach it, but the sparkles below her caught her attention, so she dipped her face down searching for those twinkles. She kept her gaze on a fixed point to figure out what the shadows on the bottom were and dove down to see them up close. The satin dress stretched out like the tail of a fish, just as though it and the waters were the same, and the coolness of the water made her feel as if she wasn't wearing anything, as she steadily advanced into the depths. And the closer she got, the clearer the images became. Many corresponded to objects quite corroded by the passage of time and the effects of the water. In the distance, she spotted a more or less familiar silhouette. She reached out to touch it with her hand and realized that it was an old wooden hut, covered with vegetation which had grown over it. She tried to open the door, but it was stuck, and her lungs were beginning to need air again, so she swam back to the surface.

When she surfaced, she saw that there was something hiding in the bushes, so she kept her head down with her nose close to the water and swam stealthily towards the shore. But when she got there, the figure had disappeared; vanished into thin air. The young woman decided it was time to get out anyway. She tried to reach dry land without disturbing the water too much in case the lurker was still there. Besides, it was beginning to get dark, and she had to go back without lingering or she would be left out in the open without any light.

Once ashore, fear invaded her being. Someone was definitely watching her from the shadows. So, she began to walk towards the mansion, slyly looking around her from out of the corner of her eye. Then, just after she had crossed the first line of trees, she spotted something moving to her right, not far from her, causing the leaves on some nearby branches to sway, and she could hear the breaking of twigs. Sasha felt her heart skip a beat. This wasn't the time for thinking but for instinct; and her instinct told her to run as fast as she could, as if her life depended on it. With adrenaline coursing through her bloodstream, she amazed herself at the speed she was capable of running and jumping through the trees, as she fled from something unknown. Despite having reached the safety of the lawn in front of the house, she did not stop but continued, panting and heart pounding, through the door. She sped across the hall, and randomly through the house, dragging the exquisite train of her dress, now full of leaves and somewhat stained with dirt, to leave a wet trail wherever she had passed.

"What am I running from? What are you afraid of, Sasha?" she asked herself. Being completely out of breath, her pace slowed, and finally she stopped. She leaned against one of the walls, before letting herself slide down it, while she gasped for air, trying to reduce the palpitations in her chest. After a while she paid heed to the features of the room, she now found herself in. It had large chandeliers, and the furniture was protected with white sheets. Everything was covered with a thick layer of dust. She realized that she had never before been in that room which seemed not to have been used for a very long time.

Death

Sasha picked herself up off the floor and looked around the mysterious room. The feature that most caught her attention was a large fireplace. On the pilasters were reliefs of female figures with long-hair and a tiara. They faced inwards toward the center of the frieze, from which an oval stone protruded. The young woman, curious, approached in order to contemplate the gorgeous sculptures. She touched the silhouettes which had been perfectly carved in marble, their texture smooth and polished; clearly, these were the work of a master craftsman. With her fingers she caressed the oval stone on the frieze, to which the carvings pointed, and it changed color. "What's going on?" she asked herself stunned by the enigma. She massaged the stone until it had completely changed color; the granite had become a jet black that contrasted with the white stone of the hearth. Instantly, the floor inside it shifted to one side and left a gaping hole that looked like the entrance to a hidden passageway.

Sasha didn't hesitate to squeeze through it. Holding on to the edge with her hands, she found her body dangling in absolute darkness, not able to touch the bottom, even with the tips of her toes. She kicked at the void. Nothing. After a while, with no strength left in her arms to haul herself back up, she decided that if this hole was there, it must lead somewhere. So, it was just a matter of faith to let go and see where it took her, knowing that if the bottom was too far away, she would lose her life. But it could also be a test of courage, and only those who passed the test would gain access to the secret. She was so captivated by this idea that she quite overcame her fear and with her new confidence, loosened her fingers and let go.

To her surprise, the distance was only a few centimeters, and she let out a small shriek of surprise, which was quickly cut off when she discovered a faint bluish light under her feet, as if physical contact with what seemed to be small boulders, radiated some kind of energy that made them glow. And so, it was with the silky, long-drawn train of her dress, which seemed to activate a subtle glow just wide enough for one to navigate oneself through that dreary strait. "Mind-blowing," Sasha thought, smiling, twirling, and lighting up the ground in her wake, which gave her an unfamiliar but pleasant sensation, which coursed through her entire being. "Let's find out where this leads to."

Fortunately, the tunnel only had one possible direction, and Sasha headed down it without the slightest idea where she was going. Ahead of her, she heard the crooning of someone singing in a sweet, soft voice like that of a mermaid. The melody lured the girl to a small opening at the end of the tunnel, which was covered with natural vines of all sizes, hanging down like a curtain and camouflaging her. Peering through the vines, she saw a large room with a high ceiling and a large glass vault with steel decoration, through which creepers and exotic plants crept, like an underworld jungle.

Drawn by that melodic voice, Sasha did not hesitate to enter the room. Brushing past the vines that blocked her view, she could see where that beautiful song was coming from. In front of her, right in the center of the fantastic room, there was a huge pool, luminescent like the stones she had been stepping on, but emanating a much more intense light that was activated by the hand movements of the young woman lying on its edge. She was dressed in a white nightgown, which was covered by her very soft, long, pink, wavy hair, her skin as white as snow.

The woman stopped singing and Sasha hid behind the nearest vines.

"Sasha, is that you? Come, come closer," said the young stranger.

"How do you know my name?" asked Sasha.

"My dear, I know everything about you," replied the girl in a familiar tone.

"Grandma?!" After the question, silence enveloped the room, and Sasha came out of hiding.

"It's about time, my child. Come, don't be afraid," said the girl, studying her from the pool.

Puzzled, Sasha approached her a little fearfully.

"Who are you?"

To which the young woman responded by flashing the sweetest smile she had ever seen on anyone's face as she spread her arms wide.

"I thought you'd already figured it out, dear. Come here, come on," she said.

"Grandma?" Sasha sat down next to her. Then, strangely enough, the stranger wrapped her arms around her. "Lara was right! I've gone completely crazy after the blow," Sasha thought aloud.

"The bang on your head had nothing to do with it, my dear, but everything in this life happens for a reason. bigger and better for all of us. The boarding school accident is what brought you here, but that's not what's blinding you, dear," the pink-haired girl explained.

"But this can't be real. I must be dreaming. Maybe I'm still on the floor or in a coma after the concussion. Saying this, Sasha slapped herself in the face. "Owww!" That obviously wasn't hard enough to wake me up, I need another one," she said.

"Mother of God, Sasha, is it really so hard for you to see your grandmother looking so sexy?" asked the girl while holding her hands.

"What!" exclaimed Sasha.

"I was just kidding," the pink-haired girl apologized.

"How is this possible? I mean, I don't understand at all."

"There are many things I haven't told you about a world you don't yet know, but the time has come for you to learn where you come from and to know the whole truth. But for that you must be prepared," explained the youthful Grandma.

"Prepared? Prepared for what?" the supposed granddaughter wanted to know, frightened.

"I have failed you. I thought... I thought you would be safe if I kept you away from all this, if I kept you out of my past and living in ignorance. It was the wrong decision, and it makes me guilty of not having prepared you in time for what is to come. But I never thought that events would unfold in this way," she excused herself, her eyes misty with sorrow.

"Grandma, you're scaring me," Sasha replied, pretending to accept her as such.

"And you must be, my dear," Grandma told her, staring into her eyes as she gripped her shoulders tightly.

"Okay! I'm scared," Sasha confessed.

"Yes! You must fear! You must! Being frightened is a feeling of caution that heightens your most primitive instincts, alerting you to danger. Be frightened! Be worried! But don't ever freeze. Use it to be prepared because we don't have much time. I have to explain everything to you from the beginning, starting with your origins, which will shorten our training period." Although she was terrified and her face reflected an expression of stupefaction, Sasha saw that the young woman who claimed to be her grandmother spoke with conviction about her ramblings.

"A long, long, long time ago," she began to speak, stirring the water with one hand and lifting it into the air, creating a pillar like a that was ascended like small tornado out of the pond, which she transformed into a sphere that she held in her hands, "there were some beings with magical powers. In reality, what they had, my dear granddaughter, was a very deep connection with water; that is, an understanding of this element so profound and of such extreme complexity that it allowed them to dominate everything that was constituted of this compound." The grandmother looked at her granddaughter over the bubble she held between her palms, floating in the air, as she pulled her closer to her. "Sasha, give me your hands!" Grandma held her granddaughter's hands gently and, spontaneously, the sphere rose to the level of their eyes, so that they could only see each other through the transparent liquid. "Now look inside the bubble, my dear, and no matter what happens, don't let go, don't talk, and don't move. Just watch and listen. Are you ready?"

"I don't think so, but I guess I don't have a choice, do I?" replied Sasha, her breath catching and her pulse racing.

"Good, little one, because I need to concentrate and for that you must trust me. Then you will be able to know the truth and to understand where you come from. To achieve this, I can only do it one way. Come on, time is running out. Take a deep breath, without forgetting not to move, don't talk, and whatever happens, don't let go of me. Just watch and listen. Now, bring your face close to the sphere and put your head in it," she commanded.

"But, Grandma, I won't be able to breathe!" exclaimed the girl.

"I told you to trust me! There's no time, Sasha! Put your head in the water and don't let go! Just watch and listen as much as you can. Now, do what I told you!"

The young girl held on to her grandmother's hands, held her breath and stuck her head in that floating orb of water. Grandma held her tightly and studied her with a steady gaze. After a while Sasha shook her head, blinking, sending signals that she needed to come up for air, but the young-looking old woman continued to hold her without paying the slightest attention to her obvious signs of suffocation. She was being left to suffer even as she tried to free herself in vain. She was desperately shaking her head from side to side, trying to get herself out of the blister that seemed to be stuck to her skull, but she was held in such a way that it was impossible for her to free herself. It was then that she panicked.

She urgently needed to escape to get oxygen. She was experiencing convulsions, but her grandmother was still standing there, holding her with steely determination as she cold-heartedly watched her die, seeming to be not the least bit affected by the situation to which she was subjecting her. It was as if she didn't care about her granddaughter's life. It was as though she could not see the girl's desperation to breathe. Sasha opened her mouth to exhale all the air she had been holding before inhaling water until it flooded her lungs. The last thing that crossed the poor thing's mind before she died was to humiliate herself by beating herself up over how stupid she had been to fall for such a twisted trap. How could she have so foolishly trusted the young stranger by whom she had been betrayed? Then she lost consciousness and her heart stopped beating.

The young woman who claimed to be Sasha's grandmother continued to hold the corpse's hands, observing her supposed granddaughter with her torso hanging from the sphere that held her skull so tightly. She continued with her macabre plan, filling the bubble with water from the pool, enlarging it to stabilize the cadaver and prevent it from falling to the ground. She stood motionless, studying the face of the girl, whose mouth was open, her hair floating inside the watery globe, with indifference.

"You're ready now," said the grandmother, placing the deceased in the pool. I hope you'll forgive me, little one," she whispered as she submerged the girl's body.

When the body of the young woman sank and settled on the bottom of the tank, the woman put her hands in and closed her eyes. Then flashes of light began to emanate from her fingers and spread throughout the pool, causing the corpse to spasm, contracting with each burst of light to which she ceaselessly subjected it, until she managed to make one of those almost electric shudders move Sasha's fingers. Even so, Grandma did not stop; she persisted in transforming her granddaughter" body, her machinations becoming ever rougher, until she succeeded with her brutality in making the girl's eyes open wide and remain undaunted under the water, unblinking for a few minutes. Suddenly, as if it were a miracle, the girl woke up in agony, desperate to rise to the surface to get some air. But as the girl was no longer submerged in the water, she was waving her arms senselessly, inhaling oxygen as if she lacked it, although she was in a dry environment.

Something strange was happening. She looked at her hands; they were pale as snow. Then she looked around, confused, as her last memory was of being trapped inside a water bubble. But now she was in completely different surroundings, a place she had never been before. Disoriented, she walked to a glass column that seemed to contain liquid, where she saw what could only be her own reflection; but it did not look like her. The person she was looking at was a young woman with long white hair and abnormally large, almond-shaped, black eyes, without pupil, iris, or sclera. She was wearing a very special outfit: a long-sleeved dress made of a very thin fabric. Upon closer inspection of her face, she discovered that she had a gem attached to her forehead. It seemed to be part of her body, located just above her eyebrows, but she stopped paying attention to it as soon as she heard someone approaching. Quickly, she ran to hide.

"We must not," she heard one of the approaching voices say. "I don't care what they say or what they think, I was brought here and then raised here. I may be different, but I am one for you and I love you. I love you with all my heart. I will talk to your father, I will talk to everyone, I want to be with you, Mihara. I'd rather die than live without you. You are my life, and you always will be. Always. And no one can change that," said a strange but beautiful young man approaching a girl who was leaning against a wall, looking at the boy with tenderness. Shyly, Sasha, who was blushing slightly, watched them from a spot where the couple could not see her.

The sweetheart had features similar to those she had distinguished in the reflection of her own face, but, unlike her, this woman was tremendously beautiful. The woman's eyes were just as large as hers, but pearl colored; her abundant white hair was somewhat wavy and very long; and her skin pale like hers, which implied that she was of the same species. The gem on her forehead was turquoise and her attire was different, much more exquisite than that worn by Sasha. This indicated that she might be someone of a higher position, who seemed to be rejecting the boy without wanting to, as they looked very much in love as they kissed and embraced passionately. The moment did not last long though, as they were rudely interrupted by a group of men who seemed to be part of an official guard. They appeared out of nowhere and surrounded the couple, while the young man covered his beloved with his arms, protecting her from that encirclement.

"That's enough," a man was heard speaking authoritatively from the shadows. "Boy, you'd better step aside. You have broken a law," said the older man, with long hair and big eyes like the girl's, but of a different color.

"A law? Love shouldn't be based on laws. That doesn't make any sense. We love each other and nothing and no one can change that. But you could change the law. You have the power to do so. Open your eyes! She is your daughter, and she loves me too. She loves me as I love her. And I would never hurt her, sir," protested the boy, who had been seized by the arms like a delinquent.

"You arrogant pup! We took you in, educated you, taught you our customs, our arts, fed you and took care of you as one of our own. And this is how you repay us?" replied the girl's father.

"If you truly saw me as one of your own, I would have the same rights as you. Why did you take the trouble to do all that for me if you didn't see me as an equal? You knew from the beginning that my whole life would be a lie. A lie that is not credible to anyone. You never treated me as an equal, but you dared to propagate that lie as though even you believed it. You even tried to make me believe it, but I have lived the truth in my skin.

"But no one dares to tell him the truth to his face because it doesn't lead to dialogue or to his assuming his responsibility. Anyone who is not on his side, he eliminates, period. What equality do you see there? The way you have treated me today is worse than any that you would dish out to any other animal in the outside world; even insentient coral is more valuable than I am in your eyes. You only had one deceitful purpose for my life. You didn't raise me, you used me!" the boy replied angrily.

"Father, please let him go, I beg you," the frightened young woman implored.

"Mihara, you are not to blame for anything," her beloved declared.

"Please, father…" the girl beseeched.

"Mihara, let's get out of here together. Don't listen to your father, let's get out of here, you and me."

The girl approached him, hugged him, and whispered something in his ear. Then the young man began to cry, begging his beloved not to do it, while the guards roughly separated him from her.

"Mihara, you will face the consequences of this act as an example to your people," commanded her father, holding her tightly by the arm.

"Let her go!" shouted the young man helplessly trying to free himself from the guards, who quickly knocked him unconscious and left him lying on the ground, while his beloved screamed and struggled to get free to go and help him. But her father prevented her from doing so, dragging her away from the prostrate boy. It was clear that he was not going to let her go.

The Trial

Sasha's vision began to blur and within seconds she found herself standing in a hemispherical room. Everything around her, including the floor, was made of glass, giving the sensation of being submerged in the middle of the ocean. She immediately concluded that this was an underwater world where, through the glass, she could see sea turtles swimming around the outside of the room, which was illuminated by fluorescent corals. The variety of species that lurked in the waters that besieged the outskirts of that chamber was extraordinary. She had never seen anything like it. But these were not the only creatures. The chamber was filled with people, all the same race, pale as snow and with huge almond-shaped eyes, like the young girl who had been arguing with her father in her earlier vision. Unlike the sea creatures, she could not classify them with any category she knew.

Suddenly, the crowd which had gathered in the chamber began to beat the floor with the long sticks they held in their hands. It seemed that they were waiting for some important event. The sound of the banging echoed throughout the hemisphere, causing the sea creatures to stop and look into the dome. The people parted, forming a corridor at one end of the chamber, whence the sound of chains being dragged over the floor could now be heard. It was so crowded that Sasha had no idea what was happening. She began to move forward, making her way through the crowd, until, without realizing it, she found herself in the front row. Remembering her grandmother's words about keeping her distance and remaining discreet, she tried to move back, but the people at her back had formed a solid wall behind her.

She noticed that the man next to her was becoming suspicious of her presence there, so she bowed her head so that her hair covered her face. She was captivated by the wonders of the magical ocean fauna that lay beneath her feet. Shortly thereafter, she was awakened from her stupefaction by an eerie silence that filled the room with an almost palpable tension, which caused her to look up. Before her stood the young lover from earlier. He was now chained and surrounded by men in armor carrying spears. These soldiers, who formed a barrier between him and the crowd, roughly brought him to his knees.

The people who had congregated in the chamber became profoundly serious as they moved in complete silence to form another corridor. Sasha felt cold sweat on the nape of her neck as she struggled to control the fear aroused by the intensity of the moment. It was then that she saw the girl of her earlier vision, barefoot and dressed in a white shift, advancing slowly towards her beloved who now lay prostrate on the floor. When she reached him, she embraced him.

"Mihara, my love, please don't do this," he implored her. She smiled and gently caressed his face.

"I love you and I always will love you," she responded, before moving to stand in front of an altar at the other end of the room. There, five of these beings, aged, with long white hair and beards, awaited her. These seemed to be the elders of the place. In the center of this Sanhedrin of five, sitting on an ornate throne, was the chief elder. Looking closely at him, Sasha recognized him as the man who had torn the girl from the arms of her beloved in her earlier vision. He was the father of the poor girl, who now prostrated herself before him and in front of all those people, while her beloved lay chained behind her. Obviously, they were to be judged and publicly punished by the girl's own father.

"Father, I adjure you before all here present not to harm him. I beseech you, father, I beseech you, I beseech you! I will do whatever is required and I will bear the consequences, but he must be released."

"Mihara, no!" cried the bound young man in an agonized voice.

"The law gives you the right to change his assignment, but one occupation must be exchanged for another. Are you sure you wish to sacrifice your own destiny to save that of this being?" asked one of the elders, rising from his seat.

"No!!! I won't allow it!!!!" interrupted the boy, trying to free himself from the shackles.

"My love, my sacrifice will not be greater than yours; they can't kill me, but if I don't do this, they will kill you. Please, please, my love, we have no choice," she told him after running to him and hugging him, which forced the soldiers to stop the beating they were giving him for trying to escape, if not to shut him up once and for all.

"That's enough! The decision has been made! This being is sentenced! He knew the rules and broke them, without caring about the functioning of our regime or our people. He has sullied my daughter! My daughter!!! A future great lady of Argua who will never be able to reign because she is so weak and immoral! Nor will she ever again be able to be part of us!"

"Mihara, you are an aberration within our community. You have ruined the honor of your family. You have abandoned your own kind for the love of a being who is descended from evil. It is intolerable! And for this, you will be punished. Punished by me, your own father, and by your own people. You are to be made an example, so that no one else will ever again dare to break our indissoluble laws."

After this the old man approached her with his arm outstretched. The girl was petrified.

"Father... Father, please," she cried desperate for a sign of her father's love, but the man rushed at her, grabbed her by her head and forcefully covered her forehead with his hand. The young woman was completely paralyzed, with her arms loosely hanging down, staring at the ceiling, and all the while letting out a terrifying scream.

The boy desperately pleaded with them to stop, but nobody paid him the slightest heed, except for one of the five elders, who hurried over and sealed his mouth with some kind of magic that he expelled from his staff. The elder then wrapped the boy's head in seaweed, leaving just one eye, through which he could watch the unfolding horror, while his beloved screamed in pain. Mihara was left floating in the air in a horizontal position. The sadness of that beautiful and unfortunate soul was reflected by the phosphorescent fauna that previously swam so freely outside. She was paralyzed, staring into the room, and as her body light gradually faded, so did theirs, as if what had just happened had somehow affected all of them, as if they regretted what had happened. They gave the girl a moment of recognition and respect.

Rage coursed through Sasha's body, and she had trouble concealing it. She tried to keep her composure so as not to cry at the helplessness she felt. It was at that moment when, under the darkness and silence that now overwhelmed the place, the gems attached to their foreheads began to give off a faint light. The boy's tears of grief and frustration at not being able to reach her beloved, gagged and bound as he was, like some wild beast, were simply ignored.

After a while, the room lit up again, giving more visibility to the scene. It was at that moment that the young girl could be clearly seen lying on the floor with her father standing over her, scowling at her with hatred and disgust. The girl's appearance had changed. She now showed human features. Although she retained the same hair, it was a pinker shade. Her skin was flesh-colored and her eyes, which were closed, were of a normal size.

Mercifully, the girl, who had remained languid in the center of the chamber, began to move indicating that she had not been killed. But she seemed to be exhausted and in need of help. Unfortunately, as everyone in the room silently respected the punishment, there was no mercy for the weakened girl, who was getting back up on her own as best she could. She stood looking frightened as she analyzed her body as if it were not her own.

"What have you done to me, Father?"

The man opened his fist and dropped the gem that had previously been stuck to his daughter's forehead onto the ground.

"It was necessary. You are no longer part of this community, Mihara. You are no longer my daughter," he snarled scornfully.

The young woman looked at him with tears streaming down her face. Completely devastated, she put her hand to her forehead to touch the small indentation that had formed, like a scar, now that the gem was no longer there.

"You can no longer stay here. You are to be banished to a place from which you can never return," one of the elders informed her.

"Father, no! It doesn't have to be like this! Father, I'm still your daughter!" cried the poor girl, desperate for her father's love and understanding.

"No, not anymore," he replied coldly.

"Well, then, if a father and an entire community are capable of doing something this cruel to one of their own, just because they love someone different, I'd rather not be a part of it. You are monsters! Shame on all of you! No matter how far you send me, father, you will never escape the secret remorse hidden inside you. And when others look at you, they will always see the inflexible dotard who sacrificed the transcendence of blood and family in adherence to bizarre, archaic laws," Mihara replied, standing up to her father and humiliating him in front of the whole community.

"Take the boy," ordered one of the five.

"Master, he..." answered one of the guards, "no longer...".

"Is a peon of the guard daring to question the orders of one of the sages?" another of the five challenged as he approached the soldier, tapping the ground with his staff.

"No, master," replied the soldier, bowing his head.

Then another of the guards grabbed the immobilized boy and dragged him to an orifice like a transparent tunnel that appeared to be a means of entry and exit to the oceanic exterior.

"Father, you promised! You're going to break a promise in front of the whole community?!," the young woman exclaimed. "Your precious law itself forbids the breaking of a promise. Our word is what made us who we are! We don't make mistakes, remember?" she reminded him.

"It was not we who made the mistake, it was you. Therefore, since we cannot and must not kill our own, through this act of Shawá, you are condemned to banishment without your powers and divested of being a lady of Argua," he explained, trying to regain control of the conversation.

"You're right, I made a mistake... I made the mistake of loving," Mihara answered sadly.

"So, you admit before the whole community that you made a mistake by loving someone you shouldn't have?" her father asked triumphantly.

"Yes, now I see everything clearly and I admit to having made the mistake of having loved a man capable of murdering an innocent person. I declare that I have made the mistake of loving, with all my heart, a man who is capable of banishing his own daughter, and taking everything, she was from her," she replied heroically.

"That's enough!" her enraged parent thundered.

"I attest to having made the great mistake of having loved a man unconditionally, just because he was my father and through sharing his blood; and for having loved all of you in this room, just because you were my people, before I knew that you were capable of doing something so mercilessly cruel to one of your own. And, above all, I am guilty of being so blind that I failed to save the only future and the only hope left for our beloved Argua!" she went on, overwhelming the culprits.

"Do it now!" shouted one of the five. A soldier immediately lifted the boy up to throw him down the crystal-clear well.

But the boy managed to fling his face against the spear of one of his guards, tearing away the seaweed that covered his face and removing the gag that had prevented him from speaking. In a trice, he was immobilized again.

"Banish me with her if you don't want to see us together, but don't separate us, please!" The desperate boy pleaded.

"You coward! And this so-called being was the one who was going to save us all? An individual who doesn't even know how to bear the sentence imposed on him by our people, which was always his destiny, with dignity?! You're just a miserable misbegotten product of evil. We should have sacrificed you as soon as we learned of your existence, instead of taking you in, feeding you and educating you, you ungrateful brute," the girl's father roared.

"You call this fostering? Tricking a child into believing he is one of your own; training him every day in isolation from the rest of the beings in this fortress; and for what? For the sole purpose of sacrificing him when the rest of the community deemed it was right and proper!" the young man riposted.

"You have sentenced yourself, boy. Now do your duty with dignity."

When the guards seized the young man again, dragging him towards the aperture, Sasha noticed that the soldier who had previously questioned the sage's order, grabbed the prisoner's hand in a very strange way, moments before the young man was thrown down the shaft

"Father, no! Nooo!!!!" shrieked Mihara as she watched her beloved slowly sinking, struggling with all his strength to break free of the chains that prevented him from swimming. She ran towards him, eluding the guards, and clung to the glass that separated her from her beloved, misting the floor with her tears. "I love you," she mouthed as she watched him disappear through the glass floor into the darkness of the ocean.

"It is not necessary to make her suffer more than what the mandate of the sentence dictates. It is not a matter of torturing or taking revenge; it is a matter of fulfilling the law," explained a sage approaching the young woman and placing his hand on her forehead. Immediately, there was a flash of light and she fell asleep, falling to the ground with the tears still spilling down her cheeks. Let's get it over with before time runs out," he urged, making her body levitate to the center of the room.

The sages gathered in a circle around the girl and placed their sticks against each other to create a pentagon, with the girl suspended in its center. Then they closed their eyes, and their gems began to glow, creating a luminous sphere around the torso of the girl. The light became more and more intense, until its brightness was so brilliant that nothing could be seen. When light died, the people were able to observe that the young woman had disappeared, though there was still a faint sphere floating in the center of the enclosure they had created.

Unexpectedly, a woman came forward and broke the pentagon created by the sages' sticks, which fell to the ground, their ends breaking into small pieces of coral that scattered everywhere. The emanating light that previously contained the young woman disappeared with a great explosion, which caused a moment of panic among the crowd in the room, who screamed in fear and threw themselves to the ground.

Sasha tried to visualize what was happening but found it impossible because of the hustle and bustle of the moment. Between the large flash that had blinded her and the screaming people running from side to side, she had a hard time looking for her target, so she tried to get closer to the elders. Despite being pushed from all angles, she could see the woman who had interrupted the act, lying unconscious on the ground with one of the dismayed sages bent over her as the remaining four elders looked on in concern.

Then, suddenly, someone pushed Sasha and she fell backwards, and she found herself inside the same tube in which the boy had just been sacrificed. Although she pounded on the glass incessantly and screamed for help, wasting all the air she had left, no one saw or heard her because of all the commotion. Then, having sunk below the bottom of the shaft, her thrashing was only agitating the water around her, as she was pulled downwards by a strong current that she could not fight against. She looked at the bottom of the ocean, which seemed to have mysteriously been transformed into a gem-stone floor. So, she put her feet on it and stuck her head out through the surface of the pool, gulping big breaths of air, and feeling exhausted. She looked around, traumatized at recognizing the place, but confused as to how she had arrived back in the mansion, in the same room that the secret passage had led her to.

She quickly examined her body with resolve and realized that she was once again herself, in human form.

"Sasha?" The girl turned around and saw her grandmother as she had seen her before everything happened, with the physique of a young girl. Still panting, she swam towards her effusively, with tears in her eyes.

"Come here, little one," Grandma purred, hugging her tightly.

"It was you. The young girl was you," the Sasha said as she touched her grandmother's rejuvenated face and hair.

"I loved him with all my heart," she replied, holding her hand tightly so she could feel the pain in her eyes. "That happened before I met your grandfather before I knew this world. I was different in every way, my dear.. It took me a long time to understand what had happened to me. Everything happened so fast, and it was so strange to me," Mihara explained.

"But, Grandma, how could your father...? I'm so sorry," apologized the granddaughter, still stunned by what she had witnessed.

"Do you remember the stories I used to tell you when you were little?" asked Grandma.

"About Argua?" -Sasha asked.

"Yes, about Argua. Do you remember?" insisted the young old woman.

"But I thought they were just stories, Grandma..." she answered.

"No, my child. Everything I told you was as real as what you just experienced," replied her grandmother.

"It's not possible. None of this is possible. I don't understand any of it, Grandma. I have to wake up from this dream," Sasha contended.

"I know that right now it is difficult to accept, but you must believe me, and please forgive me for having made you suffer, my dear. You must understand that it was the only way I could show you the truth. You had to see it with your own eyes, so that you could understand and, above all, believe," Grandma confessed with great anguish.

"I thought you wanted to kill me. This whole thing is surreal. I must be going crazy. None of this is real, is it? I keep thinking that the knock on my head has affected me somehow. Maybe I'm really locked up in an insane asylum without being aware of it. Please, if anyone hears me, I do know I'm hallucinating! If anyone hears me, I'm still sane! I know none of this is real. Oh, help me!!! Please, help me!!!!!" her granddaughter sobbed, fearing she had gone mad.

"My dear child, my little girl!" Grandma hugged her, but Sasha struggled to break free. "My dear, I'm afraid you leave me no choice." And with a delicate touch of her index finger on Sasha's forehead, she induced sleep. "Shhhh! Rest now, little one."

Helpless, Sasha fell straight into the rem phase of sleep, dreaming of the mysterious book she had found and tried to decipher with Carol. But this time, when she soaked the pages with her wet hand, something evil emerged from their blankness;

a black ink that spread over their entire surface and then leaked off the pages and out into the world. She watched in horror as the dark stain spread through her friend's house, and as it crept into her room, stealthily sliding, and splashing along the walls and floor, like a wet shadow trying to catch her. The sleeping girl, trying to warn her friend of the danger, kept calling Carol's name out loud. They had awakened some ghastly thing that inhabited the tome, and now that thing was mercilessly pursuing Carol, stalking her unawares. It came upon her while she was taking a bath and covered her body in black stains like the pustules of bubonic plague. Then the black stain started coming out of Carol's eyes, her ears, her mouth, and nose, choking her with the darkness that had been released, and which was now emanating from her friend's body, spilling onto the floor, flooding the bathroom, and seeping under the door.

The nightmare had become suffocating, ensnaring Sasha, who was sweating feverishly and babbling like a fish out of water as she watched their friendship perish.

Chapter III
A Family United

After her horrible nocturnal ravings, Sasha awoke the next morning lying on the bed in her room in the mansion. She opened the curtains to let light into the room through the large, circular stained-glass window, which reached almost to the floor and surpassed her head in height. Through her window, she could see the entrance to the mansion, the lush woods and much of the lake. The formidable views filled her with optimism, injecting her with a small shot of well-being that mitigated the unease she had suffered during the night.

As every room on that floor had the same round windows, the illumination and panorama in each were of an unrivaled exquisiteness. "What a knock you took, Sasha," she thought trying to come up with a rational explanation for feeling so weighed down by the suffocating distress induced by her delirium. It had been as though a giant python had slowly gripped her, preventing her from having any role in the horrific scenes that unfolded before her eyes. In struggling against the constriction, she had pulled a muscle and felt terribly stiff. She felt utterly exhausted. Nonetheless, attracted by the smell of freshly baked bread, eggs, and coffee, she got dressed and went down to the kitchen.

"Good morning, dear," her grandmother said, smiling at her from the back door of the kitchen.

"Grandma! You look great," she replied, relieved to see her looking aged again.

"Did you expect me to be different?" Grandma answered with a smile.

"Believe me, I prefer you like this, I mean... I'm sorry, I've had a very intense night," she apologized, sitting down at the table.

"Didn't you sleep well, dear?" asked Grandma.

"It's just that I had a lot of dreams... well, more like nightmares," she explained, resting her head on his hands.

"Well, you can tell me about your dreams over breakfast. I've asked the help to take a vacation so we can make up for lost time. Would you like coffee or tea?" the old woman asked.

"I think I'm going to need a good, strong coffee. Thanks, Grandma, I didn't sleep very well so I don't feel at all rested."

Grandma poured her coffee and sat down next to her with a cup of Ceylon tea.

"Tell me about those worrisome dreams, my dear."

Sasha inhaled the aroma of her Jamaican Blue Mountain coffee; it gave her a certain comfort. She idly watched the eddies in it from where it had been stirred.

"How strange!" the teenager exclaimed in surprise.

"What?" her grandmother wanted to know, blowing on her tea.

"Well... the coffee," she answered.

"Don't you like it?" her grandmother asked, puzzled.

"No, it's not that. It's the surface... it's moving as if it were trying to create an image." The moment those words had left her lips, she thought that maybe she should have kept those mystical thoughts to herself.

"And what image do you see?"

Sasha bent over the coffee, watching it closely.

"It's... it's..." The girl jumped in fright. "James!!! You half scared me to death!" she said berated her brother.

"I had to blow on your coffee! I couldn't help myself. What were you doing looking at the cup like that?" he asked.

Sasha couldn't restrain herself any longer and jumped into her brother's arms.

"How I have missed you," the young woman confessed with tears in her eyes.

"What is it, Sasha?" he asked, worried.

"What are you doing here, James? Shouldn't you be at boarding school?"

Grandma looked at her grandson and nodded her head. "And which would you like, James, coffee or tea?" she asked.

"Oh, I think I'll have both, thank you," he replied with a mischievous grin.

"I think we should all sit down, Sasha," said her grandmother.

The young girl looked hesitantly at her grandmother and brother as she took a seat.

"Is something wrong?" she asked.

"Sasha, we need to talk."

Strangely, without understanding what could have happened, she sensed a certain tension in the atmosphere.

"Is it because of me? Since the blow to my head, I think I've lost my mind a bit. I've done something weird, haven't I?" the young woman asked, torturing herself.

"Tell me, sis, what is normality? The concept of what is normal depends on what each society imposes and accepts as such. Or what one believes to be normal, right?"

James started laughing and, looking at her gleefully, grabbed her hand.

"I don't know. I guess there's no such thing as normality, but there are generalized norms, or perhaps personal tastes, which govern what is deemed common, or not, and by those criteria, I certainly do not fit into what is considered normal. You, on the other hand, have always known how to fit in, adapting to every situation perfectly," she lamented somewhat dejected.

"Sasha, I have known how to act and adapt to every moment, but you, on the other hand, have always been brave. I have always admired you because you have not cared what anyone thought of you. You have been true to yourself, whether they accepted you or not, and that takes a lot of guts, nerve, and intelligence, as well as originality. To be your own person requires creativity and thinking for yourself."

Grandma took the coffee pot off the stove, put it on the table and took Sasha's hand. With the other she grabbed her grandson's hand, creating a family triangle.

"James, there's something wrong with me. I know there is," the girl sighed.

"My dear, tell us about the dream you had last night," the old woman insisted.

"Is it that important?"

Grandma and James exchanged a glance. Then they looked at Sasha.

"What's going on, Grandma? Say something, James; you're worrying me," she exclaimed, knowing they were hiding something.

"There's nothing to be worried about, little one. Everything you dreamed last night really happened."

Sasha thought she was being made a fool of.

"Forgive me for not laughing, it's just that I'm so tired after last night. I didn't sleep well and I'm not in the mood for jokes. But thanks for trying to cheer me up in this... peculiar way."

Both James and his grandmother sat silently looking at her seriously.

"Sasha, do you remember when you went into the lake yesterday?" asked her brother.

"How on earth do you know that?" Sasha asked a bit puzzled.

"Because I was there, of course," the boy replied.

"But how long have you been here? And why didn't you tell me you were here?" she reproached indignantly.

"I came a few days ago at grandma's request because she needed to tell me some things. And I stayed to help her when you arrived," the boy explained.

"Were you spying on me? What kind of twisted game is this?" Sasha dropped their hands and got up from her chair to leave the kitchen. But she sensed that something was blocking her way, something invisible, planted in front of the door through which she wished to escape. The young woman bumped into it and fell backwards onto the floor.

"What was that?" Sasha asked in confusion as she picked herself up, but without receiving any answer. "Okay, that's enough. You're scaring me," said the girl who was becoming quite upset.

"I don't think we should have given you coffee, dear," the old woman commented, taking her granddaughter's cup. I'd better make you a lime tea, or maybe two."

James looked at his grandmother smiling, holding in his laughter as he tried to avoid Sasha's glare.

"Grandma's great, isn't she? You know, as a man, I have to admit that when I met her looking so young and beautiful, I had a hard time remembering she was my grandmother. I almost asked her out! Can you imagine? My own grandmother! Yuck, gross!" he confessed to his sister.

"I'll take that as a compliment, you shameless little varmint. You've certainly taken after your grandfather," replied Grandma, carrying on a conversation with her grandson. Neither of them had reacted when she had fallen over; just continued their bizarre conversation as though she were not there. She stood dazed and petrified, trying to figure out why it was impossible for her to move towards the door, while she heard her family talking about what had happened in her dream; the one she had not yet told.

"What happened last night?" she demanded.

"Last night, my dear, you witnessed a dark passage in my life."

Sasha's lip began to tremble from nerves and stress.

"What do you mean, Grandma?" she asked with difficulty.

"My dear granddaughter, I'll answer whatever you ask me, but it may be too much for you to assimilate right now, since you have not yet accepted that the dream you had was real."

Sasha was outraged.

"This is madness, Grandma. Don't you understand that what you're telling me is utterly impossible? And you, James, how can you play along with an old lady who has clearly gone loopy? Have you both lost your minds? If this is a joke, it's in very bad taste. As you can see, I'm not about to fall for your lousy game of lies and surreal fantasies. Honestly, trying to make me believe that you come from another world, one that exists underwater, from which you were expelled and turned into a human as punishment for being in love with a being of another race.

"Do you think it's nice to make me believe that I was physically there somehow? Did you drug me? What did you do to me?" she replied resentfully.

"I think you mean 'how did I get to see it', don't you, Sasha? You wonder how long Grandma has had the elixir of immortality and youth, which I hope to inherit, by the way. We could make a fortune with that secret!" James said to her as he waggled his eyebrows up and down.

"Little rascal," replied the old woman, slapping him on the shoulder with a newspaper.

"It was a joke! You can't scold me for something I inherited from you! You see, Sasha, Grandma may sometimes look like a beautiful young woman, but her brain is still somewhat prehistoric. We'll have to improve the rejuvenating formula."

Grandma reacted by hitting him again with the newspaper, this time on the head.

"But, Grandma, do you want me to stay like you or what?" complained the boy.

"Now do you understand why he came first, Sasha? Come on, sit down, and let us explain. Your amusing brother will palliate any information I can give you with his humor. You must be together in this because it affects you both equally," she affirmed.

"What affects us?" asked Sasha emotionally.

"We mustn't let anyone see or hear us. So please sit down and calm down, dear." Grandma looked out the kitchen windows and then partially closed the curtains, leaving the room in half-light. "Sasha, come sit down. Oh, don't be so stubborn. Just go with the flow... Or it will be worse."

But the young girl remained planted by the door, looking at her brother and grandmother.

"Worse, James? How could it be any worse? You're both crazy. None of this makes any sense. Maybe we're all crazy, maybe that's why Mum and Dad abandoned us. It must be genetic."

James usual affable look changed. It became serious and penetrating.

"What's wrong, James?" Sasha wanted to know.

"I can't get used to it, no matter how many times I see it," he said.

"See what?" Suddenly, the young woman felt a gust of hot air on the right side of her head, a gust so strong that it moved her hair. The poor girl, who was petrified, had the impression that something was breathing on her. She held her breath as she tried to steal a glance to her right. "James, is there something next to me?" she asked.

He stared at her, his face pale, as he rose from his chair.

"Sasha, don't panic and breathe normally. It'll be all right," said her brother.

"Mother of God, what is it?!" she whispered.

"Nooo, no, no, no, no. Just stay calm. Calm down," James said, approaching his sister, who remained completely still, paralyzed with fear, her hair rising every time she felt that warm breeze blowing against the back of her neck.

"Sasha, I love you very much. I have always admired you and trusted you completely, not just for being my older sister, but because you have always made me feel sure of myself by your side. But since our parents left us, you have closed yourself in your own world and stopped trusting others. I ask you to trust me now. Do you trust me?" he asked, looking into her eyes as he held her hands tightly.

"What's going on, James? Tell me what's going on, James." she demanded, her tone dropping as she gasped for air.

"Okay, now you really, really need to calm down. I think all this has been too much for you and it may not have turned out as we thought, but... it's too late to rectify it, so I ask you to trust me, okay, Sasha?"

The girl took a deep breath, a very deep breath, and blew the air out forcefully into her brother's face.

"Okay... Someone didn't brush their teeth this morning," James said holding his nose and looking disgusted. He was trying to distract Sasha.

"James, please do it now before your sister has a heart attack. Come on, stop playing," Grandma quietly told him from behind her newspaper.

"Remember when they told us that mom and dad had disappeared? They told us they had had an accident, but they hadn't found the bodies. And we were so naive that we thought they would come back. Even after the funeral. We were always hoping they would show up at the door. And do you remember what you told me when I cried every night because I thought they had abandoned us, when I realized they wouldn't come looking for us? You calmed me down, restored my faith that someday, on the day I least expected, they would come back, even though it wasn't true.

"You stood strong for me. You made me trust you. You gave me hope to go forward without looking back. Well now I'm asking you, even though you stubbornly refuse to believe anything we have told you since you arrived, insisting on clinging to your own personal experience, which was the only reality you believed in, until last night, when you actually were in another place just as real as this one, but refuse to believe it. I beg you to trust me and do exactly what I tell you, OK?"

The girl nodded wearily.

"Just have faith and trust me for once, like I did with you. Promise me that you will trust me no matter what," he insisted.

"I trust you, James, but you're scaring me."

"Calm down, okay? I'm with you, I'll protect you. Trust me," he soothed.

James held her tightly by the shoulders and forced her to slowly turn to her right. He then prepared to hug her, if necessary, to immobilize her, in case she attempted to run away.

When the young woman turned, she could not believe her eyes. Her heart began to pound rapidly. Such was the shock that her mouth hung open, but she wasn't able to make even the slightest sound, even though she was screaming her head off inside.

James calmly continued to hold her in his arms, trying to pacify her, as far as possible, given the situation. "Are you all right, Sasha?" he asked, concerned.

But she did not answer. She was so frightened that she couldn't even blink.

The Creature

As she turned to her right, her view was filled by a large mat of black and white striped fur. She could feel the heat of that beast standing in front of her, just a few centimeters from her face; her nose almost touching the hairs of the animal's huge chest. She watched the rise and fall of its furry chest as it breathed in and out, all the while feeling its strong breath on her. She finally managed to close her dry mouth and swallowed hard, as she screwed up her courage and raised her head little by little as she studied the gigantic body of the creature. She was more and more amazed as she looked up, even though she was also tremendously terrified. The creature stared at her with its four eyes, which were hazel and outlined in black, its huge eyeballs overlapping each other, asymmetrically. Each eye had two pupils and two irises, which were as bright as crystals, and arranged in pairs on each side of its magnificent face. Below its large snout, sharp fangs protruded from each side of its mouth, and terrifyingly were exposed even when its mouth was closed. Beneath the mouth hung a curious knob of white hair.

"It's an honor to finally meet you, Sasha," the animal said in a deep, deep voice, bowing its head and placing its enormous talon, with its long feline extensions, on its vigorous chest, in a most polite manner. "My name is Rasnar, Guardian of Talos, and I have come to pay my respects and to serve you in this terrible battle that is about to begin."

Sasha let out a nervous laugh, which was cut short by the beast's intense gaze and its intense seriousness.

"Battle?" repeated the poor girl in astonishment as she tried to process what she had just heard.

"Well, yes, mmm... You see, Rasnar, we were about to tell her about it just when you showed up," James apologized as he plonked himself down in his sister's chair. Sasha, who believed she must still be hallucinating, couldn't take her eyes off the animal.

"Relax, James, I'm sure Rasnar understands perfectly," Grandma replied.

But the beast said nothing in response, didn't even look at them, it just stared transfixed while wiggling its tiny ears, which were disproportionately small for the size of its head.

"What is it, Rasnar?"

Suddenly his eyes, which were shining like four black pearls, began to transform into a bluish hue, similar to the ocular reflection of a cat when it is dazzled in the dark. His hair stood on end and from his talons emerged large claws sharp as daggers, although they looked more like spurs. Then, to the surprise of everyone in that kitchen, from his back opened enormous and powerful wings, so beautiful and imposing that next to them the most graceful or magnificent angel would look like an insignificant bushtit.

"I am not sure. We must be cautious. I will set up a guard at every border point in these lands, for everyone's peace of mind. We will need plenty of space to train the chosen ones, my queen," informed the beast."

"Queen? Does that make me a prince?" James asked playfully.

"I am no queen, James. Neither are you a prince nor Sasha a princess, and I would be obliged, my dear Rasnar, if you would not call me that," the old woman remarked.

"Forgive me, Lady Mihara, it is possible that, during your exile, the passage of time has made you forget the suffering and the conditions in which your kingdom lives. But the people for whom you once advocated and stood up to in the face of injustice, sacrificing your own welfare to do so, have since that day been paying dearly for what they did, both to you and to the only hope we had of saving Argua.

"That feeling of injustice against which you fought, even against your own father, thus questioning the highest authority in the thirteen realms, in front of his own people, is what both your people and all of Argua need now."

The old woman stood up, holding tightly on to the back of one of the chairs.

"That day I lost everything. I spoke for no one but myself and my beloved. I was not defending a kingdom or fighting for a cause; I was merely selfish and immature. And for my arrogance, he paid with his life. I am no leader, much less a queen, and neither my words nor my actions should inspire anyone. I was just in love, and therefore blinded. I was an ignorant child who was led by her heart instead of using her head.

"I gained nothing from it but a broken heart and the loss of everything I knew, and the pointless death of an innocent boy. If that makes one a queen, may the gods have mercy on us, because the future of our kingdoms will be doomed to misfortune for all eternity," said Grandma sorrowfully.

"My lady, that is not true. You stood up for what you believed was right even though you knew the risks, and that made you powerful, even though you were banished. What happened that day changed the people and, after your disappearance, the only thing that was talked about in the whole Kingdom of Argua was the bravery of the Lady Mihara, daughter of the chief elder and future Lady Shawá of the Shwanír Fortress. By sacrificing yourself to preserve our ideals and overthrow the arcane laws of the kingdom, you became their heroine. Those laws, which had degenerated over time and were only perpetuated by a silent acquiescence, were established, and imposed by a handful of elderly men to oppress the kingdom's many subjects.

"On that day, which was so fateful for you and your beloved, hope germinated across the nation," reasoned the beast.

"I was blinded by my youthful passion, Rasnar. Instead of saving him, I sentenced him. Because of me, an innocent young man died, and I would not wish that burden on anyone, not even my worst enemy," the woman replied.

"You had the courage to stand up to an entire community ruled by the Exalted Five to save the life of that young man, a boy whose fate it was to meet that same end," the Guardian contradicted.

"I made a mistake, Rasnar, a terrible mistake."

"No, my lady, you had the audacity required to break the rules, to change the established order, to erase and rewrite what was already written. Without realizing it, you reshaped the laws agreed upon by the thirteen realms of Argua, for whom your own ancestors gave their lives. It was neither out of immaturity, nor out of pure selfishness.

"I know you did not do it as an act of rebellion, much less to break the established peace. You did not even do it to gain power. You simply did it because you truly believed in it. You did it because, that day, a grave injustice was going to be committed and, despite knowing the consequences you faced, you put your life at stake by openly opposing the leaders. What you were unaware of is that you accentuated a flaw in the regime that raised both doubt and hope in every inhabitant of the kingdom. You are the strength and spirit of Argua, the inner voice that made them say 'enough' and want to fight for change," he said firmly bowing to Mihara."

"Rasnar, I am not a queen. There are no kings or queens in Argua. Remember, thirteen realms without monarchs. The twelve domains are still communities governed by a council enthralled by fear of the thirteenth kingdom. Everything remains the same. The inhabitants are scarred by a mandate imposed by a tyrant, to whom Argua submitted out of cowardice; a despot, who continues to humiliate the communities with absurd laws written in the blood of innocents and with the impotence of cowards."

"I will not be the one to commit another terrible act in the name of one of the kingdoms, let alone in the name of all the beings in the thirteen realms. So much innocent blood has already been shed for the lust for power of a few, and I will not be the one to take part in another massacre like that one." The woman looked at the beast containing her rage, her eyes blurred with tears. "You have the wrong queen, Rasnar. I have no ambition.

"By throwing myself into exile, I chose to be nobody. I am no longer part of the Shawás, or any community. How can anyone imagine my saving the entire kingdom of Argua?"

Rasnar hung his head.

"Forgive me, my lady, for if I had any doubts about you, I have none now, my queen," the Guardian of Talos remarked tirelessly.

"My dear friend, I am no queen. Please, you must accept that," she interrupted him, settling the matter, for she was exhausted.

"We are royalty!" shouted James happily.

"No! You are not! You don't become something because one person or a group of them tell you to. Not at all!" his grandmother retorted furiously.

"But Rasnar said you are! And if you're a queen, Grandma, I'm a prince, obviously," replied the boy in high spirits.

"No, it is not by lineage," Rasnar said, looking at James. "Nor can it be by anyone's imposition. She is a queen through being the voice of a people; through reflecting the spirit of the people; and above all through being held in the heart of each individual in the kingdom. Being a woman capable of sacrificing herself for what she believes is right, despite having everything against her, she has been the motivation of generations and generations and has filled her people with faith.

"You, Lady Mihara, are Argua's only hope," the beast insisted, trying to talk some sense into her.

"Their only hope was a boy, an innocent young man, who was assigned a cruel fate that annihilated any possibility of salvation," recalled Grandma.

"You and I both know he was going to die anyway, my lady. His fate was written before he was even born. Everyone made sure that it would be, whether he fulfilled his destiny or not. Unfortunately, the sins of the father are often unjustly suffered by the children. The vengeance, anger, rage, and despair of those present contributed to the Shwanír Fortress sentencing itself and everyone in it with that terrible act.

"Though the past can never be fixed, we can and we must learn from it to change our present and save our future," Rasnar said.

"I have neither the power nor the strength to embark on such a journey, my friend. Not even by regaining what I once had could I face the one you know," said the old woman.

"What if I told you that not only could you get back what you once were, but also that you would not be alone? Would you change your mind?" proposed the Guardian, trying to convince her.

"Enough!" Grandma snapped, tired of the subject.

"Silence, everyone. Something is wrong," reported Rasnar, moving his ears to perceive what was happening outside.

The Milkman

At that moment there was a knock on the outside door of the kitchen.

"Hello? Anybody home?"

Grandma looked at Rasnar as she approached the door and in a trice the beast disappeared, becoming invisible once more.

"Yes? Who is it?" asked the old woman from behind the door.

"Mrs. de Courdeil? Good morning, I'm Henry, the milkman, remember me? I knocked on the front door as I do every morning, but no one opened it, and I didn't want to put the bottles on the doorstep without checking to see if anyone was home. It would be a waste to leave all this fresh milk out in the open, wouldn't it?" he explained.

"Oh, Henry! Good morning, sorry we didn't open the door. I was having breakfast with my grandchildren," Grandma answered as she opened the door. "Would you like some tea? For your trouble..." she offered kindly trying to normalize the situation.

"Thank you very much! I'd really love a cup of tea, ma'am."

Grandma proceeded to pour tea for the milkman as he settled himself at the kitchen table.

"These are my grandchildren, Sasha, and James. They've come to see me for a few days," she said by way of introduction.

"Nice to meet you. Next time I show up, you'll know who I am. We can't let the rich, fresh milk I bring you every morning go to waste," commented the man who seemed to have a monotonous conversation. "What was that?" the surprised milkman asked, getting up with a start.

"Are you all right, Henry?" the old woman asked solicitously.

"I thought I felt something on the back of my neck. But I must have imagined it. Well, I'd better get going or I'll be late for the rest of the households and without the milk they won't be able to have breakfast!

"I guess we'll see each other again if you guys stick around for more days. Nice to have met you," the milkman said as he hurriedly gulped his tea, burning his mouth and throat. In the end, he left half of the cup and strode rapidly towards the kitchen door. He turned the knob to open the door, which opened no more than ajar before it slammed shut with such a jerk that it wrenched his arm. He continued desperately struggling to the door as if nothing had happened.

"It must have got stuck again," Grandma said nervously as she walked to the door and opened it without further ado.

"There we go. Sometimes it seems like this door has a life of its own," the old woman said with a false laugh, trying to gloss over the odd situation while she kept an eye on Rasnar as she was the only one who was able to still see him once he had become invisible. But her glazed expression, as she stared into the emptiness, made her look like a madwoman.

"Well, have a nice day!" said the milkman, walking briskly to his milk truck.

"Rasnar! You can't do things like that here," Grandma scolded bolting the door and putting her hands on her hips, very indignantly.

"I didn't like him," the beast defended himself as he made himself visible again.

"What did you do to him?" James asked grinning widely.

"I just blew on the back of his neck. I wanted to make him nervous," said the beast, laughing.

"Sasha, you are very quiet, my dear," said Grandma, observing her granddaughter, who was still sitting petrified at the table.

"Was this here before?" the girl asked pointing to the place at the table where the milkman had been sitting.

Without a word, the Talos Guardian jumped over the table and out through the large kitchen window. The children ran to peek out to see what was going on as Grandma walked out the door.

The beast's large wings spread and slowed its landing on the milkman's truck, which it then grabbed it with its large claws and immediately lifted into the air as it took flight again with the milkman screaming inside the vehicle. Then the monster released the van in mid-flight and the man flew out like a crash dummy, but Rasnar caught him, the way an eagle catches its prey, hooking him by the foot with one of its talons, when he was just inches away from touching the ground, where he would have ended up like an egg that had smashed against the pavement of the mansion's driveway. The milk truck, on the other hand, ended up crashing onto the lawn in front of the mansion, breaking every bottle of milk it was carrying.

The Guardian flew back towards the kitchen door, with the screaming milkman hanging upside down from his big talon, before letting him drop so that he could open the kitchen door, the same door he had not used when he left the kitchen Then, as he was entering, he caught the milkman with his tail, wrapping it around his head covering his mouth and silencing his screams. In this way the beast dragged him inside.

"What are you doing, you brute?" Sasha shrieked angrily.

"Far out! Have you seen yourself? What a beast! In the best sense of the word, not because of your looks, you know..." exclaimed James, exalted at having seen the Guardian of Talos in action for the first time.

"Give me a room where I can be alone with the human," growled the beast.

"Rasnar, not here," Mihara answered.

"You no longer have a choice, my queen. They know," said the Guardian, looking at the symbol on the table.

"I'll take you. I know a place I dreamed about last night," said Sasha.

"Thank you, but there's one thing I must do first," said the Guardian, leaving the man on a chair.

"If you need to go to the bathroom, you have a whole forest of trees out there for yourself and you have our permission to mark them as much as you want," James offered, trying to be funny. He was referring to Rasnar as though he were a little animal that did his business outside.

"You have to cover his eyes and mouth and tie him to the chair," Rasnar explained nonchalantly, leaving James in charge. I'll be right back.

The beast released the milkman. Given the force with which it wagged its tail to free him, it knocked him to the ground. Then it went out the kitchen door and flew into the sky, opening its wings. From up there he enjoyed a perfect view of the entire mansion and its affected territories. Then he let out a roar so loud that it reached the ears of the people in the nearby villages. The neighbors thought that a storm was approaching and spent a few minutes watching and commenting on the appearance of the sky, surprised not to see a single cloud.

"What is he doing, Grandma?" James asked once the milkman was gagged and tied to the chair.

"He is protecting us."

At once, Rasnar began to let out roars that shook the floor beneath the family's feet. The roars projected sound waves that ranged over the mansion's estates and skirted the dozens of acres of the manor. Then he came down to earth, rattling the leaves of the trees like rain sticks. Next, he sat down right in front of an ancient elm tree, his back to the house, and adopted a cat-like posture, his tail brushing the grass gently as it snaked from side to side. And there he remained for hours, vigilant, like a sentinel, his head held high, watching the treetops, but especially that of the old elm tree.

"What is he doing now?" Sasha asked, looking at him through the broken window.

"He's talking to the trees, my dear," her grandmother replied.

"Do trees talk?" James was surprised.

"They talk, they dream, they sleep, they laugh, they cry," the old woman answered with emotion in her eyes, educating her grandchildren about what they were not capable of seeing as humans. "Certainly not like you and me, but they do feel all the emotions we can experience," she clarified, observing her grandson's astonished face. "Do you and I, when we feel, do so and show it in the same way?" she asked, creating a dilemma in the boy's adolescent brain.

"No, but I mean... Trees spend the day still and silent, they are not intelligent beings like us, who can hold a conversation, have feelings and do activities," said the young man convinced of his reality.

"Do you really think so?" The old woman approached James from behind and squeezed him against her as she pointed through the window to the woods. "The trees hear us, my dear grandson. They watch us, like silent spies that no one pays attention to, and some of these trees have been watching us for over a thousand years from where they stand, watching us be born, grow and die, generation after generation.

"Do you think that you, at sixteen years old, are smarter and have a better understanding of life and our daily lives than they do, just because you can interact as a human with other humans in this world where you think you are the center of everything?" The boy was perplexed by this new concept of reality. "All beings on this planet, from the largest to the smallest, are alive, James, and having life implies having feelings, thoughts, dreams... As well as feeling pain.

"Being alive implies being conscious; being in communion and in balance with the world around us and with everyone else. But not everyone is able to understand the ways in which other beings perceive things or how other species communicate because they depend on the deficiency of what their eyes can see, and their brains interpret. Just because other species do not flaunt their communication in plain sight so that anyone can perceive it, does not mean that they are inferior beings or do not exist.

"The being who thinks he is more intelligent than others, does so out of ignorance and a lack of understanding, and thus feels superior. But his superiority is illusory as he becomes the weakest link in the chain. This is due to the paucity of his intellect and his lack of emotional intelligence; he quite simply does not have the capacity to understand the functioning of the other living beings that cohabit the planet with him.

"It may be that the ignorance of the human being towards his own species and other beings on this planet makes him avoid reality in such a way that it nullifies the capacity to perceive the processes of the other species that coexist with him. Due to his illusory superiority, he is confident that he has the right to pontificate about everything that he regards as less equal and, thus, he classifies them as inferior, inanimate, or soulless things. But his overweening ego clouds his vision, and his tiny brain fills his mouth with nonsense, which he spews out like stuffing falling from a cushion with holes.

"In short, what human beings are not able to perceive or understand is nullified by them –unless it can be used to their benefit, of course– thus completing the closure of their mind to any understanding of the great multicolored variety of the whole, as it stagnates in their monochromatic world. Those of us who can see the world as it really is, try to help them open their eyes. We attempt to teach them to expand their mind, to train their brain like a muscle, and live and learn in a healthy way. But if that fails, we take pity on them for the terrible mental diarrhea they suffer without even realizing it. The truth is that most people tend not to put themselves in the other person's shoes when they reason; nor do they assess the effects of how they were raised and educated, or the environment in which they move; and least of all, ask whether their brains have been damaged by the cold, gray and shallow prevailing system.

"Acting selfishly often takes precedence over peaceful communication by which conflict can be avoided and mutual respect fostered". James clasped his grandmother's hands lovingly to his chest as she continued to speak a little more calmly, even though you could tell the subject was warming her blood.

"Many millennia ago, humans lost their connection to the land, but it wasn't always that way, James. There was a time when they communicated with nature and wildlife, as Rasnar is doing right now. Though it seems that legacy no longer exists. No one seems to have the time to devote to understanding or respecting what surrounds us, not even for the people or beings we hold close, like that precious elm tree. It has seen many lives here but is treated as non-sentient, as an object that camouflages itself within its environment, like the air that is so necessary for survival, but goes unnoticed under its cloak of invisibility until it is urgently required. Only when something becomes scarce or disappears do people truly appreciate and value it.

"Unfortunately, this lack of culture and intolerance has corroded people's souls and made them immune to observing and understanding other forms of communication and life," said a very saddened Mihara.

"Can I get back what we lost as human beings? I want to stop being ignorant and apologize to that elm tree for having climbed on its arms when I was little; for when I carved my name on its forehead. Do you think it will forgive me?" the boy asked interested.

"Well, an apology is never unwelcome, my dear, but I warn you, that tree has a very bad temper," replied Grandma with a smile.

"Well, I wasn't going to approach it now anyway. Rasnar seems to be finishing up his conversation and without him as an interpreter I'm clearly not going to be able to communicate with the elm to explain that I had no idea it had feelings. It's alive, but I don't know... I've never stopped to think about it like that. The tree is going to think I'm an idiot." James burbled on while the milkman waited, gagged, and tied to the kitchen chair.

Once he had finished his chat with his fellow woodlanders, the beast burst through the window again.

"All right, buster, you've taken out the window. If you didn't want us to be out in the open, you've already shot yourself in the foot, because if we leave it unfixed, someone from outside will have to come and mend it, understand?" the old woman chided.

Rasnar took one of the tables used by the servants to stack the trays they collected and nailed it against the window frame. In this way, he left it blocked. Only a few small spaces were left free at the edges through which the light entered. The milkman strained his neck to move against the ropes so as not to look at the beast.

"Well, there was too much light in the kitchen anyway, wasn't there, Grandma?" James said, trying to make peace as he thought of what the beast might do to her if she angered him anymore.

"Take me to where I can chat with this human," Rasnar said as he wrapped his tail around the milkman's head and neck.

The man let out high-pitched moans as the Guardian dragged him across the floor, still tied to the chair.

"With the strength you've got, maybe you could lift the chair a little, huh? Aren't you a bit dazed by the annoying noise you're making towing it around like that? Or are your ears too tiny to hear it?" James opined, covering his ears as Sasha led them through the corridors of the mansion.

"Here we are," she said, standing in front of the door of the unused room with the magnificent fireplace.

She let Rasnar, who was pulling the chair with the milkman tied to it, pass, followed by her brother, who continued to complain about the noise, to which her grandmother appeared completely indifferent.

"An empty room? I could have done that myself, there are about fifteen in this house," James commented.

"This one is special," Sasha explained, approaching the fireplace, with the carved women and the gem in the center of the frieze. This is it." And placing her hand on the mantel, she caressed the gem with her fingers, but nothing happened. "Maybe I didn't do it right; maybe I should have touched it in another way." The four observing her were confused as they watched Sasha feel the carved women.

"Don't be childish, James," Grandma scolded him, trying not to laugh at the boy's teasing his sister by fondling the marble females.

"I don't understand, I thought it was real, with everything that has happened and that you have told me... I'm confused," she said.

"No, my dear, you're not confused. It is what you think it is, only that day you swam in the lake and when you touched the stone your hands were wet. Only a water lady can communicate with the gem and for that you need a means of communication as a conductor," her grandmother reassured.

"Water?" James asked as he slapped Rasnar's butt. "Before you kill me for breaking the human-guardian code, I want you to know that your bottom is still wet with dew from when you were sitting out there on the wet grass for so long. And you did say we were short on time, so, quick fixes!"

As he spoke, the boy approached the gem, pawing at it with his wet hand. Instantly, it changed color and the floor of the fireplace slid aside revealing the access to the subway passage. Well, looks like I'm a water lady too, my dears!" said the boy, waggling his eyebrows and making feminine poses that imitated sculpted women.

CRACK!!! A resounding crash echoed throughout the room, startling everyone.

"The chair wasn't going to fit through that hole," Rasnar explained when he saw that they had been stupefied by his smashing the chair on the floor. It had broken into so many pieces that he was able to slide the milkman through the hole without any problems. The man, who was unconscious from the blow, had pieces of rope and a piece of wood stuck to his clothes.

"Are you sure the Guardian is sane, Grandma? Or is he just a tough guy because that's his nature as a beast?" James inquired.

"He is a Talan, the Supreme Guardian of the Talos Garden," the old woman replied respectfully.

"So, he's a gardener," exclaimed the boy.

"The best!" Rasnar boasted with a humorous twinkle in his eye.

The siblings jumped down the shaft and into the darkness, leaving their grandmother go down last, as she was the only one who knew how to close the trap door, and, besides, she needed their help if she was to get down without breaking anything.

Once they had passed through the tunnel of luminous stones, which made the beast glow as it passed, they entered the room with the pool, where Rasnar hooked the milkman on to one of the vines that overhung the wall. He then went to the pool where he had scooped up a bowl of water, which he emptied over the man's head to revive him.

"Hello, milkman, do you know who I am?" The man, still dazed by the blow and immersed in an accumulation of emotions, tried to focus his eyes on the voice, but when he saw the monster speaking directly to him, he let out a ridiculous shriek before fainting.

"I don't think your appearance is helping, Rasnar, will you let me?" Grandma went to the pool and climbed into the water and submerged herself. When she emerged, soaked from head to toe, she had become a beautiful young woman. She approached the milkman who was hanging unconscious from the vines and gently stroked his face until he came to. The man raised his face to look at the girl.

"Hello, milkman," she greeted him in a sweet voice.

"Who are you?" the man asked, astonished.

"I can be the most fabulous of your dreams or your worst nightmare. Which do you prefer?" she said.

"Hmm, my... dream?" stammered the man.

"Are you asking me, milkman?" Mihara answered, taking control.

"My dream, my dream," he spoke quickly.

"Jeez! With grandma?" said James, astonished.

"Why did you mark the kitchen table, Henry?" Sasha asked.

"I didn't... I didn't want to. I don't know what happened," the man answered, bursting into sad and desperate tears.

"We know, Henry, we know. But we need to know what this all means and why they want to hurt us. You understand, don't you?" Mihara insisted gently.

The confession

"I don't want to hurt you, I never thought of hurting you, I swear! Yesterday, when I was parking the milk delivery lorry...

You see, I do several shifts at work, and I also have several other jobs, because I desperately need money to support my family. I had just finished one of my shifts, when a man approached me. I could not see his face or body, as he kept himself hidden in the shadows the whole time. He asked me to approach him. At first, I ignored him, thinking he was a crazy on the loose in the village, but his words were very convincing. When I looked at him, I saw that he was holding a costly gem in the palm of his hand, and that caught my attention. He offered it to me in exchange for doing a very simple task. I should have realized that it was a trick.

"You have to understand that I am exhausted from working so hard for a pittance and I saw it as a stroke of luck. He showed me that precious stone and told me it would be mine if I helped him find a woman named Mihara. He explained that she was a friend from the past and that he had been looking for her for years. I told him that I had a customer with that name, and I could give him the address. But that was not good enough for him. He insisted that he had to be sure that the person I was talking about was the same person he was asking about. I did ask him why, if he was such a good friend, he did not come himself to talk to you. In reply, he told me that, being so weak and tired after his long journey and the years of searching, he couldn't face risking it not being the right Mihara as that would break his heart into a thousand pieces.

"At some point in the conversation, the man moved his hand into the light; it was very pale, with skin so clear and thin that you could see all his blue veins through it. He insisted that I take the precious stone, that I had earned it, and that it was already mine because of the information I had given him. He said he was very grateful for the help I had given him, because he had been waiting a long time for this moment. So, I reached over and took it. As I did so, the man grabbed my arm tightly. At first, I thought it was his way of thanking me, but when I discovered the mark on my skin and how it was spreading across my body, I understood that behind that strange handshake he had used, there was some kind of black magic." The man, in spite of being held by the creepers, stretched out his arm until he managed to pull up his sleeve with the vines and showed them his arm, which had a grotesque appearance. It was covered by a black stain that extended through the veins of the forearm and protruded in lumps through the pores of his skin. "At the time I was not aware of what he'd done to me, because I didn't feel anything, but when Mrs. de Courdeil offered me the cup of tea, her hand brushed mine and I felt something change. It was then that I saw the stain was spreading rapidly up my arm and I thought I was going to faint. I panicked and leaned on the table to try to conceal my fear and calm myself down. Then I saw the symbol appear on the wood of the table. I swear to God, it made itself. I don't know how, and I can't explain it, and I know it looks like I made it all up because it's completely surreal, but I promise you on my children's lives that it is the God honest the truth. Please help me. Help me!" begged the man in tears of despair.

"Let him go, Rasnar," Sasha ordered.

"It's too dangerous, we don't know if he's telling the truth," the beast replied.

"Let him go. I trust him."

The Guardian moved the claw causing the vines to release the individual, who fell to the ground and then go to his knees, looking very shaken and beginning to weep.

"Don't cry, Henry. We all make mistakes occasionally. It's about learning from our past mistakes and fixing them in the present to improve the future. Right, Rasnar?" Sasha told him, repeating the beast's words.

"I'm terribly sorry. Can you forgive me?" asked the milkman.

"You are forgiven, Henry. We'll fix your arm so you can go back to your wife and children, and with the money you've earned you can start a new life and forget everything you've seen so far," Grandma announced, looking proudly at Sasha.

"What did he do to me? Is it some kind of poison?"

Grandmother and granddaughter examined the milkman's arm together. It looked very bad.

"It creates a kind of safeguard for your obligation, which compels you to finish the task for which you gave your bond. If you break the deal by not complying, you will pay the penalty with your life. The blood in your veins will gradually petrify and your body will turn into a rock coral," explained Mihara.

"What if I get rid of the object?" the man asked desperately.

"It isn't that easy. It's not material, but your word. You made a promise in the presence of what you craved, and by giving your word in exchange for the stone, and, although you were unaware of it, you consensually sealed the contract, which is guaranteed with your life. The object, which was used to convince you, is merely a means of payment for the bond that binds you as, but it is not the knot to be untangled to free you from the curse.

"Tell me, do you still have the stone with you?" she asked.

"In my pocket, ma'am. Let me take it out to show it to you."

The man reached into his pocket, slowly pulled out his closed fist, which he extended toward Mihara's hand. He then placed the thing on her palm. The moment the object touched the skin of the now young old lady, the entire room was illuminated with a burst of light, even though the stone was protected by his hand. The light it emanated was so intense that it blinded them all.

"My queen!" Rasnar shouted, slapping Mihara's arm, knocking the stone from her hand.

She instantly regained her old age, looking worse than ever. Then she slumped to the ground. James went to her aid while

Sasha reached for the gem to grab it, but the beast gave her a gentle shove which prevented her from doing.

"No, none of you must touch it," he explained with authority.

"Please forgive me! Please forgive me! Forgive me, please, I didn't know this would happen! I swear! The gem must be poisoned! I really had no idea! I would never do anything like that!" exclaimed the milkman.

"You're lying!" James shouted from where he was holding his grandmother who was lying on the floor.

"He's not lying," Rasnar corroborated, looking at the object. "However, the stone is not poisoned. It is a gem from the Shwanír Fortress, and it is only granted to the most outstanding of the kingdom of Argua. It is one of those gems that choose the wearer when they have earned it by personal merit.

"It could have belonged to either a male or female Shawá, but from what I can detect, it is much more powerful than that. It is strange, as it is impossible that it belonged to one of the five sages. They are all still alive today and the only way to lose a gem would be to tear it out of the head of a Shawá while they were still alive, which would destroy them both. Besides, the great power required can only be attained by a group," the Guardian informed them.

"What if it was ripped from someone's body after their death?" Sasha asked hesitantly.

"After the death of a Shawá, the gem fuses with the deceased and sends out roots of the same color as the stone, which are spread throughout the body, petrifying it for its transformation. Their bodies are then buried under the Margue, where they regenerate into beautiful reefs that maintain the forms of the Shawá s they once were, replete with the energy of the one who once lived. In this way, they bear fruit again in the cycle of life under the depths of our ocean as beautiful corals of energy.

"That area of the Margue, used as a Shwanír cemetery, is always illuminated. Its strength is so powerful that ships are forbidden to sail over it. Even fish and other sea creatures respect it as a sacred area. They say that it is an area covered by splendid underwater hills of luminous corals of strange shapes and colors that represent each Shawá buried in it, and to enter there, you must be able to withstand all that huge concentration of spiritual dynamism. It would take far more power than has ever been heard of. Such power does not exist, in either our world or this one," answered the beast.

"So, if stealing such a gemstone is totally impossible, it has to be a fake stone that was created to deliberately poison my grandmother. Who could have done such a thing?" James asked angrily, holding Grandma's hand. "I hope for your sake, milkman, that my grandmother wakes up. I don't want her to take the secret of eternal youth with her," said James hugging his grandmother with tears in his eyes.

"James, there is no such thing as the elixir of youth, but if you have your grandmother's genes somewhere, deep, deep down, deep in your soul, you may have inherited it somehow, even if you don't merit it," Rasnar scolded James for his attitude.

"Will she live?" James asked, chastised.

"Look for yourselves. What do you see? Does she look the same?" the Guardian challenged.

"It's true. She has changed," said Sasha.

"No, she hasn't changed; she's changing, like when a caterpillar is in its chrysalis and emerges as a butterfly," Rasnar corrected.

"Oh no, what in God's name is she turning into now!" -cried James in a panic.

"Descendants of Mihara, stand aside," the Talan commanded.

The siblings moved away to let Rasnar take a closer look at their grandmother, who was growing paler and paler and her hair whiter and whiter. Then he gently picked her up with his talons and tucked her into his wings. Then he carried her to the pool and jumped in with his talons held together in front of him, as if praying, while his huge wings continued to hold Mihara, who was in a deep sleep.

As soon as the grandmother's body, which was as rigid as a diamond, touched the water, the pool began to glow with her torso in its epicenter and her skin took on the appearance of fine crystal. The Guardian let her sink to the bottom. When the old woman's body had reached the bottom of the pool, he opened his hands and dropped the stone onto the lady's forehead. At that moment the gemstone began to emit flashes of light and the pond crystallized like ice. Fortunately, Rasnar had gotten out at just the right time, before the water froze completely, but Mihara remained isolated inside.

"What have you done to her?" James wailed.

"I placed her where she must be," Rasnar replied, resting his claw on the boy's shoulder.

Sasha walked over to the solidified pool and looked at her grandmother glistening at the bottom. It was a beautiful, but sad image. She then put her hand on the ice to say goodbye to her, but when she touched the icy surface, a torrent of nonsensical images flashed through his mind, muddling her thoughts.

"Those are your grandmother's memories and those of the person to whom that gemstone formerly belonged. It is not only Mihara who must change; the stone must also change, to harmonize itself with the soul of your grandmother and her powers."

After uttering these words, Rasnar turned back to the milkman.

"What will become of me now?" Henry asked the beast.

"Your ambition to be wealthy will be frustrated, because you won't be able to take the gem, but you will be able to finish what you started and save your miserable life," Rasnar advised.

"It's all your fault!" shouted the young man looking furiously at the milkman.

"Stop it, James! Don't you see that revenge, anger and hatred will only rip you apart inside. They only blind you so that you make even more mistakes?" Sasha warned him, looking at her brother with tears in her eyes.

"Now you must succeed your grandmother," said the Guardian, bowing to the young woman who was appalled by his words.

"You said that one was not a queen by lineage," James reminded the Guardian.

"Yes, so I said. But I have not chosen her for lineage, but for her words and for her heart. I hear the same voice that once was Mihara's, when she was her age, and for being, like her, a lady of the water," he explained.

"I'm a Waterbender too, aren't I? Besides, I'm the only male," James protested scornfully.

"It takes more than that to be a leader, James. Your destiny will be different, but no less important," the beast replied.

"Rasnar, what are you saying?" Sasha asked fearing she already knew the answer.

"My lady, how much do you know of her past?" he asked.

"Well... I thought I knew everything, but I don't seem to know anything. Our parents died when we were little, and Grandma sent us to separate boarding schools. I honestly thought she didn't love us. I never heard from her until yesterday. I thought our parents and grandmother had abandoned us," the young woman confessed.

"My lady, if I may, I would like to give you and your brother some advice," the Guardian offered.

"Continue," James commanded regally, his voice dripping with sarcasm.

"You are both descended from a mixed bloodline, as you know: you are part human and part Shawá but, although my lady Mihara never told me, you are clearly the descendants of another great caste in Argua, one, as you know, that is in the depths of the Margue, for that is where the Shwanír citadel is located, ruled by five immortal sages. Their people have the greatest longevity in the whole kingdom; hence they boast of having more knowledge, claiming their wisdom is superior to that of others, for they have had more time to study, to train, and to observe. They are the great Masters of Water, as well as many of the other natural elements that surround us.

"For those reasons, many believe the Shawá to be the most powerful race of all the realms, but, even with all their power, united with the Exalted Five, they could not stand against..." the Talan's voice froze.

"Against whom, Rasnar? I need to understand what's going on. You understand that, don't you? I have been dragged back to this cold, empty mansion, and the last memory I have of this place is the loss of our parents and being abandoned by our grandmother. Then there are the endless nightmares which leave me unable to distinguish what is real from what is fantasy," exclaimed the girl, glaring at the beast, full of fury.

"You turn my mind upside down with your fantastic ideas and images that manage to overturn my rational idea of what I considered real. You scare me with your stories and, to top it off, you now tell me that I must go to war; a war I'd never heard of, but I'm supposed to care about, just because a stripy monster with wings has chosen me to be queen of a fictitious kingdom, in a future in which I may already be dead!

"So, it seems you want me to go from being the biggest loser in high school to leading an army, win a war, and then rule an entire imaginary territory, just like that? I'm sure I'm locked up in an insane asylum having become completely deranged, or I'm in a hospital hallucinating under the effects of some strong medication because of the blow to my head I got at the Queen Victoria School, as none of this makes any sense at all," she complained.

"Zotrak," Rasnar said.

"What did you say?" shouted James, bursting out laughing.

"The other part of the lineage from which you are descended," the beast explained.

"We're descended from what?" James asked, confused.

"It is the name of evil, born of the darkest darkness and black magic. A dastardly demon, the worst there can be." Rasnar approached the pool and sat on the edge. From there he watched Mihara gleaming and glimmering under the great sheet of ice. "People hide their true name for fear that when they speak it. They will be cursed with a horrible death, like the one who killed his own mother on the very day he was born.

"That's why people call him Zotrak. A ruthless killer of everything that has life: animals, plants, children, women, and men... Even his own family.

"He managed to seize power in the kingdom thanks to the regime of fear that he established through terrorizing the population. He does whatever he wants, when he pleases, without limits, without morality, without heart, without conscience or remorse. His power is so great that not even the Exalted Five, together with the members of the Council of Argua and the rest

of the realms, deploying their very best warrior, could successful-
ly confront him.

"But after the storm, the sun always shines again. After years
of suffering and darkness, there was a tiny clearing in the sky
through which a small ray of light penetrated, lighting a spark
of hope. You know, I was once told that every cloud has a silver
lining; an aphorism your great-grandmother taught me. Though
pain, rage, bad memories, and revenge sometimes do not let us
see the message of that saying clearly, time leads us to discover
the true paths and the significance of the teachings of our elders.

"Living in fear under a regime of violent repression, in which
envy and intolerance are virtues, is not living. Though it is not
easy –it never is– it is not too late to seek change, no matter how
difficult it may seem. To be happy, we must free our minds from
every supervening imposition, whether of our own or others'
making, and learn to be tolerant." The Guardian looked at Sasha
hopefully. "You are that voice now, just as your grandmother
once was, and it is your voice that will keep that spirit alive in the
people and ensure that this message does not disappear."

"Rasnar, is that Zotrak my... our great-grandfather? Do we
have that monster's blood in our veins?" she asked in worriedly.

"Did you know our great-grandmother? Which one?" James
asked, dumbfounded.

"Yes, Sasha, you are descendants of the evil one. And
James, I knew, and was a very good friend of your human
great-grandmother, the mother of your grandfather, Charles,
Mihara's human husband," he said.

"But how is that impossible? Grandma came from the lineage
of Waterbenders, they didn't mix with other species. What you
say doesn't make sense. I was there, I saw how she was forbidden
to be with her beloved before she was banished, and that boy was
definitely not evil," she insisted.

"And how could you have known our great-grandmother if she was human? What relationship did you have with her? How did you know her? Wasn't she frightened when she saw you?" she continued.

"In answer to your first question, yes, they did. One Shawá in particular crossed the barrier of races, although no one knew to what extent, but I see it clearly in you. I am sure that she fought for that equality without even knowing that she was pregnant, and that she did it only because of the love that bound her to that young man, who was condemned to his unjust fate to pay for the sins of his father.

"Your grandmother refused to accept this as a natural law of life. She claimed that if you do not know the son, you cannot judge him by the acts of the father. She asserted that only the deeds one personally does to others should be taken into consideration and nothing else. But even though the boy's past and present were impeccable, for the sages, by loving a Shawá lady, he had crossed the line and that a was enough of a crime for them to sentence him to death. Because of their fear of breaking centuries of tradition and culture, they were unable to embrace evolution, open their minds to other times, other circumstances and other visions, something your grandmother did naturally," he answered.

"Then the dream was real," she said, interrupting him.

"Sasha, we took more time with you because we know how sensitive you are and we didn't want it to be too hard for you to digest, but now I feel lost and so do you," James said. "This is beyond us, but we'll get through it together; I'm not going to leave you alone. I need you, you know? You are my only family. Better than I could ever have chosen."

The girl grasped her brother's hand tightly and nodded with a soft smile.

"I feel the same way, James. Thank you, brother." Then the girl looked at the beast, holding her hand tightly in James'. "Rasnar, I was there, I saw it all, I could have done something to save my grandmother and the boy, but instead, I was paralyzed," the young woman said, admitting her cowardice.

"That was real, it just happened a long time ago. Your grandmother wanted to show it to you as quickly and directly as possible, so that you could understand what happened. It was done through an alteration in time, within a memory in which you could not have changed anything at all. It is called mnemo objective transportation. The water masters, the Shawá s, use water as the enveloping medium to allow them to immerse themselves in that which they want to see or experience. But it can only be done with those who have the water gift. It has never been done with anyone who did not have that grace, as the consequences would be fatal," commented the Guardian.

"So, I could have died," said the young woman self-pityingly.

The beast burst into gales of laughter, its deep, booming voice, producing an echo that reverberated throughout the house.

"You think it's funny?" she snorted angrily.

"Oh, yes! Yes, it is! You clearly know nothing! I had no idea you knew so little about yourselves. This shows that a tree continues to grow, even if it does not know its roots. But think how lost it would be if it tries to shed its leaves without being deciduous," Rasnar replied, unable to stop laughing.

"What do you mean by that? I don't think it's funny. I could have died. Do you find death funny?" she challenged him.

"No, my lady. What amuses me is how ignorant you are of your abilities. It amuses me that a descendant of one of the most powerful lineages among the Waterbenders could be afraid of what gives her life meaning. It's the equivalent of my tearing off my wings because I think I'm going to be harmed or killed if I fly. Do you understand?"

Sasha let go of James' hand and looked at Rasnar with fury in her eyes, her fists clenched tightly to hold all her anger in them, so as not to lose her mind.

"Then teach us! Show us everything! I'll bear whatever it takes! I don't want to be laughed at for my ignorance. I don't want any more surprises or any more unresolvable mysteries that make me doubt my sanity. I want to learn everything even if it breaks my heart. No matter the effort it requires from me, or anyone else come to that, I want to learn. Whatever it takes. It won't last forever, so I'll get through it!

"I'll do whatever it takes to end all this, because that's the only way I'll ever be allowed any peace or happiness. So, tell me, how much do you know, and how much can you teach us if we're as powerful as you say?"

Rasnar watched the young woman's spirit come out in force and smiled.

"Step by step. First, we must remove the loose threads. Tell me, milkman, do you want to keep breathing?" The poor man, who was catatonic, looked at the beast warily. "I see you're not too keen on the idea. Well, luckily, for you, my queen must put her training into practice. Sasha, from now on I will be your trainer. Take a rock and put it in your mouth."

This was not at all what Henry expected. It was absurd that the girl would put a rock in her mouth as a means of torturing him. But then he thought it was maybe all a hallucination brought on by the stress and fatigue of so much work.

"What? But what kind of training is that?" asked James with a chuckle.

"Why are you laughing? It's for you too. You'll both receive the same training," Rasnar replied sharply.

"Yes, sir!" said the boy, wiping a stone on his shirt and putting it in his mouth.

"Now you must concentrate on it, licking it like candy, without swallowing or chewing it."

Hearing this, he spat the stone in indignation at the tasteless joke.

"Hey, that's going too far, it's not like I'm an idiot," the boy protested.

However, Sasha's cheeks lit up as if a flashlight was shining through her flesh from inside her mouth, showing the reddish color of the blood under her dermis.

For while James was making a fuss, the young girl, keeping her word to the one she now considered her mentor, had followed the beast's instructions, even though no one was paying any attention to her. The girl was determined to continue with the training because she longed to finally understand her past, present, and future life.

"Now visualize a precious stone, the first one that comes to mind, and spit the stone into your hand," Rasnar instructed her, seeing the young woman had agreed to respect him as her teacher. Then he placed his huge talon on the girl's shoulder.

"Is that a sapphire? My goodness, we're going to make a killing!" James exclaimed, picking up stones and stuffing them into his pockets after seeing what his sister had spat out.

"Well done, my lady. Now give me the sapphire, please."

And without a word, Sasha handed the precious stone to the Guardian. The latter approached the milkman and placed the precious object on his hand, leaving the dying man completely bewildered.

The Pact

"This is for you. Though we can't give you back your gem, we can give you another one of great value to help you resolve your present difficulties and to enjoy the future. Thanks to it you will have the financial security to be able to spend time with your family," Rasnar told him.

"Sir, I don't deserve it. I have only brought misfortune to this house because I was blinded by necessity, and I will pay for it with my life. I feel the poison is taking me to the other side. But my wife and children deserve better. I know it is a lot to ask, especially after all the harm I've caused, but please, I beg of you, take the stone to my wife," the man replied, haggardly.

"No, milkman, you will live. The curse will disappear as soon as you finish your work. The poison only begins to take effect once you start the deal, but as soon as you finish it, keeping your word, it will cease to exist without leaving a mark on you; that is, you will only die if you do not fulfill your task," the beast explained.

"But how am I to finish the job? Haven't I done enough harm already? I have poisoned Mrs. de Courdeil. I guess that must have been the man's hidden purpose. If I had known, I would never have agreed to his damned deal," the dying man lamented.

"No, that was not its purpose, neither the stone nor that man spread poison to anyone. Mihara is in a chrysalis for having had the audacity to touch the gem, a that stone did not belong to her. The person to whom it previously belonged was far more powerful than the man who brought it, and the power the stone contains is far greater than he could ever wield. He is sacrificing himself for the greater good; for something he believes in. If I'm not mistaken, his ideal is freedom and, just like me, what he seeks is a queen.

"But it is also possible that I may be wrong. Perhaps he is one of Zotrak's evil stooges; one who is willing to senselessly sacrifice himself for him, in this world, which is so far from his own, though I doubt it. So, you must return to him, if he is still alive, to tell him that the mission has been accomplished. If he is not already dead, you must bring him here without delay. Now go and complete your mission, Henry."

The milkman stood up and, staggering, infected by the stain that silently coursed through his body, tried to shake hands with the beast, to which the Guardian responded by sticking out his talon and imitating the man, placing his outstretched hand next to his.

"You shake hands cordially to greet or close a deal, Rasnar. You should shake it like this," James explained, treating him like a fool.

It responded by emanating energy from the claw, which rendered the human unconscious.

"That's why I didn't want to hold his hand, smartass. I couldn't let him remember where he had been," explained the Guardian.

"I won't forget, don't worry," replied the boy, swallowing hard.

"But if he doesn't remember, how will he accomplish his mission?" Sasha asked.

"He will only remember that he made a deal and that he must finish it urgently by bringing the other party to the mansion. I will take him outside the house so that when he wakes up, he will think he has had an accident on his way to the manor. I'm sure that when he sees that no one came out to help him, he will assume that there is nobody here, that the lady of the house and her servants took a vacation. Even so, he will bring the one we need to meet to us here."

And with his tail, he dragged the milkman across the floor until he reached the wrecked milk truck. The siblings were left alone in that room, with just the glow of the pool to light the room, a reflection of the state of their grandmother, who seemed to be made of white glitter at that moment.

The boy sat on the edge of the water, admiring the stones he had earlier picked up from the ground and greedily stuffed into his pockets to turn into jewels. Sasha watched him as she pondered his reaction when he discovered the stones turned into gems, instead of worrying about his grandmother, who lay in a deep coma underwater.

"Hey, James, you do know that the rocks will always be there for you, right? There are plenty of rocks in the world and you can be very rich," she said, forcing him to rethink.

"I know," said James with a mischievous grin.

"You're my brother and I love you more than anything else in the world, even if you sometimes get on my nerves. And I don't want to lose you, little brother. I don't care what happens to me, but I couldn't bear it if something happened to you. This whole thing, it's... This story is overwhelming. I see Grandma and I find it hard to believe that it is really her, but the truth is that, as surreal as it may seem, it is real and it is our story, one that we were deprived of a long time ago and that is now being revealed to us as an obligation.

"Look, I don't want to force you to join me in this adventure, because that decision is yours alone to make, but I want you to know that whatever you decide I will always support you."

James stared at her for a while, hesitant, and then fixed his eyes on his precious stones, knowing that she had already made up her mind. But he had to try to persuade her, didn't he?

"I don't want to leave you alone in this, Sasha, I don't want to abandon you. Come with me, please. This fight is none of our business. Hey, we can get rich! We wouldn't have to go back to school, we wouldn't need anything; we'd live the life we wanted, without any more disappointments or humiliations or misfortunes.

"We could pay the best doctors to take care of Grandma. Anything is possible now, sister. Whatever happens, wherever it happens is not our problem, understand? Remember what Grandma said: 'Children should not pay for the sins of the fathers'. You and I lived in a real world; our life wasn't the best, but we got along fine, and now we have the chance to finally improve that life. Do you really want to complicate it with more problems; problems that are not even ours? Heck, we don't even know where Argua is; that's if it really exists at all. It's all too crazy," said her brother.

As she listened to him trying to convince her with his platitudes, Sasha fixed her gaze on her grandmother's submerged body, which now glittered like a million diamonds. Somehow, inexplicably, her grandmother was still alive.

"We didn't know anything about anything until grandma suddenly showed an interest in us a few days ago. If I'm honest, I thought she didn't even remember us, but our bond is different, we've always had each other. Just you and me, Sasha. It's clear that all grandma wanted was to use us. Then that giant flying furball comes along and tells us that it's our duty to sacrifice ourselves for people we've never met and know nothing about, and for a society that banished our grandmother. What have they ever done for us? As far as I can see, they've brought nothing but misfortune to our family," the boy spat.

"James, I must stay. I want to know where I come from. Until yesterday, I used to throw stones like a caveman, but today I discovered that I could turn them into sapphires. Who knows what else we are capable of? Can you imagine breathing underwater or flying? We may even be able to save lives!" With her words, the young woman managed to captivate her brother, so she made one last attempt to express what she felt was her duty and try to accept James' decision, whatever it was. "I must stay to find out what happened in our family, find out where we came from, find out who I am and what I'm capable of, even if it means making a sacrifice.

"If it is true that there are innocent people suffering under a regime of despots, and that all our family misfortunes began because of those injustices, I want to fight them and change things, even if I have to sacrifice myself the way grandma did. A seed doesn't look much, but it germinates and becomes a plant, which, in time, bears fruit and propagates. There are seeds of change growing inside each one of us, and if they grow roots, then even a stump will be difficult to eliminate. If we manage to get those seeds inside a few people, it will not take long for them to pass them to others, who may only need a little push to start a new process that triggers a change in everyone's life. And as those seeds are passed around and develop new roots, there will come a time when those principles are shared by so many that the movement will have become invincible.

"I think if we tried it together, it would happen even faster, but I can't stand aside for my own comfort, James. If I do, the misfortunes of others will spread, the injustices of the world will increase and only a few will enjoy a bitter happiness because of the abuse of an elite. Besides, I need to know more, there is another world out there we don't know about. We are not alone in this universe, James. Imagine that!

"I just realized today that we know nothing, absolutely nothing. I can't go back to school and go on with my life ignoring all this, acting totally normal, even if we were loaded with money, you understand? It's clear to me now. I need to know, so I completely renounce the luxury of living banally without any commitment, oblivious to the realities of this world or any other. I don't want to live in a comfortable but closed environment, in which I feel safe but empty. I can no longer live in ignorance, evading reality, turning a blind eye to what is happening, not knowing who we really are or what we can do," the young woman reasoned.

"Sasha, I..." James couldn't even look his sister in the eye. His eyes filled with tears because he didn't want to leave her alone. He wasn't like her, that's why he begged her to stay with him, for fear of losing her forever and being alone.

"It's OK. I totally get it," his sister soothed him, hugging him. "You know I love you more than anything, James. Don't worry, everything will be fine," she said as if she was saying goodbye to him.

"James, it's okay. You're not a coward for wanting something different. We've literally been dragged from one world to another. We've had another reality imposed on us overnight, demanding far more of us than anyone in our situation could be expected to handle, so you're perfectly within your rights to do what you want. Anyone would understand that," she comforted.

"I'm sorry, Sasha," he apologized.

"Just relax. I'll be fine. If you want, I'll help you make sapphires right now, so you'll be happier going towards that future you're looking for, little brother. You're going to shine more than ever," she said smiling sweetly. "Hey, I haven't seen you make any gems yet! You've got to try it! Let's see what comes out of that big mouth of yours," she said, encouraging him.

"Probably coal," James replied, laughing through the tears that still streamed down his cheeks.

"I'll tell you what, in case you're just a charcoal-making machine, I'll help you make sapphires. But in return I want you to do one last thing for me. How about it?"

"Obviously," James agreed, feeling guilty for letting her down.

"When the pool froze with Grandma in it, I touched the surface and different images came to my mind like a tsunami. I think, as Rasnar said, she's processing her memories and those of the person that gem belonged to. Somehow, through the connection we have with water, it made me see them.

"It's possible that it wasn't a fluke and that she's trying to show me something, James, but from what I could appreciate in those few seconds, it's all jumbled up right now. Maybe there's just too much information for me alone. It must be difficult for her to show me what she wants in a simpler way given how weak she is. Alone, I am not strong enough to receive it, but if we do it together, we might be able to make it work.

"I need your help, brother, even if it's just one attempt. I need to tie up the loose ends."

James took a deep breath and nodded.

"We can't lose anything by trying, can we? In theory, the water is our friend, but after everything I've seen in the last few hours, I've become aware that anything could happen," said the boy nervously.

"Then you are going to help me?" she asked excitedly.

"I owe you one, sister. And, although it doesn't look like it, I have to admit that I'm a little intrigued. I'm also from this family. Who knows? Maybe I'll find out who I'm descended from," he smiled bashfully at Sasha.

"Everything will be fine, I think," she replied, taking his hand.

"If we make it through that hurricane of memories, whatever happens, don't let go of me, okay?" James asked.

"I will never let you go, no matter what. I promise you that when this is over, I will make you a mountain of sapphires, even if I have to run out of saliva to do it," she said grinning.

"Well, let's get it over and done with," said the young man, rubbing his hands together and taking a deep breath. He had stood up suddenly creating a cascade of stones which clattered to the ground.

Sasha stood up and grabbed her brother's hand. Then they knelt together in front of the pool and placed their free hand inches from the ice. James looked at his sister with doubt and fear in his eyes. They counted to three and touched the ice at the same time with their palms.

Through that icy layer they saw their grandmother's body undergo a convulsion. Immediately, cracks rippled out over the surface of the ice, and their vision began to blur as they entered another dimension. It was at that very moment that Rasnar returned to the room and encountered the siblings' blank eyes. From his hands emanated a faint light that was eclipsed by Mihara's body, which gave off some kind of energy that the grandchildren had generated by touching the surface of the pool.

The cracks were gradually breaking apart the frozen surface, so the beast reacted with alacrity, placing its talons on it to communicate with the siblings through that icy bond, trying to reach them during the trance they were experiencing at that moment.

"Lady Sasha, Lord James, I don't know if you can hear me, but whatever you are doing, you must hurry. The chrysalis and your grandmother's life are in danger from the energy force you are creating together."

Then the Guardian moved away from them and, with a gentle movement of his wing, caused the ivy in the room to form a curtain around them for safety. In the meantime, he silently awaited the return of the youngsters to full consciousness, watching to see that the situation in which they found themselves did not cause the ice to collapse on the old woman, who now looked younger than ever.

From the subconscious side where the siblings were, things were not looking good, something which could be seen from the outside. They were digging their finger into the ice so hard that no blood seemed to be running through them. Sasha and James were receiving an uncontrollable whirlwind of images and sensations, throwing all kinds of senseless impulses into their minds.

"Jaaaames!" Sasha shouted from an unfamiliar place, wrapped in uncontrolled thoughts and memories, caught in the core of an anguished tornado of jumbled memories that was dragging her away from her brother.

"Sasha, hold on to me!" James cried, Hold on!"

Chapter IV
Memories of a Gem

Rasnar watched the free hands of the siblings moving ever closer to each other until they reached the point where they met and intertwined, emitting a small flash of light that began to melt the ice. The Guardian knelt in front of the pool, and with a slight movement his wings, which he held erect with the tips touching, he began to create a hemispherical bubble to cover them all; a dome of energy that would keep them safe and lessen any further damage they might do to the ice.

It was the maneuver he used when he saw that the flowers of the garden of Talos were in danger, and he needed to protect or heal them. Producing it required a specific gift, as well as years of training, and a relentless power of concentration. Of course, as the Supreme Chief of the Talans, Rasnar was a grand master of the technique.

But this action left them vulnerable to external threats while they were in this trance-like state, so it was usually done under the protection of third parties, who watched and protected him during the process. On this occasion he had no watchers, so he placed himself as Guardian with the risk that, in the event of an attack, he would put the lives of Mihara and her grandchildren before his own.

But the young people were oblivious of the danger Rasnar was in. For them the situation had changed. They were in a gravity-free environment, levitating in nothingness, with the sensation of floating in water without feeling it on their skin.

"My little ones, I am sorry that your destiny is this. Now I fear for you and there is not much time left, so I will try to channel as best I can all the energy and memories of this gem to find myself in harmony with it, but it requires a great effort, and my body weakens by the second.

"If the worst should happen, I know you will do the right thing, and remember that I always loved you with all my heart," Mihara declared, managing to reach the minds of her grandchildren.

"Grandma, please don't leave us. We need you! Argua needs you!" cried Sasha.

"The stone I carry with me is very powerful. It belonged to the lady Riyah and her visions are intense. You must be prepared for whatever you will encounter. Be strong and always stay together; always look out for each other. And, please, be very careful."

Suddenly, the explosion of memories disappeared, and a calmness accompanied by an intense silence enveloped the siblings. They could feel a cool breeze on their skin and ground beneath their feet was firm. To their surprise, they found themselves in a kind of landscape, unlike any they had ever seen before. It was covered with what looked like cropped grass and gray stones, which were soft to the touch like velvet. The stones seemed to have come from another world, possibly having fallen from the sky centuries ago and anchored themselves to the earth they had crashed into.

"Where are we, Sasha?" James whispered, looking around, dumbfounded.

"I have no idea; I don't even know who Riyah is. Do you?" she asked.

"No freaking idea," James replied.

"What a strange landscape. It looks like we are on a foothill of a mountain, but I've never seen anything like it," said the young woman observing the surroundings.

"We are very exposed," said James, dragging his sister behind a rock, where they lay on the mossy ground.

It was then that they became aware of the great cataract that issued from the summit of the mountain; its waters cascading down the mountainside with a great roar and a curtain of spray. The micro-droplets filled the air, sprinkling the landscape with a fine mist that made the intensely brown, sticky soil viscous, so that with every step, the siblings sullied the deep green of the mosses that covered that land.

Suddenly, they heard a man scream. It was not a yell of fear or pain, but a war cry. They looked up at the sky and could not believe their eyes. A colossal beast of unparalleled brilliance, covered with black crystals that produced emerald-green reflections when backlit, was flying over them, creating a shadow so great that it turned day into night. James thought that it must be the equivalent in size to at least eight Boeing 777s. Both Sasha and James thought it was the most astoundingly impressive thing they had ever seen. It covered the sky with its immense wings, from which protruded translucent spikes through which the sun's rays passed, creating a spectral glow. As it approached the siblings, it sprinkled them with a glittering, dark green dust that evoked memories of the fairy tales they had loved in their infancy.

Unfortunately, just then, that marvelous creature let out a shuddering scream as it crashed to the ground with great velocity, expelling a puff of purple smoke and what looked like black flames.

"I think he's hurt," Sasha opined.

"And what do you want us to do? Go help him and end up as charcoal? He's a drakon!" said James in terror.

"I know! But he seems to need help. He's in pain!" she replied.

"Wait, can we help? I mean, I thought we couldn't interact in the memories," he interrupted.

"That's true... But look at him," the young woman insisted, embarrassed.

"Sasha, look at the waterfall!"

The waterfall had opened, just as if two curtains of water had been pulled back, to reveal a woman with long bluish hair and large, hazel eyes, which were almond shaped, but without any sclera. Embedded in her forehead was a bottle-green gem. She was wearing a white dress with green sparkles, which twinkled like the dust the beast had dropped.

"Do you think that's Riyah? Grandma said that the gem was hers and since they are her memories, it would make the most sense. But they could also be Grandma's, although that woman is clearly not our grandmother, even though she is a Shawá," Sasha argued.

"When you say that, you realize that we're Shawá s too, right? Because what you see is what's in our blood, even if we don't look like them," James replied.

"Wow, I hadn't thought about it like that. It's just that she seems so different from us...."

The woman approached the drakon, which was lying on the ground bleeding a strange liquid that looked like purple molten glass.

"You are as beautiful on the inside as you are on the outside, my beautiful Rombar," the woman said to the fallen beast.

"Did she just talk to the drakon? She's crazy! She's going to end up barbecued if she gets any closer!" James blurted in surprise.

The drakon turned its huge head towards the woman and tried to sit up, using its wings for support, and resting its gigantic skull next to the woman, who was minuscule in contrast. She could be gobbled up in one lick, like a grain of rice, if the animal so wished.

"Get out of here before they see you, Riyah!" the beast urged. "I'll cover you with my wings to hide you while you go back to your people!"

"The drakon just spoke," James said without blinking, wide-eyed.

"Let me help you, my friend," said the woman, approaching the reptilian titan without any sign of fear. Then she put her hand on his neck.

"Riyah, I am the only one left of my people and my destiny is written. Evitur will not be long in coming. If you stay with me, you will meet the same end as me," protested Rombar the drakon.

"If this is to be your end, let me help you avenge your kind and let the death of your lineage not be in vain," offered the Shawá Lady.

"Listen to me! My end is at hand, and if you don't leave, yours will be too." The woman stretched out her arm and the animal bent its head to rest it on the palm of her hand. Then she recited a few words, and the beast completely lost its strength. Its wings fell to the ground, its legs bent, and its eyes closed, despite its effort not to let its soul succumb to the darkness. Riyah, my friend, what have you done to me?" asked the drakon sorrowfully.

"You will die, Rombar, for that is your destiny and I alone cannot change that, but you now harbor a poison that will spread to whomever you harm. Make a wound deep enough to introduce your drakon powder into his blood and the spell I have cast over the cells of your body will spread inside whoever you injure, cursing him and his loved ones, just as he harmed yours." After these words, the woman turned away with tears in her eyes. Turning back to the drakon, she continued, "You, my friend, will avenge your race. Be strong, Rombar. I promise you that you will always be remembered, for you and yours will not disappear from memory as long as I live, and my gem endures. I will keep you alive in my memory forever," said the woman.

"Riyah, go! Go before they arrive," the drakon ordered, forcing the young woman to retreat behind the waterfall.

Shortly thereafter, some wild-looking men appeared. They were led by a man twice their size, whose body was prodigiously muscular. He had blond hair and a rugged appearance and carried two axes with sharp blades in his large hands.

"Evitur, ignorant barbarian, exterminator of species, you will die and yours with you for what you have done to me and mine," the beautiful dying creature valiantly threatened.

"You filthy beast! You're the only one left. The most sought after, the hardest to catch. But not for me, because I'm going to finish you and that will be the end of drakons in these lands, forever."

And with a thunderous cry, the hunter's men cast chains, which were propelled from the cannons that they carried on the backs of the horrible monsters that they rode, over the great Rombar, in the hope of trapping him under them and thus immobilizing him. But the drakon, garnering the last of his strength, took flight and escaped from those steel nets. Unfortunately, as he was unable to move his wings properly, he fell to the ground not far from where he had taken off. His breathing began to slow and, utterly exhausted, the great animal dropped his head. However, the pain that weakened and tormented him was more than physical, it was also mental. His frustration at the incomprehensible injustices done to his

race and his impotence in face of that terrible immorality af-
flicted his soul. His broken heart, which he barely kept going
with ever weakening palpitations, and his body exhausted
by having be constantly alert and on the run, could make no
further resistance.

The great Rombar surrendered to those evildoers and lay
where he fell, right in front of the hiding place of the siblings,
who were still huddled behind that big rock. The dying gaze
of the beast's emerald eye pierced their pupils and perpe-
trated their souls, filling them with a feeling of sadness and
overwhelming pity.

Unable to control her impulses, Sasha approached the extraordinary creature and stood just inches from its huge, closed
eye. Then she placed her hand under the animal's tear duct and
soaked it in its tears of lament.

"I'm terribly sorry, Rombar," said the girl with great sadness
in her eyes. Instantly, the drakon opened his huge eyelids and
looked directly at the young girl with his large eyeball, as if he
could see and feel her.

"This is not right. It's not right, you evil bastards!" James
cursed, approaching the drakon as Evitur's men appeared on
the other side of the great stone to begin dragging the titan away
with the help of their beasts.

Rombar's huge body was carried away from the boulder. The
scene was so atrocious that it was difficult to witness it without
imagining one's own death. Submerged in a horrible, heartbreaking sense of helplessness, the siblings could only watch as
the pack of cowards dragged the beautiful creature away to its
death. Their leader laughed as he stood beside the drakon and
tore off a crystal scale with one of his axes as the beast continued
to agonize. Despite their impotence, an immense rage began to
invade the minds of Sasha and James.

"Psychopathic degenerate!" James shouted, clenching his fist to try to restrain himself from any further outbursts, while he watched those barbarians butcher the poor animal.

Suddenly, Rombar let out a heart-rending scream and, with huge effort, swung his tail at Evitur, giving him a lash that ripped his face open and threw him to the ground. Evitur got to his feet laughing as he spat blood out of his mouth and wiped the blood, which was flowing from the wound and gushing out of his nose, from his face, as if the whack hadn't affected him at all. It was as if he was actually enjoying it.

"Thank you for this gift, Rombar. Now I too will be a legend. This nice farewell souvenir you have marked on my face will prove that it was me who killed you, the last of your race," the barbarian bragged, wielding his weapons menacingly.

Then, Evitur ran towards the beast and delivered a sharp blow from his two axes on the it's huge neck, causing the black shield of crystal scales, which covered and protected the green skin underneath, to fly off. He immediately, slashed deep into the exposed neck, causing the wonderful creature to expel its last breath in a great blaze of intense purple fire as its magnificent head crashed to the ground and its soul escaped its body. Thus ended the life of the last drakon left alive in the entire Kingdom of Argua.

"Now you will forever be merely remembered as a mythological being, while you join the rest of your kind wherever they have gone!"

It was then that the lady Riyah reappeared, climbing up on a rock, without the men noticing her presence.

"Evitur the hunter! Cruel ignoramus, I curse you and all yours! That was the last drakon of his lineage, like the thousands of other species you have exterminated for filthy lucre and the pleasure of bloodlust. You don't know what you have done, but

I will make you pay for it. You shouldn't have let yourself be cut, scoundrel," Riyah admonished with a malicious grin.

"Soon you and yours will be the ones that are hunted, and you'll suffer in the same way as your prey. You are going to get a dose of your own medicine, albeit far less than you deserve. "

"Who is that woman? Catch her!" the hunter ordered his men.

"Now you will pay for your sins," Riyah threatened him with satisfaction as the men ran towards her. But just before they got to her, the lady threw herself into the river created by the waterfall and disappeared right before the eyes of those degenerates.

"Sasha, your hands!" the youngsters looked at each other and discovered to their astonishment and fright, that their bodies were beginning to disappear.

"James, give me your hand! I think we're going to another memory."

The siblings materialized in a dark forest. They found themselves with their hands and knees submerged in the mud that covered the ground of that vision. Before them lay a small clearing that was difficult to see because of the darkness of the night and the abundant rain that was falling on them, despite their being well protected by a large tree.

"Sasha, look!" They tried to move, but they were anchored to the muddy, cement-like ground.

The ground before them began to shift and heave as if some animal was scrabbling its way out.

"Stay as low as you can, James. Hide!"

"I assure you that no matter how much I want to get up and start running once that monster that is trying to get to the surface comes out, I won't be able to. I'm as deep in the ground as the roots of the mansion's elm tree," he said, trying to get off the ground.

"I mean hide so he doesn't find out about us."

"Do you see anything?" he asked his sister as she tried to pull her legs out of the slime.

"No, it's too dark. Wait... I think I see something white."

The mound of earth that was forming like a giant molehill began to fall away from the sides and from the depths of the loam emerged something long and shiny. At first it was hard to see, but then it became clear to both James and Sasha that what was emerging from the bowels of the earth was the body of a young woman.

"I assume that her memories continue to live on through the gem, despite the death of her body. If that is not possible, then it could be grandma trying to intertwine Riyah's memories with her own to better explain the story of this Shawá Lady."

"The truth is, I have absolutely no idea. Besides, it's hard to determine anything for sure in this gloom and with so much rain. It might not be Riyah."

The woman, like a corpse in its coffin, lay motionless on the ground with her legs together and her arms tight against her sides. It was as if the ground had expelled her from its interior in a state of unconsciousness, and despite being fully exposed to the outside air, she remained there flat and motionless for a long time. In fact, she was so still that she looked dead. But she was not completely lifeless, since she seemed to move along the ground as if she were being dragged, though there was no visible sign that she had been grabbed anywhere for her to be pulled in that way.

"Why doesn't she get up and walk?" the boy mused as he observed the lady's dress and hair getting muddier as she passed over the wet and slimy stretch of ground.

"James, I think she's dead," she replied.

"She could be in a deep sleep like Grandma, couldn't she?" he commented.

"I don't know, and how do you think she did that, appearing from inside the earth? Do you think she was taking a nap underground or what? We must find out. There are so many things we need to clarify. Above all, I want to know how Riyah's gem came to fall into our hands...or rather grandma's" she said intrigued.

"Sasha, I want you to know that I will not leave you alone. I'm sorry for what I told you before. This matters to me, and if those who have killed that drakon are the ones to blame for the misfortunes of our people, then we will give those criminals something to think about."

Sasha was grateful for his words. She needed her brother by her side, but that moment of absent-mindedness cost them the body, for when they looked back, it had vanished without a trace.

"Where is it?"

It was difficult to see anything clearly, but the white of her clothing gleamed on that rainy night, yet there wasn't the slightest hint of it now.

"We've lost our way, James, and I don't think we can repeat this memory. It can't happen to us again."

The rain stopped and the earth began to shake as the they started to fade away.

"Hold me, Sasha, here we go again!"

Everything was moving, but the scene didn't change, and they remained anchored, with their legs sunk in the mud and their bodies translucent.

"What's going on? Something was wrong. James, look! In the river!" Sasha said having located Riyah's body as it emerged from the torrent and returned, sliding the same way, to the hole from which it had emerged, where the soil started to pile up on Riyah, covering her body. It looked as if she was being swallowed by the earth. "It's as if the memory is being rewound. Everything is going backwards in time, but much faster. But it's all happening too fast to make sense of any it."

Now nothing could be seen in their surroundings, only darkness, mud, and rain. At that moment, a light appeared in the distance. When the light drew close enough, they saw two horrible creatures who were walking backwards toward them: one of them was pulling a wagon and the other, who was babbling, was riding on it. As soon as the vehicle stopped, he jumped off and stood next to his companion.

Leaving the wagon to one side, they began to dig at the spot where the lady had been interred. In no time they had dug a substantial hole, from which began to emerge what looked like corpses piled one on top of the other under the ground, which the creatures put in the wagon.

"Good heavens, James. Riyah was dead. It's a mass grave. She was probably killed and then dumped in there with all those other bodies," she said analyzing the gruesome scene.

"How could she get out of her own grave if she was dead, then?" the young man questioned, confused.

"I honestly don't know. But look how many people were in there. They must have brought all those people piled up in the wagon and then thrown them in that pit like trash," she opined.

"What kind of vermin would do such a thing? I'm going to kill that hunter. I'm going to kill that hunter. What was his name? Evitur! That psychopath is a dead man," he exclaimed angrily.

"James, we don't know if it was him, and besides, you can't even kill a fly," replied his sister.

"It's obvious, isn't it? Those must be his men, the ones who are in charge of hiding the dirty laundry," he argued.

"They look more like monsters than men. What are those things? They don't look like Evitur's assassins," she asked.

"Sasha, they're leaving! And we're still stuck on the ground, we won't be able to follow them!"

The young woman looked at her hands, puzzled. They seemed to fade away. The mud began to tremble with a slight earthquake. Seconds later they found themselves, covered from head to foot in mud, in a kind of dungeon. The cell they were in had basalt walls, which were hung with chains and shackles, a floor of a blackish brown volcanic sand. The cell was secured with corroded, rusty iron bars. It was very cold, damp, and dark. The dungeon's only illumination came from a torch attached to a column at the entrance. The sound of water drops falling from the ceiling could be heard, echoing from one end of the cave to the other.

The dungeon must have been connected to the outside somehow, as you could hear the rain from a heavy storm beating down, which explained the leaks in the ceiling and the floor being full of puddles.

Unexpectedly, they heard a woman sobbing. The sound was coming from the back of the cell. Neither of the youths had thought to look in that direction, having materialized facing the bars. Turning around, they saw that the large chamber they were in was as deep as it was wide.

"James, don't let go of my hand," said Sasha, holding her brother tightly.

As they followed the sound of weeping, the darkness gave way to a faint, warm glow that lit the far end of the cell. It came from a torch fixed to the wall, beneath which a wretched-looking woman lay on the floor, with her head and the upper part of her body leaning against the wall. Her legs were stretched out, her feet bare and dirty, her arms resting on the waterlogged floor. Her dress was torn; her body was badly bruised and covered in cuts and abrasions; her battered and bruised face was disfigured:

clearly, someone had given her a very severe beating. She looked as if she had been thrown down, and too exhausted to move, lay just as she had fallen.

"James, it's Riyah. Who could have done this to her?"

"Damned monsters! I'm going to help her, I can't take it anymore," said the boy, stepping forward towards the prisoner.

"No, James! I'm certain this happened to her a long time ago, so there isn't anything we can do for her anymore.

Then the Shawá began to move the fingers of her hand with difficulty, as if she were pointing towards a sluice that was next to her, through which the rain that had seeped in from the outside was drained. Then she began to recite some words in such a low tone that not even the siblings, who were standing right next to her, could understand what she was saying. As she intoned, a lot of water began to enter and flooded the entire floor of the cell. At that point, without further ado, the memory began to fade in front of the watchers.

"No! Not now! We need to know what happened!" Sasha exclaimed.

But before the vision completely dissolved, they could see that the girl was making a last effort to place her hands on her belly, which was half exposed by a large tear in her dress. From her abdomen came a small speck of light like a firefly that floated in the air, which she directed with her hand towards the water, where it disappeared with the swift, eddying current down the sluice. The young woman let her hand fall to the ground. Though her eyes were open, they stared vacantly into the darkness.

Although the memory was moving from side to side as if they were losing the signal, they were able to observe the traumatic scene with total clarity. Just before the vision faded completely, they heard the sound of a door and footsteps.

"James, someone's coming!"

But before they could see who it was, the memory disappeared, and everything started spinning around them as though they were in a whirlpool, from which their bodies were suddenly ejected back into the secret room in front of Rasnar.

"Hi, guys, how was your trip?" he asked.

"Rasnar! We can't be back yet; we haven't got all the information! It was all mixed up and there were some men with a drakon and..." the siblings exclaimed together.

"Let's try again, Sasha!" James urged anxiously.

"No, you must rest," the Guardian ordered tenaciously.

"Well, let's take a break, have something to eat and then we'll give it a try," he replied, upset.

"And what do we do with Grandma?" Sasha asked as she watched the pool sparkle over her sleeping grandmother.

"Mihara needs more time. It's a battle between her and the gem. As long as she is in her chrysalis, we must not disturb her," the Guardian argued.

"But how much time does she need? Because she is going to wake up, isn't she?"

Rasnar looked at the two youths and then looked into the pool that illuminated their faces.

"I honestly don't know. Only she knows what she's going through now."

Being Shawá

"The magic of the gems is very powerful. Each lady and knight of the water is assigned to receive a stone, but only a few are selected for this great honor. To begin with, they must exhibit a series of gifts beyond the ordinary for the Shawá race, show outstanding wisdom and be strong enough to withstand the power of having one of these gems meld with them. It is not the Shawá that selects the gem, but the gem that chooses who it will fuse with. Furthermore, the gems are not all the same: just as they vary in appearance, so they differ in the qualities they possess.

"This particular jewel, the one Mihara now wears, is tremendously powerful. It belonged to someone uniquely talented, as this gem is the first to have ever unified with a person to whom I was not originally assigned. She was somehow able to detach her own entity from the stone while letting it retain the energy fusion and magic within it that would allow it to fuse with your grandmother. Only someone with inordinate power could accomplish such a feat. Even your great-grandfather, powerful as he was, required the help of the other four sages to remove the gem from his daughter's head and, not even with their combined power could they preserve the magic in the stone. To have the knowledge and skill to pluck one of these jewels from the head of another Shawá without losing powers forged as one in stone, would mean that they were the bearer of an enormous talisman of power.

In other words, if you simply ripped one of these jewels from the head of a randomly chosen Shawá, the powers contained in the gem be lost, which at that moment would be those of the person himself and those the gem with whom he was unified. As the gem is the energy core of both, you would in turn kill the soul of the Shawá in question, who would become worn down physically and mentally until they died. Depending on the time spent fused with the stone, death would be more or less rapid; it could even be sudden, not just for the bearer but also for whoever tried to seize the gem.

" You Shawá s are immortal for a reason, guys. In your blood you carry the gift of longevity, although it is latent, lying dormant in your DNA, until it can be verified through your being found worthy enough to be accepted by one of these precious stones, which is the equivalent of an eternal life. This is something truly exceptional, which can only be fulfilled when that condition arises in the individual, since the gems only show their power and come to the entity, when he wins it as Shawá. It is the stones that choose to be called by the feminine energy, which flows through the air and water in every particle of our planet, attracting them like a magnet. They are lured by what will make them grow, increasing the powers they already carry within them, and complementing their deficiencies with the Shawá 's aptitudes. On many occasions, talents that neither the chosen Shawá nor the gemstone had before.

"It is, therefore, the purest and healthiest union of relationships; the greatest bond of love that could ever exist. They discover each other, meet each other, grow together day by day and merge into each other, unifying into a single entity, despite being two completely different elements. They complement each other so perfectly that they need each other to survive and evolve the being they have created together.

"Therefore, although your grandmother seems asleep, she is struggling with all her might to combine with a gem that did not originally choose her, but for whatever reason, and I am not sure about this, the stone has been entrusted, at the will of the being to whom it belonged, for the future queen Mihara. This means that however stubborn the jewel may be, since it knows far more than us and understands the risks of something as complicated as achieving a meld with someone who was not destined to it. Through some kind of superior grace, it is striving to adapt to the new body and the powers and the type of energy that your grandmother possesses, despite her being practically human now. The meld will only transpire if Mihara can prove to the gem that she is worthy of possessing it.

"I deduce that the force that binds them now in that tug-of-war is what remains of the person to whom the gem once belonged, which helps the jewel to connect with Mihara," the Guardian explained.

"We believe the gem may belong to a Riyah."

Rasnar looked at the kids in astonishment. Suddenly his hair stood up as if he had just felt a strong shiver and he sensed an inner murmur that caused the appearance of a kind of crest that extended from his head to the tip of his tail, causing it to rise on his head.

"Why would Grandma want to merge with that stone if it can kill her?" asked Sasha.

"Your grandmother did not choose to merge with the jewel. If you remember, Mihara only touched it. It was the gem that wanted the union with her, which clearly indicates that, whoever they are, they sent it on purpose. This means that we are in danger. Whether the messenger's intentions were good or bad, we have been located. But what worries me most is that whoever sent it must be possessed of unheard-of power to have been able to get the gem from the lady Riyah, with her powers still preserved within it," Rasnar spoke in dismay.

"Who could do such a thing?" asked the young man.

"I honestly don't know, but it's something we need to find out." After that, he raised his wings and grabbed the youths by the shoulders and guided them from the room. "All this has given me an appetite. Let's get something to eat. We need to get our strength back and we have a lot to talk about."

Meanwhile, at the other end of town, exhausted, the milkman parked the wrecked vehicle in the company's parking lot while thinking about how to explain the inexplicable disaster to his boss. His entrance into the garage had been far from discreet, however, as the engine sounded like a broken-down tractor.

Once the milk truck was parked, or rather, what was left of it, the Henry stood in front of the vehicle looking at it in a daze, having not the slightest idea what could have caused such a disaster. He put a hand to his head and the other into his pocket. Instantly he felt something hard like a stone. When he pulled the object out of his pants, he was perplexed to find a beautiful sapphire resting on the palm of his hand.

Excited and surprise, the man tried to restrain his emotions by maintaining his composure, quickly hiding the jewel in his briefs for safety, mentally estimating the gemstone's market value. Next, he returned to his wrecked vehicle, which he examined closely, but at the end of his inspection, he was still none the wiser as to what had occurred. Then with a big smile, he imagined his boss's face when he paid for the repairs, and how little of the fortune, which was now his, would be used up in doing so.

"You look like you've had a good morning, milkman. Though you wouldn't think so from the state of your milk truck. An accident?" a dry and rasping voice asked.

The milkman turned around. Behind him stood the hooded man, speaking to him through blue lips chapped by dehydration, skin pale as a dead man's.

"You... You...," Henry stuttered. "You poisoned me! Why should I help you?" he demanded angrily.

"Because if you don't, you'll die. But I think you know that, don't you? Tell me, where did you get that sapphire, milkman?"

The man held his crotch with his hands and crossed his legs.

"You paid me with a poisoned stone! The agreement was to give you the information in exchange for the jewel, nothing more," he replied accusingly.

"Exactly. I gave you the gem, milkman. Now you must give me the information and lead me to it," replied the mysterious man.

"I don't remember the woman you are looking for. And though I don't remember the sapphire, it was in my pocket, so it's mine!" said the milkman, pulling his buckle tight to fasten his pants. I don't remember how I go it, but I know the sapphire is mine. I just want to give it to my family so they can live as they deserve," Henry insisted.

"The stone, milkman, was not poisoned. Where I come from a man's word is signed with the seal of his life; we give no ground to traitors, for no one breaks a law if he knows that he will die for it, do they? So, tell me, milkman, I have done my part, will you do yours, or would you rather die?"

The milkman began to sweat all over, which made it easier for the poison mark to spread across his neck and begin to run up towards his face.

"Complete the deal or die, milkman?" said the hooded man, knowing that time was running out for both of them.

"What do you want from Mrs. de Courdeil"? the infected man asked in agony.

"Mrs. de Courdeil?" queried the concealed one.

"Yes, Mihara de Courdeil," he replied.

"Tell me where she is."

Then he grabbed the milkman by the arm, his fingers sharp as thin sticks, and dug his long blackish blue fingernails into him.

"At Courdeil Manor, a few miles from here. Anyone you ask can show you the way, no sweat. Everyone knows that house," answered the human, observing that the man's skin was cracking.

"But I don't? So, you, my friend... You will show me the way to her," the being ordered authoritatively.

"As you can see, my milk truck is wrecked, so I'll tell you where the mansion is so you can go by yourself. I don't want to go back there. That house is haunted, you know. I got there with my milk truck in perfect condition and came back with it in pieces," replied the milkman without stuttering.

"And with a large sapphire, don't forget, milkman."

The man let go of the milkman's arm and clasped his hands together, rubbing them together as he blew on them. Immediately, fragments of dead skin floated in the air. Then a small light emerged from between his palms like a tiny flicker and in the blink of an eye, before Henry could react, the two men found themselves standing before the outer fence of the mansion. The milkman gave a yell and hotfooted it back town without a backward glance.

But a little way down the road, he saw that the stain had disappeared, and he stopped and turned. "Thank you!" he shouted in the direction of the manor. He had regained his strength and was jumping in the air with joy, not realizing that as he did so, his beloved sapphire, for which he almost lost his life, slipped out of his briefs, and fell to the ground. When he realized what had happened, he ran back to pick it up and put it back in his briefs, holding his pants tightly as he ran with a slight limp, caused by the discomfort of carrying the sapphire there. Euphoric, he headed for home by the quickest route.

"They're here," Rasnar told the siblings as he stood up from the kitchen table.

"Who?" they asked fearfully.

"That's what I'm going to find out."

Rasnar, tore out the wood he had placed over the kitchen window to replace the broken glass, and flew out through the opening he had just made.

"Really?! We've got to teach him how to use the doors," said James trying to put the wood back across the window and failing.

The hooded man stared at the gate. With his hands outstretched, he was trying to open the entrance gates, but his magic was useless, as an invisible barrier protected them, and the spell he used only bounced back against him, propelling him back a few meters and destroying all the bushes growing behind him.

"I think the window is the least of our problems right now," Sasha complained, looking at James uneasily as Rasnar made himself invisible just before he reached the railings. He landed on them in front of the mysterious man. Then he took a leap and, spreading his wings, hovered over him.

"Who are you, hooded man?" he asked from above like a shadow in front of the luminous star.

"And who are you?" the man retorted, covering his face, blinded by the lightning.

"I see you fall apart when you look straight at the sun. That only means one thing," said Rasnar.

"You seem to know more about me than I know about you. You are such a coward that you conceal yourself where I cannot see you. Be brave and show yourself! the mysterious man taunted.

"I still don't know whether you come in peace or for war," the Guardian replied unruffled.

"Ah, that is difficult to answer, since I'm here at two o'clock," he replied.

"I'll make it simpler then. In the name of what war do you come?" Rasnar insisted, maintaining his elevated posture.

"A humble servant desires peace, but to find peace there must be war. My question is: do we have what it takes to enjoy peace after war?"

After hearing these words from the hooded man, Rasnar crossed the wall of protection he had created and descended on the other side of the gate. Making himself visible again, he appeared before the mysterious man with his wings outstretched to protect the stranger from the sun.

"Rasnar, supreme Guardian of the garden of Talos".

Immediately, the hooded man knelt before him.

"A faithful servant bows before you. I apologize for not showing you my face. As you know, where I come from, we not only fall apart in these atmospheric conditions, but our lives are in danger under their effects, and our appearance ceases to be attractive, even to our own eyes," he apologized in embarrassment.

"Do not bow down to me, I am no more or less than you in this time of war," said the Guardian.

Meanwhile, Sasha sat at the table nervously holding her hands.

"What's troubling you, Sis?" James asked.

Last night, apart from the dream I thought I had with the story of our past and grandma, I experienced another vision, and I don't know if it was real or just a nightmare. That's what's eating me.

He seemed stunned by it.

"I don't know if I can help you, but you know you can count on me for anything. Why don't you tell me what you saw?" he asked.

"I have a friend, she's my best friend... Oh come off it, Sasha, she's the only one I have. She's everything to me, James. Ever since we were separated and sent to different boarding schools, I've spent years alone and she's been my only family," the young woman confessed.

"I understand. You're not the only one who's been alone all this time, Sasha," the boy replied, meaningfully.

"Forgive me, James, I didn't mean to sound like a victim; it's just that I'm worried and I need you to understand how important Carol is to me," she explained emotionally.

"Carol? Is she pretty?" The boy asked, hormones instantly rampaging.

"I think you'd like her a lot. You have the same sense of humor, but she'd eat you alive."

"You know, Sasha, I came here before you arrived because clearly, I'm the strongest and I was needed to help you digest everything that was going on. I've been through what you've been through, but alone, and maybe during that time I heard something."

Friendship

"I know Grandma sent someone to protect her, I overheard her talking to Rasnar about it. I think he sensed something, and Grandma got scared. She immediately called the boarding school, and had you come back, because the headmistress must have told her what happened to you and alarms went off, because she immediately asked her for a favor, something about taking care of or watching someone. Then Rasnar disappeared and you showed up here with the driver," he explained.

"Protect her from whom, James? Is it because of the book?" she asked.

"What book?"

"Before I came here, I had a book thrown at me. At first, I thought it was from one of the girls at the boarding school. Not that Carol and I are very popular; notorious yes, but not well liked, so to speak. It had a strange title on its cover, like a riddle, so I looked through its pages and they were empty; that is, all the pages were blank. In fact, at the time I thought it was stupid and I threw it angrily at the wall thinking that someone had thrown it at me to hurt me, since I almost got my nose broken from the blow," the young woman recounted.

"Ahhh! Hence the big schnozzle! I thought it was your new look, to make your face more interesting," he blurted out, acting silly.

"And from those comments you would get along with Carol. Well, the thing is, the book bounced, but I think it wasn't because of my strength, it was because it wanted to get back with me, so I ended up tossing and turning in bed over the title. I don't know why. Then an idea came to me, and I cracked it. Carol was with me when it happened; it all happened so fast that we didn't have time to think about what we saw on that sheet of paper. I thought something evil was coming for us, we both did, until the headmistress showed up and we didn't have time for anything. I didn't even get to say goodbye to her, James," she said, hurt.

"But what did you see that scared you so much?" asked the boy.

The book had blank pages, until I touched it with my water-soaked hand. Suddenly black ink appeared, as if it was coming out of my hand and soaking into the page, and what looked like a smudge became a drawing of Carol and me looking at the book in the library, as if we were being portrayed at that very moment.

"It took us a few seconds to realize it, but when we saw it clearly, we both felt fear running through our veins. I closed the tome immediately, but I think it was too late, I think I opened the door to something evil, I awakened something, James. I did something with the water, with my hands, something that unleashed some kind of dark magic that I can't stop, and I think whatever it is that I've done is after Carol. I'm really worried. I had a dream about her last night, and she was dead, James. I need to find her," she said in dismay.

"Okay, calm down. I'm sure grandma tied up the loose ends before going to sleep. But it's also true that I hadn't heard anything about a book until now. Maybe we should tell Rasnar about it, he might know something," the boy insisted.

"I don't want Rasnar to know anything. If he knew he would have mentioned it to me, don't you think? What if I've done something wrong? Besides, I don't know where the book is anymore. The boarding school maids collected my things, and it wasn't among them when I opened my trunk. It's possible that Carol has it, that they put it among her things, since that's how it appeared in my dream, on her bed, releasing ink that flooded the whole house and drowned her.

"James, she would give her life for me; well, maybe not her life, but she would fight for me like a sister, just as you would fight for me, and I would fight for you. I must find her," the young woman asserted.

"Okay, well, let me think. Grandma knows everything, but she's not available right now, so we'll have to find another method, and you don't want to tell Rasnar about it either, so we don't have access to that trump card either," he said, thinking about the matter, looking for a viable solution.

"It's not that I don't want to tell them, but if I've unleashed something evil, what am I going to tell them? They trust me to save Argua," Sasha explained.

"Well, think hard about how to tell him, but we have to tell him. Hopefully he may already know, or he may not, but for our sakes, for your friend's sake and for everyone's sake, we should let him know, because whatever that book is, I don't think we should keep that kind of information a secret. In the meantime, I will think of a way to find your friend without the help of the great Guardian, but whether we find her or not, you must tell, Sasha."

James disappeared for a few minutes while his sister racked herself with remorse. After a while he returned with a book in his hand and dropped it in front of her on the table, thereby kicking up a pile of dust that made the girl cough.

"A phone book?" she asked in surprise.

"Can you think of anything better?" he replied.

"We have to tell Rasnar," the young woman finally acquiesced as she looked at the huge directory in front of her with irritation.

"And then they say books aren't effective these days," James said with a big grin on his face.

Meanwhile, on the other side of the mansion walls, the Guardian was still dealing with the situation.

"My lord, I'm just a peon, I'm nobody," said the mysterious visitor.

"Nobody, you say? Yet you sacrifice your life for an ideal, for freedom, for others... And you are nobody?" Rasnar answered.

"My lord, I only managed to find you," he apologized.

"For now, my friend, for now." Rasnar leaned down and rested his claw on his shoulder. The fellow raised his head and looked at him with his huge almond-shaped white eyes. His pale skin, corroded by the sun, was wrinkled like cracks in the dry earth of a desert, but inky blue, and his lips had practically disintegrated. Protruding from the hood, was a white tuft of hair with a blue-gray reflection that seemed to be fading, which hung down over his forehead "You came to the right place," said the Guardian as the pawn smiled faintly in response to such gratifying words. I'll take you inside. You and I have much to talk about."

And in the blink of an eye, already on familiar terms, he lifted the man off the ground with his talons and flew with him towards the gates of the mansion, where the siblings were waiting, peeking out of the kitchen door.

"I open a door and you have to go through the window. It's not like we're living in a cabin, it's a mansion! The door's a hundred feet away, stupid!" the boy shouted through the broken kitchen window. He was very upset.

"James, don't be rude!" Sasha scolded him.

"But it's like he does it on purpose to annoy me!"

Her brother went out to call the Guardian through the kitchen door. There he ran into the hooded man, who as soon as he saw the boy, covered his face.

"Humans! There are humans!" he exclaimed.

"Who's the ugly friend you've made for yourself, Rasnar?" James asked.

"How do they know your name? The law forbids them to see us, Guardian!" he complained indignantly.

"It also forbids a Shawá to leave his people and his kingdom to commit treason, yet here you are," replied the beast.

"I see your point, but I am not a Shawá."

Rasnar put the man on his back and, with a leap, reached the side of the kitchen door.

"Wow, that's a new technique, gravity-free jumps, and hobo abductions? What else you got up your sleeve, furball?"

Rasnar gave the boy a lesson in respect by clipping him on the back of the head. Then he went into the kitchen.

"Who is it, Rasnar?" asked Sasha with a knife in his hand.

"Another human..." sighed the hooded man.

"Yes, two humans. And what are you, you creep?" James scoffed.

"Why did you come here?" asked Sasha gently.

"I will not talk to a human about my business," replied the stranger.

"Quiet, Shawá, I assure you that she is trustworthy. They both are, even if one needs more discipline than the other," said the Guardian.

The man stood there, his face hidden under his hood, as Sasha offered him a chair. She then motioned for her brother and Rasnar to sit down as she took a seat. Once they were settled around the table the visitor started to speak.

"I made a deal with a human to give me some information, but I see that he lied to me, since I was looking for a specific being and I found a Guardian and two humans. As for what I am, no, I am not of your species. I am a peon of the royal guard of the Shwanír Citadel of the Margue. Well, I was," the hooded man reported.

"And you don't have a name, peon?" asked Sasha.

"My name? My name..." he reflected.

"The peons of the Shawá guard have no name," Rasnar explained, looking at him.

"I once met a young man and befriended him. He was the only one who saw me as a person and not as a function. From a human point of view, I was just one of many like worker bees in a hive. But he saw me, not as just another insignificant insect among so many others, like we were clones, and he spoke to me of his dreams, of love... With him I learned to see and to feel. He made me see myself as a unique and existential being," he confessed with emotion, which was evident in the tone of his voice.

James turned to make a joke about the relationship of the hooded man and his friend. But Rasnar nipped his intention in the bud with a swipe of his tail across his face.

"Oh, come on, Rasnar! Haven't you got any sense of humor, Talan?" the young man ejaculated in response.

"One day he asked me if I could have a name, what name would I choose and I answered: "I don't know." I wasn't even aware that I was an individual or, as you say, a person. He said to me: "If you can't make up your mind, I'll call you Nose."

"Without knowing why, I endlessly repeated that name and felt for the first time my insignificant existence in that world," he recounted.

"Your name is Nose?"

"The hooded man, with only his disintegrating mouth showing, smiled.

"Now I'm not a peon anymore, so I can have a name," he replied.

"Well, Nose, tell me why did you try to kill the milkman and my grandmother?" asked the girl.

"Grandmother?" the puzzled peon repeated.

"Yes, you sent the milkman to poison her with the stone you gave him," James clarified.

"I didn't try to kill anyone. The milkman made a pact with me. Where I come from, we seal pacts with a promise of death. I respect your grandmother, even though I don't know who she is. And I assure you, I certainly didn't try to kill her or anyone else."

Rasnar put his claw on the hooded man's shoulder.

"Their grandmother is the Lady Mihara."

The peon gawked at the Guardian.

"It's not possible, she was banished without her powers," he exclaimed.

"And human-looking, Nose," said the beast.

"But even if they took away her gem and her powers; even if she looks like a human; she still retains her essence, and so is still a lady Shawá! I have sensed her power during all these years of searching. That's why I was able to track her here even though I was so weak. But with the power I detected in her, she can't be human, and it would be quite impossible for her to mate with this species. It just wouldn't work," Nose argued.

"I think you should see something," said Sasha.

The four of them went down to the secret room where Mihara was submerged in her chrysalis.

"What happened?" the peon asked shocked.

"As you say, there is still the essence of the Shawá lady she once was, but only a soft fragrance of her, without her powers and without her natural appearance. She is now merging with a gem that is not hers. You know these factors could kill her."

The hooded man approached the pool and placed his hand on the ice.

"No. No, no, no, no... This was not supposed to happen," he wailed, appalled.

"I'm sorry, Nose. For now, all we can do is wait for her nature to be powerful enough to merge with the stone. It has never been done before, so the odds are..." suggested Rasnar.

"What if she dies? I will have sentenced our kingdom, all of us!" cried Nose.

"No, my friend. You have given us the only chance to restore Mihara's powers. If that happens, it will be the birth of a queen, the voice of Argua, and if we succeed, it will be all because of you, Nose," replied the Guardian.

"I thought... I didn't know she would be so weak, so... human," he apologized.

"Nose, where did you get the gem?" asked Sasha looking at the creature.

"I had the jewel of the lady Mihara in my hands, but I was stupid. Stupid peon! Stupid nobody! What was I thinking..."

Sasha approached the man and hugged him.

"You are somebody, Nose. You are and will be whoever you want to be. What you did was not wrong, it was a good deed for someone you loved," the girl reassured him.

"How do you know what I did?"

"My grandmother, Mihara, before all this happened and she went into that chrysalis state, showed me things from her past, and I saw you. You were that soldier of the guard who gave something to the boy who was drowned. You gave him my grandmother's gem, didn't you? The stone of his beloved. He was the friend you mentioned, wasn't he?" said the young woman, leaving everyone surprised.

"I... I saw what they were doing; I was supposed to follow orders, but it wasn't right," he said. "Still, I let it happen, and I killed him too. And now I'm killing her," he said almost weeping.

"No, Nose. You only tried to help. It was those men, the Exalted Five, who did that to him," Sasha replied.

"I saw Mihara's gem sliding across the floor and, without thinking, I grabbed it. People were screaming and running." The soldier took off his hood to get a better look at the teenager. "I let him die; my only friend; I let him die."

Despite the horrifying aspect of the man's face, the young woman looked at him without disgust and hugged him tightly. She shed her tears on his tanned, almost shattered cheek, which slid down the inside of the cuts on his face; deep cracks created by the arid dryness of his skin.

Suddenly, James alerted his sister that the man's face was changing; the wounds were healing, and after a short while his appearance was totally transformed. He retained small scars, light lines like fine veins that marked where there had once been an injury. Although his skin was still white, it no longer looked dehydrated or broken. His fingernails became lighter and showed a polished surface, which eliminated the fear of holding a monster's hand.

Seeing how they looked at him, he felt a strange sensation in his body. He looked at his hands and touched his face in amazement.

"We have already discovered another of your gifts, young Sasha, one of great use and value," said Rasnar, looking at her with pride.

"But how did I do it? I've cried a thousand times and it's never happened to me before," she was surprised.

"When your grandmother passed her memories to you through the water, you could have died, but you didn't, because the water kept you alive; otherwise, you would have drowned, which means that the blood of a Shawá runs through your veins, little one. It has always been there, but the power has awakened late, though it is of no less value for that. With good training we will find out what you are capable of," explained the Guardian.

"But how can that be? Mihara was stripped of her magic, so her offspring, who are mixed with human ancestry cannot retain power," the peon commented astonished.

"They are not solely human descendants, Nose," Rasnar warned.

"What do you mean?"

The Talan stared into his eyes, leaving him to figure out the riddle on his own. Suddenly the soldier's eyes widened even more than they already were, and he dropped his jaw in astonishment.

"It can't be...

As the words came out of his mouth, his eyes misted over with tears.

"What can't it be? Rasnar?" Sasha asked.

Nose looked at Sasha and held her hands, grief-stricken by the feeling that at that moment was breaking his soul.

"I am very sorry; I hope that someday you will be able to forgive my people. And me."

Quickly, Sasha let go and turned away from him. Then she looked at the peon and the Guardian in anguish.

"What do you mean; what do you mean?"

James was sitting on the edge of the pool with his hands over his head, mentally exhausted.

"Go sit next to your brother, Sasha, please. We owe you both an explanation. Every being should know where he comes from and who he is so that he is aware of his importance and the role he has in this universe.

"Fortunately, or unfortunately, you have inherited certain gifts that not everyone has; possibly, a power that neither I nor anyone else so far has ever seen, for as far as we believe, there is something great to be discovered within you. But all remains to be seen," said the Talan.

"How can you assume what we are capable of? We are only children! I have just discovered that I can magically turn rocks into precious stones and heal wounds with my tears, but I have been and always will be a mere human," the young girl replied.

"No, Sasha. Three lineages run through your veins, and all three are among the most powerful that have ever existed. There is no other case like yours; there never has been and there never will be. If they knew of your existence, they would exterminate you. To them you are an aberration, a blasphemy, a corrupted being. They would annihilate you out of fear of what you might be capable of doing," explained the beast.

"Sure, we could stone people with sapphires and then cure them with tears. Ohh, what a horrooor," the young man said sarcastically.

"No, you don't understand, James. You are an ecumenical threat. If word of your existence got out, races from this world and other planets would come to stalk you and, without proper training, you could certainly end up disturbed by evil. Given the power of your genetics, it would be catastrophic, so we must keep it utterly secret," said Rasnar.

"But you said you were going to train us. How are you going to train us if you don't even know what we're capable of? Maybe we only know how to do those two things, I might not even know how to do that!" James protested angrily.

"You are right, I have no idea, but I am willing to risk my life to try, as you are our only and last hope. If you allow me, I will train you to the best of my ability, fighting by your side until the end. Until now you have been mere humans, a contemptible species, but with great talents for the creation of both prolific and destructive weapons, something that does not make your race weak. However, from this moment on, you will never be the same again. You will never feel the same, you will never think the same way and you will never behave the way you have behaved until now. If you decide to trust yourselves, as I do, you must be prepared to embrace the change, for there will be no turning back. But it is your decision.

The siblings looked at each other in silence. Then Sasha stood up and immediately pulled her brother's hand to stand up.

"We are in", she announced.

The Margua

Rasnar nodded as the siblings approached him.

"But before we get down to it, we need to understand our past and what is happening. We deserve an honest explanation; not the crumbs you have given us so far. I am fed up with all this, fed up! So, you will clarify in detail the truth once and for all, because in order to lead, as you ask, we need to know. You cannot lead anyone in this life if you walk blindly," Sasha insisted.

Rasnar sat down in front of them like a feline and dropped his wings, which rested on each side of his body.

"Well, it will take us quite a while to tell you everything in one go. Any particular questions to start with?" he wanted to know.

"The first thing we have to be clear about is whose descendants we are, because you say we have blood from three of the most powerful lineages in existence, but we don't know what they are. Well, I assume that the Shawá s must be one of them, and then the human, which counts as a race on this planet, not yours, so what is the third one?"

Rasnar looked at Nose, who nodded as he stood up and walked over to a moderately large bonsai tree and removed the golden bowl that acted as its pot. With the container in his hand, he approached the siblings and asked them to sit in a circle around it.

The Shawá sucked the tip of his index finger and felt the bottom of the bowl. Then he covered the receptacle with his other hand. From the place he had touched with the tip of his finger, water gushed out until it filled the entire vessel.

"How did you do that?" James asked, amazed.

"If you want to know what lineage you are descended from and where you come from, I will show you, for the place from which your grandmother comes was once my home. But mere words cannot describe it."

Nose placed the tips of his fingers on the surface of the water, then placed his outstretched hands on the sides of the pot and looked inside the container. It was illuminated by a kind of spiraling white mist. As the mist spread around the outside of the element, a blue image, like a small 3D picture, formed and was reflected in the water, occupying its entire volume.

Instantly, something glowing covered the scene completely, but it quickly moved away. It could be clearly seen that the indigo background was an aquatic environment and that the figure that had appeared as a snowy spot was a huge sea turtle with a fluorescent coral embedded in its shell, which glittered in that ocean. After the reptile, more species of animals appeared, each one more fantastic and sublime than the last. All of them gave off some kind of luminosity that illuminated the sea in a hypnotic way. The sibling, who were captivated by what they saw, remained silently immersed in it with the sensation of swimming slowly towards that glow.

They noticed another fainter and warmer light, like fireworks in slow motion, at the bottom of the neat scene. The closer they got, the clearer it became. It was a formidable underwater citadel, mostly built out of some transparent material, since its walls and ceilings almost exposed the activities taking place inside. Thus, they deduced that the beings that inhabited it were the fabulous creatures that swam around it, filling the scene with light and graceful movement. The underwater citadel had domed roofs which were linked to each other by triangular-walled corridors with overlapping peaked roofs, which created an amazingly complicated interlocking geometric effect a clear sign of the superiority and magnificence of its people.

The floors of the city were mosaics built out of various materials such as amber, pearls, corals, all kinds of shells and mother-of-pearl, as were its columns, though many were formed of glazed tubes through which animals from outside passed. Other sections were decorated with marine plants, which had been planted and cultivated to ornament the vicinity with seaweed trees or flowering corals. A slightly different flora, which seemed to be sentient as the flowers opened and closed as people passed by, was also visible on the walls and floor. Some, with brightly colored with thick petals like the legs of starfish, even moved as if they were breathing.

These flowers fascinated Sasha, who watched the images in amazement, spellbound by the waterfalls that let the water from the extrinsic ocean enter the interior of the rooms. They were used as portals to the citadel or as screens of various shapes and sizes, through which information could be transmitted by means of projections. Those that were only objects for adornment were smaller in size, some filled with pretty lozenges that seemed to give off some kind of scent, as they were not only refreshed by them, but also perfumed. These were presented one on top of the other, creating rows of water jets that in some cases had miniatures of flora and fauna swimming through them, leaping in the air as they passed from one to the other, until they got tired and dropped into the shallows of these springs, where they rested until they launched themselves back into the game, like salmon when they try to swim up a river against the current.

The furnishings: benches, stairs, lamps, fountains... were works of art; rich in marine detail and with inlays polished to perfection. Each private dwelling was designed to its owner's taste with marine material which fostered their greater comfort and well-being. The materials included wood treated by the sea, corals of the preferred type and color, a variety of stones, mother-of-pearl, crystals, shells, bones, spines, and horns. The shells were of all sizes and tissues, changing color according to their surroundings like cuttlefish, and some could even heat the room. They looked like glass creations through which the beauty of the exterior could be admired, but could be camouflaged if the residents desired, thus adapting the techniques of the cephalopods for the protection of the Shwanír citadel and its privacy. Of course, these peculiarities varied according to the status of the family that dwelt there.

These strips were not generally used for ceilings, as most people used to build them from a single piece of translucent white stone, polished and cut from a single block, meticulously custom-made for the room in the shape of a hemisphere, with a small opening through which an interior waterfall passed. From the outside they could be interpreted as balconies through which water currents flowed, just as it flows within the sea itself; access points through which the beings that inhabited it could both enter and leave the dwelling, like a front door.

The method used to prevent intruders was a barrier created by the Shawás themselves, under the supervision of the five sages, who thus kept control of all the entrances and exits throughout the fortification, both public and private. This encouraged protection and respect for authority in their society. The fountains were large circular basins, some with small circular bowls stacked one on top of the other, were in all the squares of the citadel, and these were the places where they could share information and memories through live images, just by putting their finger on the water that filled a basin. The civilization was silent and peaceful since they had no need to emit sounds through their mouths.

Manifested in the images Nose showed the siblings were other fountains attached to columns and walls, which were scattered throughout the citadel. At one of these, a loving couple were sitting on the edge of the fountain with their fingers on the surface of the water resting in one of its smaller vessels, which was surrounded by a much larger central one. She was showing him memories of precious moments between them. At the same time, from the larger receptacle, general information about the city was emitted by the Exalted Five, information that was also revealed through the hemispherical butt of transparent, drop-shaped algae plates that hung from the ceiling, all of which were connected by the same water filter through which the images were sent to the Shawás from the council chamber of the sages.

Although each sage had a separate office, they congregated in this chamber. There, each one had his own throne, constructed from the distinctive material of the elder to which it belonged, marking his discipline, and with his gem embedded in the upper part of the large armchair. On the right of each of these chairs, at ground level, was a hole with water in which the sages rested their staffs and sent information to the entire Shwanír community through the torrent that flowed to the fountains, lamps and waterfalls scattered throughout the huge fortress, thus controlling the society through the element by which they were all connected.

On the other side of the throne, on the armrest, was a shallow indentation filled with water. By placing their hand on the surface of this hollow, the sages were able to project images to whomsoever they wanted to see them.

But those were not the only halls for the five elders and Shawá leaders; there was also a huge, tiered hall that Sasha recognized instantly from the memory into which her grandmother projected her. That was where the people of the city gathered on important occasions, like the trial. In that great hall, the Exalted Five sat, each on their own personal throne. The thrones, which were made of white coral and reflected the personal taste and style of their occupant, were located in front of the tiers filled by the audience.

In the center of the room was a beautiful mosaic which, as it rested on an earthenware base, could be opened to allow an immense fountain to rise from below the hall. Marked on the fountain's edge were five points, one for each sage, where they prostrated themselves. They could either use the fountain to work in unison or individually project images onto it using the dip in the armrest of their throne. Though all the thrones operated in the same way, only these thrones could be used to connect the sages to that particular fountain.

This was how the Exalted Five informed the Shwanír Fortress Congress and the Council of the Kingdom of Argua of their requirements in a direct, visual manner. The fountain was also used to convey information to the townspeople who gathered in the chamber to discuss civil issues, projects, laws, or other various matters. The information was also filtered through the torrents so as to reach the crowds who could not be present as they roved through the citadel; even those who might be found outside the fortress could be alerted through a signal, exclusive to their kind, that rippled over the ocean.

The same procedure was followed for the animals that lived outside the fortress as for those that lived in the Margua, where they swam freely through the condominiums of the Shawá kingdom. However, the method used was different; it used marine frequencies. The ability to communicate with the fauna of that abyss was one of two gifts common to all Shawá; the other was the ability to communicate iconically through the medium of water.

The siblings noticed that a tube-like passageway extended under the deep waters, stretching from the great city to almost the edge of their kingdom. It gave the impression that it was a beautiful and extravagant highway cemented to the bottom of the sea and discreetly hidden by the sand that fell on it.

The boundary was marked by gigantic golden gates at the level of the seabed, the tops of which were uncovered on the ebb tide, when they revealed splendid inscriptions in amber. These inscriptions warned any, who might wish to pass, the terms on which they could enter the Shwanír Fortress: "Only those who respect our laws with their whole hearts will be able to pass; else these gates will forever remain sealed". Moreover, the gates were protected by ferocious beasts.

Whoever wished to pass, unless they were a Shawá, would have to exceed the limits of what is endurable in holding their breath and withstanding the great pressure, because of the time needed to descend and rise, due to the depths to which they would be forced to dive down to. But even were they to achieve the impossible and manage to touch the gate with a finger, if they did not fulfil the requirements of the inscriptions, the gates would never open, and they would drown. Such an attempt seemed impossible, not to mention suicidal, to the siblings.

The visual representations in the bowl, passing before their eyes like a sandy treadmill began to show the Margua falling away into the depths. Immediately, it showed them the surface of the sea, over which they quickly glided, as if they were flying at full speed, until it brought them to the shore of a land of pink sand, whose tiny crystals gave off small pinkish white sparkles.

Beyond this beautiful beach, stood a row of gigantic trees similar to weeping willows, but larger and full of snow-white flowers, whose petals were like nacre, but so fine that they were almost translucent. They hung like necklaces from their long, slender, reddish branches, like silk threads that rose gently with the sea breeze and exuded an aphrodisiac nectar that intoxicated the coastal air with its exquisite fragrance.

They could almost smell this perfume through Nose's words as he described the sublime bursts of a crimson pollen that floated along the shore and landed on the sands, creating the pink effect of the sand on that shore. The extraordinary buds that emanated from those trees were like strings of floral beads, which when wafted by that warm, gentle breeze, knocked together and produced a peculiar sound, like a melody of delicate shells and fine crystals, which soothed and calmed one's inner self.

Suddenly, this Zen state was broken as the image zoomed up into the sky to reveal a huge expanse of land with terrain so diverse, strange, and exceptional that even floating islands were not unusual. And, despite a lifelong diet of fantasy, both in books and movies, the variety of species, which was as diverse as their habitats, was far beyond anything the siblings could have ever imagined. Then the vision rose to the apogee of the firmament to reveal a superb map of Argua.

"That's it. A brief visual display of the Shwanír citadel, the Margua, where your grandmother was born, and the extension of the kingdom of Argua, with its twelve realms," said Nose, ending his presentation, "Do you have any questions?"

"It was amazing! I'm so glad to have joined you guys," James exclaimed excitedly.

"It's the most beautiful thing I've ever seen in my life," Sasha said ecstatically. "But you said that we are descended from three very powerful lineages. Which is the other, the one that is neither Shawá nor human?"

Nose looked uneasily at Rasnar, who signaled that he should show them the truth, fully knowing the risk they were taking.

Evil

"I have only heard about him. I have never seen him in person, but I have seen the memory images of those who did see him: great warriors who fought against him generations ago; mortals who sacrificed their lives to donate their memories to the five sages, who have been projecting these same scenes throughout the citadel of the kingdom, generation after generation, so that our history and immolation would not be forgotten. Even so, we have suffered the repercussions of that day when everything changed."

"You must understand that I can only project before you what I have had revealed to me, that is, what I learned from the projections I saw and, thus, being a figuration within a representation, it cannot function as an objective mnemoportation," explained Nose.

"I have a question: can the visions be manipulated or are they always as the person saw them?" asked the young woman.

"The images are shown as they were perceived by the person who is disclosing them. But perceptions always vary; not in concept, that is never altered, but as with any moment or situation in life, through differences in perspective. Thus, where the perception of the first receiver is at variance with that of the original emitter, the projection might be considered erroneous in some aspects. Depending on the perspective of the observer, and how many times it passes from one mind to another, these can be transformed, but the iconographies will always remain the same. It is far easier to see than to explain.

"In any case, it is an immutable law that all memories and unaltered projections are inserted into black pearls, which are kept under the emblem of the Shawá s inside the great fountain in the common room. These black pearls are extracted from the depths of the barrier reef at the edge of the Shawá cemetery. Their collection is very risky; a perilous task that only the learned can undertake.

"These pearls are brought to the fortress inside impenetrable capsules made from naturally occurring bivalves that are composed of perfectly symmetrical, equal-sized shells that can seal hermetically over the soft parts. Only the Exalted Five has the power to open these shells, which have the ability to contain any kind of energy, thus, protecting the world; or to conceal the greatest secrets of history which are contained in the black nacre spheres.

"These renegade pearls, which contain remnants of the energy of our ancestors, are able to retain even the darkest memories linked to the lord of evil, and the most terrifying and dangerous projections. Encapsulating them in the pearls prevents us from putting ourselves in danger, from exposing our own powers and mind to that negative energy, which is steeped in dark magic, and thus avoid a lethal destiny. Created specifically to protect the memories taken from the worthiest of individuals, who sacrificed everything they had to help us garner the necessary information for the study of Zotrak as he passed through the history of Argua.

"When a projection is not one's own, that is, a representation of something that was not personally experienced, the person showing the images must be objective about what they saw, or the information can be distorted in a way that could manipulate the viewer. However, in this case, there is little to misrepresent," said Nose.

"How can visions be perceived in different ways if they are projected exactly as you received them?" young James wanted to know, puzzled.

"It's very simple. It all depends on your state of mind, your preferred way of thinking or your own experiences. Also involved are your level of objectivity and empathy, as well as the difference between having a flexible personality or being narrow-minded. For example, you can witness the death of an animal and be hungry or you can watch it die and lose your appetite. Although the image doesn't vary, the message conveyed can be interpreted in one way or another: either according to your own state at that moment or through the act with which the person, whose memory it is, was occupied. This leaves you free to assimilate what you witness according to your own ideas or as the protagonist understood them.

"So, since this projection of another projection has gone through at least three channels, some details may be lost and variations from the original objective mnemoportation may unwittingly occur," Nose replied.

"I think it is the same here on earth. The legacies and iconographies transferred by our mass media systems are often manipulated. If you decide to reject them, you risk remaining ignorant, but if you pay attention to them, you risk being misinformed, because you are fed with preconceived and adulterated ideas about gender, religion, culture, politics and so on. Both positions are toxic for individuals and their society, but especially for women of any race, who are written off, even in schoolbooks, where they don't even appear as part of history," said Sasha.

"It is a very difficult task to change a society, irrespective of the world, since whoever is in power will pull the strings as he fancies, to manipulate the majority or even the emitter himself.

Therefore, we must be well informed and trained to recognize which threads to hold on to and which to let go of.

"Transforming a society that has lived under a culture and education that has been repeatedly manipulated and imposed over generations, throughout history, is no easy task. It takes centuries of good endeavors to achieve it. If anything, it has been proven that human beings have a masochistic nature, as change is only ever achieved through drastic means. Sudden change only occurs when there is mass suffering due to some crisis. The desperate, in their ignorance, fall for some con because they are blinded, intoxicated with personal dissatisfaction, while the rest of society, not only listen to, but defend with great determination, even the most foolish utterances expounded by the most villainous individuals or egotistical groups."

"How difficult it is to find an honest leader, who is genuinely concerned for the wellbeing of all without nullifying the rights of any, who does not take what has been earned through hard effort or give it away to those who do not deserve it," Rasnar replied.

"It is not enough to just talk about it, because people won't know how to listen. It is not enough to show it, because they won't be able to see it. They must live it, feel it, in order to understand. Only then will the veil fall," said Nose.

"Let us show them the truth about their lineage, my friend," Rasnar proposed.

The siblings approached the surface of the bowl that acted as a screen but saw nothing but a kind of black dye moving across the bottom of the pot, until all the water in the bowl was covered with a black smoke that appeared as powdered dye and mixed with the liquid in the pot. Nose's fingers changed hue, as if the color of the paint inside the pot was spreading through his hands. Then the Shawá let go of the pot and spilled the water, which spread across the floor. This caused all those present to jump to their feet to prevent the liquid from touching their skin.

"What on earth was that?" asked Sasha, frightened, looking to Nose for an explanation. But he was too busy rubbing his hands against his clothes, desperate that the pigment would not stain his skin as he stammered from the fear and hysteria of the moment.

Rasnar approached him and held his hands tightly in an attempt to stop his panic. "Nose, look, take a good look at them! There is nothing, nothing!

The peon looked at his hands, held by the Guardian's talons, and they were in their natural state, white as milk, with no trace of ink or paint.

"I thought... I thought he had found me... I..." Nose stuttered in a daze.

"We've all seen it and it scared all of us," commented young James, trying to calm him down, and calm himself as well.

"What happened, Rasnar?" asked the young woman.

"We don't know," he replied, "People don't even dare to think about him. He is like a non-existent image for Shawá society, even though it is very present in everyday life. These projections concentrate a great negative energy that only the Exalted Five can process and project, or at least that is how it has been until now. As I told you, to be able to emit the memories of another being requires a great gift, and the images Nose was going to show you belong to beings who sacrificed their lives for the good of all. Not having the power of the Shawá s, the only way they could transmit their memories to us was by dying, and although they did so of their own free will, that terrible energy remains concentrated in their images."

"Has there ever been a case of someone not wanting to show his memories to a Shawá?" asked the boy, terrified.

"Well, they were aware that they were likely to die, even if they hoped that it would not happen. For many, taking that decision showed great courage and won them the greatest honor life has to offer giving up the most precious thing that they possessed for their people and the Kingdom of Argua.

"I know it's hard to understand, but in extreme situations and desperate times, when means are scarce and the need for imminent change is frustrated, even when the change achieved would be minimal, the tormented wretches, blinded by their exasperation, are willing to take whatever radical option they believe viable, irrespective of the cost to themselves, for the sake of the common good." Nose replied.

"You drowned them... you murdered them all," said Sasha, practically whispering the words, which came out of her mouth with horror and shock.

"Not exactly. They volunteered. By sacrificing their lives, they let us see what they had seen objectively and study it carefully so that we could put an end to evil. Do you remember the words engraved on the golden doors, welded to the floor of the Margua, which I showed you in the images of the bowl? "Only those who respect our laws with their whole hearts will be able to pass; else these gates will forever remain sealed". The men who sacrificed their lives did so with a single purpose, and the gates were opened to them because they went to the fortress with pure intentions, from the heart, to help us and open the eyes of all... They made that decision. No one forced them," he explained helplessly.

"Were their sacrifices worth it? Were they worth it to those poor lost souls or their families? Did their deaths help you in any way? Because, as far as I see it, if you have come here to earth to look for us, it is clearly because their deaths were in vain," cried Sasha.

"It served to provide us with the information necessary for us to study his character and analyze the tactics he used in his day. These are kept in our archives to explain the historical actions undertaken, both by us and by Zotrak, and to form a specific model of the demon, his qualities, his powers, and his norms, which are now forever engraved in Argua's consciousness. They serve to remind us that, even though we have fought him we have not yet won; evil is still lurking there, spying on each of us every day that passes, whether we see it or not.

"As much as we have become used to living under an oppressive and enslaving regime, safe in our bubble of security where we lie blind to the reality hidden for generations, these sacrifices help us to remember what happened and what must never happen again. To end the suffering we have endured, what we are prepared to do, whatever the means, persevering in the study and cultivation of our survival, is to fight, not just for a better future, but for a better present.

"When the time comes, thanks to the data collected from these honorable martyrs who will never be forgotten, we will put an end to evil forever," Nose clarified to the young woman.

"And why didn't the Shawás make their own projections? They don't have to sacrifice themselves to project a memory or an image from their memory," asked young James.

It requires a much more varied study than the Shawás' experiences with you-know-who," replied the peon.

"The demon? You mean Zo..." James couldn't even remember the name.

"Don't mention his name! He has already been mentioned too many times today. We Shawá must not think of him after we have seen him in person or been seen by him, understand?" a fearful Nose scolded them.

"Why not?" Sasha asked.

"I have been seen... I have been seen, Rasnar," Nose wailed glaring at the Guardian as he became more and more nervous. He was pulling his hair and rubbing his hands against his clothes

"Are you saying that because the water darkened?" asked the boy, trying to understand what had happened.

"We can only look at images of those who have seen him. If we showed one of ours, he'd know and he'd come after us. He'd come after me! But I've never seen him... I never even think of him in case he might detect me. I don't even say his name! He must have sensed me somehow through the projections, or his dogfish have followed me, so they know of our plans, our whereabouts, and I have put you all in danger. They may be searching for us through their magic, Rasnar," said Nose with concern.

"Shawá ... do you think a zork could have followed you all the way to Earth?" the Guardian asked the man, his serious tone of voice indicating his concern.

"I don't know. But if so, we are all in danger and we must leave here immediately!" proposed the peon.

"But we can't leave Grandma here!" her granddaughter replied indignantly.

"We're not leaving her or going anywhere, Sasha. Most likely what we saw was a warning, to scare us. He likes to know he has the power and everything under control; he feeds on fear, so the more scared we are, the sooner he will find us and the sooner he will destroy us.

"He is a being who is hated by all, so he must always be alert and cautious. That is why his best weapon is to provoke fear, since it is a deficiency unknown in him. He is able to smell the alarm of any living being, even if they are on a distant planet. He enjoys the suffering of others; he feeds on it by terrorizing his victims with threats and actual abuse; he is a discreet killer, a silent assassin who tortures for pleasure, feeding his maliciousness by slowly, and tremendously painfully, peeling the layers of your skin from your body. He is a typical narcissist who plays with you until he ends up destroying your soul."

"Nose, do you think they could have seen you leave the kingdom? You know it's forbidden. If someone had discovered you, word would have spread quickly," the Talan asked with interest.

"But Rasnar, you also left Argua to look for Mihara," said Nose.

"Yes, but I made it public. Because I don't trust anyone, I camouflaged it under a plausible fabrication so that it wouldn't arouse suspicions of any kind.

"I have not shared this information even with those closest to me. Absolutely no one knows that I am here with you. If they were to find out, the garden of Talos would be in grave danger and if that were to happen, the human race could become extinct and our system, and your world, would collapse and vaporize," the Guardian said.

"How?" the siblings interrupted in unison.

"I will go out to protect the mansion now."

Rasnar left the room through the secret passageway to the unused room. As the sun was setting and he wanted to finish before dark, he ran along the boundaries of the manor and its grounds at great speed, shedding hairs from his body by brushing and slamming his torso against the trunks and tops of trees, rubbing himself against the walls surrounding the grounds of the property and the walls of the manor. Then, every hair shed from his body that touched wild or paved ground, huge plants grew and tangled everywhere. When the hairs touched the flora, each tree doubled in size and its long, branches extended and tangled themselves, sprouting flowers whose enormous buds created shelters like huge umbrellas.

When his hairs touched the flagstones, abundant creepers burst out and completely covered the outside walls of the mansion from back to front and reached as far as the dirt drive that led down to the great entrance gates. This whole area was covered with a vast blanket of wild hawthorn, which made the place appear ruined and abandoned, deterring inquisitive humans by its awful appearance. For non-humans, the protective field created by Rasnar rendered the manor completely invisible, and no matter the angle from which it was viewed, all that would be seen was a dull and empty landscape.

Chapter V
The Council of Argua

After finishing his task, Rasnar re-entered the mansion through the front door, sniffing the pleasant aroma coming from the kitchen, where the siblings had cooked, and set the table, for the four of them.

"What is that smell?" Nose wondered, attracted by that strange scent.

"Haven't you ever tasted human food?" asked Sasha with her head over the stove while stirring a pot full of sauce.

"No, but the smell gives me an appetite," replied the Shawá.

"How sweet you are, Nose, I hope it tastes just like it smells! I'm not much of a cook, but today is a special day," she said.

"Thank you very much, guys. By the way, where is Rasnar?" he wanted to know.

"Hey, you don't have to thank her for everything, okay? Chicks dig tough guys more, you know?" James hesitated, stirring the salad in front of the window with the kitchen tabletop built into it.

"How little you know about women, James," his sister remarked.

"I'm here," the beast replied, appearing behind Nose.

He was blocking the doorway to the kitchen, leaning against the frame, while the youngsters kept their eyes on the food, playing the role of cooks. Although they had been conversing with the peon during all that time, they had not taken the time to answer him even once by looking him in the face, so that by the time Rasnar appeared and the siblings turned to serve the meal, both were stunned by the presence of the Shawá.

"Thanks for the help, guys. I feel much better."

He, who once looked like a worn man, was now devoid of peeling. He had removed the layers of grimy skin and dirt that covered his body with soap and water. He had also shed the rags in which he appeared at the mansion, which is why the Arguan had a completely different appearance: his athletic physique and a superb face whose features, despite being somewhat strange to the human eye for having white hair and huge hazel eyes without iris or pupil, were attractive. He had a charming smile that did not give way to wrinkles, but was healthy with smooth skin, which gave him a much younger appearance.

"All right, everyone to the table! From now on this is going to be as close to a family as we've ever had. It looks like we're going to be spending a lot of time together, so we'll behave like one," Sasha opined.

"If it's going to smell this good every day, I won't object!" said Rasnar sniffing the air.

The four sat at the table eager to try the food, but soon Nose got up and ran out of the kitchen door. Rasnar reacted by letting out a huge laugh that disturbed the siblings, who watched as it came out of his huge mouth with gigantic fangs and sharp teeth while he extended his big paw until it reached the Shawá 's plate. He threw all the food in the bowl into his maw and guzzled it down in one gulp. He then let out a tremendous belch that was accompanied by a meatball that flew out of the bowl and ended up hitting the corner of one of the kitchen cabinets, where it bounced back into James' glass.

"Such manners, Rasnar!" James scolded him, laughing with disgust.

"What a shot," the girl marveled, observing the golf ball-sized meatball completely intact.

"Mmmm, I'm in glory," said the beast sitting badly on the chair with a puppy face, surprising the siblings, who did not expect this authority from someone who was their Guardian. Therefore, they reacted by laughing at him and with him. They all felt the same peace invading their minds and relaxing their bodies. It had been a long time since they had enjoyed such tranquility or laughed so much. At that instant they thought that maybe the situation they had been dragged into might not be so bad after all. Then Nose returned to the kitchen.

"I think I have to get used to this food little by little. Forgive me, I didn't mean to offend you. I'm not used to this kind of food," he confessed in a depressed mood.

"What did you eat before, fish food? Because I have a little jar. I had little turtles as pets when I was little in an aquarium and oddly enough the jar is still here. I've seen it before when I went up to my room. It's amazing, everything is just as I left it years ago," said the boy.

"James! Don't be rude! Of course, he doesn't eat fish food, does he?" Sasha replied.

"What is fish food?" asked Nose.

"Wait a second and you'll see!"

The boy ran off in search of the jar. Soon he appeared with it in the kitchen.

"Really, James? I can't believe it," she snapped indignantly.

"What? The guy comes from the ocean, right?"

Nose looked at him, shaking his head in refutation.

"From the sea? Who cares... What difference does it make to a fish? Even though you're in a citadel, you live underwater; basically, you make the same life as they do, right, so the food must be similar."

The Shawá took the jar and, after sniffing it, began to lick it. Inevitably, his companions fell apart.

"What are we laughing about?" he asked, laughing in a silly way.

"We have to open the jar!" explained Sasha in a huff.

Immediately, the peon opened the pot, embarrassed, and a smell of rancid shrimp stank up the room. The others reacted by pushing the dishes away from Nose and holding their noses.

"Wow, that has completely spoiled my appetite," James acknowledged.

"Mmmmmm. So much flavor!" enthused Nose, sucking his finger that he was putting in and out of the jar.

"Man, you had a certain attractiveness, you could have gotten a human girlfriend, especially wearing my stylish clothes, but with the breath you'll get after eating that, not even the trout will want to kiss you."

Despite the foul smell lingering in the room, the four continued the evening laughing and enjoying each other's company. They seemed to have found their place in the world, like a happy little family welcomed into a safe home, and for a moment they forgot why they were there, the external horrors and misfortunes of their past. Just enjoying the moment, an occasion that might never be repeated.

Once the meal was finished, Nose, James and Rasnar cleared the table while Sasha lit the fire in the main room, where after dinner, they would quietly sip tea and discuss unfinished business, as it was the perfect place to relax by the warmth of the logs and the warm light of the flames.

The four of them gathered in that white marble room, full of mosaics created with fragments of beautiful stones adorned with golden metals, somewhat maroon from rust; surrounded by walls covered with green tapestries and picturesque furniture of turquoise velvet and wood painted in weathered gold. Walls whipped softly by the light of huge, worn-white colored lamps, marked with a kind of greenish tartar that covered their metallic areas which had a floral appearance, surrounded by small bulbs like fireflies. The room, like the whole house, was covered with ivy on both the walls and the floor, enclosing a white marble hearth with small black lines marked on it. It had a spectacular design, which was at the same time effective because of the huge firebox that warmed the immensity of the great room with its high ceilings and wabi sabi beauty, like the rest of that exquisite mansion.

The Guardian sat in front of the fire in a long-backed armchair, with two holes that divided the backrest into three peaks like a trident; holes through which he inserted the wings, which made it easier for the seat to accommodate his back.

"That strange chair seems tailor-made for you, Rasnar," said the young woman.

"It doesn't look like it, it is," he smiled placidly. "This is not my first visit to this house. In fact, I may have spent more time here than in Talos, which is why your great-grandmother was generous enough to design this throne and have it made expressly for me, so that I could discuss matters more easily, since your couches, chairs and sofas are not made for large beasts with wings like mine," the Talan Guardian explained.

Great-grandmother? You mean grandmother," James corrected him.

"I thought you couldn't leave Argua, so you had to make up an excuse to come," the girl recalled.

"Well, guys, you still have a lot to learn. Times were not always as controlled as they are now. At the beginning of the chaos, when our kingdom began to falter, we could still risk committing acts that are now considered unpunished. As you well know, I come from the garden of Talos, so the motive I used to come to this world was not illegitimate but is even more important than the fight to free Argua, for one goes hand in hand with the other. Or rather, the whole solar system and our lives depend on it. Do you think the thirteen kingdoms would have given me permission otherwise?" asked Rasnar.

"Thirteen?" Sasha echoed in confusion.

"Yes, it would have been impossible to be here in this day and age without the authorization of the council of the twelve kingdoms of Argua plus the approval of the damned thirteenth, since with his tyranny and the espionage to which he subjects the rest, I would have ended up being betrayed. We would be in danger. Instead, as I did, by informing everyone of a purpose that affects even Zotrak himself, I managed to circumvent any suspicions he might arouse regarding my departure, something that would allow me to flow from one planet to another without putting anyone at risk. Still, we must be careful.

"There are things of such importance that make even the unnamable one himself tremble and kneel. Things that not even with all the power of the thirteen kingdoms can we control."

The siblings listened in silence, letting their imaginations run wild, interpreting, and visualizing every word the Guardian uttered in his deep tone of voice. Then the beast sat up in his armchair, emitting a soft roar that he projected towards the fire, transfiguring each word he uttered into a series of illustrations on the flames that reproduced images as they articulated his story. Those present observed what looked like a map of outer space with our solar system, but this one curiously contained more planets than the children had studied at school.

After that disconcerting scene, in the following one, figures appeared as he continued to speak. Immediately, a vision was shown in which Rasnar was seen gathered in a room with more people, or rather, with other beings. In it he appeared surrounded by different species. At that moment he was addressing a specific being. Everyone else in the room was paying attention to what these two were discussing, until the subject of the dialogue splashed across the room.

"The Sun is the center of the planetary system. The Earth and other bodies revolve around it thanks to its energy in the form of light, which sustains almost all forms of life and determines the climate. It is the brightest star, which decrees both the day and night of the terrestrial planet, among many others.

"We must remember that this star was formed 4650 million years ago, with fuel for another 5500 million years. After that period, it will start to get bigger and bigger, until it becomes a red giant that will eventually collapse under its own weight. It will then become a white dwarf, which will take 1 million years to cool down. But this whole process has accelerated, endangering us all," reported Rasnar.

"They say that it was formed from clouds of gas and dust, which contained residues of previous generations of stars, among them our home, the ancient Argua, something to consider," commented one of the beings present, with long floral hair like vines full of life, so elastic that they wrapped his face like hair and descended curling all over his body until they reached his feet. They covered him like a dress of a jungle green with colored tips like a skirt that covered his feet.

"What Saluac has just said is true. And it will happen again, and we will lose our precious domains once more. I remind you that this council was created to safeguard the twelve kingdoms, not to let them die a grim fate because of words written for the people and conditions of old, instilled as sacred and unbreakable, which have not been updated to the times we live in now and our throbbing needs.

"I respect the effort of our ancestors, but we must remember that these lands took a long time to be formed, since it was thanks to the properties of that gas, that from its stellar disk later emerged the planets, asteroids and comets of the solar system, thus being able to rebuild from the ashes the new Argua. The few inhabitants of the ancient kingdom that managed to survive compiled the customs and treatises for our progress, detailed and handwritten on papyrus..."

"We must learn from the past so as not to make the same mistakes, as we could once again become prisoners of survival as nomads in space, waiting for a new planet to re-form with the necessary conditions for our settlement on it. Do you want to be bound by ordinances that will lead us once again to wander into nothingness, dragging our people into suffering or extinction? If we let these laws override our free thinking, preventing pro-gressive actions, we will have fallen to the same catastrophic end once again, and this time rest assured that there will be no resurrection with the new generations. Not one of us will be left to try to recover what we have now and what our ancestors worked so hard to rescue; nor will any of our descendants survive to even consider a future where the concept of Argua can proliferate," said Rasnar.

"And what do you propose? Breaking the laws and bringing us to an even more drastic end?" the speaker had a slightly elongated skull like the ancient Egyptians, with one eye closed between her eyebrows and the other two in their natural position with respect to the human aspect, but with an almond shape outlined in black on the sides of her head. There was no trace of an ear on her.

Her pubescent torso was uncovered; she wore only a sling at the front of her neck, which fell down both sides of her back, crossed at her hip area and descended her between her legs to her feet.

"But, Wio, if humans continue destroying the Earth, at this rate, the day will come when the Sun will exhaust all the hydrogen in its central region, converting it into helium before the hour, thus changing the cycle foreseen in the prophecies," quickly replied one of the five sages of the Shwanír citadel, his race easy to identify by his clothes, his long hair and his long white beard, apart from the particularity of wearing a black gemstone stuck in the middle of his forehead, which combined with his large hazel eyes without iris or pupil, something characteristic of the Shawá s.

"The Earth will die at the hands of humans much sooner than we think, and not because of the Sun, as it is written," said Rasnar trying to convince those people who surrounded him in the act projected on the bonfire.

"We must prepare ourselves, not just give up!" said a being with a beard, eyebrows, and long grayish eyelashes, which were tangled together and lined up with his peculiar mane, from which came out a large deer antlers like branches of a tree that descended his back as they reduced in size. They ran down his spine and across his skin, covered with a fine hair of an aged brown color, which covered his hands with long fingers that ended in small hooves decorated with silver inlays.

This species wore a transparent cloth tunic with skeletons of dried tree leaves embroidered on it, attached to his body by a silver brooch hooked to one of his shoulders. The ensemble was matched by a crown of antlers emerging from its head, with silver-plated tips.

"No, Corosso, we cannot alter the facts. What must be will be and the kingdom of Tajhra will respect it. We are committed for everything to follow its course as it has been, in the hope that it will return to its natural course, fulfilling the prophecies," spoke the tallest being in the image, who had long jet-black hair and an extraordinary athletic physique, so much so that he seemed to have more abs than usual.

But that was not the only peculiarity of this man, since, in addition, he had four arms decorated with simple golden bracelets that stood out with the pink color of his body, which he covered by wearing a pair of bloomers of a slight mustard color as the only garment. He showed bare feet with six toes on each foot.

"To promote tradition by exposing ourselves to these individuals? You know that is forbidden, Rasnar! I am with Numec, the Arguans will never be part of the terrestrial life or contact with that planet, let alone ever be seen by a human. It is the law! And you know the consequences that will befall you and your kingdom if you break it," shouted an upset giant beast with dissimilar hair spread all over his stocky body.

He seemed to be accompanied by a woman of similar appearance, though tall and strong, with a charming frown and fangs protruding from her mouth. She wore over her shoulders a vest of blonde hair that spilled out of her skin and displayed the same over her large cuffs.

"Brost and Carnála, don't you realize that we must fight for our kingdoms, for our people, and not for the humans? I agree that they deserve their fate, but by letting them die we will come to the same end: we will die with them."

"You must come to your senses, like Wio and Numec, or do you want the kingdoms and people of Cryscol, Tepnos and Tajhra to disappear forever?" said Ashima of the Tunani kingdom, a woman with a turban that covered half of her visage and only showed delicate drawings engraved on the complexion of her face.

She had a brown hair lightened by the sun that highlighted her cat-like honey-colored eyes, which contrasted with her skin, of a golden tan and full of tattoos that ran along her half-exposed body, since she was only wearing long johns, low on the hips, with slits on the sides, and a kind of sling that covered the upper part of her torso. Attached to the sling was what looked like a wooden slat, and on top of it, a rolled-up mat.

"Ashima is right!" shouted several of those present, joining the cause.

"Her words are worthless! Have you forgotten that she's a changeling? She can take sides with anyone!" opined a fop arrogantly.

"I am a daughter and descendant of the Tunani kingdom. Being changeable does not change my roots; being what I am has nothing to do with having a clear and objective reasoning, especially when one is a councilor of Argua.

"The kingdom of Preciosas has a clouded judgment; they are blinded by the shining stones they greedily hoard. I remind you that one cannot possess what does not belong to one, for everything concerns the earth. Therefore, we must show gratitude, and not drain it to its death with meanness. Instead, we must proportion what it gives us and replace what we take from it: that is caring for her fairly and reciprocally. If it were up to you, Sranik, you would avenge Argua as humans do with their planet, obfuscated by greed and hatred for other races, just like you. Should we exterminate you too for being of the same ilk as Earthlings?

"You are fortunate that we are not as self-interested as you, for if we were, you would be at the top of most people's list, Sranik, and possibly none of us here would exist, maybe not even Argua. For one will always need the other, but you and your realm are too poisoned by your ego and false appearance to understand; weak and obsessed with precious objects! You are lewd and selfish beings, completely banal, full of prejudice, with airs of superiority aggravated with delusions of grandeur. You always demand something in return for any compassionate act, because everything you do is for your own purpose and no one else; you are heartless beings and lack kindness and humility."

"You are nothing but narcissists who camouflage yourselves when you need something, or rather desire something on a whim, so that you can absorb as much as you can from people who are truly extraordinary in every field. You lack the necessary ingenuity and talent, despite making a tremendous effort to appear otherwise. You merely copy from others and claim the credit for yourselves".

"You and your fellow men are so far removed from reality that you are no longer even aware that you only rub shoulders with people in a superficial way. You have to lie and pay to obtain their attention, showing them a face that does not exist and wearing it as a mask that deceives no one but yourselves. You are utterly immersed in that loneliness that you so deserve, which is the result of a life of deceit, since good people, those who show you honesty and benevolence, soon perceive your true odor of putrefaction," Ashima answered, leaving Sranik on the floor.

"I smell envy and resentment. But what can you expect from a kingdom where everything is merely sand," he said, trying to show indifference.

"One can have better or worse qualities than another, but not be superior or inferior, something that you more than anyone should know, since, without your stones, you are nothing. I affably respect what you did for the town of Preciosas, but it seems that power has gone to your head, and you have forgotten that you did not do it alone. You think you are better than all those who helped you and therefore worthy of a crown?"

"May I remind you that there are no kings or queens in Argua, or should we be worrying about the possibility of an alliance with you-know-who? Be careful with those pretensions of grandeur, Sranik, they could end up betraying you, the way you usually do to others," the Tunani councilor scolded him.

"Words of a changeling," Sranik dismissed, having nothing solid to argue with.

"I accept you as an equal and in doing so I am demonstrating the good roots of my people, even though you do not deserve it. My standing here as a changeling is a demonstration that it matters neither what I am nor your opinion, and I remind you that to be part of the Council of Argua, all of us here contributed something to the kingdom at one time, and most of us did so as a team. Although I would gladly agree to a duel with you to make you recover your memory and humility and to make you swallow those foolish words you spew like poison from the opposite orifice from the one out of which they were emitted," Ashima pointed out to him.

"This council is sacred, Sranik! If you are not capable of respecting your fellow councilor, you are not worthy to be here. You earned your place here as much as she did, and in Arguan territory, don't forget, we are all equal. Do you think your kingdom is superior to the Tunani ancestral kingdom? Your beloved stones and their lands are bound to this one in brotherhood. Without them, you are nothing."

"And that applies to all the kingdoms of Argua. So, the kingdom of Tepnos will not accept the kingdom of Preciosas until it shows fidelity in its words and will act accordingly with deeds. I make it clear here and now that we will support the decision to go to the human world, in spite of overriding the prophecies and breaking the law with this action, as, this time, they will only be broken for greater causes.

"As soon as the problem has been fixed, if that is possible, we will return to our customs and respect the traditions. But it is clear that there is a defect in one of the kingdoms that could harm the sacred values which unified our nations as equals for the greater good and created this assembly. This is something that must be fixed, because if not, young Sranik could get carried away with hubris, among the many other epithets that precede it, and end up spitting on his own plate. And we'd all rather eat sand than a virus."

Ashima looked at Wio gratefully as Carnála and Brost crossed from Sranik's side, nudging him lightly with their shoulder as they passed, making their change of stance clear to him as they joined the cause by standing next to the changeling.

"I expected nothing less from the kingdom of Cryscol. The universe breeds them, and they flock together," said the Preciosas councilor with contempt.

Brost's beast responded by roaring with rage, ready to give the intolerant Sranik the beating with all his fury he deserved, but Rasnar quickly stepped in front of the Cryscolian, stopping him in his tracks.

"This is neither the place nor the time for this kind of quarrel. Remember, Sranik, that, in your eyes, I am also a monster. You don't want to face me too, do you, or have you forgotten who I am? Because in your eyes, aesthetics, and material things aside, I am still far superior to you in power, strength, values and clearly in intelligence, so it's up to you," the Guardian exclaimed.

"Forgive me, Rasnar. I have nothing against changelings or any other species, but we must be realistic and objective about the decisions we make in these times, without taking sides with anyone out of empathy," Sranik replied, lowering his head to the Talan.

"You of all people, Sranik, should appreciate what a beautiful and unique gem this girl is," he said as he touched the face of the young Ashima, a masked, red-haired woman in a black dress.

"Possibly you are losing your faculties, my friend. Being surrounded by so many gems of the same caliber has made you lose your taste for the exquisiteness of the inimitable, the unique and disparate in front of you. It seems that your distinguished reputation has gone to your head, and you have settled weakly into a bubble of comfort that has caused you to lose the spark that once could be seen in you," the woman finished extolling."

"I apologize for my words to the kingdom of Firenel, land of lava and fire. My most humble apologies, lady Nunnara. I have great respect for a woman who can turn coal into diamonds using only her hands or her beautiful hair, for not stressing the fact that she was able to refuse the hand of the one I shall not name and be unharmed.

"I am a faithful servant and admirer," confessed Sranik humbling himself before the council and the woman, who was looking at him behind a veil that hid her eyes, while keeping her hand on Ashima's chin.

"It is a great step to be able to apologize for once in your life, Precious Advisor; a quality that narcissists lack, although you might be acting falsely in order to get something. Whether out of fear, material acquisition or convenience, it seems it's not too late to learn from past mistakes. However, it's not me you need to apologize to," Nunnara commented, making Sranik stand up, embarrassed, in front of Ashima.

"The kingdom of Ostrevo will support the unanimous decision, but speaking only for myself, as a member of the Council of Argua, I demand a public apology from the kingdom of Preciosas to all the territories of our great kingdom or, failing that, the resignation of its councilor for the unseemly affront of its leader, as this kind of behavior dishonors the council and the people it protects" Corosso, the being that looked like half deer half tree, proposed.

"And our kingdom accepts your motion, Corosso. As a councilor of Plásegar and a member of this council, I demand the same of the kingdom of Preciosas and its leader, since it has no place for me, nor for any living being of the kingdom I represent, to be part of an assembly in which equality and tolerance are not implemented," said the plant woman.

"Saluac is right, what is the point of having a council to protect the kingdom of Argua if the members of the council itself are divided and part of it does not even respect or accept those it is supposed to protect? I can speak for Cascadeld, and we will also support that motion. We bet that Ashima will make Sranik swallow his words and the ego that precedes them when she whips his ass in a hand-to-hand clash" opined an attractive young man, winking at the changeling.

"Your methods of courtship never cease to amaze me, Suka. I give you my sincerest congratulations on your skill in the art of debate, and if your suggestion is taken up, I'll bet everything I have on Ashima. But confrontations and apologies aside, which the young changeling and all beings outside the preconceived, normalized standard that Sranik has in his precious gravel brain, clearly deserve, as a member of this council and the council of Hurapolis, I must remind you that we have not been summoned to have nursery fights, but have gathered here because our kingdom is at risk of extinction.

"The planet Earth is dying, and the solar system will go down with it. Perhaps because humans are taking an example from the conduct of this assembly by behaving like children, putting banalities first and wasting time on superficial nonsense, thinking only of themselves instead of the well-being of the universe," said a hooded, infant-like woman as she levitated and spun on herself, moving from one side of the room to the other like a whirlwind.

"Thank you, Aiixs. It seems unbelievable that the wisest words of this council came from the youngest member, a great lesson in not judging by appearances."

"I speak on behalf of the kingdom of Picmeral. Enough of this wasting time on trash that should not even pass through the thoughts of any being. We demand that a new assembly be opened where we rectify the conduct of this council to focus on what is really important. Time is running out fast and it is not in our favor," said a gentleman who at first glance seemed to boast long hair, but with a more careful look, it was clear that they were fins which rested on his shoulders, rising like a crest as he became more and more upset with the conversation.

"It's not that easy, Innunu! Breaking the laws could bring serious consequences to the kingdom and seriously harm humans!"

After this, all the members of the Council of Argua continued to discuss and debate Rasnar's stance on the crisis and his concern about overstepping the bounds of what was considered correct according to Arguan law. Since the thirteenth kingdom was included as sovereign, it forced the council bodies to allow it to participate. This complicated the situation even more, as everything had to be processed and re-pressed in some way so as not to provoke the wrath of this pernicious demon, who did not attend the first meetings because they were clandestine, according to the unanimous decision of the twelve. Only subsequently, was the thirteenth kingdom included.

Everything was studied, as, with their presence silence and falsehood would invade the rooms in which the initial meetings were held, without reaching a solution. But the cursed kingdom had spies in every corner, which made it difficult to hide information from the great fruit of evil. Because of this, and the fear of being discovered, the kingdoms lived in societies in constant tension, fear, and repression, under a suffocating tyrannical regime to which many preferred to surrender rather than raise their voices and be captured, tortured, or even killed.

The Zorks

Suicide was preferable to being imprisoned by the vassals of evil since the vastness of their limitless depravity was the fruit of the worst nightmares of the most powerful and strongest of the Arguans. Its cruelty and immorality reached a confine of mysteries, with powers impossible for even the bravest and fittest of the twelve kingdoms to combat. And secrecy was practically abolished, since the procedure followed by the thirteenth kingdom was to send its henchmen all over Argua; dark shadows that remained silent and retransmitted live and direct to Zotrak what happened and was said by each of his kingdoms, and even in some congress where he managed to sneak in, letting the lord of evil broadcast his words through the momentary possession of these spectral beings that he sent in his name.

"Who are you to decide anyone's fate! Are you gods? You despise humans, but you speak like them. The thirteenth kingdom has made a decision: to summon the five wise men to be ready in two days, before the new moon, and to accept the request of the Guardian.

"By then, we will be one day away from the Moon being between the Earth and the Sun, so that its illuminated hemisphere cannot be seen from planet Earth. In this way we will be able to hold the alteration ceremony as soon as possible and with the utmost discretion," a whispering voice sounded from the shadows of the antechamber. It seemed to come from beyond the grave and echoed throughout the room, reverberating in the ears of the council members like chilling murmurs in the back of their necks.

Meanwhile, the gloom continued to speak with a low echo, as if it was shuffling around the corners of the room, until suddenly, in the blink of an eye, the specter entered the body of the Tunani councilor and took possession of her powers transforming her into a man and reproducing the words of the demoniac through her vocal cords; forcing poor Ashima to show her changed appearance. He prostrated her in the center of the room and lifted her above those present, then exited and dropped her like a rag doll on the floor.

The appearance of the young Tunani was just as beautiful as that of the woman, with the same tattoos, the same long brown hair, the same-colored eyes, and a sinewy body. Although he was taller in stature, the clothes seemed to have been designed to look the same on both sexes.

"Ashima!" shouted several people as they ran to help him.

The boy awoke in a daze, held in the arms of Saluac, who wrapped her liana hair around him, although she left his body exposed as a flower stalk with the silhouette of a woman, with limbs with which to articulate her floral complexion with the flexibility of her vegetal physiognomy.

The pink vines in her hair seemed to be healing Ashima from the inside, while Carnála, the beast woman, following Saluac's orders, opened the changeling's mouth so that he could expel the pieces of evil that lay inside him poisoning the poor Tunani, now a boy, with particles of the black magic used to possess him. Thanks to the treatment of Plásegar's councilor, he was able to expel them from his body emitting a sound with which he shuddered. Therefore, out of his mouth and nose came out expelled fragments of dark evil Zork poison that quickly Nunnara, the reddish-haired lady dressed in black, kept between her hands with some kind of energy.

At that moment, her beautiful mane, perfectly pulled back in an elaborate hairstyle, unraveled from the immaculate braids she wore and lifted toward the ceiling as if there were no gravity. Firenel's councilor dropped her hands to her sides, holding the malevolent molecules inside a ball of resistance that began to rise toward her hair, now stretched into the air. The mane parted in several loops and began to wrap around the dangerous sphere, flipping it until it was suffocated with the maneuver of a python. In doing so, it managed to make it disappear completely. Then small flames burst out, leaving the tresses charred. Then they instantly regained their natural color, as if nothing had happened, leaving everyone present there speechless as Nunnara's mane once again showed its original braid.

After several seconds, the silence in the room was interrupted by Sranik, who seemed to want to show that he was above it all by trying to play down the importance of what happened to poor Ashima with that Zork.

"Humanity, what does that word mean, does it make sense? Humans are beings, who believe they are superior to all races, capable of wiping out populations of their own species to leave them with nothing. They are born killers both of their own species and of others. And they do it for mere amusement! The mindless cruelty of the terrestrials is boundless, as is that of the thirteenth kingdom; a selfish species that cannot see beyond what it wants for itself, a race that will tear from its roots all life, flora and fauna that may be in its path just to get what it wants, both from the material and that which should not and can never be possessed, for it is endowed with a soul," said Sranik with revulsion, possessed of the most human-like features. Shiny-skinned, with ash-brown hair and eyes as clear as water, only that when he spoke a double tongue was visible, with two cobbled rings pinned to its tips. He wore clothes adorned with precious stones and the most sophisticated fabrics.

"Preciosas' councilor is right. The planet is falling apart, and humans don't want to see it because they only look out for their own comfort. It kills the essence, the life and soul of every living being or ancestral object that is part of this universe," Nunnara replied, her hair once again in a large braid twisted around her head.

This lady's charred skin was so black that the very coal seemed clear beside her, rough but beautifully polished with little glints of diamond dust, while her eyes remained a mystery, hidden under that dark, thin veil that seemed never to be removed. It left only the chapped lips exposed, with a delicate obsidian-like sheen.

"The humans you seem to love so much, Rasnar, have long since lost touch with the earth. Nunnara is right: the spiritual power they had disappeared when they became ambitious, they became machines incapable of flowing, of feeling or seeing what cannot be seen with the naked eye. They no longer have the ability to connect with what comes from within each being, they have no understanding beyond the coexistence they have created in a protocol, routine, functional, cold, and banal way. Few are able to achieve respect and humility towards what surrounds them and even towards their own brothers; they do not even wish to empathize with those who do not have the option of expressing themselves as they do.

"They have dissipated even the slightest aptitude they might have for admiring the beauty of other beings and the importance of these in the universe," opined Picmeral's councilor, a fellow with holes on both sides of his face, scarred gills; well erect despite looking older, but not enough to deprive himself of wearing a very plain and tasteless flesh-colored djellaba.

"No one and nothing in this world is expendable, Innunu. Everyone and everything in the cosmos is there for a reason, whether good or bad; even the least important gesture of the least valued person can have a collateral effect and cause a huge change in the universe.

"Those whom we hate, untouchable and invisible, even if they seem to us to be unimportant, or are or are not pleasing to us, should be free to live as they please and as they are born, as long as they do no immoral harm to others, for their work is to awaken a change already written, a series of events destined to pass for a purpose. It is the natural cycle of life, which repeats itself with the same pattern over and over again; a pattern from which we do not learn but succumb until we learn to accept.

"And although we believe that it lacks common sense to respect certain individuals and even help them, what happens in this life and the next responds to a greater good, to the collective good, so whether it is now or in twenty years, everything will make sense and we will be able to see its repercussion. However, we must rectify the mistakes and apply the concept of humanity which has been lost. That is not to say it is something they cannot recover," the Hurapolis councilor challenged, leaving everyone silent not only with her words, but because the young woman displayed the characteristics of a girl and a boy; that is, her gender and age were not clear at a glance. She expressed herself with the maturity of an old man through the body of an impuberal, something impossible to decipher, especially when her head was completely shaved, and she spoke with a biphasic voice.

The young woman was wearing long pants with a shirt that matched her outfit, decorated with a hood that she kept taking off and putting on as if she were suffering from a nervous tic.

She did the same with her sleeves, which she pulled up and down again and again.

Strapped around her hip s wore a sort of leather fanny pack that curiously she never touched at any time, so it looked new. Not like her boots, which were open and worn, indicating that she had worn them for a long time; ragged from the constant movements of her feet, which she kept moving from one side to the other. She evidenced tremendous hyperactivity.

"And act like the human Aiixs?" answered Suka, the tall, stocky boy with a broad back and strong limbs, short hair and ears pinned to his head. He seemed to have membranes between his fingers and under his arms. They were visible when he raised his limbs while expressing his opinion to those present. These membranes stretched like lateral flaps, which gave meaning to the design of his shirt, which was quite wide, with long straps and open armholes down to the hips.

"No, Suka, not human behavior, but the concept of humanity. Or our world and its beauty will disappear," said the Master Shawá looking at the boy, who had squatted down; anxiously observing the sexless subject, which implied that the immense energy of Aiixs made the Cascadeld councilor tremendously nervous. Like many other members of the council he had bare feet, only his had the peculiarity of having membranes between his toes.

The Garos

The siblings and Nose were still in the room watching Rasnar's words like a movie, while the images of the enigmatic confluence of the twelve kingdoms that had been thwarted by the thirteenth disappeared and brought the room to a new scene: Rasnar was flying over beautiful lands filled with huge, radiant colored plants; an immense variety of lush phosphorescent flora. A huge garden of titanic flowers, most of them closed into huge buds that gave off light, both from inside and from the small details of their leaves and petals. Each one of them was different from the next, unique in tenor, size, shape, and luminosity, but the most extraordinary thing, if there could be anything more astonishing than that unparalleled flowering image, was the existence of the creatures that roamed its grounds trotting between the aforementioned stems to protect the flora from any external threat.

These Guardians were difficult to spot, as they were perfectly camouflaged in that habitat, but the Talan used the fire to show the siblings some of these amazing quadrupeds running and even flying around the beautiful place.

"This is my land, my home. Our work there is key to the existence of the planets and peace among the beings that inhabit them. The Talans protect the garden of Talos, where the Garos are born. This involves working as a gardener and, at the same time, being a reputable warrior, for we must guard our flowers and the precious treasure they contain from any possible external threat," Rasnar explained to them.

"The Talans will maintain peace in their lands, thus preserving harmony on planet Earth. In this way, balance is spread throughout all the societies of the universe. In this way, the natural course of the growth of these flowers is respected. They grow from a small bud in the ground to a huge capsule, and when they reach maturity, they become a gigantic and beautiful flower that will open, releasing the Garo from within," explained Nose, fascinated by the subject and bursting into the scene created by the great Guardian.

"After a small flash of light, a tiny luminescent sprout emerges from the sacred soil of the garden of Talos -which is also called the garden of the Garos- that is immediately spotted by the Talans in charge of its tracking. After this, it is transplanted with great delicacy in a safe place, where it will be under the constant protection of the Guardians of Talos, the soldiers that you were not able to perceive without my help in the images I showed you before.

"Well, once this task is undertaken, the tiny plant grows into a flower of colossal dimensions, as you can see. Despite their size, they remain closed because inside they are giving life to a new Garo, so the plant will only increase in size as it enlarges that of the creature inside.

"Just so you understand, this creature is the physical reflection of the beginning of a new human baby's disposition right at the moment of its birth on planet Earth, so you can imagine how many flowers there are in our garden and how many Garos we must protect in its innermost recesses. I guess now you can understand why it is so vital to guard them with our lives," Rasnar explained to the siblings.

"This means that for every human birth, two lives begin their course; one is that of the infant and the other that of the Garo begotten at the very instant that the little earthling first opens its eyes to the outer world and becomes conscious of itself. So, while one begins to develop its disposition, the other will not see the light of the sun until its connection has finished forming its essence, that is to say, one increases as the other develops. They grow at the same time, only that the human does it in a free space, while the Garo does it imprisoned inside a flower and unconscious, since its characteristics are determined by the personal particularities and conscious decisions of the human. It can be said that the latter depends on itself while the Garo depends on the human for its development.

"But when the human child has fully formed his own person, his true essence, what makes him who he is, unique and special in his own way, that is to say, has forged his character, the Garo will be expelled from inside its plant," Nose interrupted again despite the looks that Rasnar was giving him, since this was his field, but the peon continued talking excitedly about the subject. "Until that day, the Garo is forming physically and mentally inside the cocoon. Its evolution depends on the development of the essence of the human to which it is linked, so during the growth of the infant and until its person is formed, the bud will germinate at the same rate as the terrestrial one. Some reach disproportionate proportions, since each flower is unique, as well as each Garo it conceives.

"Mind you, they all have one thing in common: they all give off an inner light that at dusk illuminates the land of Talos with a rainbow of unparalleled shapes and colors; a beautiful sight that only Talans are lucky enough to see.

"They also say that when you pass near the flowers you feel the aura and even get to perceive feelings, sensations and even visions of humans when you touch their petals. Is that true, Rasnar?" -Nose asked him intrigued looking at the fire, as he hoped to see the images of the cycle.

"Yes, as soon as the nature of the earthling reaches its fullness, the flower attached to it will open its petals and the fully formed Garo will emerge from within, shedding motes of pollen through the air like little flashes of light. And when this precious dust disperses into the air you can finally see the Garo. That's when you appreciate the magnitude of what you felt when you touched each of the plants as they were growing. You will appreciate the moods, all in their own way, as distinct as they are exceptional.

"But that is only a reflection of the great power of the human being, for each of these flowers and their Garos are only the sparkle of the girl or boy to whom it is attached. It will be a rare time when the process doesn't leave you both awestruck and ecstatic," said Rasnar with a gleam of emotion in his eyes as he projected his memories onto the flames.

"Each Garo has the same mission, but how it does it will depend on the actions of the human to whom it is linked and the events that happen to that human during its passage through life. That is to say, a Garo is born through and for a cause until its death, like a Guardian angel, and will go in search of the being to which it is linked. This happens as soon as it is expelled from the lozenge, so he will only see the land of the Talans for a brief moment, since at the moment of emerging from his cocoon, he is immediately transported, spiritually and physically, to its person to act as guardian of both the human soul and its own.

"This is because the acts of one have repercussions on the other, as if they were one and the same. Simply put, if one dies, so does the other," said the peon as the siblings looked at each other in fear.

"Well, it's not exactly like that, Nose. If it is the Garo that dies first, the consequence will not be the instant death of the human being to whom it is attached, but that person will sink into a deep sorrow that he will never be able to decipher, since, without further ado, he will feel such a great emptiness that he will experience an immense state of loneliness and incomprehension that will plague his soul. Humans call it depression or neurosis.

"The lack of Garo in the life of the earthling to whom it is attached is equivalent to losing a part of himself, which will leave a hole that he will never be able to fill, and he will be immersed in a deep sadness from which he will not be able to escape. He will live blinded by this state of confusion, which will eventually lead the person to make the decision, in most cases, to end this suffering by ending his life, although nowadays, despite not having found the answer to these diseases, humans have found chemical ways to make the loss of the Garo more bearable. Even so, although they continue to live, the person is in a state of penance, in the throes of death, which ends up lengthening the time of sorrow, just a little bit of the terrible anxiety, but sooner or later, all end in an appalling way.

"Overcoming the death of a Garo, which is very rare, is a sign of extreme fortitude and great courage. However, there are cases of people who, after a lifetime of constant struggle with themselves, managed to get out of that horrible vortex created by the vacuum created by losing their Garo. They are not many, but there are some; an extraordinary phenomenon deserving of a section in our lands dedicated to these humans, venerated as the most sacred of all the places in our garden, since in it are the shoots of the Garos that have been able to be reborn. But these resurrections never bring back the being they were before they died, but rather the Garo returns to us with more strength and beauty than before.

"As a Guardian of Talos, I have never forgotten a Garo, despite having seen it only for an instant as the flowers opened, but when the bud of a reborn emerges, both its energy and its strength are so powerful that it becomes impossible to forget who it was and what it has become.

"They are such fascinating creatures that I could not resist following the course of every one that has ever existed, revered almost as gods and, from what I discovered, extremely difficult to track, even for a powerful being like me. Like the humans to whom they are attached, they are the ones who make them rise from their ashes, from the darkest and gloomiest of mental hells in which they find themselves after the loss of their Garo, without even knowing of their existence nor the reason for their suffering.

"These are earthlings of extreme power and sensitivity, have a high level of intellect and great emotional intelligence. They are strong, courageous, quite creative, with great maturity, wise by birth, with prodigious instinct and implacable intuition. But the most curious thing of all is that they are not aware of it, not even after having overcome the severe challenge both personally and socially, struggling completely alone, without the help or understanding of anyone else. They are transformed into beings capable of perceiving what others cannot, something that turns them into misfits. Therefore, even my presence in front of these people can be risky, even for me.

"You must understand the magnitude of this fact. Since the rest of the humans who have lost their Garo, no matter how hard they try, end up sentenced to continuing their daily life but without the essence that characterized them, who experience a meaningless life, a bodily existence like a zombie that walks without peace or happiness. For these poor souls, nothing will have any value, there will be no more smells to perceive or tastes to savor; nothing will activate their senses or produce pleasure, since everything becomes non-existent after the death of their Garo.

"Of course, they don't know this. For them, one day everything simply became dark without any explanation. In this way, they become invisible to their loved ones and, due to lack of understanding or means, and being far away from everything they loved, from what they were and knew, there comes a day when they decide that living without vitality is not worth it," explained the Guardian, making the children understand the importance of his work and that of the Garos in their world.

"We must tell people! How are they going to help these people if no one knows what's wrong with them? They must know about their existence, Rasnar. Humans must know the importance of their actions, of the decisions they make in life, taking into account the existence of the Garo. It is up to us to let them know the consequences and repercussions of their actions, how these can destroy the two beings, so that they understand their importance.

"Otherwise, the decline of our actions could lead to the extinction of both races, dragging the earth to its end! said James in grief.

"But if our actions are consistent, they will make people prosper and will have an impact on the vast and beautiful garden of Talos, which will illuminate the coldest nights with the purity of its warmest light. Those are the values you should know, James, not the existence of the Garos."

"Human nature could lead them to hunt their own creatures to cage or exhibit them. No, what should be done is to instill good values, of love and respect, in the children of our world," Sasha replied.

"The Garos cannot be seen or heard and will not contact the linked being or any other Arguan or human, since, by law, no one should ever know of their existence. But if the people of planet Earth would listen to their intuition and common sense, if they would take just a few minutes a day to listen to nature and let themselves be carried away by the perception of the energy of their environment, expanding their heart and soul to open their eyes and senses to what cannot be seen or touched, they would perceive that the Garos are always by their side. These would embrace the being they are attached to, wrapping them in a huge mantle of good deeds, letting them know to each of those people who opened their mind to the universe that they have never been and will never be alone. Even though they belong to two different worlds, the connection between the Garo and the human exists.

"The person who achieves this bond with his Garo is intoxicated with the energy of the cosmos, which fills him with an extraordinary strength. So much so that he believes he is capable of doing everything he sets out to do in life, to enjoy a better world for everyone.

"But if they lose that link, they have, because they have disconnected from everything around them except the banal, then that which they know will disappear, for the Garo is the Guardian of the Nexus. Their life depends on it. If this were not so, it would be the end because the terrestrial would become more blinded and would walk without values, lost in his own selfish being."

Suddenly, the image was cut short by a memory in which another Talan appeared.

"Rasnar, my lord, has returned," said a winged horse of sorts, bowing its forelegs with a curtsey. It was clear that being the Guardian of Talos was a rank of great importance.

This new being was the leader of the watchmen that make up the guard of the garden of the Garos; a kind of zebra of great size, whose black stripes shone like oil, with fluorescent reflections of greenish blue. A winged species with a tail populated with feathers similar to those of a peacock, but with the difference that at the end of each one of them was revealed the drawing of an eye, so that together they completed a total of hundreds of watchful stars that did not protrude as eye lobes, but rather were part of the design of the plumage. The image clearly showed how they moved, observing, and patrolling everything around them.

At night, when darkness fell over the garden, when it was illuminated by the vegetation that inhabited Talos, the watchers shone camouflaging themselves among the beautiful plants, perfectly mimicking the floral spectacle, with their tails up to see better. For this reason, as soon as they were born, this race of Talans was designated as part of the watch guard; a position of honor, since not only could they better perceive the days and nights, as well as the colors and lights that adorned the garden of Talos, but they could naturally hide themselves completely in that marvelous visual manifestation. Thus, when the misfortune arose of having to fight or pursue a threat, they had everything they needed to win the battle.

"Yes, I am back, but this is no time for rejoicing, for the worst is yet to come," Rasnar replied regretfully to the watchman in the images.

"But it bodes well for the advancement of our purpose, doesn't it?" asked the winged zebra.

"It matters not what one thinks. In two days, my task will be decreed, or we will all be sentenced, and although the whole will take sides in the decision, the responsibility of the universe now rests on my shoulders," replied the Guardian.

"I understand, sir," replied the watchman with concern, lowering his beautiful wings.

"If it is for the good of all that one must pay, so be it... I will receive whatever punishment is necessary; destiny will prescribe it. My will is already written. I cannot maintain a neutral stance knowing that our land and all others are dying. Even evil itself has been able to see it burst into the room to make my function a fact, so the council will yield to my request.

"The fear of what might happen, in letting the laws that protect us be broken for once, is better than the assured loss of the universe," Rasnar remarked.

"My lord, what will you do if the council does not accept your request? Despite being under Zotrak's order, you know there is always the possibility that they will find a way to convince evil otherwise," said the lookout.

"They will accept. There is no other choice. It is that or death. The beings of our cosmos will suffer skin wounds before they lose their lives."

The fire subsided and the image faded.

"Is that true? Is the solar system dying?" asked the boy.

"And as you have already seen, the Sun and the Earth are the main sources of life, not because they are more important or essential, but because your planet is the sickest one right now, and it is affecting our universe at great speed, making us all in danger of mass extinction," the Guardian mentioned.

"You convinced the Arguans to send you here to try to fix that situation, didn't you? Then what are you doing here with us, shouldn't you be fixing it?" James said worriedly.

"Yes, I convinced the leaders of the thirteen kingdoms, but I did not do it solely for that purpose. Whether you like it or not, I killed two birds with one stone: this issue was a good excuse to move freely between the two worlds and be here with you without arousing suspicion, since the unnamable one must never know of your existence or of any of the plans of the rest of the kingdoms.

"Even though they all have to pay tribute to the thirteenth, the twelve will back us up and defend us against the tyrant as soon as you have been trained and are ready to hunt him down. But for now, he must remain among us. For if he whom you already know were informed of our present situation, knowing who you are, he would send spies to this planet at the next novilunium, and you would be quickly annihilated. For this reason, I told nothing of what I intended nor of your presence to any of the kingdoms.

"Sometimes there are things that it's better not to think about, just to be on the safe side. You can't trust anyone these days. There are many traitors, and every precaution is too little," said the Talan.

"But Rasnar, the chair you are sitting in shows that you came here earlier to meet Grandma and her mother-in-law, our great-grandmother. How is that possible? Were there no Zorks or evil allies back then?" the young woman wanted to know.

"You must understand that being Guardian of Talos, I have the power to come to Earth whenever I please, to maintain the balance and to make sure that the Garos are safe and in full natural function, as they should be, but this is something I have always kept secret. When evil took power in the thirteenth realm, it was decreed that no one could ever leave Argua, for whoever attempted to do so would be sentenced to immediate death, without trial. In this way it has tyrannically controlled the population of our planet: with the exception of myself, the rest of the beings can only access your world through a ritual arranged by the five sages on a new moon" Rasnar pronounced.

The XIII Kingdom

When it became clear to us after the war that our world was to change forever, the kingdoms of Argua, through the Council of Twelve, met in stealth and made the decision that we would keep secret the gifts possessed by every being in each of our kingdoms; talents sealed underground, where they would remain forever buried for the safety of all, until the day of justice came and we could strike and take back our lives.

"Since then, if at any time it should be or become of exceptional necessity to use any of those powers which we should never show, those gifts which make each of us unique, we are first obliged to consult with the council and receive unanimous consent. If this is refused, it could not be carried out, even if it meant killing a part of us, leaving the attributes useless for life.

"This is the new oppressive functioning of our society since Zotrak appeared. Fortunately for me, Talans are of a reserved nature, so we do not show what we are capable of either freely or by participating in Argua's games; an advantage at this point, since no one knows our powers and abilities. Now that you know this, it is obvious to understand that the times I came to your planet I came by my own means, unknown to anyone but myself and your family.

"In this way, no one knows whether I was there nor that I can be here when I want to be. All thanks to my humility, to keep the qualities of my gifts secret and to be cautious with them, without rushing to put my superiority and the variety of my powers before others, not even during the games of Argua. My ancestors dictated a law that no one from the kingdom of Talos should ever participate in them, for it prioritizes in our blood to do good for a far greater purpose than to be revered or flattered for our prowess and virtues.

"All of this allowed me to keep the odd ace up my sleeve, both for myself and for the community in Talana. But unlike Talos, before the appearance of evil and the war it provoked, the rest of the kingdoms of Argua manifested their mastery by exposing their best warriors and students, competing with the leaders of other kingdoms, showing the world the magnificence of the most unprecedented powers, as well as the majesty of ancestral techniques," explained Rasnar.

"In Argua's games, you mean, can we see them, please?" asked Sasha.

"Yes, in the good old days the kingdoms held games and festivals both in their domains and in no man's land. The population of the kingdom would congregate around Lake Naruh and there they would reveal their attributes, recreating them in a magical display before other Argua species. Those were truly lavish times," Rasnar replied.

"The Talans never exposed their talents and powers, really?" James asked.

"We are guardian warriors. The work we do is of great importance to the universe, so we cannot risk our position.

"In addition, we are discreet by nature, observant, strategic and cautious, we are on guard at all times. Order and security are our priority. That is why we were the only ones who never took part in the games; at least, not as participants, since as spectators we were always present.

"We have used the games as a means of informing ourselves, to keep abreast of developments in each realm, keeping us alert to any changes or possible threats, positioning ourselves two steps ahead of the others, discovering the qualities of the different territories and their people.

"I, as part of the Council of Argua, was once obliged to participate in the opening ceremony of these games, but because of my status as a Talan, I could slip away and observe from another angle the progression of the ultimate festivity without getting involved in the rituals of the council," the Guardian confessed.

"I remember the days of the games. They were good times... It was a glorious time where peace reigned, and each kingdom shone on its own with a unique light. I still remember the feeling that came over you; you could feel the energy of Argua flowing as one, in pure harmony.

"It was the only time we were allowed to leave the Shwanír Fortress and enjoy the diversity of our peoples in no man's land. There we all respected each other as equals," said Nose wistfully.

"I know, like the Olympics for us, right?" James said.

"Well, not exactly... These games were not created for competition. We did not have an athlete to represent us, but rather each sovereignty made an annual presentation of its beauty and chose those who could bring something beneficial to the whole of Argua. The inhabitants of each of the twelve kingdoms could present their gifts or their creations as an offering to the progress of the beings of our planet, but these were only chosen after undergoing hard tests that sought to prove their worth.

"It was a time when territories came together for something far more important than proving their own greatness. Every act was by and for the kingdoms of our beloved Argua. It would be the equivalent of all the countries and peoples of planet Earth coming together in a celebration that sought to share contributions and innovations for the betterment and welfare of your world and all living things on it," Rasnar replied.

"We have twelve kingdoms, but none of them has a king or queen. Each territory has its council, formed by the most outstanding beings of its people, those who contributed something to their people in the games. But the unfortunate appearance of Zotrak changed everything. His attack on the Kingdom of Margua destroyed us and the attempts of other kingdoms to help us were in vain because of the depth of our waters and the difficult access to the fortress. The terrible power of which I will not mention eliminated many of the best warriors in that battle, as well as in many others before that attack.

"War broke out when Argua was not ready. The Shwanír Fortress was barely standing. The kingdoms suffered great losses that would scar them for life. Then there came a point when we could fight no more. It was the end of us, or so it seemed....

"Until the most beautiful and powerful of the Shawá ladies, the great Riyah, sacrificed herself for the survival of the twelve kingdoms," Nose interrupted, putting his hand to his chest in respect.

Silence reigned in the room; only the crackling of the wood on the fire could be heard.

"I don't know, did you know her? Because we saw her when grandma showed us some of her memories through the gem you sent us, when we joined hands on the ice of her chrysalis in the pool," commented Sasha.

"And what did you see?" asked Nose, distressed by the memory of that lady.

But the young woman did not know how to respond, as what she and her brother had observed was not easy to digest, especially for someone who was clearly broken by the loss of that woman.

"I thought a Shwanír Fortress peon was not allowed to associate with a Shawá Lady or anyone else in general," Rasnar commented.

"So, it was and so it is," the peon replied as the Guardian opened the left wing and draped it over Nose's shoulders.

"Her loss was a tragedy for all of us," the Talan confessed.

"And with your sacrifice, did you stop the war? Because if so, I don't understand what you say we're up against," said the teenager.

"No, James. Riyah offered herself in sacrifice for the sole purpose that the unnamable one would accept peace between the rest of the kingdoms and him, and that he would stay in the thirteenth. That there he would reign as he pleased, without intervening in the other twelve.

"Thanks to her cunning and her Shawá s knowledge, she forced the agreement with the evil one under a death pact, which the tyrant did not know about. If Zotrak had known about Shawá s customs and qualities, there would have been no deal on his part. That's why it is so important to learn about other cultures and study your opponent, because you never know what they can do to you or what they can bring to you," Rasnar recommended.

"The shrewdness of the Shawá Lady managed to stop our kingdom from being at war. Her sacrifice endures today even though she has passed away, since, by giving herself as an offering, she kept her word, forcing the evil one, in accordance with the Shawá pact, to keep his word or, failing that, pay for it with death. A deal that no one knew if it would work, since the powers of you-know-who, like yours, are yet unknown. But if the Shawá pact affected him as it did the milkman, you too are susceptible to that power.

"The problem now is that, due to lack of knowledge about the species, their death may never come, since we don't know the full extent of their power or longevity," Nose acknowledged.

"If he were to break his word and leave the thirteenth realm without using the Zorks, his body would probably quickly poison like the milkman's and with luck he would die. Or, at least, we think so, since that day the evil has been locked up in its co-dominions and, as far as we know, has never left them. For this reason, we believe that, in some way, dealing with Riyah affected him.

"One of the strategies that would overthrow him would be to provoke him to get him to break the agreement, to make him leave his fortress, as hopefully, this would end his life. In doing so, we would take back our world, what was once Argua.

"The Shawá Lady managed to ensure that as long as evil remained in our lands, it stayed out of the way and did not get involved in the affairs of the twelve kingdoms. But he found other means: telekinesis, telepathy and various dark magics, to demand his wishes by tormenting the population with his cruelty, creating an oppressed society. He appeared throughout the twelve kingdoms practically unseen and without risking his life; he showed himself through his specters, his Zorks, so that the possibility of making him leave was annulled.

"Anyway, no one would dare to face him without the help of a large army of his own kind covering his back. That is why you must train yourselves, to get strength and hope," Rasnar reported.

"Anyway, the pact has a trick and Riyah did not realize it: the pact loses value in the thirteenth kingdom, so that in its territory he could defend himself in person. This place has become his life insurance, his fortress of protection. He has the assurance that hidden there he remains safe thanks to his advantageous powers and mastery of the area, which is unknown to us. He took it from the Kingdom of Firendel and now it is fortified with black magic, so if we were to attack him within its walls, he could unleash his fury and win without breaking the pact.

"Despite the fact that to anyone's eyes it may seem like a prison, he has managed to handle himself well, complying and respecting the rules of the treaty he made with Riyah, turning the kingdom into his fortress. From there he torments without having to move from the throne he snatched from the Lady Nunnara.

"For now, he is the most powerful being we have ever known, so attacking him will be no easy task. Besides, he is not foolish enough to leave his sovereignty at the risk of his life. For this he uses his minions, whom he possesses whenever and wherever he wants, whom he uses to transport himself mentally from one place to another and interfere in the affairs of others," Nose reminds them.

"Before the war, when that was a Firendel area, accommodated to their needs and customs, it was a different kingdom. After the expulsion of its people, once they won the battle against their leader, the other kingdoms did their part to help them to recover from the ashes, the fruit of their food, and start another life in a new home.

"Lady Nunnara was the only warrior in the history of the bloody days who managed to face evil in person and not die on the spot. She became the sole possessor of the notions necessary to fight it. Unfortunately, she too was changed and although she survived, she was never the same again.

"Her exploits were such that Zotrak himself still craves her as a wife, not only because she is the only woman capable of withstanding his power, but also because she would be the perfect mate to rule over the rest of the kingdoms and spread his venom over the twelve to unify them into one, his own, under the rule of terror. She would then burn down homes, render their lands infertile and enslave their people.

"After the pact, Lady Nunnara is, in his view, even more important to his work; a key piece given his situation, as he cannot move. Thus, if he were to get that alliance, he would have total control to move through the lady, nullifying the kingdom as we know it.

"But she will never join him, even though she lives in a perpetual hell having to endure the fury and torment of Zotrak's uncontrolled power, enduring the physical and psychological torture to which this psychopath subjects her from a distance to try to manipulate her. Some say that the Lady stays alive because her skin can withstand temperatures so high that even she does not know how high she can go. There are rumors that her body can be recomposed from the ashes, hence her current appearance.

"It may be that this quality gave her the ability to be the heir to the throne of Firendel, not as queen, but as leader and advisor of Argua, a position that in her kingdom is ceded every hundred years, when the birth of an exceptional baby occurs right after the death of the previous leader, like a reincarnation, but with different abilities.

"To find out, these creatures are subjected to several tests culminating in that of the throne, prostrate in the depths of the lava of the great heart of Argua: only the one who survives is the heir to the gifts that make him worthy of the fiery masteries, something that makes them unique in the twelve realms.

"Lady Nunnara was the only one of her kind to pass every test without so much as a flinch. The limits of her endurance to physical pain, mental endurance, or the powers she possesses are not yet known; what is known is that she is a superb leader for her kingdom and an exceptional Argua advisor.

"None predicted what was to happen, but Firendel has become the perfect realm for evil to create a small fortress. No one saw it coming; neither she nor her people can ever forgive him. The day Zotrak took the people of Nunnara's lands from them, appropriating them as his lair, he not only destroyed the homes of these people, but he also annihilated them, whether they fought against him or not. He left an image of death and decay everywhere, a scene that not only lingers in the memory of the Firendels. The corpses of the men, women, and infants whose lives he took that night are still scattered like skeletons over their lands, a cemetery without graves. A difficult thing for loved ones to process. Zotrak keeps it that way as part of the decor after the conquest.

" Could have joined him to protect herself and keep her people alive, albeit subjected to the dictator's tyranny, but instead she confronted him in person. No one had ever done that before, especially not alone. She was willing to sacrifice her life for the sake of her people and paid for it by losing her eyesight, among many other things.

"Miraculously, she survived the battle against the most powerful being of all time. So, after that, she proved that she was not only chosen for her gifts, but for her values and morals, which stood out greatly among the other candidates to the throne of Firendel, because they were just and immovable, and she faced evil alone to protect her people while the others fled. In doing so, she gave them the time and the advantage they needed to escape from evil and its minions, behavior that honors her.

"Many lives were lost with the unforeseen appearance of the Zorks' shadows, which terrified and eliminated the people who remained on the border of her realm, and that Nunnara sensed the energy and heat of any species. But these wraiths, from what she told us, are impossible to detect even for her. They have been designed for evil surely by allies of Zotrak, and that gives him an advantage, since we do not know who they are. Clearly, he knows us and has analyzed us to create weapons that are impossible to fight.

"To prevent these Zorks from following her people, even though her people were escorted by great warriors both from her kingdom and others willing to help them, she had to face those invincible evil phantoms alone. The bravery, courage and powers of the warriors were not able to defeat them, and they were falling like flies.

"The Lady could not bear that genocide and defended her kingdom as much as those heroes and heroines, while her people tried to flee as best, they could. She was devastated when she saw it abandoned, surrounded by depraved spirits against whom she fought until she was exhausted, prostrate on her throne, awaiting the arrival of evil itself. The coward appeared before her when the poor woman had no strength left; even so, the lady resisted and came out alive.

"Nunnara is the one true heir to the heart of Argua, with the strongest gift ever seen, the bravest spirit and the most certain integrity in the history of the twelve kingdoms, both old and new Argua. But it is to Riyah, the Shawá Lady, that we owe our survival, that of our kingdoms and that of our people, for her kindness gave us the opportunity to organize a rebellion with which we will proceed to regain what we once had and was taken from us," Rasnar exclaimed.

"By then Riyah was part of the Council of Argua, but in a more independent way. She had earned the respect of everyone, but, due to her introverted personality, she never wanted to take part in public events unless it was necessary, nor to make herself known by showing off to the Arguan societies, so she only attended meetings where issues of vital importance to the kingdom were discussed.

"Faced with the imminent destruction of Margua and the other territories that were trying to help them, she made a decision and made it public in front of the committee. No one had the audacity to contradict her argument or offer a better solution than the one she proposed, so after the announcement, poor Riyah walked alone to her fate while the kingdom of Argua covered itself in shame in silence.

"The Lady came out of the Shwanír Fortress across the water, levitating over the sea towards evil itself, until she was planted in front of it. The retinue that protected him did not touch her, for the Lady's power was so great that none of the Zorks could harm or restrain her. And when she approached the unnamable one, she dodged the attacks she received because of the aura of magic emanating from her body. Those attacks were blocked by beasts and animals with which she shared a special connection.

"But do not think that the sacrifices of her friends were to her liking. For even she could not restrain them, for their love for the Lady blinded them. Riyah could only hear her own heart breaking into pieces as her beloved fauna gave up her life for her. But the creatures were not the only ones who sacrificed themselves, as the plants were immolating themselves for the lady, surely provoked by the support of Eyíre, who with great pain was protecting her as much as she could until her end."

"It was absolutely clear to them that no one could overthrow Zotrak without getting some kind of pact. Thus, without the sacrifice, the war would have continued until the total destruction of Argua and all its beings," Nose explained.

"But... I don't understand why she had to sacrifice herself. Why not propose that pact without having to give her life for it?"-James asked.

"The reason Zotrak attacked the Shwanír Fortress, the most complicated to attack because of its difficult access, is precisely because Riyah was in it. That was no mere coincidence," Rasnar replied.

"What does Riyah have to do with that monster?" the young woman asked.

"That monster, Sasha, was created by her, and it was too great a burden on her righteous soul not to punish herself by sacrificing herself for others and for the greater good," the Guardian told them, leaving them speechless.

"How? It can't be... But we saw her in the memories Grandma passed on to us; she was a good person! We both noticed that she defended the last of the drakons against some savages," James replied.

"Rombar? Did you see Rombar? How lucky you are! Though wretched the moment you had to witness, but lucky in turn... I would give all I have to see Riyah and the last of the drakons again," Nose confessed.

"That was precisely the moment when our destiny changed its course. Although Riyah did not crave evil, she paid dearly for her desire for justice and revenge," Rasnar said.

"Evitur... She put a curse on him, didn't she? He's... He's Zotrak?" Sasha asked as Rasnar sat up, staring into the fire. Then he let out a soft roar, projecting onto the flames of the fireplace the images of Evitur after the attack of the drakon Rombar, which caused wounds on his face.

In these visions the barbarian was seen as a normal man. He arrived at a stone house, built in a circular shape with earth on its sides and moss covering the roof, which gave it the appearance of a small hill or burrow from which smoke was coming out. From the outside, the house could only be distinguished from the field by a curved door covered with skins that protected the interior of the house from the cold. It was full of badanas covering the walls and floor to provide warmth to the dwelling, with herbs to mask the smell of the animals hanging from the ceiling, which was supported by a stone column in the center of the hut. Next to it were the embers, where they cooked and heated the dwelling. And there, sitting by the fire, was a sweet-looking woman who seemed to be waiting for the hunter, worried. In the representation, she could be seen tucking him in gently, embracing him when she saw him arrive. It looked like a loving home where a healthy married couple lived.

The Conception

The following projections illustrated moments that followed one after the other as the months went by. They reproduced daily life in the hunter's abode, a normal life, only now, unlike before, the scarred Evitur's beloved was pregnant, about to give birth. The images stopped at the moment of delivery, hinting that something was beginning to go wrong. Suddenly, darkness descended on the interior of the hearth, with a dark cloud blinding those present. Then a horrible portrait was shown, showing the barbarian's wife bleeding to death after conception, as well as her midwife, who was lying on the floor covered in blood.

The face of horror reflected in the face of the savage Evitur produced a terrible shudder that ran from head to toe across the skin of the siblings, who were attentively observing that tragic vision over the fire. The great hunter and ruthless killer of beasts, the one who feared nothing, was for the first time in his life dismayed after losing his beloved at the hands of the monster he held in his lap, his own blood, his firstborn and only son.

Riyah's words echoed in his head with every step he took towards the cliff near his house, on which the village was settled; he walked covered in blood through the humble streets towards the precipice, dodging the townspeople, who came out of their homes horrified at the sight of the man with the creature wrapped in a blanket over his beefy arms stained red like a butcher from a slaughter. Desperate, already on the brink of the abyss, he threw his son into the void in the presence of all his people, who, before such an atrocity, cornered him like one of the beasts he had hunted on so many occasions, as if justice was finally being done for so many species he had pursued to extinction. As a consequence, by barbarian tradition, they had to tie his hands and feet in the shape of an X to judge him, with four ropes that came out of the ends of two huge wooden poles located on a stone altar.

In the meantime, the event was announced to the people with drums beating; in this way, the crowd could attend the trial if they wished, for they had been informed in a public manner with the sound of the drums. Their power was such that they resounded throughout the territory, their vibrations were felt in the chest of everyone who walked through those lands, since these acts always involved the whole of their people in the trial and during the sentence.

In Evitur's case, after the opinion and evidence gathered by those present, he was found guilty by an absolute majority. It was decided that for each murder committed, he would receive an axe in the spine. Culturally, they believed that to put to death a murderer of their own was to show mercy; on the other hand, to strike him in the back for the crime committed, if it did not kill him, would render him useless for life and useless to society. For them it meant a penalty even worse than death itself, since it would lead him to a life of lamentation and suffering, degraded to the subjection of a permanent disability that would incapacitate him to lead a dignified life. The sentenced person was forced to swallow his pride and beg for alms for his own survival from those who had judged and punished him, because by leaving him crippled for life, it would be impossible for him to survive otherwise. Although it was rare that someone survived having committed three murders in the eyes of the people.

The moment of the trial began with Evitur tied in the shape of an X on the altar. Behind him, an executioner held a huge two-edged axe in his hands while the people gathered before the tabernacle. The act began in the presence of men, women, and minors, as everyone took part in the ritual. The crowd shouted the crime committed against the midwife, with which the barbarian received the first axe. He tried to focus his gaze beyond the crowd, on the border where the cliff broke with the horizon of the sea, but something caught his gaze and penetrated his thoughts, which is why he had to turn his head towards the crowd, even though he had no intention of doing so.

There, in the crowd, stood the culprit of all his misfortunes, standing in front of him, smiling with satisfaction. She looked him in the eyes without blinking as she recited each of his true crimes, reminding him of each of the species he had exterminated. She slipped into his mind thanks to the sweat on the hunter's forehead, who was forced to listen to her words, her voice, which sought justice for those who were once friends and who had disappeared as victims of that conscienceless barbarian.

After the first axe, despite being supported only by the ropes that held his joints, the man continued with his head held high, staring at the Shawá without even blinking, enveloped by the shouts of the people, who enumerated the alleged second crime. At the sound of his beloved's name, Evitur closed his eyes in anticipation of the next blow, but this time the cracking of his back was barely audible, as a terrifying scream of pain, rage and revenge came from within him as if his soul had been expelled in horror, blocking out any other sound that could be heard in the surroundings. Even so, the hunter continued with his gaze on the young woman, who was hiding among the people enunciating mercilessly in the mind of the subdued man the names of his slain companions.

In spite of the shifting shrieks of the court, the extreme pain he had to endure, the accusations of the crowd and the penetrating words of the young Shawá, his angry contemplation of her harassed Riyah with fury. But she did not even flinch, she continued to stare at him unblinkingly, reminding him of the species he killed for money and pleasure. Then, just before the third slash, the lady whispered to him:

"Now, for your last crime, the murder of your own blood, the fruit of your love for your beloved, your only son. And so, your lineage has ended, extinguished like so many others that you mercilessly eliminated."

And with a sharp blow, the last heartbeat of the merciless one sounded, which extinguished the images of the fire. The fire diminished its intensity until the figurations that were forged in them disappeared.

"So Zotrak is Evitur's son? But also, his wife's and somehow Riyah's, isn't he?" asked the confused boy.

"So, Zo... was it a human baby?" said Sasha hesitantly.

"Would a human baby kill his village days after birth? No. He is only the son and fruit of evil," Rasnar answered.

"Maybe if you piss him off too much, he can burst everyone's eardrums by crying at full volume," exclaimed James, who was met with silence from those present. "Sorry, it was funny in my head," the boy apologized, embarrassed.

"But you said Evitur threw his son off a cliff. How can a baby survive that?" Sasha asked.

"His wife's pregnancy was the result of a spell created by the desire for revenge that blinded Riyah with rage, used on Rombar without taking into account that it would take the lives of innocents, starting with Evitur's wife, who on the most beautiful day of her life, the day of the birth of her child, lost her life at the hands of what she cared for and protected during the entire gestation period; months of deception, engendering a murderous monster, sentencing herself under a false veil of gentleness. That which he threw over the cliff was never a baby.

"You must know that in one of his combats Evitur was so badly wounded that he nullified any possibility of having off-spring. It was after this traumatic event that he became the ruthless annihilator of species. We suppose that for this reason the hunter did not kill the creature with his own hands when he should have done so. But who would have known that by throwing it over that cliff he would sentence the whole of Argua.

"After being thrown into the void, the bundle fell into the deep, cold waters on the west side of the Margua, where huge waves continuously crash against the high walls of its cliffs and cause the fall of large rocks that tumble and are piled one on top of the other, exposed in plain sight as soon as the tide goes out, by the suction of the water with the entry of new waves. But the body of the wicked creature miraculously dodged those rocks and was saved from ending up smashed against the ground. It was submerged in the foam while it was dragged by the strong currents of its waters, without the option of breathing oxygen and suffering the freezing of its naked body.

"The instinct of the little monster instigated it to steal the oxygen particles from the Larus shark that had engulfed it, thus gaining strength to eat the animal from within, which gave it the strength to withstand the cold of the dark shades of the Margua. But the creature's effort to overcome these conditions caused it to mutate and expand its organism through this space, altering its cells and provoking in itself the rupture of the fibers. Then the water boiled until it evaporated.

"During the remaining days, hundreds of dead animals appeared along the coasts, some with bites that pierced their torso. It seemed that a new predator was loose in the sea and this one was not killing for hunger, but for pleasure, something new, unknown, and unexpected for the citizens of Argua. The beast slaughtered uncontrollably wherever it passed, and the water became so warm that it annihilated specimens acclimated to the cold nature of its depths.

"But the threat was not the problem of our waters; the monster was preparing to take revenge and as soon as the day came, he did not hesitate to go straight to the village where he was born. There he saw the figure of his decaying father hanging from the poles as an example to the village. The anger unleashed in him by that traumatic image made him lose control of his actions, discovering for the first time one of his many powers, with which he razed and exterminated the entire village mortifying and devouring its inhabitants in a way even more cruel than the one they had used with Evitur. He did not leave a single living being in the territory, he killed everything that came his way, be it men, women, children, animals, or plants.

"After that, his power increased. He discovered that not only did he feed on the flesh of our beings, but that the fear and horror he inflicted on others increased his strength. He realized that the more he slaughtered, the more power he gained, revealing a variety of new and extraordinary qualities that surfaced in his being; qualities that grew with the pain and suffering of others as an unstoppable dark power.

"If he no longer had a conscience or scruples, that only intensified his homicidal content, for he enjoyed his atrocities with an ambition for power, recreating himself with a terrifying clairvoyance of macabre creativity, surpassing the limits of aberration, going mad everywhere without mercy," Rasnar finished his account.

"But why did he avenge his father, if his father threw him into the void?" James asked in confusion.

"Some believe that the great hunter and species killer was such a brute that he did not even flinch when he saw the midwife and the love of his life die at the hands of his own son. He was simply stunned for not having predicted such a situation even in his worst nightmares. According to legend, on the day of the conception of evil, what Evitur felt was pride for being the progenitor of that creation, a being even more barbaric than himself, so when he threw it, he did so in order to protect it. After doing this, he returned in search of the corpse of his beloved. Then he discovered that the body of the midwife had disappeared," said Nose.

"But why did the people accuse him of the midwife's murder if the body was no longer there?" continued the boy questioning the Guardian.

"By all accounts, the midwife did not die at that instant, but lay dying, and the moment she sensed danger, she pretended to be dead to save her life. That is the scene that the people of the village saw. The hunter was cornered and so the girl was able to escape by crawling along the ground until she was well away from the ruckus.

"By all accounts, she ended up taking refuge in the lost woods, as no one ever saw her again," said Nose.

"So, if she didn't show up again, how do they know this story?" Sasha wondered.

"Because the midwife was not just any woman. The great reputation of the barbarian allowed him to surround himself with many of the most influential and powerful people of Argua, whom, in turn, he blackmailed over making public the assignments that they had entrusted to him. If that information had come to light, it would have terribly tarnished the honor of many individuals, who had discreetly entrusted him with dirty jobs, which gave him tremendous power over them.

"So, before the birth of his firstborn, unaware that this was the fruit of an artifice rigged by Riyah, he sealed a pact with the priestess Fraya. If he hunted down her twin brother, she would help him during the birth of his child, not only with the delivery, but by granting his baby a great gift, whatever power the father chose for him. Evitur, of course, accepted and immediately began searching for Eyíre, the priestess' brother.

"As an enthusiastic father, he did not hesitate to choose as a virtue that his son should live up to his name and far surpass his father's dreadful prowess, that he should be stronger and more bloodthirsty than he was until he became a legendary beast of the hunt. But this gift literally countered his words and caused the creature, already evil and monstrous in itself, to lose empathy; an ability that would have somehow curbed the cruelty he inflicted on his victims.

"This unfortunate event destroyed any possibility that would have left the evil being mentally vulnerable. He had been blessed with extreme corpulence and became a horrendously difficult anomaly to bring down. Fortunately, as he willingly secluded himself in his realm, his potential was stunted, or at least did not increase at the speed and magnitude with which it could have. Still, when he can, he enjoys small captures made by the Zorks, with which he amuses himself inside his fortress. Despite being stunted, his fullness is still extreme," said Rasnar.

"Why would anyone want to see their brother dead? What did Eyíre do to her to deserve that?" -Sasha asked.

"Dead? Who said dead? She didn't want her brother dead; she wanted his magic!" the Guardian confessed.

"What Rasnar is trying to say is that Fraya's ambition for power blinded her in such a way that she thought it was better to keep for herself what her brother did not use," Nose clarified.

"What powers did her twin have? Were they like the good witch and the bad witch?" the boy wanted to know.

"No, James. In this life it is not all black and white, nor is anything or anyone only good or bad. Fraya's ideas were very generous to Argua, as she and her sister blossomed into the best duo in the games period. For a time watching them together displaying their skills was as exquisite as you could imagine. Beautiful, brave, strong and with extraordinary gifts that they used for good; a team second to none. If watching one of the sisters was dazzling, imagine enjoying the spectacle of the two of them. It was like watching the fauna and flora of the kingdom in total harmony, merging in complete perfection since they were little. They ate up the audience with their incredible initiatives and Argua revered them for it.

"Until one day, with the appearance of another young woman, everything changed," Rasnar said.

"Wait... You were talking about a twin brother before, and now you're talking about sisters, as if they were two girls," James interrupted quizzically.

Chapter VI
The Arguan Games

"Oh, I understand you got confused," Rasnar said with a chuckle.

"What's so funny?" James said, completely lost in the conversation.

"To be honest, I didn't really understand it myself. I don't even know if they were brothers or twins anymore," Sasha confessed in a confused state.

"They were both, I mean, they were twin sisters, but one of them was a changeling," Nose answered, clearing up the siblings' doubts.

"At that time, Fraya and Eyíre were beautiful and cheerful young women who dominated Lake Naruh during the Argua games. They displayed their gifts, and no one dared to compete with them, as they formed a duo impossible to match or surpass," said Rasnar.

"But when Riyah appeared, their twin power bond was severed, and with that, we don't know how or why, Eyíre was instantly transformed into a boy," Nose interrupted. "Until that day no one knew that the girl was a changeling; apparently not even her sister," said the peon, exalted.

"How is that possible? My goodness if it ever happened to me," James blurted out.

"I have a theory that when the powers that bound them together cracked because of Fraya's madness and ambition, the bond that held them together broke and turned Eyíre into the opposite of what her sister was, as a transformation out of spite.

"But the sex change did not occur until Riyah appeared on the scene, so possibly Eyíre's feelings or connection to the Shawá lady determined that she wanted to join her in the way she perceived it from Riyah; someone special who was on her level and who must have felt very lonely having as her only friends the animals she was encountering around Argua," Nose recounted.

"That is to say, she moved on from the bond that united her to her sister and changed sex because of the love she felt at the sight of a young stranger who liked the siblings..." commented the teenager, stunned.

"So, is it a girl or a boy now?" asked Sasha, confused.

"She was and still is both, since she has the power to be whatever she wants to be, like everyone else at heart; only she can totally change her physical appearance and choose the sex she wants, although no one knew it until she transformed that day. She surprised us all," Nose replied.

"It is very rare to have the ability of the changeling, not only to modify their physical appearance, but also to connect with both sexes through the inner essence. Possibly, thanks to that, the bond between the twins was deeper and took the magic to a glorious level. Eyíre was the strongest asset of the two, but no one knew it until the jig was up," Rasnar said.

In reality, we do not know if Fraya knew that her sister was a changeling and if Eyíre was aware of her condition. It is possible that she felt she was different, but who doesn't feel that way. Surely, she sensed that something made her connect differently with any being, but that feeling does not mean that you are a changeling," Nose mentioned expressing his doubts and thoughts on the matter.

"The truth is that not much is known about these beings, and the few that exist tend to keep it a secret. Since it's not a common condition, it makes people avoid them out of ignorance," Rasnar lamented.

"But Eyíre made a difference to all shifters of that time, bringing her ability to light quite naturally in front of all of Argua, proving that shifters were not only superior beings in many ways, but that they were as normal as you and me; openly declaring that they could be heroes and heroines to the world, beings from whom we have much to learn," Nose debated.

"Well, after that event, Fraya did not reappear with her twin, but she was heard to say that Eyíre was not worthy of her powers and that she should have taken them from her to use them properly, but that was before she disappeared," said the Guardian.

"Do you think Fraya might have felt betrayed by her sister not knowing she was a changeling?" James asked in dismay.

"Maybe it was the secret of their power and triumph, and Eyíre broke the bond, exposing it. Maybe that was the only thing that united them: a secret that Fraya benefited from, but that was heartbreaking for the other," Sasha opined on the matter.

"Maybe Fraya advised her to keep it a secret as a precaution and Eyíre decided she had had enough of hiding her true inner self," James proposed as a second theory.

"What if Fraya had told her to use her powers as a changeling to show them to everyone, but her twin didn't want to do it out of fear? Then Eyíre betrayed her and revealed them to the others through someone else," Sasha argued, intrigued.

"Yes! Until Riyah showed up and the twin transformed helplessly. It would make sense that Fraya would feel abandoned and betrayed by her sister, because until then she had been her only support, the one who encouraged her to come out into the light, even if Eyíre didn't want to.

"By the time she finally discovered his secret, it was too late to use the powers to the fullest as a duo, as he abandoned her for another woman. The event was very frustrating and painful for her. That's why she now claims that power for herself, because her sister never wanted to use it on her by displaying who she really was to all of Argua, despite having her full support," James understood, deciphering the plot of an imaginary soap opera about the twins' story.

"Imagine how upsetting for Fraya. When her sister finally throws off her chains and shows the world that she is a changeling, she does it for someone else, someone who was never by her side, a mere stranger," Sasha acknowledged, stoking the fire of confabulation.

"They're all good theories, but the truth is we have no idea which one is accurate," Rasnar replied to the siblings' ramblings as he scratched his chin.

"Maybe Eyíre couldn't choose... Maybe when she saw Riyah, her feelings took over her in such a way that she simply changed in front of everyone, with no way to hide it or disguise it," thought Nose, defending the other twin, opening a new topic for debate.

"Why, how sensitive, and noble you are, Nose. If my beloved had been taken from me, I certainly wouldn't have been able to see it from that point of view," said James with the utmost respect for his new friend.

"It is simple empathy. If I had been a changeling like Eyíre, I wouldn't have been able to control my impulses either, and I might have transformed publicly, just as she did for Riyah," said the peon.

"Wait a minute! What if the Shawá lady liked girls? Then she would have switched to the opposite sex for nothing, wouldn't she?" James proposed with his hands on his head.

Shifters are not gender-sensitive, but emotion-sensitive, so their transformation depends entirely on what they perceive from the other person and what is less threatening to them. In short, what they find more pleasant or less uncomfortable.

"When she saw Riyah, she must have sensed her essence immediately and changed her body according to what he perceived of her. So, in that she couldn't have been wrong. But don't put so much importance on the fact that she changed into a man or a woman, because there is also the possibility that what she understood from her was the need to show her that she was a changeling, understand, guys?" argued Nose.

"How do you know all this, my friend?" asked Rasnar.

"After the event, let's say I needed to understand and accept many things," he replied.

"Then we can be sure that Eyíre changed without being able to help it, but that doesn't mean that she didn't know she was a changeling or that Fraya was aware of it. It just means she wasn't in control of her changeling power yet, so we're in the same boat," said Sasha, looking at the ground.

"At least we know that the supposed betrayal of her twin was not premeditated. It was Fraya who betrayed her sister, not Eyíre," James said.

"I think the poor thing was blinded by the injustices she perceived around her, and they ended up affecting her so much that she lost control. She was left alone and unhinged," said Sasha, lying down on the carpet. Then she stared at the ceiling of the room, her head resting on her crossed arms.

"What a pity, with how ideal it would have been for Argua to keep the twins together, with Eyíre accepted in society as a changeling and Riyah as part of the team... It would have been an amazing trio, wouldn't it? The things they could have done together for the kingdoms," the boy lamented.

"Wow, James, you spoke like a true leader," Rasnar congratulated him proudly.

"It's a pity that events unfolded in such a catastrophic way for Argua and all our people... It could have been so simple, but, as always, we tend to complicate our lives and the lives of others," sobbed Nose, looking at the embers in the hearth.

"Hey, I know I shouldn't ask you this, but I'm curious. What happened between Riyah and Eyíre? "James asked Nose.

"To be honest, I don't know," he replied.

"Come on, Nose, we all know you were obsessed with her," said the young man, shamelessly.

"James, behave yourself, don't be so insensitive!" Sasha shouted angrily.

"Okay, you'll tell me about it another day," the boy agreed, winking at the peon.

Rasnar looked at Nose and sat up with a short throat clearing. He immediately fixed his eyes on the siblings and changed the subject.

"It seems we have two romantics among us. You may be more the heroes of the soap opera than of Argua," said the Guardian.

"What are you trying to say, Rasnar? Are you out of your mind too?" James complained.

"I mean that you are more interested in a love affair than in the very games of Argua," the Talan argued.

"That's not true; it's just that we were more intrigued by it because of the theories. You know, they are important data for the deductions of the affairs of the kingdoms, especially for the games," answered the boy.

"Well! You still have time to ask about the games, if you are interested in knowing about them, of course," Rasnar replied.

"Of course, they interest me. Who knows, someday I might be spitting gemstones out of my mouth over the famous lake Naruh." Nose burst out laughing, he let out an exaggeratedly strange laugh that left even Rasnar perplexed. "Hey, I said it as a joke, but just know that by training I'm sure I'll get jaw-dropping powers, and when all this war is over, hopefully for you, I'll be able to do something great for Argua," James boasted.

"I hope so," said the Shawá.

"Why don't you show us, Rasnar?" the young woman suggested.

Rasnar nodded with pleasure.

"In no man's land, where the games were held, the chosen ones could choose whether they wanted to go on their own or share a scene with another player. Sometimes forming duos, trios or even teams of more members, but first they had to make the request to the council, not only mentioning with whom they wanted to present their feats, but also if they wanted to exhibit them in no man's land, away from the lake.

"Sometimes a chosen one would pronounce the name of another participant over the lagoon and in front of the crowd, so that he would have no choice but to deny the public request to team up together. By announcing it in front of the entire population of Argua, he would look like an ungrateful citizen who did not wish to contribute to the cause if he refused the request. This gave both him and his kingdom a bad name, as the act of refusal was interpreted as a belief of inequality before the petitioning candidate and his kingdom.

"When such an event happened, the participants were forced to accept, as they were in front of all the kingdoms and the main motto of the festival was that we were all equal and should contribute, without focusing on oneself. Although these cases were a minority; most of those who showed up, if they did not do it individually, prepared something with another person and showed up together on the waters of Naruh to make the request for the location in no man's land" Rasnar explained.

"Was this always the case, and was there never a case where a citizen refused someone's public request not to be exposed in the games with the petitioner?" James asked.

"There were some, but we will tell that story another time. First you must understand the true essence and meaning of the games for the kingdoms. Once the participants were introduced, they could show their skills, and if they formed an ensemble, the members exhibited their spontaneity and also their teamwork skills," the Guardian replied.

"The name of the place where the games were held has a bit of each kingdom; hence it was a sacred place for all, a land of peace. Its landscapes are so varied that the collaborators could choose in which place to make their display of powers and abilities, according to their aptitudes. And over time each realm and even some of the players were also contributing things to this neutral paradise," said Nose.

"Riyah showed up on the first day of the kingdoms' festival in the last year of the games, but not as a player. Like many other Arguans, she went as a mere spectator, camping like the rest of the attendees, staying in the area in small residences reserved for the altruists of the kingdom of Hurapolis; beings of very diverse factions and qualities, for they were mongrels, individuals despised by their own for not belonging to a pure race. Creatures who had had to learn from an early age to survive alone in the kingdoms of Argua, living on their own as nomads and getting food as they could, either by begging or stealing.

"In the long run, this created gangs of abandoned and lost children all over Argua who ended up uniting among themselves, forming a great brotherhood to adapt to the world that had them helpless. They were forced to develop in our society by committing acts of vandalism that required a forced self-control, both mentally and of their vital energy. These practices led them to such extreme situations that they underwent transformations in their bodies and minds. They evolved into specimens with a new set of unique gifts and qualities that ended up defining their guild of wild creatures as another kingdom of Argua, which they called Hurapolis.

"Forced to surpass the reasoning of their courage and fortitude, intentionally brought into situations of exorbitant risk, from which they had to extricate themselves by any means and all alone, or else they would die. These developed powers at a very early age, which were adjusted to their needs at a time when they were pushed to the limit of their endurance, as a consequence of the collapse of their little spirits before the labors to which they were forced by the ringleaders of Hurapolis, the now chiefs of their kingdom.

"With no system to control them and no master to guide them, these young men created their own rules as a huge street family, constantly testing themselves with dangerous feats. Hence, some of the outstanding characteristics of the beings of this realm are their great abilities to disappear, in addition to their talent for recreating visual illusions, with unmatched physical power.

"They are extraordinary mixtures of various species and, because of the way in which they had to be raised, they have a mental resistance that exceeds the terms of the impossible, to which must be added an exaggerated maturity and a legitimate creativity acquired to subsist. As a whole, all this resulted in a mutation of aptitudes, provoked, and developed by the need to stay alive from childhood in a ruthless and aggressive collective.

"For Argua, these people were considered the confines of contingencies, for even having emerged from nothing, they learned to build all kinds of devices, mechanisms, vehicles, devices and even a kingdom with dwellings coupled one on top of the other like a great architectural chaos. Everything this kingdom does involves collaboration among them, like a community of marauding gangs that at first seem anarchic, but are governed by certain hierarchical rules, like a kind of nation ruled by mafias.

"Very few people dare to venture into it and if they do, they must already be known to request contraband objects manufactured by the Hurápolos, engineering created with stolen or illegally purchased parts from other places far from their own. But, above all, what is most sought after is the hiring of spy services, among other things.

"Because of this, the beings of Hurapolis have progressed, both physically and mentally, in a way that was strange and terribly irritating to the rest of the kingdoms of Argua. The Hurápolis are misunderstood and misfit prodigies that accept creatures that, somehow and for whatever reason, have been banished from other kingdoms, whether they were scorned souls or beings treated as waste. Any being was welcome in that place recognized as a kingdom by the council, since it was accepted as a domain characterized by giving utility to what could be reused from the rest of the places in the universe.

"They boasted a power on which all of Argua ended up being dependent. They would build areas where they would welcome the many pilgrims who would arrive disoriented in no man's land to see the great event, the perfect occasion to find and recruit more lost souls, as the Hurápolos collaborated as a team; they were inalienable individuals who were united by a greater force after having been abandoned by society. So, keeping a healthy mind and a body prepared for the day to day was one of their strongest tactics to help these people feel better and part of something, like a family. They trained daily, around the clock, with survival techniques on which they based their teachings, helping to discover and strengthen the best in everyone for the purpose of getting other realms to depend on them. They turned karma on its head, going against those who rejected and neglected them in the first place. This made them a unique and uncontrollable society for the remaining eleven kingdoms.

"Business and bartering were among their most talented maneuvers, but, at the same time, they were great examples of good Samaritans, contradictorily starting from the basis that they were petty thieves turned into better negotiators, gamblers and conspirators. Thus, if you were not a soul in pain, you had to negotiate your cards well to get a place at a good price during the days of the games.

"If there is one thing to emphasize in Argua, it is the diversity of species and classes that existed, so that if you had a good position, you did not have the need to stay in an altruistic cantonment. Depending on who you were or where you came from, you were assigned chambers and even apartments in which to stay, very well located and very luxurious, but if you did not have an influential social position, although if thrifty, you could agree on a fairly decent room in which to stay during the holiday.

"What could not, nor could it ever be, is to appropriate land on no one's land, since this territory was to be respected, cared for and protected with the same affection as if it were one's own, but without being anyone's, since it belonged to each individual equally. It was both mine and yours, in its extensive totality, and this meant that once the earthly division had been made among all the inhabitants of Argua, the portion to be acquired by each one was so minuscule that the individual who tried to appropriate that minutiae would be ridiculous. But if everyone shared that trifle, what might seem an insignificance, would acquire much more value, and not only because it had become an immense piece of land, but because of the importance of the concept of being and not being the owner of something that belongs to everyone equally. It showed the consideration, care, and appreciation of what these lands entailed being shared, it described the birth of a paradise by which to celebrate each year the greatness of the many ideals, principles, and values of this great and varied people, as beautifully diversified as they are united and cared for.

"Within the different no-man's land areas, the kingdoms decided, under a common agreement, to divide sections around Lake Naruh, next to the border of each of the twelve kingdoms, and created right there and then enclosures with facilities to congregate the original inhabitants of one of these lands, where the people belonging to their borders could meet with their own at the end of the day for the duration of the games to celebrate and cheer their players, whether or not they had representatives from their kingdom that year, since not all domains always participated.

"But these strongholds were not enough to overcrowd the entire population; although they were practically large villages representative of each department, with different quarters for the inhabitants and collaborators, most of the space was occupied by markets, taverns, teaching or meditation areas, according to the needs of their people, with facilities provided for training for those who wished to play friendly matches between kingdoms. In them they could demonstrate their powers, celebrity exposing their abilities and skills with the rest of the participants; ordinary individuals who wished to have a good time without having to be a superstar of the kingdom of Argua.

"On the first night, following the ritual of each year, the kingdoms and the beings who had come to witness the events gathered around the lake while the council announced its opening with all kinds of spectacles. Most of the members of this were also, in their day, great warriors and collaborators in the games, standing out in such a way in terms of their contribution for the kingdom of Argua, as they were chosen by the people as its leaders.

"Thanks to popular communication methods, information about the games was relayed through the councilors of each kingdom, who filtered it from the broadcast provided by the Council of Argua, which was the first to know about the changes during those glorious days. They announced both to the people who were in no man's land and to those who had not been able to attend in person and remained in their kingdoms. Thus, the councilors of Argua relayed the testimony of what had happened, whether it was announcing the beginning of a contest by a player or announcing the exhibition of a display of greatness exhibited by some kingdom or by the organization of the games itself.

"These messages were sent, with images, throughout Argua by the media channels that characterized each kingdom. For example, as you well know, the Shawá s used water to transmit projections to their people. This meant that the information was not only reproduced in installations and devices already created for this purpose, both in the Shwanír Citadel and in no man's land, but that any area of Argua with water showed the data during those days. This is just one example, as each kingdom had its own methods of reaching its people.

"Every year the same rituals were celebrated, but the shows varied, becoming more and more grandiose and surprising, without changing the customs. In this way, those present were reminded of what we were and what united us. During the opening night of the games, which I am going to show you, the twins changed the course of the history of Argua. After that year's Council speech and their welcome performance, the sisters Fraya and Eyíre participated in the tournaments. As expected, the people were ecstatic with excitement and gathered around Lake Naruh, eager to see the new performance their heroines had prepared for that year. Everyone knew that they were the best in terms of entertainment, and they outdid themselves more and more every year, always leaving the audience completely astonished. And like any candidate, they had to stand in the center of the lake so that the people of Argua could see them, especially the Council, to whom they always paid a small tribute as a sign of respect," explained Rasnar.

"Why was it done in the middle of the lake? It's not a very comfortable place for one to display one's skills on a boat or in the water," James interrupted.

"Rasnar, we should show them some pictures. I'm sure you haven't forgotten that particular day either. Let them witness the grandeur of the games. Let's go back there, my friend," Nose told him, thrilling the keeper himself with his passion.

The Exhibition

"How could I forget," Rasnar replied, dragging the armchair across the carpet to stand directly in front of the large fireplace.

There he breathed on the fire, causing the fire to undergo a series of transformations and the flames to progressively increase in size and change color. At the same time, a dense smoke rose from the fire, spreading through the room where they were sitting. Then he began to speak as a clear four-dimensional image emerged from the smoke and surrounded them as if they were inside a movie.

The smoke disappeared and ceased to be annoying; it was literally transformed into representations that enveloped them in a virtual reality. To their surprise, they were inside the games themselves, although in reality they were still sitting in the living room, in front of the warmth of the fire. The Guardian created such a realistic simulation of that day that both the siblings and Nose could almost feel the beings that had once been there witnessing the games, watch them as they walked freely through no man's land, exploding like smoke bombs every time one of these holograms walked or flew across the body of one of them sitting quietly in the living room.

The images and the angles from which they saw the beings moving around the room changed as the Guardian mentioned them, so that sometimes the perspective showed shots from the sky or from a rooftop, although they could also be moving among the masses, through the streets or into the taverns and rooms.

"Lake Naruh was chosen for the mere fact that everything that was exposed on it would be manifested in it; that is, everything that any being would be able to do on it would be reflected as a mirror on the Arguan population, thus becoming a symbolic connection for all beings, because the acts undertaken and shown there would be part of each of us, as an example to follow or a lesson to learn. We were special and possessed of that magic, even if we did not have the same gift, regardless of social status.

"Although the hustle and bustle usually appeared there during the morning of the first day, Arguans continued to arrive even after nightfall, and even on the second or third day of the games, even if they had missed the presentation and the first exhibitions. We must consider that many tried to organize themselves and informed themselves about who was participating and when they were going to make their appearance, in order to be able to ask for a free day to support their favorite heroes and heroines. Thus, they attended only to see them in action on the lake, which was surrounded by huge trees on which natural balconies grew, with long swings descending from their lianas. There the citizens of Argua stood to get a better view, while others used their powers to squeeze in wherever they could.

"As night fell on that first day, the Council formed by the most prominent councilors of the twelve kingdoms proclaimed the inauguration of the games with a speech given by the Councilor Ashima, the changeling of the Tunani kingdom, from the balcony of the tree designated just for them, the largest, whose gigantic trunk anchored its roots inside a part of the lagoon. In this area they were half submerged. Some of the privileged beings who dared to be in the front row and also the players who were presented that same year, to see their teammates from up close, would dock on a thick root that was sticking out of the water.

"Our world is not ours. Our kingdom does not belong to us, for it is all alive, and like us, it cannot be possessed. It can be admired, it can be cared for, and it can be loved... But not subdued. Like the blood in our veins, we flow freely through her lands, her waters and through the air with which she blesses us. She allows us to be free over her body, as it is natural for us to let our blood flow through our being.

"In our hands is the duty to do good, for it is given to us as quickly as it can instantly disappear. Just as without flux a being comes to its end, so without harmony among us, Argua will quickly come to its end and with it, all that we love. Therefore, I proclaim today the beginning of the games, in which each of the beings present here, as well as their actions, count and matter. And to the brave ones who dare to walk on the waters honoring us with their contributions, good luck!

"Then Ashima raised her arms to inaugurate the games. The crowd applauded euphorically amidst shouts of excitement as the council rose, causing the entire no-man's land to slowly run out of lights. Then there was silence in the area and at once one of the councilors proclaimed the entrance of the twins. You could tell by the tone of his voice that they belonged to his kingdom, by the pride which filled his mouth as he mentioned them. The spectators fell silent, waiting for something to happen under the absolute darkness. And they did not have to wait long. A few minutes after that, patches of light appeared on the lake like small footprints illuminated on the water. They were the footsteps of Eyíre, one of the twins, which not only illuminated, but also created ripples that spread until they formed flowers that opened and floated on the water like huge water lilies.

"By the time the girl reached the center of the lagoon, a huge bud opened under her feet and rose with her towards the incredible starry night sky, lengthening its stem, which kept growing towards infinity. And although it was night and there was no light, the light given off by the petals of that flora was enough to distinguish every movement that the girl created with her arms. The plant on which she was standing stopped and a flash appeared in the firmament, like a shooting star flying directly to the bud where the twin was standing, which immediately closed its corolla, thus protecting the player from that attack with a great explosion that illuminated for a few moments that darkness as if it were day again. The scene was illuminated again, and this pattern was repeated and again with the same form of the previous assault.

"During that puzzling event people discovered that petals were falling from the sky.

"Look! It's Eyíre! They're attacking her!" the audience was heard murmuring.

"The spectators looked up to see the young woman fall from a great height after suffering those insistent onslaughts that had completely shattered the bud of the gigantic luminescent flower that protected her. Her body crashed at great speed into the water, where she ended up submerged in the depths without a trace.

"The crowd began to hesitate, fearing that it might not be part of the show. Their thoughts were instantly interrupted by an explosion of water that splashed those nearest, who panicked and screamed. The crowd ran staggering, when suddenly the water calmed down and from its gloomy bottom emerged several circumferences like concentrically expanding luminescent ripples. Then small spikes emerged with a series of peaks peeking out from each of them. To everyone's surprise, they emerged from the water like the petals of huge flowers that rose skyward at great speed while dropping water from the slits in their corollas.

"It was a beautiful image, it looked like water cascades with long glowing vines drooping from the core of the bud; a real floral light show that amazed the attendees, leaving them spellbound and immediately calming the ambient tension.

"The tallest of the flowers was the last to open. Eyíre emerged from inside, with her hands open and her arms extended above her head, victorious in front of her audience. The crowd reacted with euphoric applause, even though it was not over yet, since for the twins it had only been the introduction to their exhibition.

"The Tajhran Councilor, the kingdom to which the sisters belonged, was filled with joy at the sight of the exaltation of the crowd at the rejoicing of his girls. He gave a big smile of superiority to his fellow councilors, who watched the spectacle from the large balcony.

"We are very proud of them," said Numec, Tajhra's councilor.

"Of course, in distraction no one beats them, but... will their entertainment skills be useful for the survival and prosperity of Argua?" Sranik, Preciosas' representative asked doubtfully.

"Be that as it may, the kingdom of Tajhra has no adversary in the games, whether in terms of spectacle or not. The power and prestige of the twins is unmatched," Numec replied just before another flash descended from the sky like a bolt of lightning and fell into the lake to disappear into its black pit.

"Then she rocked with such force that she swayed the great stems of the shoots Eyíre had created and upon which she stood attached to her stamens so as not to fall into the void with her aggressive shaking. She raised an arm and made a beautiful tree composed of moss and algae emerge from the water; a new creation fruit of the qualities of her many gifts with which she was blessed at birth: to create life with cells from the same environment. It was like watching the birth of the soul from the depths of Naruh, transformed into a visually appreciable figure, created from the underwater flora.

"But when it came to the surface, it was a not so pleasant image that showed the fauna that lived submerged. The top of that huge tree had trapped varieties of eels, fish, amphibians, and worms, among many other specimens that were piled on top of each other. A shiver ran through the bodies of those present as they listened from the top of that flower to Eyíre shouting the name of her sister Fraya and urging her to put an end to it. She raised her hand again, making the tree give off more light. She wanted to illuminate the bugs better. But what the audience saw next was as repulsive as it was degenerate, for the worms, eels, insects, fish and all the fauna she carried piled on her great crest were eating each other, devouring each other, gobbling each other up without even chewing, doubling in size as they became fewer and fewer.

"You could see the worry on Eyíre's face as she whispered words that no one could hear, as she was too far away. It didn't look like it was part of the script. Suddenly, the animals became one, a huge and grotesque monster, a long beast, with fins and legs that ran along its strange body; a mass so big that when it stood up in front of the audience, it made them scream with fright and try to flee to get away from that horrible and terrifying scene. The soldiers of the Shawá Fortress reacted to the alarm of danger transmitted by the people. So did the warriors of the Kingdom of Óstrevo, who surrounded the lake to create a barrier on the shore with their spears, like a defensive wall. Eyíre immediately prepared to attack the aberration, but the creature opened its mouth and let out a thunderous shriek that knocked everyone over. From inside its maw appeared the twin Fraya, crouched on the tongue of the atrocious specimen, which stretched its foul boneless form to the balcony of the Council. There the young woman bowed inches from the railing, which completely stunned the councilors standing in front of her.

"The audience exploded with euphoria, adrenaline, amazement and relief that it was all part of the performance, almost crying with emotion, but Fraya did not receive the same kind of reaction from the council. As she lay there semi-prostrate before them, her knee on the beast's tongue, they stood silently staring in shuddering awe at the monstrosity. Immediately, Councilor Numec began to clap effusively with his four hands as he stood up in an attempt to defuse the situation, but the girl sensed that the last thing she had accomplished with her new creation was to amaze them. She sensed the doubts she had just created in them regarding the techniques used with her powers and the distrust she now felt towards her person," the Guardian said in his projections.

"I don't understand, Rasnar. She exhibited her powers like the others, didn't she?" asked the young woman.

"Until that day, everything the twins showed to the public in the games was an extraordinary combination of the power of both; they recreated themselves in such a way that they were able to form territories high above the sky, and even new species with the union of the cells of the flora and fauna around them. They opened the doors to a world enlightened with hope, but that day their ability as a duo was divided.

"As I told you before, the games were not a competition, but a contribution in communion and that night Fraya did not show her superiority, but her weakness. This event caused a rupture between the sisters because of ambition and created a monster at the cost of sacrificing other species, instead of using molecules from them, as they had done before. This was not, nor would it ever be, the solution to a threat, much less a contribution to the kingdom, but rather a holocaust of innocent creatures eliminated for the sole purpose of creating a weapon with them.

"With this maneuver, which risked the extinction of our species, she demonstrated plainly and clearly that she did not mind going beyond the limits of immorality in order to gain, so that, although her intentions may have been good, the means she chose were completely wrong and they were exposed to the entire Arguan population. Then she broke the bond with her twin," Rasnar replied.

"What about Riyah? You said she showed up that day," James recalled.

"That's right, but not to participate; rather, she was forced to expose her powers during the games," said the Talan.

"I still shudder when I remember that day," said the peon, stroking his arm as if he were cold.

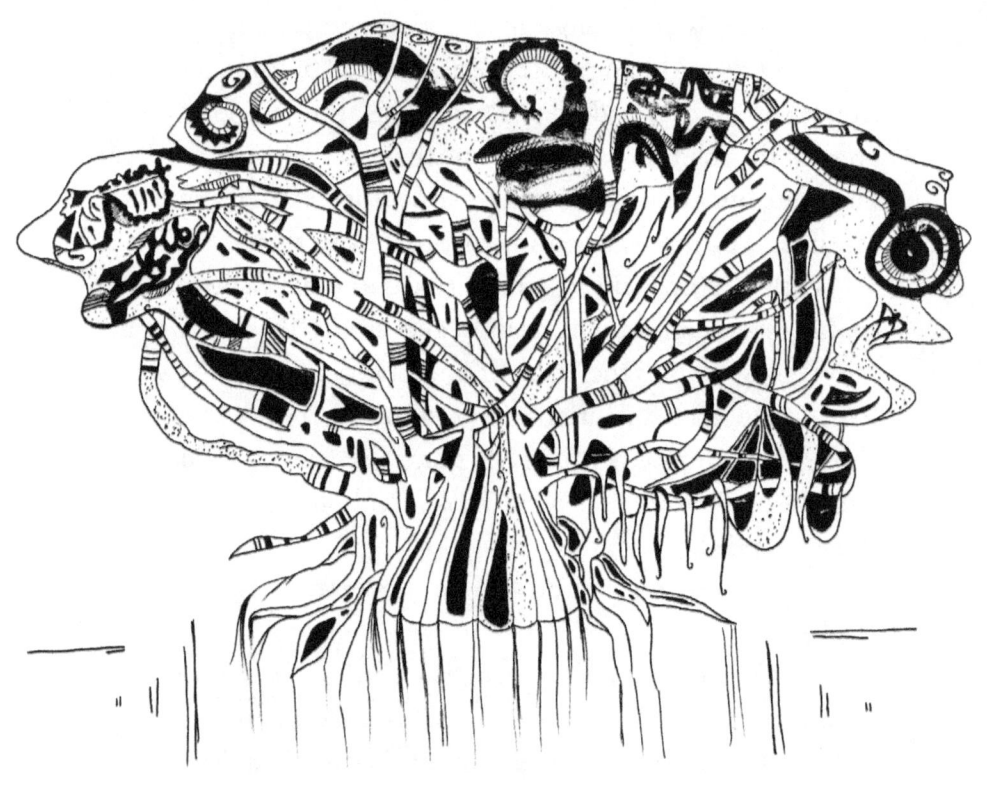

Broken Ties

"After that night, once the first rays of light came out at the dawn of the new day, a subtle tremor struck no man's land, awakening the crowd that was camped there in confusion. The people came out of their rooms dismayed by that strange earthquake and, as one more, I followed them until they stopped near the Margua. From there we could see a gigantic wave approaching the shore. We saw the young Fraya kneeling with one hand on the sand and holding her sister, who begged her to restrain herself, with the other hand.

"The council members ran towards the sisters as soon as they arrived. It was Innunu who first stepped forward and threw a blocking ball at Fraya to stop the twin, but she countered it with a wall of bacteria that was trapped inside her, like a cloud of living matter with which she returned her own sickness-filled blow to the Picmeral Councilor, who was badly injured. Quickly, Ashima began to illuminate one of her tattoos causing the sandstone to stir and raise large dunes to distract and hinder the young woman's movements, to which Eyíre countered with a solid base made of branches that allowed her to have more stability.

Numec, who was responsible for the twins as an advisor to the Kingdom of Tajhra, ran to the water and sat on the shore in a meditative posture. He then pressed the palms of his upper limbs together in prayer while the hands of his lower arms touched the water. Then he opened his now reddened eyes. Two lines like black tears ran down his right cheekbone. He immediately warned in his mind of an even greater problem, for he had sensed with his powers that young Fraya was communicating with some kind of beast approaching at great speed. Hastily, he notified those present of what was happening.

"I command you as a member of the Council of Argua and as an advisor to your kingdom to stop right now!" Numec shouted, walking towards them as the rest of the council members prepared for whatever might come from the Margua.

"Suddenly, out of the wall of water loomed a gigantic white thing. It was a buyáh, a beast we had never seen before, but of which we had all heard. It was dragging the water in its path towards the shore, creating a huge wave that would sweep over us like a tsunami. The Shawá Council member shouted to everyone present to run to safety. Most of the Arguans fled in panic amidst screams for help, while a minority, including myself, stayed behind to defend the shore and help the councilors. We lined up all along the beach, ready to receive the impact of their onslaught. But upon seeing us, the buyah accelerated his march without a second's hesitation, for he had a past to avenge and Fraya had put on a platter those who had participated in his misfortune of yesteryear; she was giving him the opportunity to take revenge and to finally get justice.

"The story of the buyáh with the Shawá s began the day we lost our old home. We had to find another one conditioned to the different species, with the needs of each one, so we built from nothing the new Argua, which we divided into twelve kingdoms. But when we arrived on this new planet, it was not uninhabited, so we had to ask permission and respect the beings that lived there, both on land and underwater. At that time the buyáh was considered the king of the Margua, but with the division of land in the new world the sea had been left in the hands of the Shawá s, who mastered the arts of water and were the only ones capable of surviving under this medium. Thus, it was decided that the greatest demonstration of their power was to build their fortress under the depths.

"But this beast did not want intruders to disturb its habitat as a mere demonstration of its greatness, so the Shawá s met with the buyáh for the sole purpose of making an agreement, but the animal made it clear that it would never give up its kingdom, since that was its home, and no one would make it change its mind. The Shawá s, who were the only species not yet settled in the new world that had been attributed to them, had no choice but to drive out the vulgar beast, but it was too powerful to defeat without facing hundreds of losses among the Shawá population.

"Confrontation was not a viable solution, so one night they sent several of our peons to capture the buyáh's calf in an attempt to bargain for dominion over those waters, but unfortunately the plan did not go as they had hoped. Although they sent the best soldiers of the Shwanír Guard, who mastered the arts of the water to perfection, they did not take into account that the enormous beast was nothing more than a helpless creature, like a child in the eyes of a human, and in the attempt to seize this poor innocent soul under the darkness of the Margua, panic seized the little giant, who was chained and dragged into its depths, where, terrified by not understanding what was happening, she sought the protection of her father.

"In fear, it towed the soldiers along the bottom of the sea, frightening them in such a way that in a desperate act to stop the creature, they blocked its way with a coral wall. Unfortunately, instead of slowing down before that obstacle, the calf tried to cross it without knowing its thickness and was left unconscious and seriously injured after the blow, since that wall had particles of a carnivorous coral. With each passing day, the wounds in her skin became deeper and penetrated to the bone. Her fate was written, and nothing could be done for her.

"The peons felt no guilt and the cries of suffering of the buyáh calf lasted for days. During that time not a soul was seen in the sea; even the plankton itself had gone into hiding, dismayed by this terrible event. Desperate, the buyáh went out to the banks of the Margua where the Shawá s were camped and begged them for help in exchange for his kingdom; he gave them his word that if they managed to save the calf, he would let them build their fortress in the depths of the Margua, without having the slightest idea that he was making a pact with those guilty of the crime. Thus, the Shwanír Citadel was quickly built, but the buyáh's offspring died a few days later, after the father had been given false hope. The depths of the Margua were silent and the buyáh disappeared, until the day Fraya summoned him and told him the raw truth of what had happened; a trap contrived by the young woman to prove to the council that her skills and being prepared for an attack were necessary for the betterment of Argua.

"Eyíre managed to get loose from her twin the hard way, breaking her heart, telling her that she was no longer her sister; something that broke both of their souls. Fraya let her guard down for a moment and Eyíre, took the opportunity to escape with a quick flick of her wrist, letting go of her sister and getting as far away from her as she could. In the meantime, the council launched its attacks against the buyáh, which continued to approach the shore without caring in the least about the damage it might feel in its body, since no aggression could be more painful than the one it had suffered for so long for the loss of its only calf. When the beast reached the arena, it attacked without restraint. They fell one after another despite their desperate attempts to stop the buyah. I must say that, even positioned with the council and prepared for battle, and despite what I was witnessing, I was unable to move or react. My legs were anchored to the ground, petrified before that scene so hard to assimilate. Then Fraya got up from the ground and shouted to the Council that she could help them: they only had to admit that they had been wrong to underestimate her ideas, the reason why she thought she had received her gift, but the councilors replied that they would never agree to it.

"Eyíre looked at her sister with tears in her eyes as the battle continued. Suddenly, a wall of water surrounded the beast, which continued to struggle against the onslaught, trying to shake off the watery barrier, but the wall continued to envelop the animal until it was enclosed in a liquid sphere sealed on the outside by a solid, thick layer of ice that rose a few feet above the ground. The buyáh was trapped inside while the beast continued to pound relentlessly on the frozen walls of that great ball. Then the councilors stopped, stunned by what had happened, since none of them had the ability to do such a thing. It was in this interval, as Fraya cried out in frustration, that a beautiful young woman appeared with her hands raised towards the globe. She approached it slowly, as if with every step she took she held the weight of the beast on her body, watching her feet sink deeper and deeper into the sand as she trudged forward.

"That young woman was Riyah, the Shawá Lady, known among her people to be withdrawn, for it was said of her that her only friends were the animals, with whom she surrounded herself at all hours. She was never seen either with her own people or with individuals from other kingdoms; in fact, she was rarely seen in person, and when she was seen, they thought she was strange for not behaving like a member of her society.

"The Shawá of the Council, one of the five wise men, ordered her to freeze the inside of the sphere, but Riyah replied that if she did so, the animal would perish. The councilors agreed that the beast must die, for its desire for revenge would never be satiated. But she refused, replying that there must be another way, that this was why they were meeting in no man's land and why they should set an example by honoring the ideals of the games. Her superiors responded by ordering her to comply, but she did not give in.

"Feeling the regret of the decision of the leaders of her people, in addition to the exhaustion from the effort she had to make to keep the bubble high in the air, with the buyáh inside, she lowered the sphere a little. The councilors began to worry, for with each passing minute, the tension and fear that the animal might escape increased. Fraya shouted at her not to follow the orders of assassins and told everyone the truth about the Shawá s: that it was they who killed the buyáh's calf to keep the Margua for themselves. Then Riyah looked at the Sage and he bowed his head in shame.

"Immediately, a tear of light cracked the young woman's chest as if her heart had been torn in two. Her power waned and she dropped the sphere onto the sand. It was at this moment that Eyíre struck her sister unconscious. She then created a whirlwind of roots with her hand with which she managed to hold the frozen bubble back in the air, thus helping poor Riyah. With the other hand she designed the structure of a cage around the ice balloon, which seemed to be melting, but in which the buyáh was still imprisoned. Eyíre slowly lowered the frame while Councilor Ashima dug a hole in the sand, where the new prison packaging was buried. But Fraya had already disappeared.

"The council took the opportunity to discuss the ground where the buyáh was buried and decide whether the beast would live or die down there. Even knowing that I was only a mere peon, I could not believe that no one cared about Lady Riyah; it seemed that the matter of the animal was more important than the heroine who had saved us all. So, I ran to her to hold her hand as she lay suffering on the grit, but the young woman was unresponsive and her once bluish hair had turned snow white. Her skin was also so light that you could see the veins pumping to the beat of her weak heart, broken by that luminescent blight that continued to cross her torso. I begged her again and again to wake up, but her eyes remained closed as his spirit flickered slower, waning like the light that pierced his chest.

"I was nobody, but even though I knew my place, that was the only chance I would have to be honest with the young woman I loved, and so I did… I told her that I had always loved her, from the first moment I saw her, even though she was not able to notice me because of who I was in the Shawá hierarchy, but I didn't care about all that as long as she stayed alive. I implored her for everyone's sake not to let herself be defeated by the beyond, that she should fight to come back to us, since she was the only hope I saw within the hypocrisy of the twelve kingdoms, because my word was worthless, but hers was not, and only she had the power to change things.

"I told her that in my daily life I felt miserable, until I saw her, and that her image alone motivated me to be a better person, to face anything, because I wanted to be more than a peon, just to protect her, even if I never exchanged words or glances with her… I remember that at that moment my tears were spilling over her face, with her body withering in my arms, until a member of the council saw me, and the others ran towards me with suspicion. Then I fled from there in fear and hid in a cave where I remained lamenting what had happened, my heart completely broken. That same afternoon the leaders of the twelve kingdoms announced throughout Argua that the games were not going to be cancelled, that despite the unfortunate incident, nothing would break the union that made us strong, but the signal that relayed the message was weak, because I received it through a small puddle on the floor of that cave. The information reached me drop by drop through a crevice that opened in the ceiling of the cavern.

"Anyway, I had no desire to see the hypocrisy of that conscienceless Shawá broadcasting to the whole kingdom, so I went out to listen to the message by any other means. Although I was not trained to perceive the broadcasts provided by each kingdom, in those days you didn't need a special gift to be able to see or hear the inquiries about the games," the peon explained.

"I am very sorry, Nose. It must have been very painful... I know it may not be the right time, but if as you say we will be one of the leaders of Argua someday, I think it is important and necessary for us to know each kingdom, even if we can't do it in person. I hope I don't sound insensitive," said James.

"You know the Shwanír Fortress, though without showing it in pictures it is difficult to express its full magnitude. However, I doubt I will be able to do so with the other eleven realms, unless Rasnar helps me, as I can only show what I have seen in person and at this time it may be too risky to show you the realms through the water, especially after what happened earlier with the bowl. You saw what happened the last time I tried," the Shawá recalled.

"I don't think the revelation of scenes from other realms will aggravate our current situation," Rasnar opined.

"What do you need, Nose? I'll get it for you," Sasha offered.

"Actually, I don't need much; if I lick my finger and place it on your forehead, I'll share the images with you." The siblings were disgusted by the idea. "Just kidding! Well, not really, but there are other ways."

Rasnar laughed and patted Nose on the back.

"For a mere peon, you have a lot of personality. I don't know how you would manage to keep all that stuff inside you during your days of guard duty in the Shwanír Fortress," the Guardian commented in amazement.

"Tell me about it," Nose replied. Suddenly the Talan began to move his ears as if he were listening to something. "What's the matter?" But the watchman just moved his hairy auricles back and forth without saying a word. "Rasnar, the door!"

"I see you didn't miss me, my dears," Grandma greeted.

"Grandma!"

The siblings ran to hug her like there was no tomorrow.

"My lady, Lady Mihara, what a joy to see that you are well. I am deeply sorry for the pain I caused you," Nose apologized.

"And you are?" Grandma retorted.

"I am... I was a peon in the Shwanír Guard, my lady," he introduced himself.

"His name is Nose, Grandma, and he's one of us now," Sasha pointed out.

"In that case, you don't need to call me ma'am or introduce yourself as a guard, dear. If everyone calls you Nose, I will too. It is a very curious name. You could have chosen any other pseudonym in this world and even your own, why Nose?" asked Mihara, puzzled. Is something wrong? I'm sorry if it was rude of me. I meant no offense; I was merely curious. I've never heard such a name before, and I lack the creativity or wit to come up with one, although I once knew someone who would have loved that nickname," Mihara said. "It's a beautiful name. I'm sorry if I misunderstood," she said with a slight smile.

"It's not that, my lady," Nose replied.

"Mihara, please call me Mihara," replied the grandmother.

"My lady, excuse me, Mihara, you have not offended me at all. It's just that I didn't choose the name, my lady," he explained in sorrow.

"Please, I'm just the lady of the house here, and as far as I know, you're not one of my servants, so I think we can even be on a first-name basis," said Grandma as she looked for a seat.

"Mihara," Grandma turned to the peon as she placed a cushion on the vacant spot she had chosen on the sofa, "the name was given to me by Aztrak."

She looked at him in confusion. Then she plopped down on the seat.

"It's been a long time since I've heard that name. How long has it been, fifty-five, sixty human years? So long that I don't even remember anymore. I'm just a lonely old woman in a big, cold mansion I call home.

"Aztrak... That name brings back so many memories, mixed feelings that I thought were gone, I didn't remember what it was like to have them. I didn't remember what it was like to have them. How could he have given you that nickname? When did you two meet? He's..." Mihara asked.

"As you well know, he passed away, my lady. Forgive me. Aztrak gave it to me before all that happened; he was the only friend I had, that I had... We didn't talk much, because of circumstances and rules... you know. But for the little we did talk, he made me feel like somebody, not just another peon among so many others," Nose confessed.

"Yes, I remember that feeling. He was definitely a special boy, wasn't he?" said the woman.

"Yes, he was. Mihara, what happened to him was not fair to either of us. I feel tremendously guilty for not having done anything about it," said the peon, ashamed.

"Unfortunately, I doubt anyone could have done much more than what was done, Nose," she replied.

"When your gem was taken from you, there was a commotion in the room and someone must have kicked your stone, which slid across the floor to me," he explained.

"Do you have it?" she asked.

"I wish I did. Unfortunately, I didn't think this day would come. If I had known, I would have kept it to this day so that I could help you and everyone... I was a fool, since at that moment the only thing that crossed my mind was to give it to your bel..."

The peon was timidly silenced.

"You can say it, Nose, to my beloved. Those present here are informed of my past. Too many moons have passed for me to still feel a lump in my throat about it," she replied.

"My lady... Mihara, if I may, I must say that the years have not passed for you, since I remember you exactly as you are now; I mean, you are somewhat more human, but you are still as young and beautiful," said the Shawá.

"Grandma, I think you should look in the mirror."

Grandma sat up and approached the mirror above the fireplace. Then she touched her face. It was like going back in time. She looked at her hands, her feet, her hair... and then she looked closely at the jewel attached to her forehead.

"What do you feel, Grandma?" James asked.

"It's strange. At first, I had to fight with the gem to get it to tell me who it belonged to, but once it knew who I was, it accepted me without further ado. I don't know where I got the strength to hold all her energy and contain her memories inside me, but once I did, the hardest part came: adopting her powers as if they were my own.

"I thought I was going to die; I just wished over and over again that you were safe. Suddenly, I felt energy flowing through my being more powerful than ever, with a vitality I never experienced even when I was a teenage Shawá. But the curious thing about it is that I do not perceive its powers in me, I do not even think I am capable of bearing them.

"If I'm honest with you, I have no idea what could have happened, I don't know how I did it, or what happened," she said in confusion.

"But you're here, Grandma, and that's all that matters," Sasha said.

"We thought... I thought we had lost you, Grandma."

The siblings hugged Mihara in tears of happiness.

"Please don't give us any more scares like this, okay? You can't leave the mansion and the family name in our care; imagine what a mess," James said with tears and his mischievous smile.

"But how long have I been asleep?" she asked.

"In real time, not much; in mental time, too much," her granddaughter replied.

"My dear Rasnar, how I missed you. And you, Nose, thank you for giving me back my vitality and so many things I had forgotten. You have given me life."

The Shawá sat down on the floor and leaned against the side of the fireplace. Then he looked into the fire.

"I thought I took it off, Mihara. I can't tell you how happy I am to see you among us right now and looking so well," he said.

"Thank you, dear. And now why don't you explain to me where you got this gem?" suggested Grandma.

"My lady, I was very little when it happened. It all happened so fast, and it was disconcerting, yet I must say I remember it as if I were there right now.

"I was in guard training, deep in the Margua, when I heard murmurs of her name through the sea waves. At first, I did not understand what they said, though I feared the worst. My heart hoped she had returned, and she had, but lifeless.

"I still remember the pain I felt in my chest, as if my heart was being torn into a thousand pieces under those cold waters, while to my ears came those horrible messages like a hurricane of whispers coming from the people who were in the Shwanír Fortress, until at last they confirmed it, and my pain was such that I plunged breathless to the darkest bottom of the Margua.

"I wanted to scream, I wanted to kill that monster, I wanted to do so many things, but none of them were allowed. Except to let a part of me die because my soul was torn to pieces. By the time

I regained my strength, I emerged from the depths and blinded by frustration, I finished off my training partners, unloading on them the anger I carried inside. I became the number one among the soldiers of the guard, something never suspected in me, so my superiors and companions were dumbfounded; they flattered me when the training ended, but I felt nothing, I was no longer me nor would I ever be the same again.

"They carried me on their shoulders to the fortress while they sang excitedly about my exploits, but I could not even hear them, for my being had been nullified, dead inside and out. I only seemed alive in appearance, with the total normality of a peon, non-existent, merely functioning without thinking, carrying out orders like a robot. I was the perfect soldier.

"After that, I picked up my equipment and was decorated. I was quickly promoted to a higher position, which brought me before the commanders and from there before the Sages, but they were busy, so they made me wait standing before the door of the great hall for hours, until at last they opened their gates to me. And there, floating horizontally above the center of the great hall, was the body of Riyah surrounded by the Five Exalted Ones.

"I remember I couldn't breathe; I thought my legs were going to give out on me. I was petrified without a word, like a good peon. At that moment, a Lady Shawá burst into the room and said something in the ear of one of the wise men. It must have been something tremendously important because they suddenly disappeared and left me alone in the antechamber in charge of Riyah's body. She was so beautiful, so young... But her body was bruised and dirty. That brute had broken her inside and out, like a disposable object.

"I wanted to hug her, talk to her... But she was no longer with us. Still, I don't know why I did it, but I went up to her and promised her that I would avenge her death. Then

I kissed her on the forehead and as I did so the gem came off her skin as if it wanted to tell me something, so I took it and hid it. When the five returned to the room and discovered Riyah's body without the gem, I was demoted back to peon on suspicion that I had left the room by letting someone enter it during my absence to steal the lady's stone. They came to that conclusion because a peon does not have the power to take the gem from a Shawá. Nor did they find it among my things. Fortunately, I was not accused of theft; I was only slandered as being unfit for a higher position, no matter what I showed from then on during my training or in the missions we were given," explained the Shawá.

"How did you hide the gem, Nose?" James wanted to know, curious.

"The only way I could: by swallowing it again and again, until they stopped looking for it," confessed the peon.

"Okay, that's what I get for asking," said the boy with disgust.

"So that's why...," said Grandma.

"My lady?" encouraged Nose.

"I remember my father being very upset that day at home. You know how hard he was when it came to respecting the traditions and laws of the Shawá," she said.

"Yes, a man of great authority and power. I never understood how they didn't perceive the energy of the gem inside me, especially your father. It must have been deactivated voluntarily to stay safe inside me," the peon opined.

"That night my father came home in a terrible rage. We knew he was having a bad day because he would sit on his throne for hours in silence; that's what we called his favorite chair. I remember him there every night, staring at the bottom of the sea through the walls of his study. Whenever something was troubling him, he would stare at the animals with that beautiful light they emanated; he said it relaxed him to the point of finding a solution to any problem no matter how impossible it seemed.

"But that day he spent the whole night lying there prostrate. I remember waking up in the wee hours of the morning to get a sihf star from the kitchen. I loved to eat those sea flowers; they were tiny, but when I put them in my mouth they multiplied and lit up my cheeks. I liked them so much that my mother used to hide them in order to ration them for me; she said that from the binge I would get, one day they would end up planting me at the bottom of the Margua so that their buds would blossom from me.

"Well, that night, as I was returning from my culinary mischief, I noticed the door of his chamber open. Inside my father, fatigued on his throne, was staring into the void, his eyes lost in the dark waters. He seemed to be very distressed about something," recounted Mihara.

"Yes, I remember it well. I guess that's why they left me alone in the great hall that day, trusting my guard," Nose explained.

"Are you referring to Aztrak's unexpected arrival?" asked the Guardian.

"That's right, Rasnar. My father and the sages announced it as a misfortune, but we had to see it as the chance we needed to be free once and for all. It must have been that night when it occurred to him to dictate the law of silence, whereby the seed of evil would be raised as an equal, but their training and their daily life would be only for and by the cause. It was forbidden for the Shawá people to mention their existence and to speak to the subject about their purpose in life. They said that thanks to the Shwanír Fortress and the depths of the Margua we could hide him from the other realms; above all, from the eyes of Zotrak and his Zorks.

"Then the legislation was announced throughout the citadel, making it clear that if anyone thought of breaking it, they would be punished with the death penalty," said Grandma.

The Imprisoned Savior

"After that speech, they put the poor creature in an aquarium. The first time I saw it, I thought how something so small was going to save us all. For, at that time, it was no bigger than an amoeba. Every day after my classes I would stop by to see it, curious to see how it changed. At first it was like a small bubble in a jar of water, but the strange entity grew at a much faster rate than me, until one day, fully formed and submerged in that liquid in a fetal position, I got so close to it that, when I touched the glass in which it was enclosed, it opened its eyes and stared at me.

"At first I was frightened, but immediately I could see and feel that something was wrong. We could breathe underwater, but it seemed he couldn't, so I grabbed one of the relics in the room and broke the glass, with the luck or misfortune that the specimen fell into my lap. To my surprise, he immediately curled up looking for my affection, but I was terrified, so I stood petrified watching him. It was then that I realized that he was just a child like me, even though his appearance was different, with long hair the color of the earth, like his skin, which was much darker than ours, small, slanted eyes, and several strangely shaped pupils.

"When I understood that he was not the monster they had convinced us of, but an innocent boy in fear and in need of affection, I felt I had to hold him. I don't know how long I held that beautiful being, but it must have been a long time, because he fell asleep in my arms. I still remember the peace he transmitted to me; an emotion so strong that I ended up falling asleep too. When I woke up, I felt my mother caressing my face. The poor thing, worried sick because I hadn't come home, went looking for me in every corner of the fortress. She was the sweetest woman in the world. She lifted me off the floor while she took the child in her arms. Then she carried the little one hidden in her cloak and took me in her other hand. Thus, she discreetly carried us home, where she put the little one in my room and tucked him in with quilts on my bed.

"He told me he was sick and not like us, that since he couldn't go outside, we had to help him to get him warm or he wouldn't survive, so I stood there watching him while my mother made him something hot to drink. Since my bed was a waterbed, I put my hands on it and made its insides boil a little to bring the temperature up, trying to help. Then my mother came back into the room with a cup and explained to me that just like any other being in this world, that one needed a loving family. Then she stroked his head while singing sweet melodies to soothe his pain.

"But it wasn't long before my father came through the door accompanied by the guard with the intention of taking him away. He shouted at his wife and at me, his daughter, that this being would never be one of us, that we should not be fond of him because he had a purpose, a destiny for which he was in the citadel. If that were not so, he would have killed him himself by now.

"My mother tried to convince him that he was just a child, but my father replied that you don't win a war by lovingly raising a soldier and that he should be aware of what the kingdom was up against. He had to choose between watching his daughter grow up to be free or helping a monster and treating him with love. Still, my dear mother did not give up and replied to my father that they could not win a war if the child died. My father approached him and observed his state of mind. He then agreed to give him enough time for the child to recover. He also informed him that once he was healed, the creature would continue with its purpose.

"So, after that argument, the little boy was taken into our home for several weeks. Mother adored him and he adored her.

He made us so happy that I didn't even mind that he had taken my room; besides, thanks to that I had got the best room of all in my father's study room, where I could enjoy every night watching the beasts swim free outside, glittering in the night like the stars in the sky, the one I couldn't go out to see, but dreamed of so often.

"The being learned his first words with us: my name and mom, which was the second thing that made my mother's eyes mist over with tears. Within two weeks my father had deemed him strong enough to begin his training, and so, without further ado, he was taken to a seclusion they built in the fortress just for him, taking him away from our home forever. But despite the security surrounding the little boy's quarters, my mother and I tried several times to sneak past the guard to see him again, though all our attempts were unsuccessful.

"By the time we finally made it, the creature was as big as I was. He had grown so fast that by the time I was in my teens, I looked like a little girl next to him. No one knew how big he would grow or how long he would live, since he was the first of his kind, so people were fascinated by him, and not only because of the rapid evolution of the curious appearance of his physique, but also because of his incredible attitude and his great personality. Qualities he got during his many trainings when the crowd crowded around the training room, which was like an arena, only without sand and without bleachers; rather, an oval classroom that could not be accessed, but could be observed from an upper area surrounded by a railing through which people looked out to not lose sight of the progress of our savior.

"Every time I went to see him, he would recognize me in the audience and do something silly to get people to cheer him on. He put on a show and was adored by everyone as a star, something that neither my father nor the sages were amused by. One night I sneaked out to go over to the hall; I don't know why I did it, as he was sleeping at that time and I wouldn't be able to see him, but something compelled me to do it. When I peeked over the railing, I saw two small lights like those in the eyes of felines when it gets dark in the daytime, and I was frightened. I took a step back and then I heard.

"Mihara, don't be afraid, I'm still the same person you once hugged. I would never hurt you; you saved my life, remember?"

"I looked out again and those eyes were still there, staring at me like beacons in the dark, not even blinking, so I asked him why they glowed like that, and he replied that this glow was nothing compared to the way his heart glowed every time he saw me in the crowd.

"A shiver ran through my body at those words, and I ran home, completely flushed. My mother heard me walking down the hall and for a moment I thought I had been caught, but then she scolded me for stealing sihf stars. After that, I stayed up all night remembering Aztrak's words, which kept repeating in my head over and over again like an echo that I could neither stop nor ignore. Then I made the decision that the next day I would focus on my own training as a Shawá Lady, and so I continued for the next few months, forcing my mind to follow my routine, without seeing him a single day during all that time, until one night I woke up from a strange dream and there were those glowing eyes at the side of my bed. As soon as I turned on the light, they disappeared. That vision made me pale.

"My parents had left the fortress to meet friends from the kingdom of Picmeral in crystalline waters, far from the Shwanír Fortress, so I got dressed and ran out to warn the guard, whom I accompanied to the section where they had placed that being. At that moment I noticed for the first time the high walls that enclosed his room and I realized that they did not allow him to see the outside like us, which made it look like a large cell full of books, weapons, and training utilities. It was then that I understood that the sweet boy I once lived with was, in reality, our prisoner; a slave forced to obey orders, unable to decide for himself as a free being. And I felt deeply sorry for him. The image of the cold, nearly dead child I once tucked in came to my mind, and it was impossible to understand how we could have done that to him.

"The truth is that when I made the decision to notify the guard it was an instinctive impulse, as I thought he had escaped and was somehow in my room. I was convinced that once we got to his cell, it would be empty, but there he remained, meditating on the bed with his legs crossed.

"What are you doing in my room? he said aloud to the guard, while in my head he said to me and only me, "Thank you for coming, Mihara. It's just what I wanted. It's good to finally see you face to face."

"I watched the guard, but they did not hear his words, those he conveyed with his mind. His lips only moved to address the soldiers.

"They only hear what I want them to hear. No one knows I can do this; it should be our secret, don't you think?" he asked me telepathically as I continued to watch him in fascination.

"I thought I was going crazy, then he turned, looked me in the eyes and in my head, I heard:

"Be calm. You're not crazy."

"And he winked at me. At once one of the five entered the room and asked the guard to explain the reason he had let me in there, so I apologized and told them that it had all been a misunderstanding, that I thought Aztrak had escaped and that was why I encouraged the guard to check it out. The wise man explained to me that I had been very lucky that my father was not in the fortress that night and that, for disturbing the order with that lie, he was going to punish me with the obligation to give one hour of class a day to that being.

"I still remember Aztrak's reaction, the way he looked up at me from his bed, smiling and pleased that he had achieved his purpose; it almost seemed as if he had planned it.

"See you tomorrow, Mihara," he whispered in my mind as he left his room.

"After that, as ordered by one of the Five, we spent an hour a day together for almost a year. Everything I learned as a Shawá Lady, I taught him and he in turn showed me his skills, which we kept very secret. The days went by, and I was looking forward to going to see him more and more. Little by little I felt more comfortable by his side, I no longer considered him a threat nor the delicate creature I watched in the aquarium. For me he was already an equal, unjustly locked up in those chambers like a prey, isolated like a beast.

"So, I convinced my father and the council that Aztrak should attend certain classes with the rest of the Shawá s, both theory and training, so that he would fight the guard and perfect his tactics for face-to-face confrontation with the unexpected, and not just the inanimate objects in the rehearsal room. This way he could socialize so he could defend himself once he left the citadel.

"Luckily, they listened to me and accepted my recommendation. All the people of the Shwanír Fortification attended the great event in question, absolutely no one wanted to miss it. And as soon as he came out of his cabin, they were in awe of his height, his grandeur, his strength, and his charm. As time went by, people accepted him as one of their own, which made the wise men uneasy, especially my father, since his skills and powers were increasing at the same time as his interest in me, as well as mine in him," said Grandma.

"It had an unfortunate ending," said Nose.

"My father sentenced himself and his people with that decree. Tell me, you who were recently in our home, is everything still as I remember it?" asked Mihara.

"Yes, my lady, only with more fear and less freedom than before, since the thirteenth kingdom is demanding more and more and uses his Zorks to intimidate. They have perfected and increased their powers," the peon replied, with a frown.

"Tell me, Nose, how are my parents? I assume that my father will remain a bitter and disheartened man of immovable ideas; it hurts me to continue loving him despite everything, but it hurts me even more that they wouldn't let me say goodbye to my dear mother. There is not a day that goes by that I don't think of her; I miss her so much...."

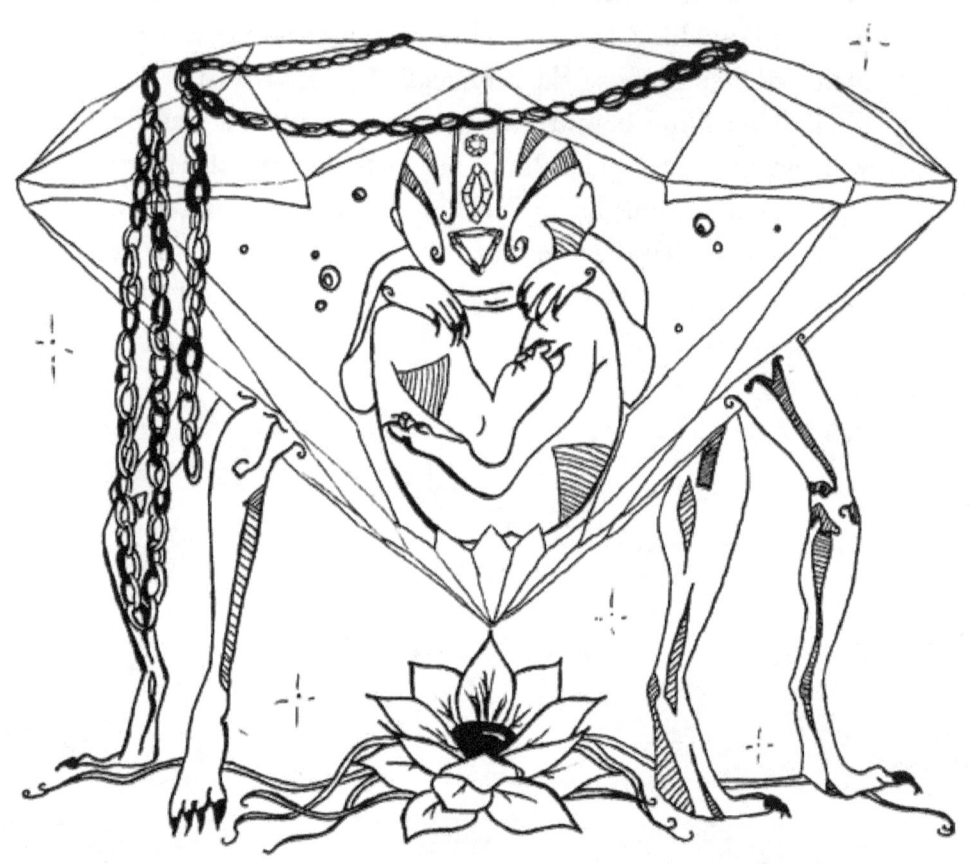

Setting an Example

"My lady, your mother, wanting to save you from exile, tried to break the circle of five. With this behavior she only managed to receive a blow of energy that left her unconscious, and she is still unconscious today. On the other hand, your father is still awake and there is not a day that goes by that he does not regret what happened. It is well known that those of Shawá blood live longer than most and that our period of youth is longer. As a result of the event, the man grew old with great diligence, so much so that one day he sat down from exhaustion on his throne in the great hall of the Shwanír Fortress and never rose again. He spends his days and nights there as just another object in the hall.

"In the Royal Guard's quarters, we peons have a little waterfall in the wall by which we are awakened only in case of emergency. One night your father, who seemed absent minded, communicated with me through it and startled, I ran into the room. When I arrived, the watery floor of the chair illuminated him with his gaze fixed on the beyond. He had been there for so long and quiet that his long hair and beard almost covered the whole of the throne. Then the old man moved his eyes for the first time in a very long time and spoke again to tell me to look for you, and in case you were still alive, he ordered me to give you the gem of Riyah. It was then that I realized how naive I was during that whole period, as your father always knew I had it hidden with me, but he never let on.

"Despite my differences with him, that day I knelt before the throne. With great effort, he explained to me that he had made a mistake with his decision, that he could not expect forgiveness from his daughter, but he still hoped that you could forgive the people who need her so much, since you are the only salvation for her people. He also reminded me that I was once a great warrior and that this was still in me, hidden somewhere. Therefore, he entrusted this task exclusively to me, making it clear to me that no one else knew of my task and that I should keep it that way.

"After that, incredible as it may seem, he opened my way to the human world without the help of the other four. He left me completely perplexed at the power he had achieved after years of deceiving the crowd, making us believe that he was retired when in reality he was in a deep state of meditation, studying and evolving in silence, going unnoticed before the ignorant eyes of the rest of the fortification, including the other sages.

"Just before crossing over to this world, he told me that once I arrived here, I would be all alone. Then he wished me luck and immediately I appeared in the terrestrial world, having no idea how I was going to get home, but knowing that, if you lived, I would find you," said the Shawá.

"You must have spent a lot of time alone. It's amazing you managed to find us," said Sasha.

"I spent months hiding and searching incessantly, but the connection between the Shawá bloods is so strong that, even though Mihara was practically a human, I was able to detect her and start an exhaustive tracking work. And although the energy I received was small, little by little it ended up bringing me to this town, and you already know the rest," explained Nose.

"But that is impossible. My father doesn't have the power to send someone to earth. It took the union of the five of us to send me here. The powers of a Shawá are not powerful enough to accomplish that task," Grandma wondered, trying to reason with the peon.

"After your mother's fall, it was some time before they ruled that she would never wake up. At that time her father thought that perhaps, if he returned home his daughter would miraculously awaken his wife from her long sleep, but the council rejected the proposal to bring you back to the Shwanír Fortress. "The law is the law," they told him, beating their sticks hard against the ground. However, your father did not give up, he sat immovably on his throne and used all his strength to fall into a deep trance for the sole purpose of acquiring the power and wisdom necessary to bring you back.

"He has spent all these years working at it by stealth, not caring about anything else; he practically became besieged, part of the decoration, to transform himself into the most powerful sage who ever lived without anyone noticing. The other councilors thought he had gone mad from the loss of his family, so they allowed him to remain there wasting away; they almost abandoned him hoping his mind would fade with time. I believe they respected his wishes to remain on the throne because of who he once was to Argua, a model for the people and the example of the wise man who would not allow himself to be corrupted even by his own blood, who enforced the law with his own daughter, thereby demonstrating to the kingdom how sacred and impenetrable our laws were. A man incorruptible to the extreme, the image of a true leader of the Shwanír Fortress.

"I will now be at your service, my lady, as I have nowhere to go. Besides, they will have noticed my absence by now. Honestly, I wouldn't know where my fate lies right now, but what is clear to me is that, if I try to return, which is not what I wish, it will be my death sentence," Nose reported.

"If that is so, we must get to work as soon as possible and find a way to return home, whether the Shawá s like it or not," said Grandma.

"Excuse me, Grandma, I'm sorry to interrupt, but I need to know something. We were talking about it before you came into the room: what happened to the buyáh creature?" James asked.

"Is that what you were talking about?" Mihara was astonished.

"Well, we were a bit lost, we didn't know anything about where we came from, so they were explaining important facts about the people's past and, to tell you the truth, I'm getting more and more curious. Do you think we'll get to see all of Argua someday, Grandma?" Sasha asked.

"I'm afraid I can't answer that for you, my dear, but I hope you can, because it's the only way to get back what was once taken from us, and you deserve to see it in person.

"About the buyáh, he is probably already dead. So many years have passed that it seems more like a myth than a reality," Grandma replied.

"My lady, I don't know if he is alive, but he is certainly not a myth. Your father could have told you the story firsthand, since he was present when the beast was captured under the sand on the banks of the Margua. It was the Five Wise Men who tried to make sure that the buyáh remained buried there, hoping and believing that it would eventually pass away, and with it, any stain on the Shawá s' moral record. But when Riyah awoke on the beach, she demanded the right not to kill the animal, for if Fraya's confession was true, not only had his home been taken from him, but he and his family had been unjustly injured and discredited, and it was not right that he should die in that way.

"It was then that Eyíre approached her, showed her loyalty and supported her cause. And when he held her hand, to everyone's surprise, it showed his changing self as he connected her gaze with Riyah's. I knew right then and there that, though I had never had her, I had lost her forever, for the connection that arose between them made it clear to anyone's eyes that it was somehow impenetrable, whether it was that masterful union or the passion with which they fought for the same cause; it became clear that they had more in common than I or anyone else could ever have had.

"After that, Eyíre explained to all present that a grave fault had been committed by banishing a creature from its own kingdom in such a horrible way and reminded them that these were not the ideals of Argua, that their lives had revolved around games that preached what was not being applied. He then asked them what they should believe in then and made them question the meaning of the games if we were driven by greed, cruelty, and accepted injustice in such a way. He used his sister Fraya as the clear example of the fight against those ideals, a person they criticized for creating a monster by force of the sacrifice of many other species. And, hypocrites, they were going to make the same mistake with the buyáh without taking into account the transgression that influenced this creature to act with so much anger.

"With those words he succeeded in showing the selfishness and the great hypocrisy of those who called themselves wise men, casting doubt on the credibility of the councilors as leaders of the people of Argua. These, after having been put in evidence, dictated right there on the sand that Eyíre and Riyah would decide the fate of the beast and that the Shawá s would pay their tribute for the sin committed against the offspring of the buyáh. A new home would be found for the great caged animal.

"The sages remained guarding and protecting the area where the sphere containing the beast was buried while the council met to fix the situation and calm the population. To restore the values until the situation was fixed. As I told you, I escaped from that situation by hiding in a cave until I received the message relayed by one of the wise men through a small puddle. But it was not transmitted well; I did not want to see the Shawá in question either, so I went in search of another means by which I could find out what was going on.

"I had climbed a long way to get to that cavern; it must have been hours since I fled from the beach before I found that place as I don't even remember how I got there, but as I gazed at the view from the top I could see the lake, the shore, and the vast diversified landscapes of no man's land, with the sun at its hottest and the planets a splendid pink behind it.

"I looked down and saw a forest of shush trees at the foot of the hill where I stood, so I descended to them in the hope that I would be granted permission to receive the messages transmitted by the kingdom of Ostrevo through its long, bare branches, which touched the ground. On it crowded their delicate fallen leaves, surely because someone had already been there just before I reached them. Then I asked one of the trees for permission, but it lifted the brush and, with a whip, knocked me to the ground.

"You are not from our kingdom, Shwanír soldier, why do you come here?"

"I got up from the ground, but its leaves covered me up to my knees, so I fell again. This time I was dragged by a branch that grabbed me by the leg until I was covered by the frond.

"With all due respect, shush tree, I just came to listen to the message from the Council, since from my medium it is not well received.

"But the branch pulled me into the forest, covering even my face with its petals. It carried me levitating and managed to flip me in the air.

"So, you admit that our kingdom is superior in method?"

"I took a second to concentrate, as my mind was very distracted by everything that happened before, but I ended up answering correctly.

"I believe that each kingdom has its hegemony as well as its detriments, but that united, no one surpasses us.

"Immediately, the flakes fell to the surface, and everything stopped moving.

"Then you are worthy to hear the message through the shushes."

"The beautiful leaves that covered the ground began to flutter around me delicately, creating shapes that presented the message from councilor Corosso. In it he explained that the games would resume that very day during sunset to end a terrible event, and that a new and better one would begin; that we would record the memory of what should not happen again, paying for our sins, and recover the principles and ideals of the games for the prosperity and continuity of Argua.

"When the message ended, the branches quickly returned to their vines, which allowed us to enjoy a splendid forest, which in turn was also terrifying. The branch that held me let go and dropped me roughly to the ground. I got up and thanked them, but the shushes did not say another word, they remained static before me, so I got out of there quickly. By the time I reached Naruh, there were so many people that I could hardly move in the crowd, so I climbed one of the beruna trees by pulling on one of its lianas, on which I hooked my foot. This lifted me up to the top from where I could admire the grandeur of the lake, with the people arranged around it and the council sitting on its balcony.

"The Councilor of the kingdom of Tepnos, a kingdom built underground, stood up and the games began. He apologized for what happened and exclaimed that we are all weak at heart, but that we must resist in order not to fall into temptation, in order not to dig deeper into the depths of our own grave, in order to strengthen ourselves with the truth, the essential and basic thing in this life, since the fundamental thing is the union of all of us, no matter where we come from or where we are going; that we be free and respect everyone equally, help each other to improve and live in peace.

"He reminded us that what had happened was a lesson for all and an example of what should never happen again. On that occasion they had been lucky, but that is not always the case, so we had to reinforce those principles and ideals, not only by preaching, but by acting. Thus, the games were resumed with a tribute to the example to be followed.

"Then a huge shadow covered the top of the beruna tree where I stood, accompanied by a thunderous sound that made my bust tremble. I looked up. Flying above me, a great black drakon swooped down from the sky and hovered over the lake like a swan. Clinging to its spinal spines was the beautiful Riyah, with her new appearance after the attack. She then descended the wing of the giant animal until she touched the water with her bare feet. She managed to silence the crowd and stun them, for Drakons were not often seen, let alone in direct contact with beings not of their race.

"A beautiful demonstration of how all the creatures of Argua can live in harmony," said Councilor Nunnara, from the kingdom of Firendel, standing up.

"Riyah responded by bowing over the pond in front of the balcony. From the interior of the lake a huge sprout emerged and when it opened, it showed the young Eyíre also offering his respects to the council, with his hands joined with those of the Shawá as a sign of alliance. The duo then announced the tragic reality of the poor buyáh, mistreated and unjustly judged, who had been left without a family and without a home, for which he deserved justice by giving him a new kingdom in which to rebuild his life. The Council reacted by rising; the leaders were somewhat bewildered.

"And what land are you going to give the beast? shouted someone from the audience.

"What domain will have to pay for the sins of another?" another person shrieked as the hubbub declared that it should be the Shawá s who should cede the Margua back to the buyáh, since they were the ones to blame for that outrage.

"Rombar, call for order, please," the young Riyah asked her imposing friend, who, with a thunderous roar, made everyone shut up.

"We are not here to take anyone's land or to set us against each other, or have you forgotten our principles and the Arguan laws?" said the great drakon, whose great and deep voice resounded in the eardrums of the audience.

"Have you so quickly forgotten the meaning of the games? We are here to prove that, thanks to our gifts, we can help and bring prosperity to our kingdoms, but to do so we must be united. Eyíre and I have decided to join forces to give the creature a new home, and what better place than here, no man's land; a place that serves to reconcile, so that we always keep in mind in our lives the right path to follow, immortalized every year in the games. As a reminder of what must never happen again," Riyah said, holding on to her partner's hand as the council members gave them their permission. They wanted to know what they had planned, leaning on the balcony railing as they watched the pair join foreheads to combine forces. Then the earth began to tremble, stones, rocks, and trees to fly; tornadoes of water shot out of the Margua and ascended into the sky, where they collided with the earth rising from the surrounding fields. Riyah's hair moved from side to side completely wet.

"From the top of the tree I began to see and understand the purpose they had outlined when darkness covered the whole area and a mirage appeared in the sky reflecting the world lying beneath my feet. Like superimposed images enclosing the same pink sky, with identical warm sunshine between the two landscapes like a sandwich of light between twin worlds.

"Then the huge sphere that had been brought through the air from the beach plunged into the lake that was held above us and, with an explosion emanating from within the marsh, the buyáh appeared, splashing all the spectators. The beast swam out of control across the vast lagoon that covered the firmament, going from side to side at great speed. Riyah and Eyíre ran for shelter under the great Rombar, which took flight and hovered between the two lakes, suspended in the air, flush with the surface of the watery base of that celestial cut, letting the Shawá send a message to the buyáh creature through her hand, whose palm touched the area of the lake suspended above our heads.

"The huge white figure reacted by stopping just at the edge. After standing there motionless for a while, it receded until it disappeared into the depths. Then, without expecting it, the snowy spot appeared again, accelerating towards the surface of the celestial lagoon, where it jumped across from one lake to the other, exposing the immensity of its body as it descended before the audience, flying from one world to another, with the setting sun piercing its hair full of white scales and revealing its fins like great bathed sails, which gave off particles of water that recreated numerous rainbows around its being in the glare of the light.

"I admit that at first I was frightened, clinging tightly to the branches of the great tree as I watched the crowd transfixed by that dazzling but terrifying image. But when I saw the grandiose scene of the monster falling into Nahru Lake, my body and mind were neutralized. The giant disappeared for a few moments into the waters of the original lagoon, only to emerge from its depths and leap into the reflection of the upper marsh. The people applauded amid shouts and whistles of euphoria. Not only could I appreciate the beauty of the moment, but also the greatness of the power that both Riyah and Eyíre, the new favorite team of the Arguans, had just demonstrated, for together they were even better than the twins.

"With that exhibition they showed the whole world that the union between opposites makes us stronger. We received a great lesson. I have never seen, nor will I ever see anything like it again," said Nose.

"And what happened to Fraya?" asked the young man.

"No one knows if she was there for certain, but from her later exploits it is inferred that, if she did not see it, she somehow learned of what happened in detail. She never appeared with her sister again; she lived isolated and hidden from the kingdoms, in a kind of ostracism," Rasnar answered.

"I would love to see the buyáh," said Sasha.

"We do not know if he is alive. It has been a long time since anyone has seen it, since none of the inhabitants of the kingdoms set foot on no man's land again after the appearance of you-know-who. Nor is the longevity of the animal known. That was the last time this majestic being was shown; it was a farewell in style, one impossible to forget."

After these words, the Guardian took one last tour of the manor and its grounds to make sure they were still safe. Meanwhile, the others left for their rooms, loaded with thoughts and images that were difficult to digest, but full of intrigue, fascination, and the desire to repeat them.

Chapter VII
Training

The next morning, before the first rays of light came out, both Sasha and James were awakened by an effusive Rasnar.

"A good breakfast before your bath will give you strength to start the training," he explained, taking them to the kitchen dangling from his claws.

Nose was waiting for them next to their grandmother with breakfast prepared on the table.

"But what time is it, you animal?" James complained, trying to open his eyes.

"The hour of the dew, dear."

James looked seriously at Grandma with a coffee in her hand.

"So, this is what our days are going to be like from now on, with dawn raids and riddles," Sasha replied.

"No, more like this," said the beast, grabbing the siblings and flying out the kitchen door.

"Rasnar! Put us down right now! Have you gone crazy, you damned pigeon? I said put us down!" they exclaimed in distress.

"As you command, my lords."

At once it opened its claws and dropped the siblings from the highest point in the sky. They tumbled down, terrified and crying for help as they approached the treetops. When it looked as if they were about to crash, Rasnar hooked them again with its huge talons like a bird of prey.

"You are crazy! How are you going to train us if you kill us?" they protested indignantly.

"The next time you complain, you will have a closer view of your precious woods," the Guardian threatened, leading them to the entrance lawn, where Mihara and the peon were waiting.

"I think they've got it, dear. Today you will have to enhance your skills with the smallest particles of water, the dew, which settles on the grass and appears insignificant. Controlling these molecules is no easy task and is of utmost importance, for if you can handle something so tiny, you will gradually be able to control elements much larger than you can imagine," explained the Lady Shawá.

"Why don't we start with the biggest thing right away?" the boy wanted to know.

"A good artist must take care of the smallest details to make his work perfect, right?" opined the Guardian.

"You do not learn the number two without first knowing the number one, so now sit on the floor, with your legs crossed and your hands on your knees, your back straight and in absolute silence. I want you to concentrate on the water, feel how it flows, be guided by the sensations of touching it, seeing it, swallowing it... Perceive it inside you as part of your being so that you connect with it as one. Once you get that, concentrate all that energy in a single drop of dew until it rises in the air.

"If you succeed, the second step will be to keep it in the air as long as you can. Once you have accomplished this task, you must repeat it with several drops, and so on until you have done absolutely all the drops in the garden."

The siblings spent hours pondering. The practices went on for days; there came a point when both Sasha and James no longer knew whether the drop, they were practicing on had moved or was a figment of their imagination. They were so focused on the same task that they began to get delirious.

Training was hard. They were forced to wake up before dawn to take advantage of the dew and continued learning the rest of the day, with attack and defense classes taught by Nose, who began by giving them the basics. But as soon as they managed to control the frost molecules, the lessons were adapted to their progress and the same methods were used in combination with their powers, which they still didn't quite know what they were.

At the same time, Grandma subjected them to exercises with gems, leaves, branches, water, fire and even tests of faith, throwing them off the roof of the mansion to see if they could levitate or fly, some of her methods became more like torture, such as putting on lead shoes and filling their pockets with stones and, with their hands tied, submerging them in the lake to see how long they could remain under water, subjected to pressure, enduring the effects of the little oxygen they received.

They had barely learned to breathe in this medium, so, unfortunately, all the results, despite being better than any well-trained human would give, were still lousy by the standards of any Shawá child. For an initiate in the Shwanír Fortress, breathing in this environment was natural, but for them it was quite uncomfortable because of the choking sensation caused by the adaptation of their body to the water. It was hard for them to get used to not receiving the breath of air with which they longed to fill their lungs; something instinctive that they could not avoid, nor to stop the impulse that they had to unlearn so as to adapt to an unnatural way of breathing. A change even more costly if we consider the level at which this task was required of them.

When they managed to more or less control aquatic breathing, and they could stand hours panting underwater, subjecting their skin and organs to the evolution of this discipline, they proceeded to learn how to walk under this element, in addition to swimming in it at great speed with the agility of an aquatic animal.

To do this, Nose relied on the knowledge used by the Shawá s, both outside and underwater, and set them obstacles, traps... They were even chased and attacked by beasts that he recreated with the help of Rasnar's illusory powers, to accustom the siblings to a near future; he prepared them for combat in a more realistic way. Also, in these cases, despite the fear inflicted on the siblings in the course of those very hard exercises to which they were subjugated, they always came out unscathed, even if they failed in their task. But the reality would be very different. Once they were in a real battle, fighting in the approaching war, they could not allow even the slightest failure, for it would mean losing their lives.

The young people were still too far from perfection to know how to protect themselves against the risks that lay in wait for them, to which they would be subjected when the reality of that hostility would turn them into protagonists. They had to be prepared not only physically, but also mentally.

The arts of the water were based on techniques acquired by ancestral marine beings, so that the primary preparation of the Shawá s from birth was mandatory. They trained with true masters who had acquired this systematic after a long life dedicated to the study and practice of these disciplines. Therefore, exercising them with the children was a huge challenge for Nose and Mihara, who were trying to get the youngsters to reach the simple level of an ordinary Shawá at the age of early childhood, without having the skills and notions of these teachers, let alone the required facilities. Hence, they used resources that would cast doubt on their guardianship both in the land and in Argua because of their handling of the siblings. As an excuse for their barbarities, they alleged the pressure to which they were subjected due to the lack of time with respect to the situation in which they were and the events that were approaching.

The siblings, knowingly depressed and frustrated, ended up more united than ever; they joined forces to make rapid progress, more easily overcoming the traps and obstacles that were so tenaciously placed. In the meantime, Rasnar watched from the sky just as Nose followed them underwater, supervising them with his hand over the lake to make sure of every move the siblings made, guiding them on their journey from one end of the lake to the other. During the daily training sessions, he would help them come out of each mission unscathed, despite changing them to surprise the siblings with something new and unexpected that would force them to discover new techniques. This was a good thing, as all Shawá s had a method. Thus, the siblings' improvisation would allow them to use that as an advantage against the predictable tactics of the warriors.

After several months of instruction, the motivation of the two grew, as did their ambition to learn more inventiveness from other realms. They sought to carefully analyze their movements objectively and to deepen their perfection, both bodily and psychic, through deep meditation and constant study in the insatiable daily combat to which they were subjected. They demanded more from their teachers and from themselves. The more they prospered in the disciplines, the more they concentrated and the more they gave themselves to their purpose. This caused them to awaken their latent powers; unknown abilities that surfaced within them and showed the magnitude of their potential.

The mansion and its grounds had become a complete training camp, active twenty-four hours a day, so Sasha and James learned to be alert at every instant. They were prepared for the unpredictable, they rehearsed without relaxing, they did their tasks with their senses sharpened and active, so that their reflexes and aptitudes, as well as their power of concentration, were developed at times, whether sleeping, waking, in the shower or urinating, eating, or lying on the couch.

They were mentally and physically exhausted by the hard daily training. The siblings' reactions to danger and their alertness to the suspicions that their instincts revealed to them, to the constant coercion to which they were subjected by their teachers, were more than brilliant. As time went by, the adolescents were exposed alone to trials that they welcomed as normal, as if they were innocent games, with the difference that in these the fun consisted of putting their lives in danger by competing between themselves to reinforce their individual and team power. The goal was to one day overthrow Zotrak and free his people. However, their agility, skills and powers were not up to the level of a true Arguan, despite their advances.

After receiving this report from the teachers, the siblings' motivation plummeted, because they understood their task as an impossible risk and began to lose control of their emotions, with turmoil and negative thoughts. They became pessimistic and, in their heads, only the past and the failure of the present resounded. They came into conflict with themselves and the world around them, something that could be categorized as depression or personality disorder. They were aware that they were descended from evil, so they thought that as their strength increased, so would the power of their lineage, which would take its toll on them like a toxin. Therefore, they had to bend their own blood, for in their genes was a darkness that had to be fought as their gifts increased.

That suffering they were going through just to free a people who rejected and banished them called into question the veracity of who their family really was, as they began to feel Zotrak as someone closer that they came to understand.

Without the strength of mental clairvoyance, the body is weak. The siblings' tutors discovered that this feeling surfaced dangerously in the youngsters and caused them tremendous concern, no longer for the future of their people, but for the emotional stability of the siblings, so Mihara, Nose and Rasnar decided that they would take a break from training and devote part of the evening to telling them stories about Argua.

They intended to tell them the truth about Zotrak, and remind them that, although they were linked to evil, they did not have to be like him. They would link to other stories about evil as a subliminal message, narratives they were not to forget, and would slyly alternate that information with other events. Like when Mihara learned of her pregnancy status after arriving on earth in human form and meeting the siblings' grandfather. She explained to them that their earthly great-grandmother took her in knowing her condition, as did Charles, who was the second great love of her life. He accepted her unconditionally; her, her history, her origin, and the baby inside her, all under the blessing of Mrs. de Courdeil, who in those days was already a legend.

She told them many other anecdotes, such as when she first lovingly tucked in her son, the father of the siblings, who would have to cope in a human world with the fact that he was a descendant of Zotrak. This knowing that the child she had given birth to carried in his blood the lethal combination of the poison of evil, with the genes of the greatest Shawá that had ever existed and the ancestral lineage of his family, and that he was the successor of one of the Five Sages of the Shwanír Fortress, which is why he had not been affected by the evil of the unnamable one.

"Your grandfather was a tremendously eccentric and adventurous man. This led him to commit acts of great stupidity and risk that one day ended his life, when your father was only a child. My son grew up without knowing who his real progenitor was and where he came from, because at that time I thought that letting him live in ignorance would protect him from suffering and external threats and he could live a normal human life.

"But the absence and the memory of the one he considered his predecessor set him on the path to the same kind of behavior and he committed the same foolishness as Charles and put your mother's life and his own at risk, until that fateful day when their bodies disappeared.

"There is not a day that goes by that I don't regret not telling my little boy the truth, but who knows if that would have been better or worse. I lost my only son, but I gained two wonderful grandchildren. You should be proud of who you are and be clear that, despite your blood, you will be whatever you want and decide to be. It is your choice, not your undoing.

After the long night talks, the siblings returned to their rooms exhausted, confused, relieved and bewildered. So many emotions and doubts invaded their souls that sometimes they could not cope with sleep and awakened a telepathy like the one Aztrack possessed and used with Mihara. Lying on their beds, they asked each other if they were already asleep. This without uttering any sound, as they did it through their minds, thus controlling not to wander in thoughts to concentrate on a spiritual conversation, which relaxed them and helped them to succumb to sleep and thus reach the rest they needed and that comforted them so much.

The connection between the siblings was so strong that they had come to call each other in their visions to experience this facet together, giving answers to their doubts and even facing their worst nightmares together in combat. Their training and dedication did not cease even while they were staying overnight, until one morning Rasnar decided to give them a break. It was the first time since they started training that he gave them a break.

But they were so hooked on the whole thing that they would never have asked. So, when James got the news, he was stymied and demanded an explanation from the guardian. The poor guy was so used to his daily routine that he had no idea where to start enjoying the time off. So, he did what he was best at and seemed to have forgotten: talking nineteen to the dozen, endless-ly questioning the poor Guardian, who promptly passed the pest to the peon and the peon passed the pest to the siblings' grandmother.

The girl raised a torrent of questions for which none of them were prepared. For this reason, it was decided, for the very first time in all the time they had been staying there, to go up to the room where Grandma used to read her books to calm them by the fire, as she did when they were little.

Sasha entered the room and noticed the jar of water containing a leaf. James reacted immediately by picking it up and mentally remarked to his sister that he had noticed it too, so it hadn't been a dream.

"Is Grandma the hooded woman we saw as children?"

Candidates

"It is Arguan law that as soon as a baby is born, it must be trained for the prosperity of the kingdoms as a whole; not only by the parents, but instructed by the territory to which it belongs, since each of the twelve domains has its own specialized methods. The children are educated in the traditional disciplines of their people, and those who stand out within this preliminary phase are sent to each of the different kingdoms for a time, where they are trained by these others until they acquire more notions with which to perfect their techniques and personal powers.

"Those selected usually end up being great teachers for their people. If we add to this that their values and wisdom are firm when it comes to respecting both regulations and traditions, without holding back creativity, they are very successful among their people. An instructive procedure that has benefited the kingdoms for generations, like the basic education of an Arguan. This has borne fruit with true facts: the best of the girls and boys who excelled during this formative period always end up concluding their education with a contribution to Argua and, consequently, become future members of the council," explained Rasnar, lying down in the cozy little room which was Grandma's study.

"Knowing this, how are we to lead the Twelve into war without being on a par with these creatures and without having contributed anything to their domain?" Sasha asked.

"So, those on the Council, have they personally collaborated in giving Argua something new or advancing?" James asked.

"Well, if you manage to be among the best in your kingdom in terms of gifts and wisdom, you will be a dominant, but if you only excel in qualities what they will do is assign you to training which will analyze you and increase your techniques so that others can study them in the future. This is how the progress works in our domains.

"And if you are of the best in both skills and techniques and have a notorious sapience, as well as having committed some feat in the kingdom for the prosperity of all Argua, then you will be an influencer. Possibly you will be nominated to a position in the council of your kingdom, to give example and welfare to your people, with the values and the new teachings, without losing sight of the old traditions.

"And if with all that you also manage to contribute something so unusual that it is considered a heroic deed for the prosperity of the Twelve Kingdoms, increasing the strength of all the kingdoms and the beings that inhabit them, then and only then will you be among the few that may be considered fit to be a member of the Council of Argua, since to hold this honor one must earn the respect of every living element of all the kingdoms," explained Mihara in a more colloquial way so that his grandson would learn the theme.

"Okay, now I understand why you respect the Council so much," the boy conceded.

"Without respect, only disorder would reign, but if the group of elected officials is influenced by fear, then it doesn't matter who rules it, for chaos will also reign. Reprisal creates cracks in the walls of any society no matter how big or thick they are, and before long, huge cracks will form and spread until they become a deep hole that will eventually collapse every last one of its partitions," said Nose.

"I will put all my efforts and motivation into this, but even so, I don't know if we will ever be up to it," said Sasha.

"I'll do it too, not because I want to be a prince or a mass leader, of course, but because now I know how important it is to all of you and what you're risking by being here with us. Besides, having powers is a blast and when this is all over, I'm going to be so polished that I'll have all the girls after me!" James joked, regaining his originality.

"Wow, I can't believe I missed that character of yours. You were so into training that you didn't seem like yourself. I'm glad you have so much motivation because you're going to need it. But we've got to get your self-esteem up, young lady, and you, my boy, we've got to get yours down before you join Preciosas."

Relaxed in front of the fire, the siblings continued to listen to stories from their tutors, but they were abstracted. Had it not been for the events that had brought them there, they would have started training again, instead of sitting around listening to stories, as their motivation was once again sky high. They wanted to make progress in learning new resources and improving the gifts that were springing up in them like weeds in a field: fast-growing and difficult to control.

Bored out of their minds, they stared blankly at the fire while Rasnar told another of his stories, until Sasha motioned James to look at her side of the fire, where a peculiar log was burning in front of her. She had noticed that the light given off by the flames was getting stronger and stronger, to the point that they gave off small sparks that splattered the floor of the room. The young man reacted quickly and extinguished them before they burned the carpet, while watching his sister. The latter smiled mischievously at him, making it clear that she had been the one to provoke this.

Astonished, because he did not want to be less, he tried to match it. He fixed his gaze on a very thick piece of wood from which a vast flame was emerging. He thought that by choosing this one it would not be so difficult to match a new skill he did not know if he had. Nor did he have the slightest idea when his sister had discovered the skill she now possessed.

He had doubts, since the siblings respected each other every time they unmasked a quality. They told each other before they told their own teachers to be on equal terms when it came to training, although sometimes these unheard-of aptitudes appeared by surprise during one of the training sessions and they didn't have time to show it to the other before it was revealed to their mentors. When this was the case, after the exercise they always shared what they had learned in order to develop it equally. In this way, not only were they great partners, but they were both student and teacher.

The boy threw himself into feeling the fire as if it were a challenge, with the same technique they had been taught to control water, assuming that power in the handling of any element and matter required the same technique. The fire burned inside him, until he was engulfed in flames. Nose nimbly extinguished them by transforming the moisture in the air into water, which he used to wet his body until his temperature dropped.

"It's obvious, you don't feel like paying attention to the importance of relaxing your mind and listening," the Guardian scolded them.

"I'm sorry, I didn't realize. You're right," James replied.

"Why is there so much hatred for changelings in Argua, Rasnar?" Sasha asked, changing the subject, rescuing her brother from the predicament.

"Hate? There is no hatred, but mere ignorance and fear of the unknown. If you're referring to the discussion, I showed you between Sranik and Ashima, that has a more personal explanation," the Talan explained.

"Do you mean to say that something happened between that dandy and the changeling with whom he was arguing?" insisted the young woman.

"That's right. Not everything is what it seems at first glance, guys. Before Sranik had so much power over his people, as well as over Argua itself as an advisor, he was a normal boy, like you and like any other boy. He went to school in his kingdom, signed up for craft workshops where he studied the types of stones and their qualities. Then he continued his apprenticeship in the art of energetic handling of these stones and trained with obsession to be the best in the Preciosas championships.

"These consisted of exposing personal aptitudes with the stones that surrounded them. They celebrated the act before the whole town with a great festivity that was supervised by an important jury composed of the best connoisseurs in craftsmanship, stones, powers, energies, and training techniques of the kingdom. And to stand out, you not only had to have innate potential, but show total dedication to knowledge about the study of the branches that encompass the active understanding of rocks; besides knowing each one of them by name, shape, color, and properties without using your sight," commented the Shawá.

"But to be selected, you had to stand out among the best students at Preciosas. This could happen voluntarily or by decision of the teachers and the Council of the Kingdom, so, once the notification was received, the chosen ones had to be prepared to pass the tests, which would be overcome with mind and body alone.

"Thus, if you were brilliant in an art or had an innate skill with a particular stone, it did you no good, as you were exposed to the public in front of a demanding committee who tested you in the enclosure of the cobblestone courtyard.

"This building is located at the end of the citadel, like a porticoed palace, in the Kingdom of Preciosas. It is square shaped with light stone floors and an altar in the center where the selected one was lodged to be examined. Between this sort of square and the arches that surround it like a portico, there is a still water channel that separates them, surrounded by an atrium of arches of alba stone where beautiful crystal plants are entangled and ascend the pillars from which the magistrate observes during the act. Above this porch, tiers are arranged with balconies where the crowd who wish to watch the spectacle congregate, although many enjoy it from a higher angle, watching from high in the sky on their famous roan birds, which are beautiful creatures used for riding. It is the national sport and is part of their school education.

"From up there they could see the entire citadel, with the tributaries of the kingdom architecturally structured as decorative elements through the orchards of the neatest city, with delicate palaces linked by floating walkways. All of this bordered by the waters of a swamp filled with boats full of attendants who watched the proceedings in the cobblestone courtyard through the arches surrounding the stalls.

"The participating student was tested with his body uncovered, wearing only something that covered his modest parts. This ensured that he could not cheat in any way. And the act began when he placed his hands on the four squares sculpted on the large stone table, where he had to be able to perceive and guess each of the stones that contained those designs, placed in a drawer in the altar. If he guessed correctly, the stone would rise showing the particular material, giving way to an interrogation about the object in question, which continued with some tests on that particular gem.

"If the participant passed the questions, he moved on to the next box and followed the same procedure until he had deciphered all of them, something that few succeeded in doing. Thus, only a few were eligible to take part in the no-man's-land games, since almost none of them succeeded in passing the Preciosas tests. But Sranik succeeded, although that was not enough for him, because he did not want to be one of the best in his kingdom and appear as a participant just to show off, but he wanted to be revered by all the domains of Argua. He wanted to contribute something that would give him the greatness he felt he was destined for. And even though people already idolized him, inside he felt a terrible emptiness knowing that he was capable of so much more than passing those tests, which didn't really classify him as someone unique or beneficial to the games. He needed to stand out at all costs, even at any cost.

"Thus, almost a year after the festival, the day came when they announced the next tournaments, reminding, promoting and encouraging the people of the twelve kingdoms to participate or attend. The territories were filled with notifications and expectations of possible contributors chosen for having gained fame thanks to their prowess, both in their region and in the others.

"As I told you before, those who excelled were obliged to improve and learn from other cultures, acquiring knowledge both in education and training in other kingdoms, so depending on their level and talent, they were trained in groups or privately at the hands of the masters of the kingdom to which they were entrusted.

"After the images were broadcast with the selection of potential players, Sranik was captivated by one of them. To his surprise, it featured an old friend of his with whom he had been battle-hardened under the teachings of the Tunani kingdom, as part of his Arguan instruction. The girl, much younger than him, had earned the respect and fame of the twelve for having gotten more tattoos than anyone in the history of her kingdom. She had even designed a new one on her body; something unheard of both as a feat and for the symbol engraved on her skin, since the drawing had never been seen before among her people. It was a power unknown to her people, an ability that made the young woman unique, even though she still had much to learn by age, marks she had yet to achieve and the fullness of control over the handling of some of those she possessed. Her actions gave her the status of a master at a precocious age and an emblem for her kingdom," said Rasnar.

"But anyone can get a tattoo, right? Depending on the endurance of your skin and your tolerance to pain, you can get more or less drawings. I don't understand what merit that has to earn you a spot in the no man's land games," interrupted young James.

"To begin with, the position as a participant was not earned, since anyone could appear on the first day and formulate their request. But knowing the general expectations of the Twelve, not everyone had the courage or was so shameless as to present themselves just like that, since it was in everyone's conscience that whoever manifested themselves on Naruh would only be to contribute something to Argua and not to gain fame, unless you were part of a show team which offered entertainment as part of the festivities. In fact, it was so hieratical that many of the individuals who appeared on the programs about new revelations and possible candidates did not even get to introduce themselves, even if they were among the best in their realm in many and varied fields. It was not because you were great that you had something to contribute, you know what I mean?"

"Cooperating was a great honor, it meant respect, so appearing in them to foolishly expose some qualities was neither to anyone's liking nor the purpose of the games," Grandma explained.

"Regarding the Tunanian tattoos, they were not done for aesthetics or for pleasure, since in their blood run the lineages of transhumants of the sand that for centuries not only learned to live with it, but to control every particle, with a deep respect for the land on which they depended to survive. They suffered the harsh conditions of living as nomads in the desert, with infernal high temperatures during the day and extremely cold conditions in their nights of absolute silence, with the clearest firmament you could ever imagine, without the slightest possibility of light pollution.

"In the land of the Tunani you can see the entire universe above you but enjoying this aspect of the realm meant having to deal daily with quicksand that swallowed entire caravans of families, sandstorms that wiped out entire acres, uncontrollable poisonous beasts unknown to most beings....

"They survive on what little they have, foraging for provisions as they wander through these arid estates dotted with the occasional small oasis where they can get water, settle down and regain energy. Until they meet another group of nomads with whom to exchange goods or acquire new ideas for the survival of their kingdom. That is why the marks appeared in these people, since they only appear in their skins after an exhaustive study and a very hard training on the symbols. The motifs learned are drawn on the sand and are quickly memorized, since nothing is permanent in this domain. By the time they manage to master them, the drawings are reflected engraved in the dermis on the area of the body linked to that skill.

"No one is known to have succeeded in acquiring all the Tunani signs. Each ideogram learned means the mastery of the magic it contains, so the young Ashima was already, by the number of figures presented in her body, a teacher promoted to councilor of the Tunani kingdom, although not the best, she was the youngest to achieve this position and the recognition of the Twelve, a prodigy with a very promising future.

"When the announcement was over, Sranik was excited by the extraordinary news and immediately wanted to contact the girl to congratulate her, so he ran to one of the study rooms, where he used to combine stones and arts, with the intention of creating new techniques for his people and submitting himself to the games as a participant. But he always ended up with unsuccessful results.

"After a long night of work motivated by the memories he had of the girl, the young man devised an ingenious method to contact her and captivate her attention: a desert rose, an evaporite sedimentary rock formed by the sand flats, with layers of gypsum, water and sand, which produces beautiful crystals reminiscent of the petals of a flower. What better way to reach a lady than with something so unique of its kind, especially when of all flowers it is the rose that symbolizes remembrance. So, the boy left the room for the geological library of the citadel of Preciosas and borrowed a piece of the specimen of the exceptional stone that was in one of its showcases. Then he ran to his house and turned it upside down looking for a remembrance of the strong friendship between them; an amulet that contained a lock of young Ashima's hair," Rasnar explained, preparing to continue the story by projecting it onto the fire.

The Message

"After sending the enchanted aerolites to the Land of Tunani, where the young woman dwelt, these curious stones moved towards her body like a magnet. Gliding on her flying carpet so that she could move through acres of quicksand without stepping and sinking into it, a survival tactic learned from her wandering ancestors, she watched in amazement as she left behind impressions on the sandstone. She realized that those marks were caused by hundreds of desert roses that left a path as they passed over the surface she flew over, like a long tail crossing the dunes. Then she remembered the words of one of her teachers, who had discovered the curious event long before her.

"When sand comes to us it tells us that a storm is coming. But when a desert flower goes after a young girl, what can it be telling her?"

"Ashima thought her master was rambling from old age, but when she found that the stones were following her, she took a moment to observe the rocks. As she approached them, they piled up on top of each other, and as she moved away, they separated, so she raised the carpet until she reached the sky. She wanted to observe them from afar. As she ascended, she noticed that the petals of these flowers were separating and decomposing into fragments that were moving from one side to another until, to the girl's surprise, they revealed a clear message: a huge figure formed by the pieces of all those rocks that covered the uninhabited surface, with a symbol that many Tunanisians carried engraved on their skin. Then she remembered the day she won that tattoo.

"As I already told you, in spite of being the Tunani who had gained the most skills, just like any other young woman, her beginnings were difficult, since she had to fight very hard to win the emblems that her complexion presents today, and this particular sign was one of the ones she dreaded the most in her day. The mere idea of facing it to gain it terrified her to such an extent that she preferred not to present herself so as not to face it.

"It all happened on a day like any other, as she was showing her foreign friend from Preciosas the wonders of the desert. They were flying on her carpet through the lands of the kingdom, having left class in search of adventure, and practiced during their explorations in those arid lands the teachings of the masters.

After a silly prank on her companion, the two fell off the carpet onto a dune and rolled down it until they were miles away from each other. The carpet ended up a few feet away from her. The huge mound separated them and, without a perspective from the sky, the orientation on the sandy ground of that monotonous landscape forced the youngsters to walk in solitary circles, completely lost.

"Ashima desperately climbed the many sandy prominences under that scorching sun, exhausted by the effort required to move through the sand, as it slipped under her with every step she took, making the climb even more difficult, as her feet sank to her knees because of that impossible mountain to climb. After hours of searching for her friend, worried for their lives, she managed to spot him in the distance from the top of a dune. He was gazing at a gigantic wall of silica clasts that stretched across the horizon like a huge cloud of undulating shapes and was about to touch the ground. Next to it the boy looked tiny.

"She shouted at him in desperation with the purpose of encouraging him to flee, but the boy turned around and greeted her euphoric for having found her and excited because it was the first time, he had seen this natural phenomenon. He was unaware that a tsunami of sandstone was going to sweep over the place without mercy. At the moment of impact, an instinctive impulse came from within Ashima that took her to Sranik, levitating over the sand, an ancient tactic used to cross areas of quicksand. It moved at such a speed that it caused a huge explosion due to the doppler effect.

"Suddenly there was darkness, which was accompanied by an incessant rumbling that enclosed them in an aggressive whirlwind of sand grains that ravaged the atmosphere and covered them with millions of tiny particles shot out like needles penetrating everywhere. Sranik, who had closed his eyes and held his breath as he endured the monstrous sandstorm, noticed that nothing had hit him. None of the little calcarenites brushed against him or hindered his breathing, but strangely he did feel his hair and clothing moving. He also perceived a very intense toning sound. Then he began to open his eyes slowly, cautiously. To his surprise, he lay enclosed in the middle of the storm, but the storm did not touch him, but miraculously passed around him like an aggressive stream of water flowing over a rock. He saw the grains of silica biting past him, like great waves flowing toward a horizon he could not see.

"Dying with curiosity, he ran his hand across that moving sand panel and scraped his skin as if it were a glass spiked brush. He reacted immediately by withdrawing it, taking a step back. Then he collided with something behind his back. It was at that instant that he saw Ashima with her arms raised blocking the cyclone. Her palms and forehead gave off light and her eyes were completely blackened, and her body petrified. A terrifying appearance that distressed him. He realized how stupid he had been and felt terrible for the poor girl who had just saved his life, who stood firm prostrate like a statue while draining her power, consuming her vital energy only to defend him, who unfortunately could only watch and wait, shedding tears of helplessness, feeling very ashamed, with his head between his legs.

"Suddenly he noticed that his hair stopped moving and the horrible buzzing sound disappeared as well, so he looked up. The young woman still stood before him with her arms raised, arranged like a motionless figure anchored to the sand, even though the sandstorm had disappeared, her eyes open and blackened. Quickly, he wrapped her in his arms and spoke her name, frightened, waiting for her to react, but her body began to convulse until she tilted her head sharply toward the sky. Out of nowhere a tattoo appeared engraved on her forehead and her body, already without strength, fell on the sand. The young woman was unconscious.

"In a panic, Sranik tied the carpet to his back and carried his friend in his arms for several kilometers in search of help, until it was impossible for him to continue with her on his back. So, he put the carpet on the sand and the girl on it to drag her to the citadel without harming her body, but unfortunately the night fell on them, forcing them to stop. He was going to have to put into practice what he had learned in Tunani, since it was well known that the temperatures at nighttime dropped dramatically and to continue walking would have been suicide. He remembered the exercises taught in the classes and made a hole in the sandstone, as the Tunani teachers had taught them, to hide together with the little girl. Then they covered themselves from the dust with the carpet. Then he embraced her, trying to cure her and himself of their physical distemper.

"The night was hard, but at the same time magical. They were able to appreciate through the small holes in the carpet's elaborate fabric a beautiful night sky and admire the stellar immensity that was uncovered with colorful enlarged planets and meteorites crossing the universe from side to side, which left a tracery of lines like a crazy brush on a black, pink, and purple canvas, full of various spheres and exceptionally positioned rings. This gave the appearance that the universe was wrapping them in a milky blanket. But by then Ashima's eyes were already closed, now outlined with a new tattoo that crossed her forehead and lips and reached down to her chin.

"Sranik felt a mixture of sadness and joy, so trying to ease his own pain, he began to speak to the girl describing what he was observing, explaining that Jupiter was pumping light like the beating of his heart, as a consequence of the great storms exploding in it. He then pointed to a particular star, small and green, and told her that if he could, he would give it to her. After a long conversation with the faded young woman, the boy fell asleep.

"When he awoke the next morning, the young woman was not beside him. He lifted the rug that covered him and there, curled up at the end of the hole, she was watching him. Although the scene was somewhat strange, he called her happily, but the young woman immediately silenced him by putting her finger to her lips and indicating something with her eyes. Guided by her gaze, he looked down at his feet, where a snake with three heads, one on top of the other, was lying.

"Frightened, Sranik moved his leg, and the animal opened its mouths, disengaging the jaws as one, splitting the faces vertically, and exhibited huge fangs, but Ashima nimbly caught it by the tail and threw it through the air, with the bad luck that it split into three and one of them attacked the boy. The girl ran towards the snake and killed it with one bite, but it was too late. The boy had the venom circulating in his veins. Fragments of the vision of a desert floor and a moving carpet were passing through his current feverish delirium as Ashima flew toward the citadel holding Sranik so he wouldn't fall off the cloth. She was saving his life for the second time. At last, before them, the defensive wall, built of rock-hard sand, began to open, and showed them the entrance to the first bazaar, where their master stood waiting for their arrival.

"When the young man awoke in a room full of cushions and windows he didn't recognize or remember, he was confused. The only light coming in came from small holes in the shape of signs that adorned the apertures. He smelled the incense that enveloped the room, whose aromatic fragrance seemed to soothe his pain with each breath. As he tried to get up, a soft voice asked him to remain lying down under the protection of the room, as it was still too early to make his heart pump more, because it would spread the poison further inside him. However, the young man paid no heed and collapsed.

"When he awoke again, he saw Ashima and their master meditating behind semi-transparent cloths hanging from the ceiling next to his bed.

"You were lucky you were together," said the man with the dark goatee and tattoos bordering his eyes.

"Then he got up and left them alone," Rasnar recounted.

"It was during those days of recovery that the young people swore eternal friendship and exchanged a piece of their hair, but they lost contact as soon as Sranik was sent back to Preciosas," explained Nose.

The Trip

"After remembering everything, the young woman sailed on her carpet through the zephyr until she reached her village, where she tried to contact the boy. But as she did not have the means to do so, she decided to go in person, so she took provisions and left a note for her teachers. Then, under the universal sea of midnight, she traveled on the carpet to the confines of his kingdom, crossing the immense desert. And even though she had made it practically all the way during the night, after dawn she knew from her experience as an explorer that she must take a break to hydrate herself at some point where she could find water. So, she hurried to reach her favorite oasis, one that she had not marked on her maps, so as to keep it secretly to herself, even though she was breaking one of the Tunani rules, for it was forbidden to go to these small uninhabited paradises without permission or an escort for fear of the creatures that lurked there. Ashima did not understand. She had completed much of the topography of her map using this Eden as a resting place and came to wonder if those stories told about these places were nothing more than an invention for the enjoyment of a few, as she herself had done.

"As soon as she arrived, scorched by the heat, she climbed down from her mat forgetting to check her surroundings. She crossed the dense flora of the oasis without a second glance, taking off her clothes as she ran over the trunk of a palm tree that was leaning on the shore, from where she launched herself. She remained like a starfish, floating on the water, relaxed, watching the light pierce the leaves of the trees as she felt the cool elixir lowering her body temperature. She reached out her arm, trying to draw the dry sand from a small bag that the Tunani always traveled with to her, but it didn't budge. She tried to use her powers on the wet sand at the bottom, but this had no effect either. Strangely, she looked at the tattoo on her hand and immediately remembered one of the reasons why it was forbidden to be in these places.

"According to the stories of the elders, in them they could come face to face with creatures that even the best warriors of the kingdom of Argua could not face, as the beasts used these paradisiacal islands lying in the middle of nowhere as burrows and created protective fields marking the flora that bordered the spot with their urine and nullifying the powers of anyone. Realizing that possibility, Ashima realized how foolish she had been to let her guard down in the heat, forgetting the warnings and teachings of her elders as she let herself be carried away by the impulsiveness of her actions. She had escaped the kingdom without notifying anyone of her whereabouts and had put her life at risk for a foolish memory of someone virtually unknown in a now blurred past.

"She began to swim carefully towards her belongings perched on the shore, but from among the large leaves that surrounded them emerged three strange and enormous wild cats with huge fangs protruding from their jaws, with hairless bodies like the skin of a reptile that served to camouflage them like a chameleon among the flora of the place and even adapt to the soil of the shore when they touched it with their paws.

"The young woman, already with half her body out of the water, tried to take a step back, but one of these creatures pounced on her and pushed her back into the water. There Ashima fought with all her strength to survive that attack; she managed to get behind the creature's back to concentrate all her energy on breaking the barrier that blocked her powers. Meanwhile, she held the animal's fangs mounted on her neck, hugging it tightly with her legs to suffocate it by crushing its larynx. But the physical and mental effort to which she was subjected was such that she noticed not only how her muscles were enlarged, but also how her body became really stronger, so that she could turn the feline under the water at will and wrap her arms around its neck to hang it with a loop of her thighs.

"Then the creature's movement ceased, giving Ashima a chance to come up for air, but as she looked out, a herd of gagres was circling the lagoon with their eyes on her. She realized that the creature that had attacked her earlier was nothing more than a hatchling and the ones stalking her at that instant were the adults. They were incredibly stout, with long tails that left the palm trees marked with barbs.

"The young girl tried to get out of the water with the purpose of reaching the sand outside, with which she intended to defend herself, but when her naked torso emerged, she looked at her body with fright, for she had the genitals of a man. On the verge of fainting from the shocking bodily change, the largest of the creatures approached him and licked his face. Ashima fell to his knees and lost consciousness. She then suffered a series of hallucinations about the history of her ancestors the changelings. Through it he learned how they lived with the gagres; both protected each other from other beings. After these visions of which she had never heard, the young woman saw herself as a strong and beautiful boy stranded on the sand, leaning on his fists, and stripped of his clothes at the mercy of the beasts.

"With her head still in a daze, Ashima noticed the huge animal bowing to her and urging the rest of the gagres to accept her as one of them. She was surrounded by the herd and bewildered her chest made a fist. It was then, when she brushed against the skin of one of those animals, that she activated her camouflage ability, which caused the young boy to change to his natural state, that of a girl, while the beasts encircled her.

"After this, weeks passed during which the young girl cohabited with these creatures as part of the pack; a family that helped her in her changing process by teaching her tricks to control her new power. From them she learned the skills of the shifter being as she enjoyed bating the pups by creating figures with the sand that appeared to be alive.

"But that innocent happiness ended one morning when the little ones woke Ashima up crying and wailing disconsolately in her ear. The girl realized that the other beasts remained hidden, camouflaged by the vegetation of the oasis. Then she knew that something was not right, so she went forward towards the outside, following the footsteps of the mother of the offspring, until she reached the top of a dune. From that place she distinguished her dear friend, the greatest of the creatures -the one who had given life to her transformation and had helped her by guiding her through the process of adapting to the change with such tenderness-, being dragged chaffingly along the burning sandy ground, hooked and pulled by two calimos;

monsters able to withstand the harsh desert life thanks to their huge clawed paws that dug into the sandstone, which favored the climatic adaptation of their body and gave them agility of movement on this medium, as the palm was kept away from the scorching surface of the desert.

"These animals were subdued by aggressors, not only for riding, but they also took advantage of their tongues to engage in hand-to-hand combat with creatures such as gagres, which were extremely rare to see, so their skins were worth their weight in gold. But no one would confront these sneaks because of the dark arts they practiced, especially since many influential people from other kingdoms sought their services to ask them for secret jobs. Therefore, it seemed that they were somehow protected, so their evil nature was only further unleashed by pushing the limits of the immoral.

"Ashima observed that the calimos were wounded, so her companion had fought to the last against the six men and their five creatures. She noticed that one of them was carrying on its back the hide that had been removed from the mother gagre. The anger that welled up in her was such that a light burst from within her that united with fine lines the tattoos on her body, which until now had been completely separated from each other, binding themselves together with threads of ink that descended to her belly, illuminating her entire being. Then she formed a hurricane of sand that was taking the exact shape of the downed beast. The animal galloped towards the calimos with ferocity.

"Upon seeing it, they began to flee, thinking the soul of the animal had been resurrected with a thirst for vengeance, as Ashima's rage had created a beast over which she no longer had control. The animal caught up with the poachers and tore them apart one by one despite their attempts to counterattack and defend against the Tunani's new creation.

"When the battle against the poachers was over, without leaving a single one of the hunters alive, the creature she had created approached the gagged calimos and freed them from their chains. The animals bowed and left the place running like terrified lizards, until they disappeared into the arid horizon. Meanwhile, the sandy replica of the mother gagre approached her skinned corpse to bury her there.

"The young Ashima burst into tears as she watched her friend's replication pick up the skin that had been taken from her with its jaws. After this, the girl mounted on the back of her handiwork and rode it back to the oasis, where the beast was covered with the scent of the excised and still warm skin of the mother gagre. She then deposited it on the ground next to the young, who sniffed it until they snuggled next to their replica on the still fresh skin of their mother. It was then that the young girl decided that the time had come to leave, to resume her journey to Preciosas. So, completely desolate, she said goodbye to the herd, but somewhat calmer as she left the cubs under the tutelage of the creature created in the image and likeness of their deceased mother.

"With the change that now inhabited her, she wondered how she was going to explain what had happened when they saw her new tattoo, a symbol unknown in Tunani history, something never seen before, imprinted on the dermis of her belly by her own creation. She meditated much on herself, for it was evident that she possessed the abilities of a powerful being, even if these emerged from uncontrolled impulses that took her to levels that seemed to alter the natural laws of the Tunani; a feat as extraordinary as it was fatal. She had to discover how to be a changeling, a skill for which she had not been trained or educated, so she was lost not only on her lonely path to inner balance, but to the outside. She wondered if she should tell or keep it a secret.

She was on her way to see Sranik, traumatized by everything that had happened, and she didn't know how he might react.

"Almost without realizing it, she reached the gates of Preciosas. She folded up the carpet and tossed it on her back. Then she picked up the board she carried with her and overcome with emotion, nervous and excited for the first time in a long time, she began to skateboard. She went through the interior of the citadel levitating on that kind of board she carried on her back, on which she had glued and embedded sand with a symbol that gave her the power to float on any kind of terrain that was not sandy.

"As she approached the interior of the palaces, people began to leave their establishments to watch her pass by. The news spread quickly and reached Sranik's ears, since the young woman was famous throughout the kingdoms of Argua. Then the crowd approached her. Her presence brought together individuals of all ages, until out of the crowd appeared her young friend, who removed the distance between her and the bustle to embrace her tightly.

"Welcome, Councilor," he greeted her, comforting her in his arms, not realizing how much that gesture meant to her after all she had been through.

"Ashima agreed to spend several days with him alone, catching up on everything that had happened so far in Sranik's life. She didn't mention her change or what had happened at the oasis. After a few weeks, the pals had not only reconnected as friends, but something deeper was welling up in them, feelings they could not control, knowing they would only harm them.

"At this point, the boy asked the Tunani to stay there with him, selfishly ignoring the responsibilities she had as a Councilor for her land. He convinced her by begging her to stay at least until the beginning of the games, so that they could present the idea he had been working on together. Then, when the festivities were over, they could live together anywhere.

"He'd received intelligence that advised him there was a possibility that he might win and be appointed advisor to Preciosas, which would mean living apart. However, she gave in, as the boy promised her that he didn't care, and said he would give up everything for her. As a result, Ashima disappeared for a long time, she abandoned her work, her training, and her studies for him; that is, she left her life aside with the purpose of achieving a common future and dedicated herself to watch over the boy and his dream.

"The kids began to work on the idea, combining sandstone with one of the symbols she knew. Thanks to Sranik's studies and Ashima's power and concepts, they showed themselves to be a duo in the games and stumped everyone with their contribution, which consisted of a series of aeroliths for individual use for the communication of the people of Argua. With them, everyone could receive information both from their realm and others, whether it was about the games or about any everyday thing, and this regardless of races; that is, it was not necessary to have the same power, or even have special skills to carry out the exchange of information, so any Arguan being could access it and use it.

"Of course, as expected, people cheered the duo, enthusiastically; they became the most popular couple in the Kingdom given their great contribution. So, Argua's advisors had no choice but to invite them to be part of their team, since as individuals they were of great worth, but as a team they were extraordinary. The lovers responded euphorically to the cheering crowd, kissing each other, but screams of terror caught Sranik's attention and he opened his eyes to find a huge beast galloping towards them in the area they had chosen to exhibit their contribution. And just at the edge of the no-man's-land border with the Tunani kingdom, he spotted several more creatures advancing toward them. Huge gagres running straight towards Ashima, captivated by her scent.

"The council immediately descended on the ground to control the situation before there were any casualties. But the one who stopped them was Ashima, who broke away from Sranik and ran towards the beasts, pushing the council out of her way. Then, before colliding with the ferocious animals, she changed form and prostrated herself in front of the head of the great gagre, who bowed to the changeling. And after her, all the beasts threw themselves with joy upon the now boy. They were the offspring with whom he once lived.

"Seized with happiness, Ashima turned to call out to Sranik so that he could meet the creatures, unconsciously changing her appearance to her normal state, but her partner had become transfixed. He was stunned and stared at her in astonishment. Then he was aware of the change in her body, of how others saw her. Her beloved shuddered, turned his back to her and quickly disappeared from the scene. No Man's Land fell silent under the watchful eyes of the crowd there as the gagres tried to ease the sadness they perceived from the young woman and brought their snouts close to her hands which fell dead at her sides. Then her belly lit up and exposed the engraving she had not yet shown to her people.

"It's a new symbol, where did you get it?" exclaimed a councilor as a cloud of sand rose up behind her and took the shape of the great mother gagre. She bowed her head.

"And with tears slipping from her beautiful eyes, the young woman mounted on the back of the beast and rode with her herd back to her homeland.

"Mother of beasts, mother of endurance!" the audience cheered and whistled as she rode away.

"But the Tunani councilor asked the excited audience to let her go. She put one hand to her belly and raised the other as if it were a claw as a sign of respect. From that day on, society's outlook towards changelings was not the same; a silent division begins to show itself publicly. This historical moment caused many people to position themselves on one side or the other; they felt envy and hatred towards these beings, because in a certain way they are unique, similar to the mother of beasts. This was causing problems in Argua, because after that everyone wanted to know who was a changeling. Some beings went so far as to distrust even their own relatives.

"Despite having been a hidden topic for a long time, when it could be talked about openly, for many shifters it was more difficult than carrying it in secret," Rasnar recounted.

"What I was saying is that thanks to the team that Sranik and Ashima formed, the people of Argua never again had limitations when it came to communicating with each other, whatever their species or the kingdom they came from. Using this new technique with the stones selected, processed, and carved by Sranik in the kingdom of Preciosas and then sent to the Tunani kingdom, to be mimicked by Ashima in communicative union with the use they were to be given, the Arguan society improved its quality of life," Nose summarized.

"Even though she was heartbroken, the Tunani councilor continued her work to help the people of Argua and used these rocks as accessories placed on her temples, forehead, neck, wrists and even as an anklet. In this way she was able to communicate with other species in the distance and kept abreast of information being sent across the realms.

"But Preciosas was not about to let the Tunani control the power of this prodigious costume jewelry, so they kept the mother stone in their possession under the custody of Sranik, who used it to make communiqués that were relayed by the aeroliths. In this way, he had sovereignty over media control and could manipulate society at will.

"Not content with this, he later wanted to expand this idea as a business, both at the request of the public and influential citizens and employed a system of grouped ceramics that would go unnoticed to anyone's eyes as mere body decoration, jewelry of all kinds for a specific collective of, shall we say, turbulent intentions. But for this he needed the Tunani alliance, or rather, he needed Ashima's help, and it was going to be difficult to convince her.

"Without the concepts and powers of the young woman, the gems were only energetic stones that required to be blessed to acquire the indicated use. She was in charge of giving the material the utility, and even the purpose: auditory or visual. Ashima was the only one who had the power to make it happen.

"As expected, she refused, but not because the person she loved had manipulated her to climb to the top by using her as a mere means, no; she did not give in to his demand because she knew the evil that a greedy person without empathy, like Sranik, was capable of causing among the kingdoms of Argua. But the Council of the Tunani territory eventually forced her to give in to the narcissist in order to achieve citizen freedom in the games, the progress of the kingdoms and, above all, the fight against evil. Thus, they made Ashima indispensable to the Twelve," said the Guardian.

The Kingdoms of Argua

"I understand. It's like when cell phones came here. The difference is that Grandma didn't give us one to keep in touch. We were probably the only kids without a cell phone in our whole generation," James said, somewhat resentfully.

"Yes, it's true. But the need for these devices has become a banal addiction. The important thing now is to know the powers of each of the Twelve, because although we understand the greatness of the breakthrough Ashima and Sranik achieved, we must reflect on the change they brought about in Argua. We already know some about the kingdoms and their abilities," said Sasha.

"Well, leaving aside the contribution of the stones to the progress of inter-species communication, which improved the time spent by young people while training or studying during their stay in other realms, the different territories have their own methods of communication with their people. Something they maintained so as not to lose the practice of the powers and avoid the disappearance of the gifts from our DNA, since like everything that is not exercised, it could be forgotten, and become totally erased from our system.

"Regarding the rituals and powers of each of the Twelve, we will go sector by sector, detailing in a summarized way the area and the qualities of their respective species, as well as the rituals that they uphold as an ancestral tradition, and mentioning their current leaders. So, when you are ready, you will know what you are facing and how to act. I look forward to that day and of proudly boasting of my work with you.

"We will begin with the kingdom of Hurapolis, which was among the first to use these stones. Its people do not represent a single species but are composed of mongrel beings with mixed powers from each kingdom. These have come to interfere with the public communications of other territories, forcing them to tread very carefully in the presence of a Hurapolese, for it is difficult to know what qualities they have, unless their appearance betrays the mixture of races of which their being is composed.

"Precisely because of the great diversity of mixtures in their realm, they were forced to create their own methods before the communicative stones came out, using objects, which they made manually, to have ways to facilitate the notification of messages. Above all, so that the Council's communications would reach all the people of Hurapolis. Although it is a kingdom with beings carrying an incredible variety of gifts, these did not necessarily coincide, as happened through genetics in the rest of the race kingdoms, so they did not have a natural communication system for all its citizens. We must not forget that it is a relatively new kingdom, created by beings banished from other lands, and they do not provide a traditional education.

"The means they employed were derived from advanced techniques of a very mechanical as well as magical nature. For example, when their advisor Aiixs had to send information from the sacred tree in which the members of the Council of Argua carried out their function during the games in no man's land, she resorted to a method composed of living ink like the blood of the Tajhrans, an element by which she retransmitted waves whose vibrations formed drawings and symbols that were projected on the liquid. According to the words and tones used on it, each sentence or phrase was recognized by the different means of communication of each species and kingdom, thus adapted by the territory of Hurapolis as a single language, readable by means of a coded system that they had to learn as part of their education. These were the only beings capable of deciphering it, as it was not taught to exchange students.

"As a receptive medium, they created screens, transmitters, graffiti and tattoos with the patterns of the mother source, through which they continue to receive these communications today, as they are the only ones that Zotrak cannot interfere with.

"After the territorial imprisonment of evil in the Thirteenth Kingdom, many individuals began to tattoo this liquid element under the skin, perceiving the messages through alterations in the dermis. In some cases, depending on the bearer of the tattoos, they came to have the power to reply from these designs. Those who did not boast this ability, had to pay the price for having the necessary dose of ink to be able to respond and act as a transmitter or, failing that, remain a mere receiver.

"There are also beings who inject this dye inside the skull and leave a dot in the center of the forehead, although there are also those who have it in the back of the head, almost at the nape of the neck. In this way, the recipient, either individually or collectively, not only receives the information, and feels it as the sender perceives it, but is able to clearly see certain images, as well as symbols that only they understand, to immediately visualize the situation or the mission; each with more or less ability to focus, as that goes with the mental capacity of the wearer. They can even activate, with more or less power, the faculty to absorb or dispatch according to their level of creativity and their decoding protocols.

"In contrast, tattoos drawn on the dermis in a superficial manner are the least private, since by observing the tattoo, any individual, whether the bearer or a third party who is familiar with those emblems, can perceive it and visually understand its meaning. This is the reason why wearers often wear long sleeves or other fabrics that cover the inked areas. Their people eventually develop a telltale tic, as they tend to show an obsession to constantly look at the engravings and anxiously move their clothing, like a repetitive fixation, something you already saw in the images I showed you of the secret meeting with Argua's advisors.

"I'm sure you remember Aiixs and their peculiar and insistent mannerisms. These movements make them seem like nervous beings, a condition that can try the patience of other individuals. Suka, the councilor of Cascadeld, as you could see, does not have the tolerance to deal with these pathologies so distinctive of the Hurapolese.

"As I was saying, according to the words used by the speaker, these tattoos alter, changing shape and dimension. Sometimes they rise above the skin or expand, and even minimize the area marked on the recipient's dermis, recreating various characters alternating at contrasting speeds. Depending on who and how the sender sends them and the condition of the collector, they must be hidden to reproduce rapid body movements without them trying to decipher them. For this reason, it became fashionable to implant the element inside the skull. This is a safer method, but it also has its risks, as it can interfere with one's thoughts and dreams, which, if not controlled, can have the effects of a drug and lead to insanity.

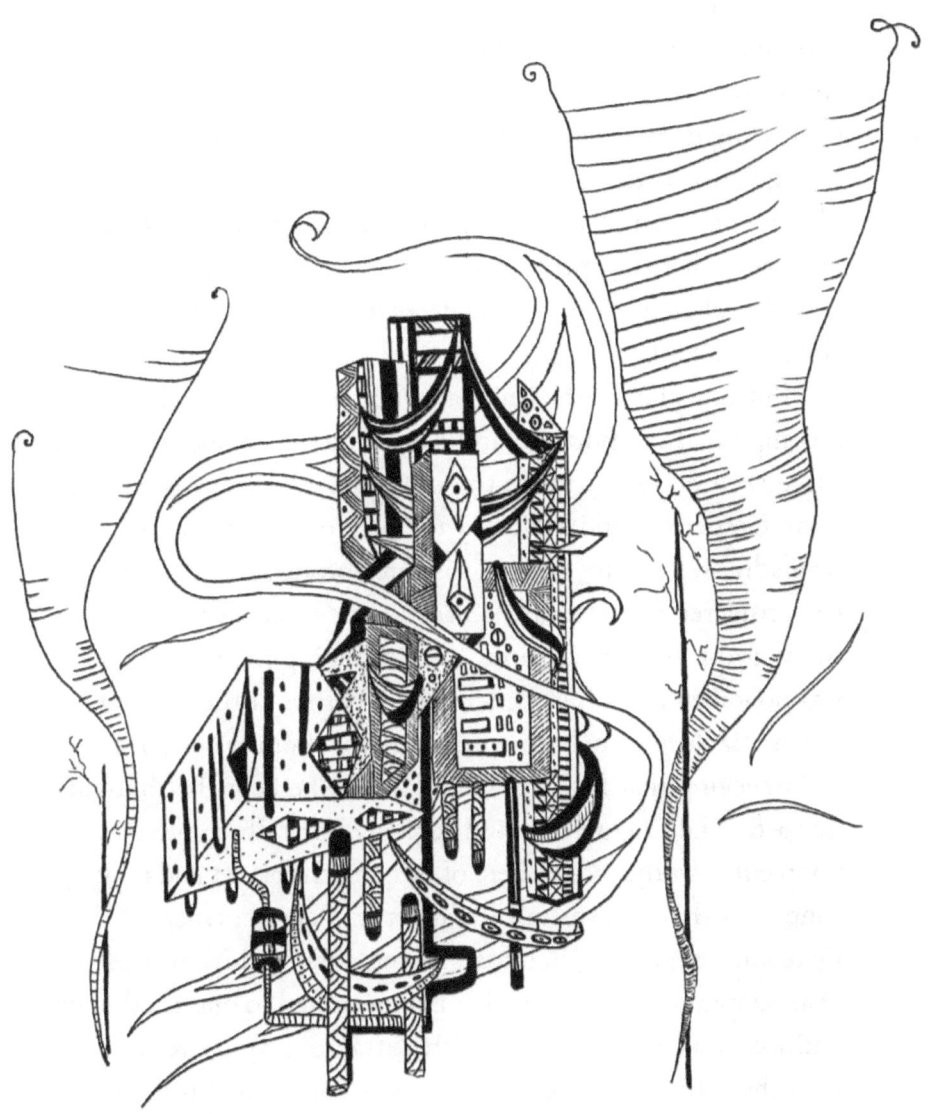

"On the other hand, the kingdom of Tajhra needs no other means than the one it naturally carries within itself, since, being a land of twins, triplets, quadruplets, etc., all are born with the innate gift of telepathy. A quality that unites them as a race through an amazing sixth sense. They are descendants of a being considered and venerated as a deity that, according to the beliefs of this kingdom, wanders through some of our galaxies. It is said that he created the Tajhrans when he was a mere nomadic explorer who, tired of wandering in solitude, chose to rest in our universe. There he spent his days studying the strategic way to align the planets, painting and decorating the cosmos like an architect or an artist.

"But once he finished his task, he felt lost. He had already accomplished his purpose and found himself alone in a huge space with no one to share the beauty of his great masterpiece with. Desperate and blinded by the pain of loneliness, absorbed by madness, the deity tore out his three-pronged tongue because he considered it useless as he had no one to converse with and threw it out into space, since by eliminating the tongue, there was no longer anything to incite those desires or the longing for the insatiable need to have someone with whom to converse.

"Believing that his grief would lessen, he kept the thoughts trapped. The tongue split and separated into three pieces and, upon entering the atmosphere of our ancient planet and making contact with what we call Tajhra, the Tajhrans emerged, like Eyíre and Fraya, who, like parts of the same seed from the fruit of an amputation, blossomed as beings united to one another or multiplied as exact replicas; with extraordinary powers, fused with the habitat and the universe because they are brothers and sons of the same being.

"When their advisor Numec officiated at some ceremony or reported a matter to the beings of his realm, he needed no object or means other than his great telepathic ability; an innate characteristic of the Tajhra realm, since the information he or any of his people receive is automatically passed between them. Fortunately, or unfortunately, they live always connected. This is the reason why individuals of this domain must always be in harmony with their environment, the ecosystem, and the beings around them, as well as at peace with themselves, otherwise there would be mass madness.

"With study and severe training of values through tough meditation, they manage to control their impulses both individually and as a group, for it is not desirable to perceive the energies and feelings of others all the time, nor those of oneself. Of course, to be able to control inner and outer dynamism, as Numec and his people do, requires great spiritual and mental fortitude. Without these faculties, the beings would enter a toxic vortex that would create irreparable damage in the worlds. The energy accumulated could destroy everything we know, since the association is not only between them, but also between the flora and fauna born of the particles of the being from whom they mutated. Therefore, they detect the aura of a being even before its birth. This ability helps them to guide the child before it is born and to help it during its growth by teaching it to channel its energy. They take into account that energy can also change with age, depending on the events and interactions in the individual's life and the way they deal with those events.

"As I told you, his people have the ability to read auras, so in his realm the unborn are classified with tasks, as are studies and trainings, since they are based on the uniqueness emanating from them. For example, indigo auras are those of the most extraordinary or, at least, the most peculiar beings; red auras always end up being the most radical; white auras are peaceful souls; blue auras are the most temperate, despite containing storms; brown auras are the bravest; yellow auras are the most energetic; pink auras are the most idealistic; and green auras are the wisest. And so on, a thousand colors as varied as unique characterize each being to perform a harmonious future among hermaphrodites.

"The study of this very special art is displayed on the walls of the teaching shrines, scattered throughout the jungle of their kingdom, where they live in harmony with nature. There they illustrate deeds of their ancestors and explain the meaning of colors in sacred and public buildings. But that is a subject for another day," explained the Guardian, somewhat wearily.

"But Rasnar, this god, is he still alive? I mean, is he our god or only theirs?" asked the young woman.

"God is the word for that which is above us; that which cannot be explained because its power and magnitude are beyond the reach of our understanding. It is also used to explain the unexplainable. And above it are beings even more powerful. What would you call them then?" said the Talan.

"I think my understanding of the world and the universe, as well as society, will never be the same for me again. I don't know whether to thank you for bringing me out of my blissful ignorance, or to feel wretched because you make me feel as tiny and insignificant as an ant," James replied crestfallen.

"Do ants seem insignificant to you? You should know that it is not size that matters. Who told you that this god you ask me about is of enormous size? Bacteria are so tiny that you cannot see them with your human eye, yet they have the power to make you sick or even kill the entire population of your earthly planet. Only simple minds assume that one's power is due to its superficial greatness, but it is even worse to accept the size of a being without ever having seen it.

"Great will be the one, who by his own means, senses, studies and verifies in person whether the information is correct or not.

One should not speak or think without verifying, or the ignorant sheep will live and die like a caged bird, in a prison that they have built for themselves, convinced that therein lies one's security and comfort," said the beast.

"Rasnar, continue to tell us about the kingdoms, please. I want to know all the details, see them, be trained in each of them and learn their methods," instructed Sasha.

"You will surely know them, since part of your training, once you reach the designated level, will be given there. That is the pretext I used to come to your planet. I devised a plan to sneak you into Argua, but only when you are ready for it.

"For the time being, I will finish by explaining to you what I can of what I know. Let's see, where did I leave off?" he asked.

"You have spoken of the means used in the games by the Shawá, of the methods of Hurapolis, of the powers of the Tajhrans. You have already told us about the kingdom of Preciosas through the story of Ashima, so we also know something about the Tunani," James said.

"Very well, then I will continue with the kingdom of Ostrevo. These deer-like beings communicate by means of a certain type of tree very specific to their area, which is scattered throughout no man's land at the request of the kingdom in order to report back. Thanks to deals made with the remaining eleven domains, these plants are located in strategic positions scattered throughout Argua, both individually and in small groups that form a grove.

"The beings that inhabit them are renowned for being soldiers capable of standing on guard for days. They are anchored by their antlers like long branches and by their legs like extensive roots, which is why they hold the same position for days until the end of their watch, perfectly mimicking, both physically and spiritually, these trees.

"But not only do they communicate through them, they also live inside the already dead trunks. They choose the largest specimens, even if they must empty their interiors to establish their communities there.

"These clumps look like three different types of plants, but belong to the same species, only its appearance changes to acclimatize to the area in which the seed from which it sprouts falls, so it grows adapting in every way to the environment in which it is. It transmits messages through the sonority of its foliage, as an alarm or call. Thus, according to the type of sound emitted, the beings of Ostrevo know immediately the type of information they are going to receive. For this reason, the acuity of their ears is recognized as exquisite. They are able to perceive the sound of flora from miles away; they receive its melody through the air and know where to go to turn on the call. They know in advance the type of information they are going to face, whether good or bad, and they manifest themselves with bellows if it is necessary to group the soldiers who are scattered all over Argua.

"Some of them pick up messages by attaching themselves to the tree trunk, using the branches as receiving antennae, which merge with the antlers, which are already a radio receiver, but only for their own species. Therefore, this ability gives them unprecedented team-building qualities. In their kingdom, they train these group techniques, recognized as unique in all of Argua, to perfection.

"The kingdom of Ostrevo is famous for its legions, from which they draw much of their economy, as they are hired by influential people and other kingdoms to effectively solve problems in other territories. And they let them be part of the local defense, as during the dark times when they were fighting against evil, when they suffered many more losses than other territories. Even so, they continued to fight with honor, like their councilor Corosso, who, despite already being old, was one of the best warriors of all our kingdoms. He was the one who communicated to his people every detail that occurred in the games. To do this, he used his extraordinary antlers, which extend from his head to the end of his spine, like a satellite system with enough power to reach all the trees in the vast regions of Argua and with the strength to recreate the message repeatedly through the forests. In this way, he manages to contact the beings of both his realm and the other eleven remaining realms.

"However, the realm of Plásegar is ruled by beings that carry flora in their genetics; that is, if a tree is capable of giving enough oxygen in a day for four people to breathe, these plant-like individuals can even be helped to breathe underwater. With faculties to heal both wounds and diseases, they can also be lethal, for they harbor the secret of restoring life and taking it away with their poisons.

"In terms of physique, despite looking like vegetables, they are neither fragile nor do they remain stoical in the face of danger as they are great climbers and swimmers. In fact, many of them dwell in this watery environment or underground. But there is an even more important quality: most of them have the power of rebirth, which gives them more courage in battle, as some of them resurface from their waste months, or even years, later. Thus, this race may seem more vulnerable in appearance, but, on the contrary, it is the most powerful, not only because of its magnificent qualities as a species, but also because it controls all the flora of the kingdoms of Argua, as it maintains a very special connection with plants and is able to understand them. For this reason, they boast an advantageous power over other domains, as they can learn everything through the vegetation, and even influence it.

"The methods of communication they use among themselves and with the rest of the beings and flora are as varied and extensive as they are complex; something overwhelming to reveal, since, as you can imagine, they are beings capable of conversing with millions of species without the study or training necessary to do so. An inexplicable ability. And they do it with the ease with which we breathe; simply because their brain and genetics are programmed to function this way. Thus, they communicate in millions of different ways for every species that may exist.

"Incredible as it may seem, their means do not enter into the Arguan training studies, as it is simply an innate ability. Even for a Talos Guardian such as myself, to enumerate their variety and not their complexity would take centuries of waiting. When the time comes, you will get to see and learn what you can of their methods in person; surely, thanks to their advisor Saluac, a relentless healer and magnificent warrior who used to use as a means of communication in Argua's games the movement of her hair to relay codes via spores to the flora of the realm, as well as to her people. It gave off a kind of scented gas that, combined with a sound that only they understand, envelops them in one environment or another, like a bubble of emotions that are perceived with images full of detailed information. They say that one can experience the most exquisite of climaxes while under one of these trances if the receiver wants to demonstrate it in order to better understand their methods.

"Because of my work as a Guardian in Argua, I asked Saluac, as the good friend that she is, to allow me to make one of those educational trips through her land, since all the members of the Council must go through it to open the mind. And with just a few moments I came to understand the workings of the universe and the existence of each of the beings that inhabit it. This helps you to understand the whole in an unparalleled and inexplicable way, it quickly opens your eyes. Then the experience remains as a memory after the trip because you are no longer able to relive it again. It only remains engraved in your being as an unforgettable experience, something that changes your life forever, something that requires inner strength and outstanding mental control.

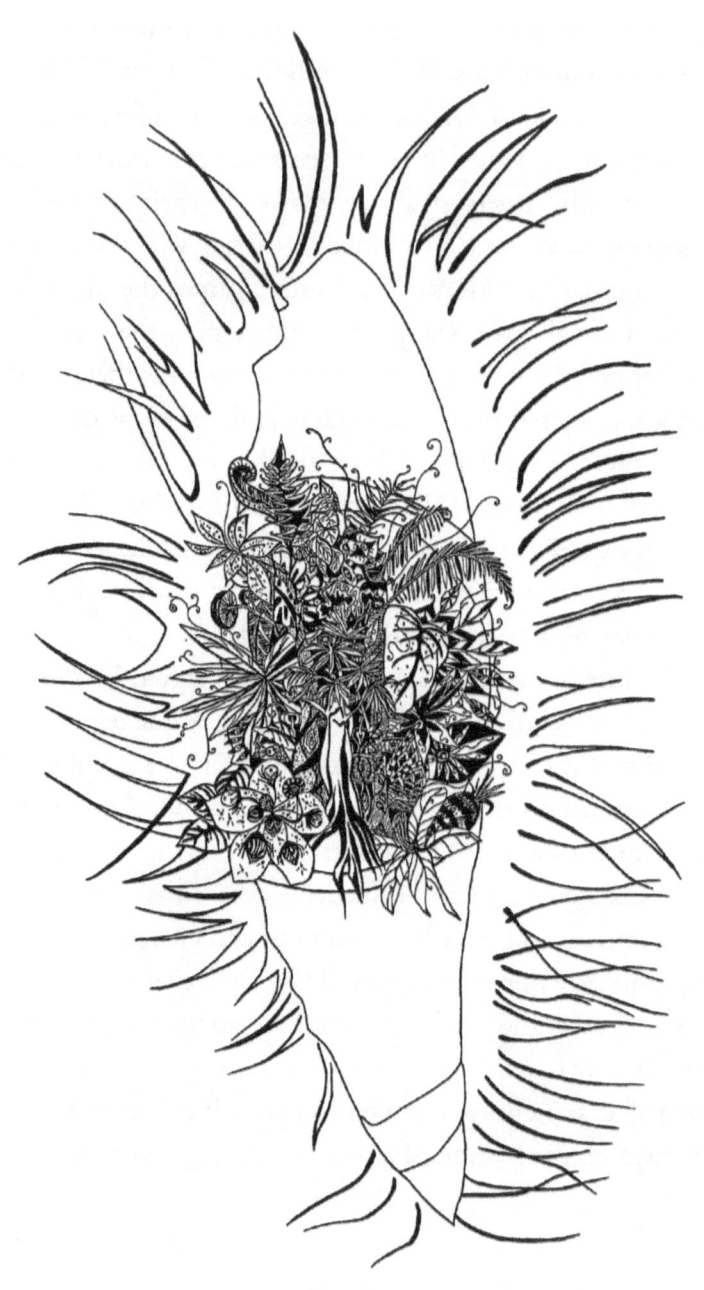

"On the other hand, the kingdom of Cryscol, a rough land of brown snow beasts, has the most prehistoric and effective method against evil. So much so that if all the energy fields were to fail and the magic and gifts of the people of Argua were to run out, this race would be the only one that would continue to communicate at a distance between kingdoms with the best functionality and speed of all. They are incredibly good at tracking, which is why this quality is one of their most requested services.

"The inhabitants of this kingdom help each other by strengthening communication as a family, they travel through the twelve domains as part of their royal training after hard training in the rocky and snowy mountains of Cryscol. There, as a test of adulthood, they learn to survive alone. They must overcome great challenges in the face of very violent adversity, but once the test is completed, they return home guided by the stars after having suffered icy storms with unpleasant encounters in which they risk their lives against fierce animals on which they must feed to survive.

"Upon their return, they are welcomed with festivity and continue their education by learning to perform as guerrillas by howling, grunting or using their body essence. They also use marks on rocks, earth, or plants, and even apply their own urine in extreme cases to leave clear messages for the receivers, which work as short codices: for us they would be comparable to one or two words, but for them it means a whole visual field. They interpret the tone and phonetics used in the shriek, as well as what is hidden in the perceived aromas that they meticulously and premeditatedly leave in specific areas. These messages go directly to the data, to the primordial question, like a numerical code or morse code, and include a very concise but sharp vocabulary.

"During the games, the councilors Carnála and Brost come out onto the balcony emitting a series of squawks. With them they report what has happened or what is about to happen and give directions on how to proceed to their people, like a great herd. And the Cryscolians respond by roaring in response.

"And to forward this information to others, they mark places or howl, as a reaffirmation of their union as a collective," Rasnar said.

"How did that pair of Cryscolian manage to become Argua's advisors?" Sasha wanted to know.

"Carnála and Brost are not a couple, they don't even come from the same litter, and what they did to get to that position is quite a long story that I will tell you when I finish explaining what you asked me to do first. One step at a time, guys," he replied.

"Don't worry, I won't forget to ask you again. I'm intrigued," the young woman commented.

"Well, changing plane, we have the Kingdom of Tepnos, famous for its knowledge based on a deep cult of silence. They are accustomed to solitude and affective distancing between them; they only relate to each other by telepathy and use telekinesis for the rest. Their councilor Wio, a prophet of superior level in these masteries, is able to channel all his energy on his third eye and with it transmit messages to as many minds as he wishes, making them hear a voice inside or introducing them in a virtual world. He is able to convince or guide his victims at will and drive them to madness. Sometimes it is enough to integrate subliminal signals in their daily lives, things or situations that seem real to the subjects, but are implanted by him, inciting his targets to proceed or give in voluntarily to the councilor's plans.

"For Tepnos, mentally sharing the perception of life, even exchanging their identity as people without making contact, is an everyday occurrence. They use their body as vessels when changing the mind, unless the subjects are changelings, as with them this method does not work. Thanks to this experience they have the possibility to complete missions, as well as to learn more about other species and the world itself.

"By law, this method must be undertaken under the responsibility and consent of the Council of Argua, and always for governmental purposes, especially when practiced by Wio, as it is considered extremely dangerous, since he could convince the masses of anything. That is why, knowing the magnitude of his power, during assemblies, and out of respect, the councilor of Tepnos always wears the third eye closed. And for moments of great caliber in no man's land, he is granted a small room in the council tree. In it he can be alone to pass on information to his people, and even, under mandate of the Council of Argua, to extract data from participants or opinions from the public, which helps to better judge the true intentions of the nominees.

He always knows where each individual stands, so when someone is in front of him, he tries to block out their thoughts and emotions. However, as much as some try to hide their truth, Wio has the ability to see behind that wall and lay them completely bare. And regardless of the background of the individual he is analyzing.

"Fortunately for us, he has a devotion to justice and honesty. In his mind the teachings of his realm take precedence, both those of the spirit and those of the mind; values ingrained by the weight of his reasonableness and wisdom. He is fully aware that power under the rule and manipulation of one alone would be Argua's undoing.

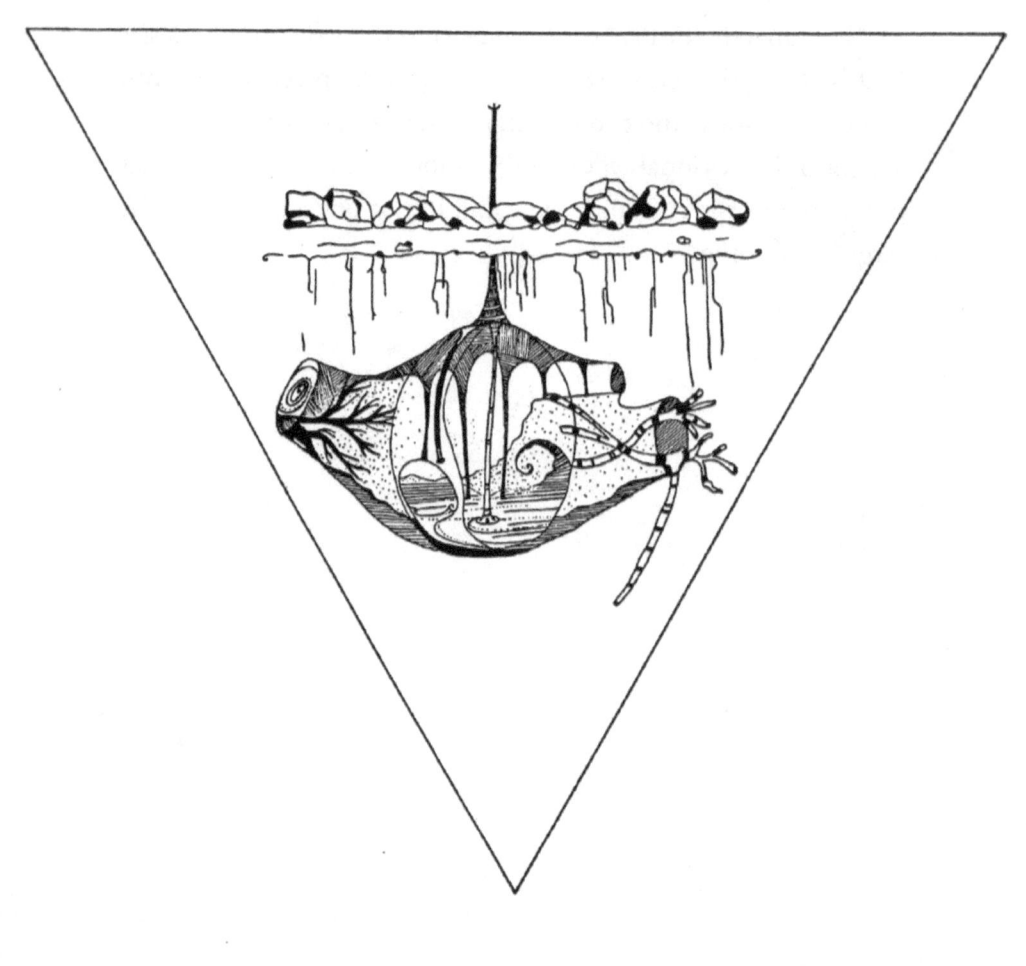

"But the greatest case of loyalty and honor in Argua is definitely in the kingdom of Firenel, the most peculiar of all territories for its distinctive use of solar energy. Its people use the heat of the earth, among many other things, to communicate with each other. This is how its counselor Nunnara broadcasts from the Games of Argua, but only to its citizens.

"The species feeds on the heat emanating from our star, but also from fire, lava and even from the heat given off by every being in this world. But do not think that they literally suck the energy off the people, they obtain it like we acquire oxygen when the heat is released from our body. Although in some cases they exploit more than we would like to give, because they use this energy to charge their batteries, that is, to strengthen their powers when they have used them excessively, something that happened a lot in the battles against evil.

"Of their entire race, only one leader is born every hundred years. When discovered, after a ritual to search, the child is treated with great care and subjected to intense testing by the masters of the Ksu volcano in the heart of this kingdom. Once it becomes clear who will be chosen to lead their lands, the infant is taken away from his family and forced to learn their most ancient teachings in a manner specific to the position. And so, he is raised for the rest of his life, under the tutelage of the Ksu masters, as they are the only ones with the power to control the sun's rays at will, as well as withstand the highest temperatures in the core of their fortress. In that place is the throne of the predestined to be leader. This seat is used as an emblem to demonstrate whether the chosen one is the true predestined one or not. If he is not, he will burn in flames and his ashes will blow in the wind. This ritual is accepted with great honor by the children and their families, as terrible as it may seem.

"Nunnara was the reincarnation of several of her ancestors and became the most powerful there has ever been in the kingdom, both as receiver and emitter of the element that sustains them all. Her gifts are of such greatness that she can set an entire kingdom on fire with a breath. She is also able to detect the presence of her subjects and individuals from other realms by means of the heat they give off, and control what they feel; she knows their exact location in a matter of seconds, even if they are in masses of people. In addition, using the connection she maintains with our star, she can even alter the nervous system of her enemies, even when it is night, because she uses the energy of the reflection of the sun in the moon, with which she lowers or increases the intensity of the vitality of the bodies that are her targets. Using this tactic, she can torture or disconcert her enemies, but she can also take their lives and make them disappear without a trace.

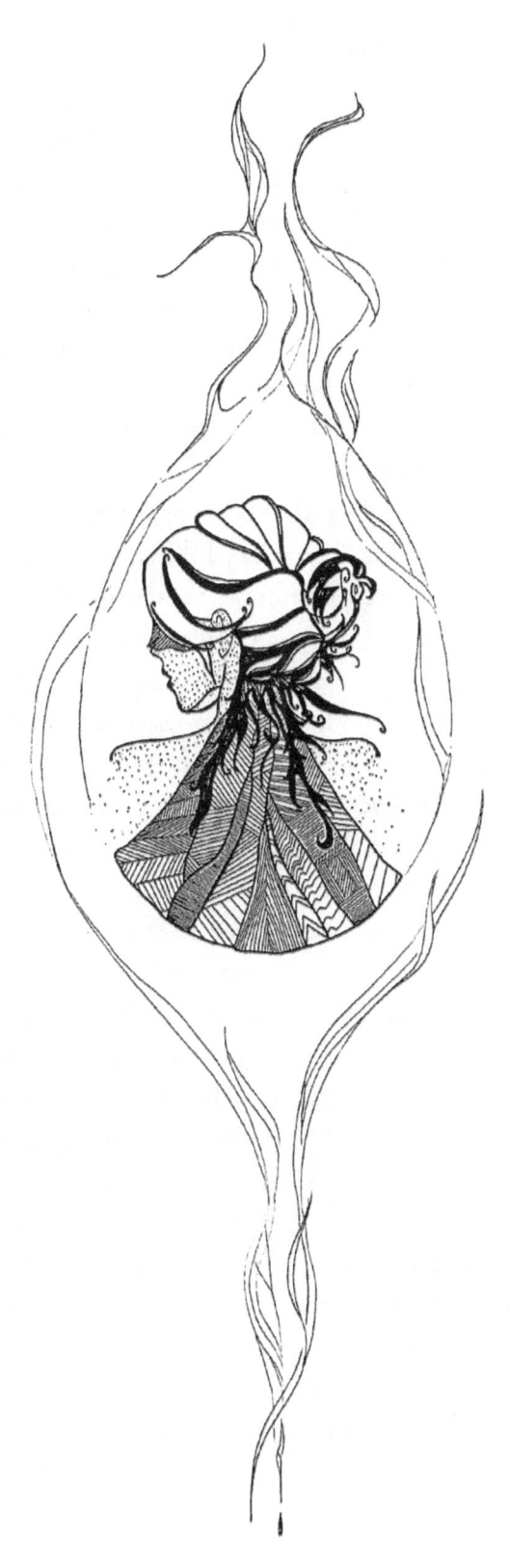

"In contrast, the inhabitants of the Picmeral realm operate by means of sonar, both on land and underwater. With it they locate their prey, beings of all kinds and even objects. They emit echoes that allow them to see clearly in the darkest of nights, whether they are in the bowels of the earth or in the deepest waters of the Margua, regardless of whether these are turbulent or unclear; no matter how many kilometers apart the targets are, they can perceive a clear image of what is in front of them regardless of the walls that separate them.

"These beings live on the shores of the Margua, in beautiful beach huts on the sea. There the children jump into the water as if it were their natural environment and can endure long periods of time under this element, an ability that makes them sublime divers and fishermen. They are also expert night hunters and develop this ability on land and in the water. But their people have a deep respect for nature, especially for wildlife. For this reason, their diet is vegetarian and they only hunt animals when absolutely necessary. When this happens, they perform a ritual of gratitude to the victim, who involuntarily gives up his soul for the survival of others. They never kill for fun; thus, their training is based on respect for the environment.

"When they are teenagers, once they have learned the tactics of their arts, at the end of their schooling, they hunt for the purpose of feeding themselves. Through this activity they learn the concept of taking a life, as from a young age they delve into survival by revering the environment and its creatures. Possibly for this reason, many do not eat any meat and feed only on algae, plants, and marine fruits from their crops, without taking into account that the flora is also alive.

"This question disturbs their councilor Innunu, one of the great leaders of these lands, the only one who can detect goals by connecting with them; notions that he tries to instill in the people so that his people can progress. However, this learning requires a lot of dedication and work.

"They also have their own method of communication, undetectable to even the most prodigious ears in the realm, soundless to any eardrum other than Picmeralis. Only the Shawás can perceive it, but only as a vibration that they identify with their language. The waves are transmitted from the front and nasal part of the skull. When they receive them, the winged mane alters and rises like a crest to better knead the perceived information. This movement alerts third parties that they are communicating with each other, even though they do not hear or understand them.

"Picmeralis don't even move their lips when conversing; undoubtedly one of the most characteristic traits of their people. Maybe that's what makes them so lethal when it comes to fishing, hunting, swimming, and gossiping, for unless they address you directly in a neutral language, they enjoy conversing with each other, making remarks about you and laughing in your face without any regard. Their faces express emotions without you knowing what they are babbling about you.

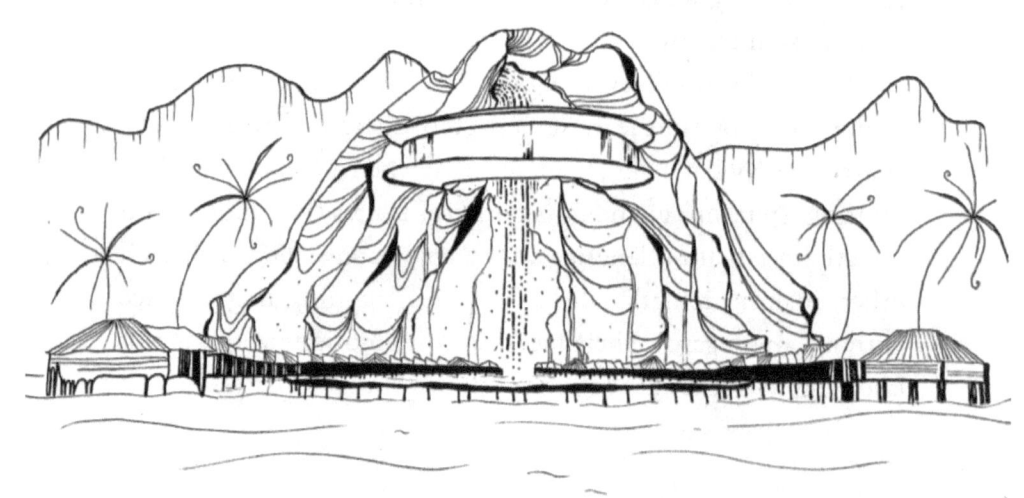

"And if you continue upstream along the river that flows into the banks of Picmeral, you will come to the kingdom of Cascadeld, the simplest of all. As such, most of its citizens use sandstones to communicate with each other, even more so than the Hurapolese, for the latter, being half-breeds, have a potpourri of gifts in their DNA that allow them access to a wide and varied system of methods.

"The Cascadelders, on the other hand, although they are a pure breed, have the unique ability to bond with birds; a method that consists in the study of both visual and verbal understanding of the famous dlirnos birds, animals with which they coexist. In fact, there is a dependence between them, and some pairs behave as a single being.

"Its citadel is protected inside a cylindrical mountain range, which hides the population between large and long rocky walls through which water cascades ascend in the opposite direction to gravity, as they are born from the core and climb furiously along its firm walls, completely perpendicular to the ground, until the raging waters reach the top. Once there, they appear as waterfalls that become aware of gravity and plummet from the top to the outside of the massive fortress. Mountains of unreachable heights that form a closed corridor where thousands of waterfalls escape from its interior.

"The citadel is protected by dlirnos that fly over its lands or keep watch clinging to the high rocks while they refresh themselves in the great torrents that fall into the void and spread out like tributaries for the prosperity of life outside the fortification. The core of the city produces the water from the rivers and lagoons of Argua; it manages them through its many branches until they flow into the Margua. This simple fact brings great value and power to the kingdom, but it also implies a great responsibility regarding the maintenance and protection of its habitat, since they are the Lords of the Sacred Spring. For this reason, they dedicate their entire lives to this purpose.

"The houses are anchored to the walls of their cylindrical mountain range. The houses hang like drops of light among the wet stone. Others are held in the air over the center of the watery marrow. And they use the dlirnos to get in and out of this place. The birds, clinging in brotherhood to the Cascadelders, communicate every event and bit of news in detail, proving to be highly intelligent animals, although their dialect is only understandable by those of their kingdom. During the games they used them to spread the information among their own. They were sent from Naruh to their kingdom. But the process of warning was somewhat slow; hence they began to use the communicative stones with more enthusiasm than the other kingdoms.

"If you noticed from the pictures I showed you of the council meeting, their master and advisor Suka had rather peculiar features: some flaps and gills. This makes him unique among his people. These are malformations that gave him the ability to fly or, rather, to glide along with the dlirnos. He also dives with them in the water, in order to observe their behavior in more detail.

"Although he is not the only malformed Cascadelder, only he had the courage to use his anomalies as an advantage to go with these birds where the rest of the citizens never dared. He lives with them; unlike the rest, who only ride on their backs. In this way he managed to gain the unanimous respect and trust of all the dlirnos of his kingdom, which gave him the power to command whatever he wanted to communicate through them to whomever and however he wanted, becoming the alpha of his flock of flyers.

"This ability gives more value and power to his kingdom; he educated both his people and the dlirnos with new techniques to make the union of both beings much stronger.

"After implementing this new legacy as part of the kingdom's compulsory education, Suka ended up having under his command flocks of dlirnos and Cascadelder soldiers ready to fight. With them he has not only applied his teachings, but those learned in other kingdoms. He has also used all this knowledge to create a tremendously effective army that does not resort to dominating its own over the flying reptiles. For respect and equality are crucial to the pact between the two sides. Likewise, he devised the writings of the famous CaDlir lifetime contract for the harmonious coexistence and prosperity of the two species.

"And finally, the most famous of all realms, a territory that belongs to each of the beings that are part of our beloved Argua: the incredible no man's land, with which we complete the twelve domains on neutral ground.

"As I mentioned earlier, the most prominent members, those on the council, would gather on the balcony of the great tree over Lake Naruh, around which the diverse specimens of Argua crowded to watch the games. In them, the aspirants of each kingdom showed their contributions for the improvement of both their land and the whole of the twelve territories. But I already told you about this and showed you images of better times, since as you well know, now the games are forbidden by the thirteenth kingdom, something that I hope we can change by joining forces.

"Well, I have fulfilled my part of the bargain with all this, and now, it's up to you to pick up the pace with the training to reach the level you need to fight against evil as soon as possible, and to be able to see the games in person as you are so eager to do. Having kept your promise, all of Argua will support you to the end and the best fighters and warriors of the Twelve Kingdoms will join you to eliminate the unmentionable once and for all," said the Talan.

"But Rasnar, we have it in our blood, in our genetics. If every time you speak of him with such contempt, I hate myself, how can the beings of Argua not be indignant about it?" said James.

"Because you will prove to them that you have nothing to do with Zotrak," Mihara interjected.

"But, grandmother, that's not true and you know it. You said yourselves that you didn't know what we were capable of," replied her grandson.

"Now we could use Numec to read our aura, you don't know how to do that, do you? Because we could really use it. So, we would know what we really are, or what we could end up being, and if it's bad...," said the young man.

"That is in your hands. We will help you in the process, but the path you take is up to you," Grandma replied.

"I wish Wio could possess us to see what we are made of. It would speed up the maturation and training process and bring out our powers or what we really are. I don't want to keep adding to my long list of failures," Sasha growled.

"When I came here, you were ignorant humans, but in a matter of days you had superpowers and an enviable understanding of the universe, and you agreed to save the lives of others without asking for anything in return. Is it just me, or is your perception of your reality distorted? Would you think the same if I told you your story as if it were someone else's?" Nose challenged.

"Life is a constant struggle; it cannot be dodged, but we have to counteract every blow it gives us in order to keep walking towards a goal. And if we fall, we should not sink or compare ourselves with those who continue to move forward. What we must do is take time to recover and get back up again, because in this life we are going to be alone, Sasha.

"Only you will pull yourself through; only you will be able to save yourself. Do you understand? The sooner you learn this, the better prepared you will be. And that goes for you too, James, although as a man, you'll have it easier. So, start changing that pessimistic attitude right away, because that is the primary training, the basis of everything to undertake any journey in this life, but especially this one. You aspire to achieve a very high goal, but you will not achieve it without your head up and your sights set on the goal, without losing sight of it. And you will not only be wasting your time, but also ours and that of the people who spent moments of their precious lives believing in you. Do you understand?" said Nose.

"Wow, man! I feel like hugging you and tackling you. That's just what I needed to hear," Sasha acknowledged.

"I think your speech has already had an effect on my sister, and if you have succeeded with her, imagine its impact on me. In fact, I'm already looking forward to training to the death. I'm worried about how long we can stay stable though. Our state of mind is what it is, so we're going to be lying to ourselves in order to end up convincing ourselves otherwise. But it's better to deceive ourselves for a positive than to dazzle ourselves with the negative, isn't it?" James reasoned.

"Exactly," confirmed Nose.

"Yes, but don't get all narcissistic and inflate your ego without humility and kindness, please. No one wants to put up with another Sranik," said the Guardian.

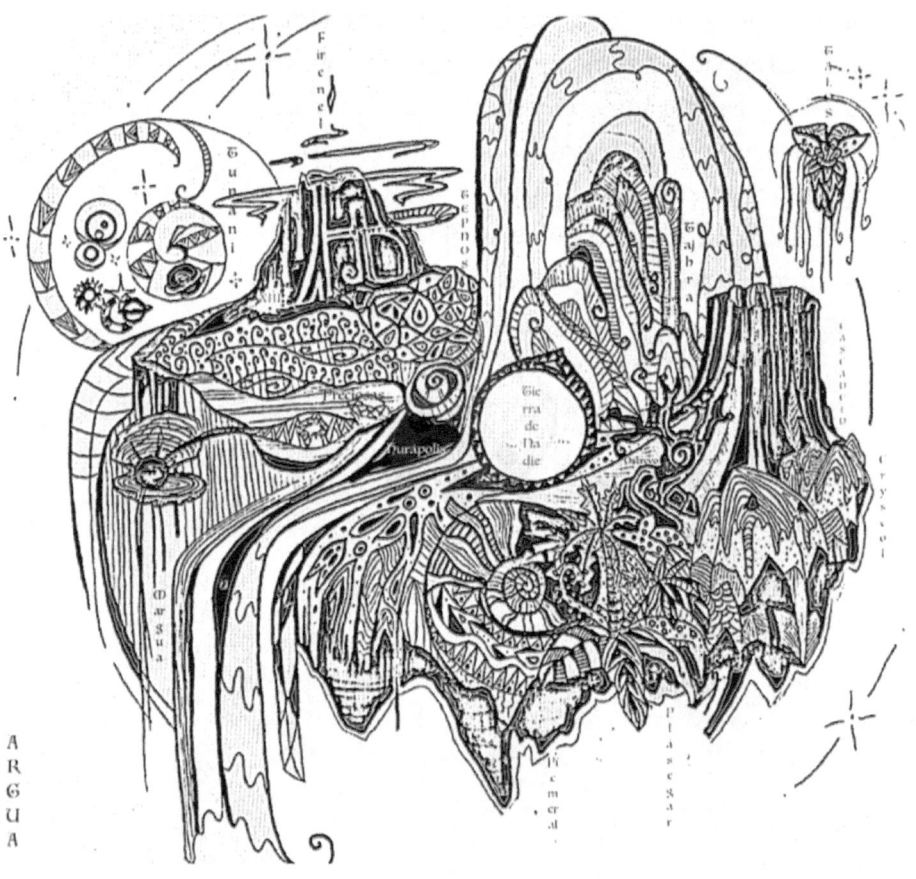

Chapter VIII
Genetics and Lineages

The teachers and students spent days in long, intense conversations, or listening to Nose's anecdotes, while taking walks around the lake, where the teens had fun in the water playing with their new skills or exploring the forest with Rasnar, who taught them about the nature of the plants. He also helped the kids awaken their connection to the surrounding flora.

Quiet afternoons of tea and cakes with Mihara were much anticipated; in a family atmosphere that favored a calmness by which meditation and inner peace tactics could be better channeled. Not only did it involve trust with their elders, but it also created emotional bonds with them and healed their emotional wounds. The next step was their acceptance of their lineage, which was shown by the revelation of authentic powers that surfaced naturally. This contributed to their empowerment and amazed their guardians with qualities never seen even in Argua.

One night, when the siblings, who were more confident and relaxed, had let their guard down, their teachers took the opportunity to enter James' room and tie him hand and foot to an anvil. After this, Rasnar took the boy and flew with him to the highest point of the sky, from where he dropped him while the young man was still asleep and unconscious. The boy felt the cool breeze of the fall accompanied by a curious sensation of indescribable lightness and gently awoke as, groggily; he gazed up at the beautiful starry sky. Drowsily, James began to realize that he was tied up and falling into the void. Quickly, he cried out for help. Then he noticed the reflection of the moon under his body in the mansion's lake and held his breath, petrified, waiting for the brutal impact. He was aware that the collision would be like hitting concrete and he would die on the spot. It would be a miracle not to perish instantly after that.

Suddenly, something strange intoxicated him and he remained calmly clinging to a past experience, blindly believing that every bad dream has its end. He remembered that nightmare he once had with Sasha. In it, after letting go of a beautiful bird, they were thrown into the void without being able to react, so the lesson was already more than learned: he had to let go without fear.

Convinced that the situation was a chimera of the same caliber, he overrode his panic and concentrated on the training he had received. He felt the water as part of his being, recreating a simulation of the wave that swept over them as children and saved their lives. In this way, he closed his eyes and put his whole being into every molecule he perceived of the element, causing it to rise like a magnet towards him seconds before impact. It slowed him down. The droplets flipped him like a puppet until they completely stopped his fall. Then he descended gently into the depths of the shady marsh.

Already anchored in the depths, he let out a breath of air as he opened his eyes. He let go of the tension caused by the effort required for such a feat and tried to free his hands so that he could swim to the surface, but it was impossible. Then he concentrated his energy again to perceive and gather the oxygen particles in the water and move them towards his face to breathe, but the first breath was not enough; he inhaled too much and swallowed water that quickly flooded his lungs. He suffered a cardiac arrest and his body remained submerged and static, anchored deep in the lake all night.

This event activated something that lay dormant, an unknown quality of his lineage; it awakened an anomalous activity in his cells, as he somehow began to infiltrate oxygen through his skin. Despite being dead, the particles of his organism were still alive and kept his heart in hibernation, alive under minimal energy, until fully charged. When he opened his eyes with the first rays of light penetrating the water, James understood that his death had awakened something extraordinary in him, a gift he had yet to master. He tried to move, but he was limp, weakened by the shortage of oxygen. So, without fear of dying again, he tried to master at once the method carried out by the Shawá s to breathe underwater, pushing both his mind and body to the limit in an attempt to survive in those conditions. At all times he remained calm in order to have total control of his subconscious.

The next morning, after waking up, Sasha went down to the kitchen where her grandmother was preparing breakfast with Nose's help. Though Rasnar was sitting quietly at the table waiting, she sensed a great tension in them. Suddenly the footsteps of someone, who seemed to have chopped feet, came into the kitchen.

"Good morning, family," greeted James, completely drenched.

The boy sat with the others at breakfast as if nothing had happened while Sasha looked at them dumbfounded, as they hadn't reacted to her brother's appearance.

"Wow, did you get burned?" James said to Rasnar as he suddenly dropped the teacup. You should be more careful; you don't want to have a nasty surprise, do you Master?" commented the boy looking at the beast with a mischievous grin on his face.

Rasnar refilled the cup again, contrite. The cup went from one extreme temperature to another and froze instantly, as if the cup were possessed. The Guardian, fascinated, turned the cup upside down and saw that the liquid had frozen inside it like ice. Then, just at that moment, it returned to its original state and spilled out onto the table, burning the beast again.

"James, when did you learn how to do all this? And why are you wet?" asked the young woman.

"Sis, you'll have to get your act together, because I've clearly moved up a level. You see, just like that. Who knows what I'll be capable of tomorrow," he boasted with his eyes fixed on the Talan, who was starting to get alert. About being wet, I just felt like having a morning bath; you know, to wake me up all of a sudden."

Rasnar looked at the water spilled on the table. It had clumped together to form the words "Thank you, assface". Then it changed quickly and showed a smiling face that immediately evaporated, leaving the Guardian stunned. He looked at James and the boy winked.

"Are you alright?" Grandma asked worriedly.

"I'm better than ever," replied the young man.

"I wasn't asking you, James; I was asking Rasnar."

The beast cleared its throat, as if something was blocking its throat and preventing it from speaking.

"Yeah, yeah, I'm just worried about the kid. He seems to have lost his way a little bit. Do you think we've gone too far?"

All three looked on in grief; unlike Sasha, who was off her game.

"I've learned to breathe underwater, sister," James confessed, softening what really happened.

"That's great, we should go to the lake so you can show us what you can do! I don't know how you managed it, brother, overnight, but I hope you'll teach me how to do it, because now I'm miles away from you and I won't be able to train with you anymore," she commented.

"Don't worry, maybe tomorrow you'll wake up and, miraculously, it has happened to you too. Or better yet, to all of us," said the young man with sarcasm and rancor.

"Okay, now the kid is really scaring me," commented the grandmother, looking at her grandson.

"I think I may end up peeing in bed tonight while I wait for him to do something to us," Nose exclaimed with a worried look on his face. Then he looked at his fellow teachers.

"My friend, I don't think anyone is going to sleep tonight," said the Guardian, watching James unblinkingly with his ears down.

The five of them prepared to go to the lake, although the only one who seemed to be excited was Sasha, who kept telling them to brighten up their faces, since they had something to celebrate, and kept commenting on how cool it would be if the same thing happened to her. James walked along crestfallen and silent. From the scene, it looked like the siblings had switched roles, which the tutors noticed cautiously, not knowing what to expect, nervously.

Arriving at the lake, they overtook the young men in horror.

"What have you done, James?" asked Nose.

"I've touched it up a bit, giving it a... retro style," he replied.

"It's been a long time since I've seen this place like this. Even my hut has been maintained, exactly as I remembered it," said Rasnar excitedly as he approached the dry meadow full of small stones and remains of what until that moment covered the bottom of the marsh, which no longer existed. James looked at his grandmother, who was silently observing the scene of the now non-existent lake. Then, dismayed, he asked her if she was all right and indicated that, after resting, he could return the water to its place, if she wished.

"I've never seen it like this, you know. The lake was created because of me the day I came here," she said wistfully.

"How did you do it, James?" asked Sasha suspiciously.

"I know it's hard to understand, but I need a few days away from the water. Do you mind training for a while in the plunge pool in the secret room until I recover? As soon as my discomfort subsides a bit, I promise I'll get back to filling in the meadow. Believe it or not, it's a piece of cake," said the young man.

"How is that possible, James? What if I can't keep up with you because of this?" said the girl.

"Don't be silly, Sasha. I can feel it inside you. You just haven't tried hard enough to bring your powers to the surface, because you don't think it's possible and you're blocking yourself," the boy replied.

Meanwhile, the Talan rolled across the plain, gazing happily at the hut that still stood, with its rusty tools scattered inside.

"Hey, am I crazy or did he say that was his shed?" said the boy.

"Yes, I heard it too, loud, and clear. Look at him, he looks like a changed man, doesn't he? As happy as a clam, behaving like any other little animal in the field. Seeing him like that makes it hard for me to regard his presence with the respect he deserves as a guard and great Guardian of Talos," Sasha confessed.

"Come on, everybody, let's go home! Anyway, no one has finished their breakfast, something I take as disrespectful, since Nose and I have worked hard to make it good and food doesn't get thrown away, got it? So, let's get going!"

"Besides, we have a lot to talk about and this isn't the best place right now," said Grandma.

"Of course, ma'am," declared the peon.

"Nose, please! You, of all people, who never eat what we cook, should be the most polite. I'm going to have to buy you an aquarium so you can eat fresh food, since it looks like my grandson just put you on a diet."

Poisoning

James whistled to Rasnar announcing that they were leaving as he rubbed his back against the grass with glee. The Guardian reacted by springing to his feet and shaking his body effusively. With a couple of jumps he caught up with the siblings, trotting jubilantly alongside them, beaming a broad smile never seen before on his face, as the tools he carried on his back, tucked between his large wings, clattered against each other.

Then Sasha stopped and asked her brother how he had done it. Then she grabbed his hand tightly to force him to slow down. But James gave her the runaround and tried to get free despite her insistence.

"James, I'm going to lose motivation with this. What you've accomplished today is incredible. Please help me," she pleaded.

"Sasha, I can't. It wasn't pleasant and I don't want you to go through the same thing," James replied.

"As you said, I'm much stronger than you. You told me so! Test me, come on!" the young woman urged.

"Please respect my decision. No is no, Sasha. If you want help, ask our great masters of cunning for it, but not me," he replied sharply.

"You mean they helped you? Why? Why did they help you and not me?" the young woman began to despair.

"It wasn't what you think, Sasha. I wouldn't consider it help; what they did was cruel," the boy pointed out.

"But how can you be so ungrateful? Have you seen what you're capable of now? Can't you see that I can't help Argua being a mere human? James, you have to help me, I've already been through the worst. Grandmother drowned me, killed me, remember? Besides, last night I had a dream about Carol. I know she's still alive, I can feel her, but something's going to her. That thing wants to get out of the book, I feel it inside me," she explained.

"You should talk to Rasnar and do it now. I don't understand why you haven't told him already. If that book is as dangerous as you say it is, it means you've let it loose in the hands of your human friend, which indicates that you're not ready to have powers or to rule Argua," he said rudely.

"Well, suddenly you think you're better than me. James lecturing me on wisdom," she said indignantly.

"No, Sasha, you're getting it all the way you want it. The craving and desire to have powers is going to your head; you just can't accept that for once I'm ahead in something," the young man blurted out mercilessly.

"That's not true! You came here first, remember? You always get your way, James, and I've been happy for you, but you don't want to cooperate. We always share everything. I've never hidden anything from you, so your attitude is cruel," she commented.

"Because you don't respect that I don't want to put you through what I went through to have these powers and you assume that your attitude towards your friend's situation is not the right one," he replied.

"You're enjoying yourself, aren't you? You just want me to humiliate myself by demeaning me, because inside you've been feeling that rage towards me for a long time. What you want is for me to beg you. Yes, that's what you want; me to beg you for your new ability so you can feel bigger and more powerful, because you have an inferiority complex," Sasha angrily protested as she pushed her brother into a tree.

James moved to the side to avoid the fight. But the siblings were so into their argument that they didn't even notice a dip and James fell roughly to the ground.

"What are you doing, Sasha? Have you gone mad?" the young man shouted.

"You're driving me crazy! All of you! I've tried to be good to you. I've tried to be patient with everyone, but I'm always sacrificing myself for others and I'm tired and fed up. You were going to leave me stranded here, to take care of everything by myself. It seems unfair to me that they give those powers to you, the coward, the traitor who was going to abandon us for some precious stones and a vague life of wealth without caring what happened to the rest of us.

"Life is never fair to me. Dad and Mom left us because of you, you know." she said.

"Shut up, Sasha! That's not true! Stop that!" But the girl rushed at him in a frenzy. James stopped her with his foot and pushed her away. "But what are you doing! This is not you! Stop it, Sasha!" In a fit of rage and blinded by senseless anger, he counterattacked, "I don't want to hurt you, Sasha, but you leave me no choice!"

To stop his sister's constant attacks, James knocked her out with a single punch to her stomach. Suddenly, Rasnar appeared with Grandma on his back and asked the boy to explain the brutality.

"What have you done, boy?" they asked in fright when they saw her moaning.

"She went crazy, and I had to stop her! I didn't mean to hurt her," the boy apologized, cowering, as Mihara swiftly climbed down from the Guardian's back to pick up her granddaughter.

"We must hurry home now, James."

The young man, on the verge of a nervous breakdown, asked if Sasha was all right or if he had seriously injured her, but the Guardian and Mihara took flight without explanation and with the young woman still unconscious.

Standing in the forest and stunned by what had happened, the boy began to levitate the drops of water on the plants around him, angrily clenching his fists as he lifted his body into the air. He tried to channel his energy by putting his whole being under meditation, keeping his eyes closed and perceiving what was around him to direct his body forward, floating over the plants in the direction of the house. By the time he reached Sasha's room, she was lying unconscious on her bed. Nose ran his hands over her body to examine the area in great detail.

"My lady, I think you should see this."

Lying with her head up and limbs outstretched, the peon held Sasha's hand and showed her grandmother the girl's fingertips, which appeared to be stained with ink. Mihara watched him quizzically. She thought her granddaughter would be writing something in secret, something that might have affected her emotionally, like a diary where she could find some clue about her current state of mind. But Nose put her granddaughter's fingerprints on her hand and the grandmother shuddered.

"With your permission, ma'am, may I remove Sasha's t-shirt?"

Mihara nodded in dismay after sensing the horror she was suffering through her palms. Then the peon moved the youngster and tilted her torso forward. Uncovering her, they stared at her back in fear. So much so that Nose let go of her and backed away from the scary cot, dropping the young girl with her back uncovered. On it was visible a huge black mark extending up and down the spine.

"What have I done to her?" James asked tearfully, overwhelmed.

"No, my dear, assaulting your sister was wrong, even if it was self-defense. But this is because of something much darker. Now help us, we must get her in without coming in contact with that thing. We don't know what it has, and it could infect us. Right now, this is not your sister. Something is taking hold of her, both Nose and I have felt it," Grandma explained.

"Mihara, we must lay her face down with her back in the air to follow her, keep track of what is consuming her to try to stop it."

After saying this, Rasnar created a protective field over Sasha's bed to keep the spread of the poison through her body slow, as they had no means to remove it and could not cure her. That method of freezing time would buy them some time. Then they left the room and left the young woman alone. Rasnar explained to the rest that they absolutely must not talk about anything in front of Sasha, as that which was dilapidating her could be linked to something evil that might be spying on them, lying in wait to know their plans and location. That's when it dawned on James that the stain was similar to the descriptions his sister had given him regarding the dreams, she had had with the book that was thrown at her during her time at boarding school. He then told the teachers the story just as Sasha had related it to him, telling them of the young girl's concern for her friend Carol.

"Sasha was very uneasy, but she was afraid to tell you in case she had opened a door to an evil being. She felt really guilty about what had happened, and especially about her best friend. Please don't blame her. She was afraid of not being accepted as part of the team, of not living up to what was expected of her because of what had happened. Possibly, that is what is blocking her from bringing out her powers."

The Guardians stood silently in thought. Mihara held her head in her hand with her elbow resting on the table as the Guardian paced back and forth, his tail whipping the furniture as he passed.

"We should split up. I'll go with James to find the girl and get that damn book back," said the Talan.

"Then Nose and I will stay at the mansion and take care of Sasha. As long as your protection field is working, we have time, but please don't take too long to come back. We don't know how long she can withstand what has been implanted in her and her soul is already at the edge of its limit," Nose said.

"I will clean and reinforce the perimeter before we leave," Rasnar replied before flying out the door to secure the manor grounds.

After this, he talked to the trees and when he finished, he turned to James and had him climb on his back. Then they set off in search of Carol.

"How are we going to find her?" asked the boy.

"With my sense of smell," replied the beast.

"How are you going to know what the girl smells like?" James was interested.

"With this," he said, pulling out of his body hair a photo showing the girl with Sasha.

"Wow, she's gorgeous," said the teenager, shocked.

"Take care, lest with all those hormones you fall and miss your date with the maiden."

Then James noticed in the background of the photo an ungraceful blonde girl.

"Hey, did you get a good smell of her? Don't get confused with this other girl, I've had enough unpleasantness for today," he replied superficially.

"I smell the person who held that picture in her hands. I can't smell the picture, you dumb ass," he scolded him, holding in his laughter.

"Yeah, yeah. I knew that. I was joking, you know, just in case. We don't have time to waste if you know what I mean."

Rasnar changed direction and descended at high speed with James clenching his jaw. He was trying to keep his composure in front of the Guardian. When he reached a park, he landed and hid behind some bushes.

"That's the one over there," said the Talan, pointing to a beautiful, terraced house with large rectangular windows and cute little steps leading up to the entrance from the road in front of the garden.

"Okay, what's the plan, do I knock on the door and stall her while you go into her room to steal her book?" asked the young man excitedly.

"That's a good idea," Rasnar replied.

So, James walked towards the house, stopped at the gate, and saw that someone was watching him from one of the windows which had the curtain slightly drawn. Still, he rang the doorbell, which rang with a sweet and very catchy little tune, so much so that it amused him, and he rang it a second time just to hear it again. But at once the locks of a second door were heard and the melody stopped. A young woman with a pierced nose angrily opened the door. She wore her short black hair shaved on one side of her head.

"If you ring once, it's enough to deafen the whole neighborhood." James looked at her and was speechless. "Are you mute? Or did you just want to annoy me with the infernal chiming that my parents make me listen to about fourteen times a day? Of course, they are never here to realize the great mistake and the terrible decision they made in choosing that tone."

"Unless you're in the mood to subdue me like in A Clockwork Orange, I don't know what your intentions are to torture me with the doorbell right now." The girl looked at him waiting for an answer, but James couldn't even breathe. "Buy yourself an mp3 player, kid." And she slammed the door in the boy's face.

Then there was a scream accompanied by the sound of breaking glass. James stupidly rang the doorbell again, though he regretted it instantly. While repeating to himself what an idiot he was, he struggled with the doors with the help of his new skills and ran up the stairs of the house until he saw Carol holding a bat. He couldn't help but stare at her ass just as she turned around. She noticed what the kid was doing and lunged at him to thrash him for being a pervert.

"Carol! Carol! Please! I'm not going to do anything to you, I was coming to save you," James exclaimed.

"What, by looking at my ass? And how do you know my name? Who are you? And who the hell is the man in my room?" she asked, about to shake him.

"Who? Is there a man in your room?" James pushed her away and tried to grab her bat, which he failed to do, so he went forward into the room to defend the girl. As he entered, he saw a man of color, rather stout and older.

"Bill? But weren't you dead? What are you, a hundred and fifty years old now?"

The young woman let out a war cry and jumped on the boy's back. He fell on the bed.

"On another occasion I would have even liked this," commented the boy, choking, his head pressed on the cot.

"That's enough!" Bill shouted with an extremely deep voice and claws coming out of his hands, his face transforming with exaltation.

"But what the hell are you?" asked the young woman, letting go of James and standing up against the wall.

"My sister was right..., although the part about you eating me alive sounded appetizing to me at the time. Well, I guess I imagined it differently," said the boy, his face red and puffy, looking at Carol.

"We just want one thing and we'll be on our way. Now we know you're safe and, apparently, you can hold your own pretty well."

"Who are you? What are you talking about?" she demanded angrily.

"I'm James Courdeil, Carol's brother. I mean Sasha's! I'm not making this up; it's just that you make me nervous," said James.

"Sasha? Is she okay? Where is she?" Carol asked concerned.

"She is very sick. We think it's because of a book that was mistakenly given to you at boarding school when you picked up your things," the boy explained.

"The book? I don't have it, I'm sorry," she answered firmly.

"We know you have it because she told us before she was knocked unconscious. She's been dreaming about you all this time, worried about you, and even kept it a secret that the book had poisoned her. She wanted us to come and rescue you from whatever had emerged from inside the tome before it was too late, and well, that's what we've come for," the young man confessed.

"Where is the book, child? We don't have time for these games. Your friend's life is in danger, do you understand?" Bill rebutted in exasperation.

"I don't have it. I buried it in the cemetery in a box. It gave me the creeps to see it, and I haven't heard from Sasha since, so after my first nightmare, I put it there, underground. It's a place where I never go, not me or anyone else... I thought it was the safest option for everyone," the young woman confessed.

"Perfect, now we have to dig up a book from the dead. Great! Absolutely fantastic! Let's go with the time counting down and you're going to make me go to pieces," James complained.

"I'm sorry. How was I supposed to know that Sasha was going to get sick, that her brother was going to burst my eardrums, and that he was going to be gutless to boot? Not to mention that he came with a mutant psychopath who was going to break into my room like a burglar!" she yelled at him.

"Okay, you're right, Carol. I think you have a lot of explaining to do when we get home, Rasnar," James chided him.

"Take us to that cemetery now," ordered the Guardian.

"Don't hold it against him, I think he's bad tempered," said James as they headed out the door to dig up the book, leaving Carol's house behind. They were on their way to the cemetery. When they arrived, Bill stopped at the gates, which were locked. He approached them and broke the chains that locked them with his hands.

"Where the hell did you get this beast?" grumbled the girl.

"Ha, ha, ha! You can't imagine how funny it is that you call him that."

The teens walked behind Bill down the driveway, stepping onto the grass of the so-called holy ground. Carol went ahead showing them the way to the place. They came to a mausoleum that had the gates locked, but the young woman pulled out a key and opened them.

"I thought you said you buried it underground," James recalled.

"That's right, but you wouldn't want me to leave it where the grave robbers might find it, would you?" So, Bill and the boy walked into that mortuary carved with sinister angels. This is our family vault; I used to hide here when I didn't want to go to polo practice."

The girl opened a wooden trapdoor behind the altar and descended the stairs. James shivered, but nevertheless tried to conceal it by walking down an aisle filled with skulls and bones piled on top of each other.

"Are all these your relatives?" James asked.

"No, they were already here when my family bought it; they were included in the package," she answered happily.

"Did you really hide here? Wasn't there a better place?"

Bill looked at James with a big smile.

"She's going to eat you alive, kid."

James gulped and tried to straighten up, puffing out his chest to play hard to get, when suddenly a short, sharp cry escaped his mouth.

"What's wrong with you?" Carol asked worriedly, focusing on his face with the light of her cell phone.

The boy reacted by leaning against the wall and appearing indifferent. He avoided touching the seeds piled on the wall.

"Nothing, girl. It's my way of expressing the thrill and adrenaline of this little adventure so much fun. Have you never heard surfers scream like that when they are exalted with excitement?" said the boy.

"Do you surf?" asked the young woman.

"Eh... no."

Bill watched him trying to hold back his laughter, but it escaped from between his lips, unlike Carol, who remained indifferent. The girl continued to make her way through the dark place. James took the opportunity to get behind the Guardian, where the girl could not see him. Then he took the opportunity to shake his head and shoulders in disgust. After a while, they came to a circular place full of skulls stuck in holes drilled in the walls up to the ceiling of the room. The girl stopped at a plot of ground in the center and pointed to it.

"This is it." Rasnar walked over and sniffed the ground. "Your colleague is a weirdo, but I think I have a certain fascination for him, although he's a bit old for me," she remarked.

"You're joking, aren't you?" James replied to the girl, who dumbfounded as she watched Bill, whose human hand transformed into a claw. Then he pulled out a box from the bowels of the place.

"That was amazing, but I'm not intimidated enough to open it and let you leave with the book without seeing Sasha first," she said, snatching the chest from Bill.

"You are the Guardian of Talos, and a mere human has stolen the tome from your hands?"

Bill looked at the boy and let out a thunderous grunt.

"And what do you want me to do, eat her?" The girl gulped. "I'm not going to hit some innocent and I can't erase her memory, because she saw the pages before us and we need that information, so tell me what you want me to do," Rasnar exclaimed.

"We'll take her," said the young man.

"We can't do that, James," the beast replied.

"Why not? We need someone on the ground, and she's reliable; there's no need to train her, and she won't attract attention, since as a human she goes completely unnoticed. That is, no one would ever suspect her. She's perfect, don't you see?" replied the teenager.

"We'll take her to your grandmother and see what she thinks about the whole thing. If necessary, we'll completely erase her memory after we find out what she knows, before returning her back to her world," commented the Guardian.

"Did you really mean that?"

James was so perplexed that he was unable to respond to the young woman. Besides, remaining silent or, rather, stoic in the face of the girl's distress gave him a certain advantage. He had already made a fool of himself. So, he looked at her and walked past her, playing the badass as he motioned with his head for her to follow him to the exit. When they reached the outside of the tomb they hid behind a large funeral sculpture. Then Bill transformed into Rasnar. He then motioned for the pair to climb onto his back. To their surprise, Carol reacted by stroking the beast's hair, which made James start to get jealous. So, he instinctively grabbed her and put her on top of the Guardian. He then forced the young girl to stick to him during take-off.

The Talan was laughing inside as he watched the way James held Carol's hands against his body. She was staring at the scenery beneath her feet and was indifferent to his physical contact. Shortly after, they finally caught sight of the large mansion covered with thick and vast flora. James thought that it would fascinate the teenager, since from the sky it looked like a jungle, but since she was a human, she saw nothing but a vast desolate land and could not make sense of what the boy was saying to try to impress her.

But the boy's disgust quickly passed when he saw the sad image of a deserted field where before there was a lake full of stars, in which he had admired the moon reflected like a mirror. Fortunately, that image and the dazed thoughts did not last long. When they landed in front of the main gate, Mihara appeared with the gem embedded in her forehead.

"Who is that girl?" asked Carol.

"Can we make the effect of the human spell not affect her?"

Rasnar accepted the proposal with a simple snap of the fingers and immediately the young woman began to freak out at the surroundings, struck by the extraordinary variety of flora that surrounded her.

"By the way, that's my grandmother.

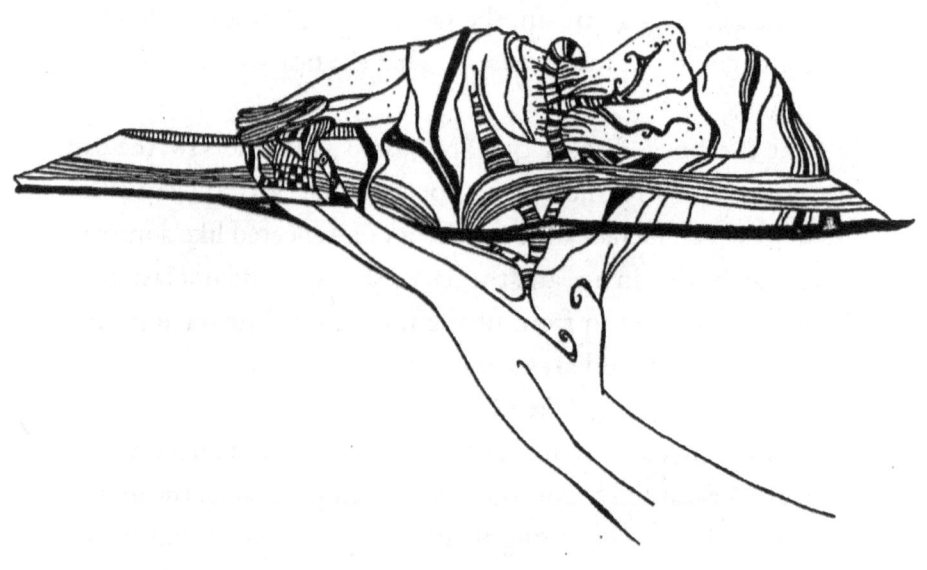

The Appearance

"Welcome Carol, how are you feeling, little one? I know you must have been going through a lot of emotions today, but I'm sorry, we don't have time to waste. My granddaughter's life hangs in the balance, and we need your help to tie up loose ends," Grandma reported.

"Her granddaughter?" repeated the girl, perplexed by the porcelain face of the pale Mihara.

The four of them went up to Sasha's room. The young girl was lying with her back covered by the stain. When Carol saw her, she rushed to the bed, but James restrained her and explained that she mustn't touch her. It was then that the box containing the book began to move and escaped from the Guardian's arm and fell to the floor, where it crawled in the direction of the fainting girl. Quickly, Mihara stopped it with her bare foot while Nose helped her by holding the trunk tightly.

"We need to get this thing into the living room. Carol, do you mind staying here to watch Sasha, without touching her, until we come back upstairs?"

The girl nodded and sat in a chair next to the bed as she watched the stain spread across her friend's back.

"I'm here, Sasha, and I won't move until you wake up, just like old times, sleepyhead."

As soon as the others reached the secret room, after climbing down the chimney hole, they placed the box in the center of the room and squatted around it. Then they carefully opened the lid and noticed inside a book with a blue cover and an enigmatic title.

"They disappear as quickly with the waves as they appear with a few drops," read James as he reached for the manual to check if the object was alive.

"James, please, we've had enough unpleasantness," Grandma scolded him.

"Grandmother, it is better for me to fall than for you to be once again prostrated in a chrysalis. At least then we'll know what happens if we touch it," said the young man.

"My dear grandson, if it were so, your sister would not be as she is, don't you think? Now, please, leave it to us. If you want to help us, bring us a pan of water from the pool."

Rasnar lifted the tome in the air without touching it and studied it in detail inside and out. He analyzed its cover and the pages, which were blank. Meanwhile, James placed a bowl of water next to his grandmother. She guided a drop through the air onto the pages of the book, but when it hit the pages, nothing happened; not a trace of ink appeared on the paper.

"My lady, I think I should be the one to put my finger on the book, as a precaution," said the Shawá.

"Nose is right," said Rasnar, watching with intrigue.

Mihara nodded and let the peon dip his finger and then rest it on the book, to no avail.

"I don't understand. Sasha explained to me what he did and the words on the cover make it clear. And without further ado, he sucked his finger and placed it on the blank sheet of paper. Immediately, a spot appeared, which darkened and expanded to form a cross. What does this mean, religion? It doesn't make sense..." the boy hesitated.

"Let's think, it could be a cross or an X. What else could it mean? Why? More?" replied Rasnar.

"More. Maybe he is asking for more water."

The boy reached into the container and dropped the water on the cross marked on the page. The liquid began to stain black, forming a new drawing. When it finished reordering itself, everyone was perplexed by the clear image of them sitting in the room surrounding the book, as if they were watching and portraying them live. The boy then turned the page and poured water on the next one. On it appeared something very different: a bound and gagged man with bubbles coming out of his mouth.

"It is Aztrack at the time of his death."

Mihara shuddered.

They repeated the procedure on another sheet, and this one showed turtles on the outside of the Shwanír Fortress. They had light coral embedded in their shells and were dragging Aztrack's body. The man had his hands tied behind his back and appeared unconscious. Grandma lost control and used her own hand to wet another blank piece of paper. It absorbed the water from her palm without a trace. After a few minutes, during which Mihara remained petrified, it showed a bit of ink, but this time it did not form a drawing, but letters: "Mihara?

"Don't answer, my lady. It may be a trap. It seems to detect only your essence; obviously, this text is designed to find it," Nose explained.

"Everyone thinks Mihara may still be alive, but no one knows for sure, let alone that she may have Aztrack offspring," said Rasnar.

"What do we do now? The drawing showed all of us sitting here, so now you know who we are and where we are," said James.

"If so, don't you think I would have deduced by now that your grandmother was here? Not only by detecting her essence, but by showing her image in the first painting drawn in the book. I think those images are just a reflection, but don't worry, all magic has a back door. That's why you must study and train, to use those flaws as an advantage."

As they debated, the letters disappeared and left the sheet blank again. Without thinking and fueled by anxiety, Mihara repeated the maneuver and a new message appeared on its surface: "Miha?".

Grandma's eyes misted over with tears, for that is what her beloved Aztrack once called her.

"Who are you? What do you want?" asked the Shawá in fear. But this time they were answered with a drawing of a forest in which there was a kind of den from which a man's arm was sticking out, with ropes hanging from his wrist as if he had been untied. Where are you, my beloved? Did you survive? Did they free you? Did they hide you to protect you or reprimand you?" Grandma questioned in dismay.

"Do you think it's a trap?" asked the peon, observing that the paper showed a huge forest and under it the word "lost".

"Is he lost in the woods?" James asked, trying to make sense of it.

"The lost forest... An unknown place where only exiles, deserters, vermin, and murderers dwell," replied Nose.

"What are you doing there?" Then some letters appeared forming the word "waiting for you".

"Ask him how he got there and who he's with, because I don't think the sea turtle could get him there, could it?"

But the book kept showing words as if Aztrack was addressing directly or, rather, only Mihara: "Come", "I beg you", "I have waited all this time only for you..., for us, my love".

"Ask it again," the boy challenged, but his grandmother was broken. The feelings she had fought so hard against and had struggled so hard to bury in order to survive that fateful trauma had resurfaced in her and still seemed to be present.

"Mihara, Mihara. This is what they want, don't let them win. We don't know if it's him, but we know it's black magic, and Aztrack would never join evil, don't you see?" Rasnar explained, holding her in his hairy arms with huge claws.

Seeing his grandmother's condition, James decided to close the book. Then he was horrified by the reaction of his grandmother, who fainted after letting out a shuddering scream. Immediately, the Guardian grabbed the woman and tucked her in with his wings while trying to wake her up, but Grandma had a blank stare, as if that had made her go crazy. So, they took her up to her room and Nose covered her with a blanket. Then he sat down next to her, checking her mental state with his hand, while James cuddled up to her on the bed.

"I'm here, Grandma. Everything is going to be all right."

Rasnar closed the door to the room and set about lighting the fire, as night had come, drastically lowering the temperatures.

The situation was not good; with the two women of the family catatonic and James despondent, Rasnar had to meditate, so he asked Nose to examine Sasha's condition to see how to proceed while he kept an eye on Mihara. The peon went to the young woman's room. There everything they had built to protect her had collapsed and the mark on the girl's back was even bigger than before. Maybe they had not done the right thing, since it was possible that they had been paying attention to the wrong thing. He pondered on the possibility of having been wrong about Sasha's ailment, of having failed the girl by wasting time with that damned book that had made Mihara sick; they had behaved tremendously irresponsible leaving the poor girl alone with an unknown human who was asleep on the armchair at the side of the bed where Sasha was lying.

"Sorry, young Carol, I didn't mean to startle you," the peon apologized, waking her up.

"Why do you talk as if you were ancient?" she queried.

"I may look young, but my manners are comparable to my age. I'm sure you would prefer that I call you buddy, as youths speak to each other, but, frankly, it is not in my nature to call a beautiful lady like you by that vulgar title. Young James, on the other hand, has all that and more to offer you," Nose replied.

"But where did you come from? Because you're clearly not from this planet," said Carol.

"Are you saying that because of my countenance or my manners?" replied the peon.

"Both, no doubt about it," Carol said flirtatiously as the Shawá looked at her, smiling and standing before her.

"Excuse me, my name is Nose. I believe in your human protocol you shake hands, right?" he explained, extending his arm cordially.

"No, man, no. My grandparents were Spanish, so my genes are programmed to give two kisses: on the cheeks, easy. You know, don't lose your roots!" she exclaimed with a silly laugh.

"Oh, I see, I beg your pardon, Carol. I am not familiar with all the customs of your world, much less have I ever been able to engage in conversation with a human female other than Sasha. Before I met her, I was always kept aloof from females.

"Again, I beg your pardon for my ignorance. My life before I met you was entirely centered on deep study and training as a Shawá warrior, so those are the only arts I know." Carol gaped, head cocked to one side, mouth stupidly ajar. "Are you alright?" the peon asked worriedly.

"Hmm? Yes, yes. Yes, you definitely need to practice this ritual. You know, where you go, do as you please," she said, getting up and bringing his face close to the Shawá 's.

He answered dodgingly with his eyes fixed on Sasha.

"Excuse me, young Carol. Your conversation is most interesting, and I would be more than happy to sit by the living room fire to learn more about the subject," he replied as he placed his hands inches from the sick young woman's forehead.

"Fire?" asked Carol.

"Yes, it's a favorite place for humans to talk, as I've found out from the Sasha and James, isn't it?" Nose replied, referring to the long meetings with his new family on planet Earth. He didn't realize the connotation of saying that to a young teenager with raging hormones, focused as he was on checking Sasha's body temperature, oblivious to the effect of his words on Carol's mind. Carol sat back down, completely numb.

"Are you a doctor too?" Carol wanted to know, melting in her chair.

"We studied some healing arts to apply on our missions or after training, but I wouldn't consider myself an expert in the field," he replied.

"Missions? As a secret agent?" she asked, intrigued.

"Excuse me, Carol, I'm going to need your help."

Without questioning him, she flung herself at the bed and settled next to him.

"Tell me what to do," she said.

"I need you to hold Miss Sasha, so she stays seated." Then Nose ran his fingers up and down her spine, pressing up and down repeatedly, causing the stain to shift and focus on the spinal cord to improve the flow of the ink. I must channel the energy that has accumulated in her back to flow into the correct channel. You see, your friend has extraordinary powers, but she cannot control them, because until now she has had them dormant and did not know of their existence.

"I think the two contributing factors have been both the lack of knowledge, as humans are skeptical about having powers and other things that Sasha has had a hard time accepting, and the emotional factor. Disregarding her lack of self-esteem, knowing that her mind was not ready, has contributed to the increase in her internal blockage, which is now so severe. Surely, she has collapsed by forcing the machinery to carry a load she was not prepared for, and a poison has been activated within her that is spreading uncontrollably through her body, consuming her from within and confusing her clairvoyance with negative emotions that do not really exist.

"I think something that seemed serious to us is as simple as mismanagement of the energy around her, such as her internal energy. It sounds silly, but it could kill her and everyone else," Nose explained.

"Oh yes, I get something like that a lot, but I manage to control it for about a week a month. Well, I've been trying to control it my whole life, really, but no one gives women credit for it; it's kind of a taboo subject," the young woman replied.

"Do you have a gift too?" the peon asked.

"Oh yes, all women have it, some more, some less... But basically, it's the same for all of us. It's hard to repress it, plus it's quite painful; a ritual we all deal with, but hey, it's not the only thing we have to deal with," Carol replied.

"Curious... Most curious... I might be interested in studying that subject. I had no idea of its existence in humans," he said.

"Well, you'd be the only man on planet Earth who would want to do something like that," she commented.

"Well, I'm not from this planet, young Carol."

Suddenly, Sasha reacted by shuddering and let out a huge gasp of air. Then she opened her eyes, which were now dark, without the usual white, completely veiled in a navy blue that frightened her friend away.

"It's all right, Carol. It is reacting to the rubbing, taming its will, and taking shape. Relax, Sasha, it's going to be okay. You've been asleep, fighting with your own gift, but now you must relax and stop fighting it; try to accept it and not be afraid of it. Everything that comes will be good." Sasha closed her eyes and dropped her head, which Carol quickly held as

Nose laid her back on her bed. I'll stay with her tonight. You can go take a relaxing bath and rest. There are many rooms in this house: choose any one of them to sleep in for the days you are with us."

"For now, you're part of our little team, so don't worry and do as you see fit with confidence," quoted the peon.

"Don't worry, Nose. I'd rather stay here with you and Sasha. She's practically the only family I have. Besides, you're very nice company to spend the evening with."

The peculiar family they had created ended up falling asleep after hours, and even sleepy, they were still taking care of each other, so Nose was not surprised when he opened his eyes the next morning with Carol cuddled up to him. The two were sitting on the floor next to the bed. Rasnar, on the other hand, awoke to the image of James and Mihara in the same position he left them in the night before on the bed.

What did surprise them was the alertness of the peon when he burst onto the scene reporting that Sasha had vanished. Carol, who appeared behind him in Grandma's room, also confirmed it, something that made young James, who did not want to be seen cuddling with his grandmother, jump out of bed.

"Good morning, Carol!" he said with a smile from ear to ear.

"But what's good about the morning? Your sister has disappeared!" exclaimed the girl.

"Relax, Carol. She's in the kitchen, I can smell her downstairs, though... something has changed," said Rasnar making the young woman run to find her friend. She went out the door followed by Nose.

"Thank you, James. Without you..." said Grandma when she had her grandson alone.

"Don't thank me, Grandma; we are family, that's what we are for, through thick and thin, always," said the boy hugging her.

"I'm sorry I wasn't there for you. I did what I had to do when things got complicated; it wasn't up to me, you understand, right?" Mihara apologized with tears in her eyes.

"What do you mean, Grandma?" James asked.

"Do you remember Bill?" his grandmother commented.

"Oh, yes, that's what I wanted to talk to you about," he replied.

"That he was here with your great-grandmother, before I arrived, and that he continues her stay with us during my exile and up to now... doesn't it seem suspicious to you?" Mihara prompted.

"It's true. I thought he was retired or dead. I don't know, Rasnar never told us how he knew the great-grandmother. I mean the one hundred percent human, and that must have been before he knew you would be expelled to these lands. I just honestly didn't get to link him with... the hunk of a man that Bill is. Knowing that they are the same individual makes my hair stand on end."

"How does he do it? Is it part of being a Talan? How did he know you would fall from the sky right here? I have too many questions to answer, Grandma."

Then Carol appeared through the door, cutting off the young man's moment with his grandmother. She warned that Sasha was no longer in the kitchen, but that she had left breakfast on the table with a message. Grandma immediately got out of bed to watch Rasnar and the peon from the window as they went into the forest.

"We should go to the area where the lake was right now, James," said Mihara.

When they reached the meadow, they wondered if the girl had lost her mind after what had happened. Nose explained to them the procedure he had used the night before to help her and both Rasnar and Mihara agreed that it should have helped her, so if she had disappeared after making them the snack it was for a different reason. Even if it was strange not to see the young woman anywhere, they felt her so close to them...

The plain still looked the same after the events of James' agonizing surprise training: an esplanade full of long, flattened grasses. But then Nose looked up at the sky and swallowed.

"Guys, look!"

And there was Sasha, floating above them as if nothing had happened.

"James! I know how you did it! You evaporated the water, didn't you? You changed your body temperature and concentrated on each water molecule! Then one by one they volatilized. I'm going to give us back the lake so we can continue training. I'll change it from vaporous to liquid again, what do you think?" After saying this, the girl gathered a huge cloud that descended to the ground like fog, leaving the ground wet. Then the girl descended from the sky and landed next to her new family. How did you sleep? Let's have breakfast while this thing finishes filling up."

And without further ado, the teenager turned and headed for the mansion quietly, leaving the others so stunned that they were slow to react to follow her home. But at once Sasha stopped and stepped back to grab Carol's arm. Carol was completely stunned.

"I'm sorry, Carol, for not telling you anything. I was very worried about you, but I was really looking forward to seeing you and telling you everything. But I was a little bit scared not knowing how you would react.

"Come, I want to show you something. Put your feet on mine, quick." Not knowing what to say, her friend did as she was told while they held hands. Then Sasha asked her if she was ready and asked her not to let go. Then she began to soar, carrying her friend with her, and circled in the air until she passed the treetops, where she stopped. "I want you to know what I felt."

At that instant, she put her hand on her friend's forehead and Carol felt as if she was transmitting information through her mind; she felt a kind of coldness run through her body. Suddenly, Sasha let go. She was miles above the ground, and she dropped her, ignoring her friend's screams as she plummeted downward, until she slowed her fall by controlling her movements in the air. Sasha stuck her head upside down in front of her face, her hair falling from gravity, her body tilted towards the ground and a big smile on her face.

"What the hell did you do to me? It's amazing! I'm going to kill you, I almost had a heart attack!" said Carol euphoric, ecstatic for the moment.

While the girls were having fun, the rest of the ensemble sighed in relief. It looked like things were looking good. Sasha had caught up to James with new powers and seemed to be fully recovered. Rasnar had gotten his tools before the meadow became a lake again. Carol was safe and now they had a human ally they could trust, with the bonus that they could pass powers to her, so she wouldn't be entirely vulnerable. And Grandma seemed to have gotten over the shock she had suffered the night before, even though the issue with Aztrack was still a sore subject.

Everything was beginning to harmonize toward a prosperous equilibrium. Even Nose, the least optimistic, was happy that everything had turned out well. Now they had to focus on getting their strength back by having breakfast to celebrate the new energetic addition to the family. Then they would decipher certain enigmas that had been left up in the air, such as Bill's identity, which continued to disturb James' mind, since he was the only one who had seen the Guardian's transformation without receiving any explanation for it. Apart from that, they had to tie up the loose end about where the mysterious book came from, find out who sent it and for what purpose.

Upon arriving at the house, after filling their stomachs with Sasha's snack, the team sat down to chat. James took the opportunity to help Mihara as soon as she got up to make more tea and resume the pending conversation between them.

"Grandma, what you said upstairs this morning, does that mean we shouldn't trust Rasnar?" asked the boy.

"My dear grandson, you must trust no one but yourself. Go by your instinct, do you understand me? One should not trust even one's relatives, because if I have learned anything, it is that family is demonstrated day by day; only time will reveal it to you," said Grandma.

"So, you were warning me?"

Grandma picked up the boy and carried him out of the kitchen, to the garden in front of the forest. She let the others have breakfast inside the house.

"Son, the only thing I have tried to tell you is that in this life there are things that just happen because they were meant to be. It is part of the maturation process: the understanding and acceptance of our past is part of our evolution. How we react to adversity is what will determine our destiny.

"You can have all this that you see before you and feel lucky or miserable. That is for you alone to decide. Whatever comes, whether good or bad, is for our good, even if sometimes things happen that are beyond our understanding. Even the most incomprehensible things happen because of something far greater than ourselves; events so colossal that the intellect could not comprehend even after a lifetime of working at it. And these events encompass even the moments that one considers the most insignificant.

"Nothing is casual, it never was. Like Rasnar's arrival in our lives. Had it not been many of us would possibly not be here now.

Those who manage the future with the planets and with life in general must make very hard decisions.

"What I am trying to say, my dear, is that knowing this should not make you lose motivation, but that you have to accept it as part of the workings of what we consider our reality. Let go of the past when you have learned the lessons it has taught us and will continue to teach us throughout the rest of our lives, and never stop walking where that inner whisper dictates. Suffering is part of life, it reminds us that we are alive, my dear," Mihara confessed.

"Did you just call me, dear?" James interrupted.

"She means me," replied his sister, standing behind him.

"I say this to Sasha because being a woman, I want her to be prepared, with the strength and knowledge to be able to defend herself from the harsh reality that our sex lives within all worlds. If you can understand this, without anger blinding you or pain overriding you, you will be able to move forward. Do not let what others are lewdly plotting take away your essence; remain alert to the signs that appear along the way, because sometimes it is not the goal that reveals the destination, but what you find along the way.

"Always keep in mind that no matter how many obstacles are put in your way, you should not slow down, as it is part of the formation of your being and guides you in the right direction," Mihara continued.

"It's the small gestures to each other that collectively change the world," Sasha said, taking them by the hand.

"Never give up, because miracles happen if people don't give up, for they break down unbreakable walls," said Grandma, reaffirming that he who knows how to stand alone is stronger. Forget about predicting what is to come, for no one knows and no one ever will; focus on building your now," said Mihara. "The greatest wonders are yet to come, but everything has a price in this life: you must be prepared for anything, for no one's journey ends until they die. And no one knows when that will be."

"But know that once we disappear, other mysteries will haunt us from the other side, when we are energy merged with the cosmos. So being honest, what we have is what you see, so we must do what we can with the present, as I did when I met Betty, the love of my life. Our existence is very short, so be clear about what you want and go for it with intense passion," said Rasnar making himself visible.

"Betty?" asked Sasha.

"Yes, it turns out that Rasnar is also old Bill. Go figure," James explained.

"She was my everything and, although our paths have parted, she will always be with me and I with her," commented the Guardian with sadness in his eyes.

"And I will always be with you in one way or another, my little ones. The love that you had and have, the love that appears and disappears, even your own affection, all this should make you strong, to continue fighting to maintain a firm footprint in the face of life. Believe it or not, if anyone dictates what you can or cannot do with it, it will be you yourselves with the attitude you adopt before the events that arise in this life," said Mihara.

"Do not let fears or feelings block you and interfere with your judgment, because if you do not free yourself from ghosts, you will make bad decisions, stumble all the time and blame others or yourself without improving."

"If you cannot show your face, accepting your mistakes as well as those of others, being able to see the big picture, you will project your own failure. It's like when you think you're going to lose what you have. Then you end up thinking you were right once what you wanted so badly dissipates, because according to you, you had predicted it, without being aware that you yourself caused the loss of what you were so afraid of losing," said Nose, contributing as a mentor to the siblings.

James, tired of the intensity of the conversation in which everyone had taken sides, went inside the mansion, pondering the possibility that they had intentionally provoked his feelings for Carol. If somehow it was all scripted, it was no coincidence. In that instant he decided to deny himself those emotions, contradicting his desires to see where following the opposite path to the one supposedly already dictated would lead him.

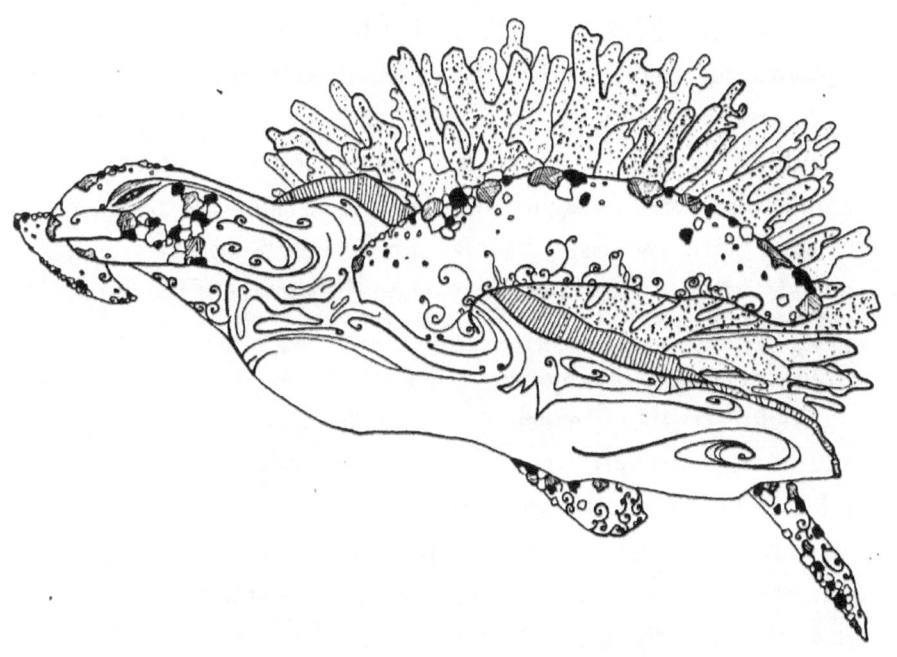

The Transformation

The tutors followed James after his escapade, so Sasha, noticing that her friend was a bit out of sorts, took her by the hand and lifted her into the sky. Then she flew over the now completely filled lake.

"Do you want to try something else?" she asked Carol.

"Like what?" the human replied ignorantly.

"This." Sasha hit her on the forehead with her hand to knock her out and let her fall with all the weight of her body into the lake.

She awoke flush with the surface, her body immobilized; she could not get out. Desperate, she thought she was going crazy amidst disturbing thoughts while she was exasperated to inhale oxygen, until suddenly she saw the silhouette of her friend outside, with her hand outstretched on the surface of the water. She implied that she was the one whose magic prevented her from emerging to breathe.

Frightened, the girl expelled what was left of the air in her lungs and was unconscious almost instantly. Her body surrendered to the current of the dark waters and was swept across the wetlands. With her eyes open, she could somehow watch the light penetrating the water and disappearing with a mist that began to cover the surface of the lake. She watched helplessly the succession of events she was suffering, unable to do anything about it. And even if Carol could no longer feel her body, she could still barely see Sasha, like a blurred image coming down towards her, recognizable by the movement of her nightgown and long hair under the water.

Then she noticed that when she touched her again, gave her a delicate touch on her chest. Instantly, the young woman's sight began to become as clear as the dry air outside and she distinguished Sasha positioned in parallel, floating above her, her face almost glued to her face, staring into her eyes with a big smile on her face and a sinister expression, her hair spread across the element like a jellyfish.

"Breathe," Carol heard in her head. Her friend was smiling happily in front of her, who didn't understand why this was happening. But Sasha continued to talk to her underwater, making her realize how long she had been breathing without oxygen. In addition, her vision improved, her sense of hearing improved in that habitat, which was no longer so cold, but refreshing. Then her friend touched her again and a tingling sensation ran through Carol's limbs and allowed her body to move, so she took the opportunity to move away from Sasha after letting out a scream, even though not a single bubble of air came out.

Perplexed by what was happening, she began to speak in complete astonishment, without finding any trace of oxygen. Her partner, tired of waiting, grabbed her and dragged her swimming like a dolphin through the interior of the lake, until Carol had the confidence to enjoy that pleasure on her own, making great leaps outward, propelling her body from the depths of the lake. But after a while the girl stopped that breath of fun and forced Sasha to sit on the bottom of the lake next to her. From there she watched the luminary coming in with the stirrings of the ripples of the water and her hair moving to the rhythm of the undercurrent.

They spent hours there, talking about the whole situation, what happened and the future plans they had, and despite what happened, Carol held her friend's hand tightly, making it clear that whatever happened, she would support her as a loyal sister, she would be by her side to help her in whatever she needed or what she could merely do as a human. But Sasha's response to Carol's nobility was not what Carol expected, as her earthly condition made her vulnerable, so aware that her life was in even more danger than theirs, who were possessors of powers, she was not going to risk it. But Carol insisted and explained to her that family is never abandoned, so no matter what she said, even if she returned her home, she would find a way to return to the mansion or wherever it was to find her.

Then Sasha picked up a stone from the bottom, wiped it a little and put it in her mouth. A small glow emanated from it on her cheek. After that she spat it out, expelling a precious diamond from her mouth, and offered that huge gemstone to her friend to rebuild her life without looking back, without having to go back to boarding school or depend on her real family; it gave her the chance to be financially independent for the rest of her life. But Carol took the gem and threw it away. She then replied to her friend that this wedding ring could not be bought, so she had to accept that it was going to be part of her adventure, whether she wanted it or not. In any case, the diamond would still be there when she returned, so to get it back she had to make sure that both she and Sasha returned home safely. If not, she would not be able to recover that valuable gift, for without it she would not be able to hold her breath for so long underwater, let alone the pressure of descending to that dreary bottom. So that would be her life insurance: a motivation that would keep her alive so that Sasha would not have to worry about her, but about herself.

After several minutes in silence, the young half-breed understood in Carol's gaze that she was not going to convince her in any way; no matter what she did to manipulate her and make her stay away from her, since her companion was determined to stay by her side, without any fear of the adversities that stalked them like an unstoppable hurricane. So right there under the water, holding hands, they swore an oath and unwittingly Sasha transmitted part of her powers to her friend, enough for Carol to survive underwater.

Perplexed after the magical connection between the two, the earthling touched herself behind her ears and noticed a series of cuts that had appeared there. Then she discovered that part of her hair was moving through the water after having come loose from her scalp.

-It's gills," Sasha exclaimed in astonishment, fearing the power she had transferred to her friend.

But when they came out of the water, the gills looked like simple scars behind the cartilage, like three thin lines on each side of the head. Apparently, these only opened on contact with the element. Since they were soaking wet, Sasha made all the molecules that were soaking them disappear, evaporate from her body. Then they walked to the mansion door with their hair and garments completely dry. James stared at Carol entering the front door. Without knowing why, the girl seemed more beautiful to him than ever.

"Look, if you need help with the girl, they say it's best to always act normal; that is, be yourself, you know? But you... don't do that," the Guardian said quietly.

The boy stared at the beast impassively. Suddenly, he remembered that Rasnar was Bill and stood still pondering on it, looking at it without blinking. At the young man's strange reaction, the Guardian presented a series of twitches in his ear because of the tense atmosphere. He stared at the teenager and moved closer to his face until he touched him on the cheeks with the hairs of his feline mustache.

"Wait a minute, maybe I'm acting weird, but let's not get tense. It's just... I'm just not used to the idea of you looking like the old Bill. And if you're him, you're... because... I mean, that Betty... Well, that's what I've heard, you know, rumors from the house. I got to know her; you know? The... The... Whatever. She was a cutie, really," James commented.

"Boy, don't you know when to stop? If you dig a hole, don't keep digging until you've made your grave. And yes, one of the reasons I stayed in this mansion was my feelings for her." James was about to interrupt him, but Rasnar stopped him. "She...," he pointed to the Talan.

"Forgive me for butting in, but who is Bill?" asked the peon.

Rasnar strained every muscle and bone in his body, which rattled thunderously as he moved them to make them creak. Then a physical transformation took place with which he became the man they were asking about.

"By the seas of Argua! How long have you known how to do that? Are you a changeling?!" exclaimed Nose.

"If I were a changeling, I would know more about them, don't you think? No, this was a gift given to me a long time ago," replied the Guardian.

"Can you choose who you become? Because you've got yourself quite a big guy for an avatar, you big lug! Someone wanted to conquer Betty in style, huh?" said the boy, smiling at Nose.

"For your information, everything you see was at the request of my beloved."

Instantly, everyone present burst into laughter.

"Those would be good times," Nose said.

"The truth is that I was given this body as a gift for dedicating my life to protect humanity. What you see is the real aspect of what would be my human self, the best gift I could have ever been given, since I am the only Arguan able to come and go to Earth and I needed to hide, but that prevented me from really knowing you. This body has helped me to be the only being among the Twelve Kingdoms who knows the truth about humans, with all your virtues and faults. This made me hate you, but also love you; you awakened in me a deep fascination, as I always wanted to know what it would be like to be part of your society.

"As a Guardian, these notions served to protect planet Earth, the Garos and our entire system, but I was to go unobserved among you, and so Bill was born," explained the beast.

"Well, unobserved, maybe; but you definitely wouldn't pass unnoticed..." answered Carol.

"That's why I had to hide somehow under the protection of someone noble and pure-hearted, someone like the lady of the house, the real Mrs. de Courdeil, Sasha's great-grandmother. What a woman. She was, without a doubt, the best and most incredible human being I ever knew. Her passing was a great loss to all of us," Rasnar said.

"What a coincidence that you were here when what happened to my grandmother, Argua and the lake, isn't it?" James hesitated.

"Coincidences only exist in one's own mind," replied the Talan.

"Who is Betty?" Carol asked. She had a hundred questions as a new addition to the family.

"Well, let's get her up to speed, champ."

Bill wiggled his ears and showed the Rasnar in him as he watched the boy, who had lost interest, walk away. Instantly, he transformed back into the Talan, and began to explain to the girl how he fell in love with the most beautiful of all flowers, how he met her and how they had their encounters.

"Well, as I said before, his great-grandmother helped me by protecting me at a time when a being like me didn't have total freedom, and even less to fulfill my task; you know, following, observing, and controlling people so that everything was in its place. No, that was not easy," explained the Guardian with a certain sparkle in his four eyes.

"Ah, because you had to keep an eye on everyone's Garos, didn't you?" exclaimed James, who had returned and wanted to be clever in front of Carol by exposing Rasnar's secret.

"You know that must remain hidden, boy," the beast spoke with disappointment.

"What are Garos?" asked Carol.

"If you want, let's change the subject and you explain to us who gave you the gift to be Bill and by what coincidence of coincidences you were here preparing the area for the arrival of Mihara, my grandmother, yes."

Carol tried to defuse the tense atmosphere. She clearly detected a confrontation between them, but she needed explanations, so she encouraged James to question the Guardian.

"There are things, boy, that you are not ready to hear, let alone understand. When that day comes, I assure you that I will tell you everything, if that day ever comes," the Talan clarified.

"What happened to the girl you loved?" asked the peon, who seemed to be the only one interested in the story of that romance.

"You know, Nose? You and I should have a few drinks alone to tell each other what we clearly can't discuss in front of a teenager with no control over his hormones. We've made too much progress to have it all fall apart over a human who is out of his league with that attitude," Rasnar said.

"Yes! Let's take the extraordinary new addition with us to bring her up to speed," proposed Nose innocently and happily, as they could spend time together.

Meanwhile, James misunderstood the peon's intentions and felt somewhat jealous. Though he was weighed more heavily by the humiliation he received from Rasnar, for he was aware that he had blundered by mentioning the Garos to a human.

"What if we start with the Garos?" Carol asked.

"She's trustworthy, Rasnar. She will never say anything about what she hears or what we show her," Sasha confirmed.

"That's not the point. If an Earthling discovers this, the consequences could be fatal, so thank you, James, for breaking, in an instant, millennia of secrecy and a lifetime of dedication guarding this sacred secret," said the Guardian.

"Wait! Sasha and I are half human, so we should have Garos, right?" James replied, joining the conversation like an intruder.

"Yes, you have them, but when the buds came out and I sensed the strange scent they emanated, I had to hide the flowers and become their personal guardian so that only I would know of your existence. Luckily, it was me and not someone else who found them. That is why I knew of your lives even before your human mother and Mihara," the Talan said proudly.

"Can someone explain to me what a Garo is?" Carol insisted.

"We have dogs! What's mine like? Is he cute? Is he a dog? I love dogs," James exclaimed.

"I think I'd better show them to you," Rasnar offered.

"Really? Can we see them?" Sasha was surprised.

"Yes, but please, Carol, what you're going to see now, don't let it scare you. It's like your guardian angel, you understand? You must act normally and accept it as part of you. Don't worry, it will make you stronger, even if you only get to see him for a moment. And never — if you value your life — talk about this with anyone," said the Talan.

"Only with you, I promise. Where are they now, Rasnar?"

The Guardian looked up at the ceiling and pointed to the position of the Garos as he told each of the young folk where to look. He then took the teenagers' hands and bit them to leave a small mark on their palms.

"The effect won't last long, but it will be enough for you to get to know them. Don't worry. They only protect you; they are completely harmless, at least to you. But I think you'd better go out and stand side by side. That way, when they appear, you will have your corresponding one right in front of you. I don't want you to get confused and want to swap them," Rasnar joked.

The youngsters walked out into the garden around the side of the house, nerves in their stomachs; still, they got into position to see their Garos. Instantly, James shuddered.

"Is that... is that mine? That... That thing is the reflection of my inner self? Oh hell!" he exclaimed, euphoric and terrified at the same time.

"Exactly, he's as honest as an owl and as mischievous as a monkey; tremendously agile both because of his four arms and his long, flexible tail, which helps him hang on to whatever area you're in. This way, it can watch from any angle and height," the Talan reported proudly.

"It's very... hairy! And it's scary. I love it! Can I touch it? Please say yes," the boy begged.

"Sure, kid. He understands what you say to him; in fact, your connection makes him know exactly what you are thinking now you do, being able to predict your feelings, desires, and movements, but, of course, he would never use them to harm you. Keep in mind that it is not your pet, nor will it ever be your best friend, but it is part of your soul, part of you. For that reason, you must take care of each other with your life," Rasnar answered.

"I just met him, and I already love him like a son."

The Garo was turning its head at a three-hundred-and-six-ty-degree angle. It held its mouth half open, with a long tongue hanging out of it. Admittedly, it was a bit creepy, but also funny; it seemed curious and shy at the same time, so James approached it with open arms to show his unconditional love. The Garo, like a monstrous version of the boy, within its bizarre forms, opened all four arms and raised its paws like a contortionist, embracing the boy with its body, wrapping its furry torso around him. It encircled him like a spring roll: the creature was the wrapper and James was the stuffing. It protected him as it did cartwheels with him across the lawn, like two excited, elated fools.

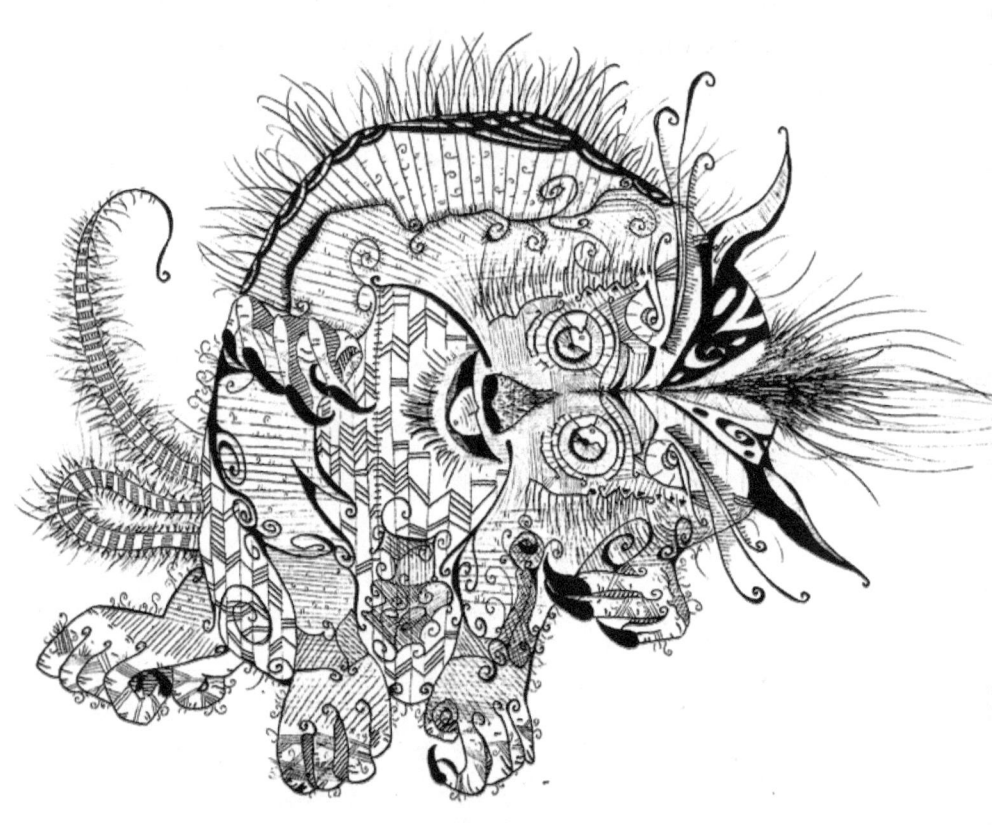

Meanwhile, the girls waited their turn nervously, eyeing the young man enviously as he circled his levitating body three feet off the ground and spoke to nothing, since they could not see the boy's face. Nor apparently their own, so they asked Rasnar if something was wrong, but he told them to be patient. Everything would come in due time.

"What is that?" Carol gasped in astonishment.

"It's your Garo, girl, your bond. You are a very lucky girl; possibly the only human in history who has been able to see her guardian spirit. The fact that you haven't seen it until now doesn't mean that it has just appeared. You should know that she has always been and always will be with you. Even if you think or feel that you have been alone until now, she has protected you and will continue to watch over you around the clock, making sure that nothing happens to you.

"They only live for you and for you, they travel to your world as soon as you are born to be physically by your side when you humans form the spirit. They make sure that your instinct does not fail you, drawing strength from within you so that you can bounce back after the falls, to squeeze your essence to the maximum, that which makes you special to conceive extraordinary things. She is by your side when you think you have lost everything.

"But don't forget one thing, Carol: you must protect her equally, with the respect she deserves, using well what she bestows on your being, honoring what she does for you. Because if you don't, you could lose her, end her life, and you'll die too," the beast explained to her.

"Is it a female?" asked the young woman with a smile on her face.

The little thing was approaching her was a kind of old-looking mouse that moved on four legs, but it stood on its two hind legs as if it had human qualities, like an old man turned into a rat. It did not look feminine at all, that is, it did not show the female appearance that has been inculcated in us.

Carol was definitely not expecting this kind of guardian angel, as it didn't look like that specimen could protect her from anything, judging by its appearance and size.

"How are you going to protect me, little girl?"

The creature reached her feet and began to circle her ankles, caressing the girl's skin with its fur. She picked up the animal to observe it closely. The Garo looked at her and curled up on her chest. Then small tears began to spill down Carol's cheeks as she smiled hugging the creature, as if she had been invaded by an extreme peace all at once.

"Do you like it, Carol?" asked Sasha without being able to see what her friend was looking at.

"It wasn't at all what I expected, but it's just what I needed. Now I understand everything. Do you know that she just spoke to me, or can only I hear it?" said the young woman.

"They can hear us, but you can only hear the beings to whom they are linked," replied the Guardian.

"What did she say?" Sasha wanted to know, completely astonished by her friend's reaction to the Garo.

"Just what I needed to hear. I don't know how to explain it, but now I have the strength and tenacity to face everything in this life. I always thought I was alone, even though I had my parents alive, and I know it's unfair for me to say this when you lost yours. But I always thought you were my only family, since mine doesn't seem to be interested in me or at least understand me.

"The Garo is the reflection of my inner self and, at the same time, what I am missing. I don't know how to explain what it makes me feel, but it understands me perfectly and helps me not to be confused, it calms my pain. Does what I say make sense to you?"

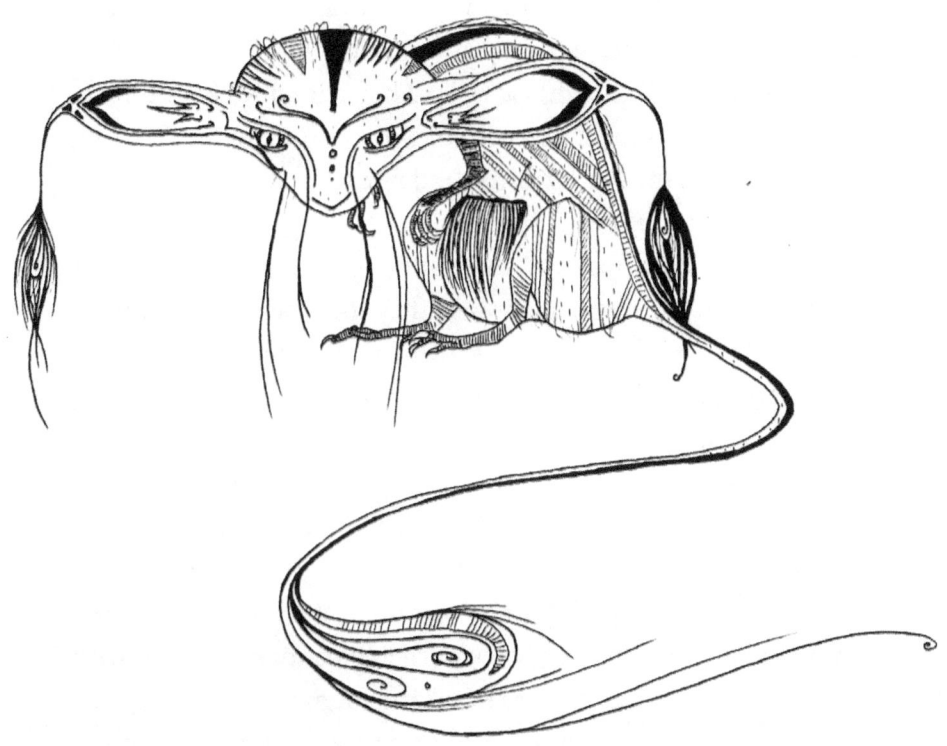

Sasha nodded her head and stared blankly, holding back the urge to cry.

"I think I know what you're saying. In fact, I don't think I've ever felt so good or so complete in my entire life."

Carol looked ahead to where Sasha was looking. To her amazement, a white creature, with the size of a horse and the head of a kind of deer, replete with strange shapes all over its body, composed of coral fragments coming out of its skin and lighting the way, was heading towards her friend with strange legs that looked like seahorse tails. They curled back and forth, caressing the grass as she passed, like something divine. When it reached Sasha, the Garo put its head next to the young girl's and both bowed in unison.

The curious thing was that, although the Garos were not what the trio expected, as soon as they met them, they all felt a deep love and gratitude towards them, unable to understand how they had been able to live without knowing of their existence, since if they had opened their minds and souls more, they would never have felt lonely. Confused at not having realized and disappointed with themselves, they discovered how shallow and blind they had been until then. When they brought their senses together, they felt the connection of their soul. Then their mind did an involuntary review of their past together. And with a flashback forced by the magic of the moment, they perceived for the first time the presence of these creatures in each of the scenes they remembered being alone. And they became aware of the influence their Garos had on each of them in their day-to-day lives. Since these beings came out of their cocoon, they had dedicated their entire lives to them, comforting them without complaining or receiving anything in return, protecting them at all costs, at all times and without exception. Living by and for them, making them strong in an unconscious way, marking with this discovery the young people forever. They drew a new perspective on their lives and the world around them, an image that took their breath away.

Just to feel that these wonderful beings understood them was beyond perfection. But it didn't end there, because, as Carol said, these beautiful spirits equilibrated the balance between what they were and what they lacked as people and provided them with well-being. They pleasantly noticed the increase in their strength, as well as the development of emotional intelligence that each of them lacked separately, filling them with affection and security. An unparalleled feeling that they would never again feel lonely or vulnerable and that they would not let go of for anything in the world.

As Rasnar said, you just had to open your mind and connect with the energy around you, and that we carry within us, to feel that strength that many lose along the way. It was amazing how easy it was to see and understand the world with the Garos, and how difficult it was to have this clairvoyance without getting to know them. Now they understood the Guardian's words, which he kept repeating, and so they respected the Talan even more. They felt really bad for those Garos tied to humans detached from that world; people who succumbed to the darkness and gave up weakly with a bad attitude towards life and other beings, who let themselves be won over by the harsh attacks of external adversities, thereby causing the death of the poor Garo. Despising a lifetime of love and dedication that these beautiful creatures had unconditionally deposited on their humans from the moment they were born.

The youngsters' hearts swelled with deep respect for this species, especially the Garos, unable to explain in words the deep connection they felt the instant they met them. Rasnar left them there. He took a seat and watched as each of the siblings spent their time with their Garo. He reflected on why Carol had been able to see Sasha's Garo. He realized that being aware of the presence of these creatures in their lives made them stronger and thought about the possibility of letting them spend a few more days with them. The siblings were experiencing a great blockage that hindered their progress. With the help of the Garos they would not have to use the drastic methods they had tried so far. Time was running out for them, and although it was forbidden by universal law for humans to know their Garo, no one knew what the repercussions would be. Who knows if the change could lead to progress for both species, and even save the planets, despite the vile human nature by which this decree was imposed.

"My lady, do you think it would be beneficial to let the siblings spend a few days with their Garos?" asked the Guardian in confusion for the first time.

"You seem to have read my mind again, Rasnar," she said.

"But how are you going to take them away later?" Nose cautioned worriedly, knowing the pain of losing something you love.

"Well, I wouldn't be taking them away; they just wouldn't see them. They would still feel them; although before I do that, I should talk to the girls, because I think it's only fair, since women are the majority in this trio.

"I will tell them that they can stay with their Garos for a few more days, as a reward, but only as a temporary thing, without them knowing that it is a test. That way they can heal their wounds, and if all goes well, who knows, they might stay by their side longer. Anyway, no one is going to be able to see them but them, so no human will know of their existence. Luckily, I kept the Courdeil Garos a secret during their growth in Talos.

"But if we do this, it could jeopardize what we've gained so far. We have no idea what the aftermath of heading down this new path might be, so for now, I don't want them to see the possibility of keeping them forever. Let's first wait to see how it affects their progress during their apprenticeship as warriors and future leaders," Rasnar concluded.

"You know that we have always been able to see them, don't you, Rasnar?" said Grandma.

"Yes, Mihara," replied the Talano.

"Well, I hope it goes well, because the truth is that I was having a hard time coaching the kids while trying not to look at their faces. Teaching gets pretty complicated when you lose your concentration, especially when you're trying to hide. Honestly, this situation is a big weight off my shoulders."

Rasnar began to laugh, until Nose interrupted him.

"Forgive me for butting in, my lady, but what will happen to Carol's Garo? If the girl is going to stay with us, even though she is human, it might do her good to have her creature with her. She seems really happy and calm. From what I have gathered about this young lady, she is desperate to find a family to take her in. Don't get me wrong, I don't know anything about her, but I sense that she is noble enough to know how to handle everything what happens here with respect and under the utmost secrecy.

"She's clearly a girl of courage and bravery, so I don't think we should take her away from her Garo, even if it's for a few more days," the peon confessed.

"You are right, Nose, but being fully human, your creature is indeed being watched by the Talans. Having her here with us could be a problem. We could be risking everything we have fought for so far and be discovered at any moment. Remember that her Garo is in the Talos garden listing, so even if I returned to my land to hide it, it would be missed. Talans never forget a Garo.

"If I'm being honest, I don't think the girl should stay no matter how much potential you see in her. The mere fact that she's terrestrial makes her very easy to track and take down. The girl poses a huge threat to us, Nose. We will be vulnerable if we keep her among us; especially living here in the mansion."

Chapter IX
Mutation

Rasnar, Mihara and Nose sipped tea at a small table on the porch at the entrance to the Courdeil house while they watched the children enjoying themselves in the garden with their Garos. But the bliss in which they were immersed was soon to end. As pleasurable as it was to watch them spend quality time with their critters, that comfort would eventually bring on another kind of blockage. Not only the young people and the beings to whom they were linked, but also their teachers, enclosed in an idyllic bubble that would take them away from their true mission on Earth. It would turn that mansion into a home when it should really be a fortress. A place to hide, thanks to the protection created by Rasnar, to carry out intensive training with a single purpose. They had to come down soon from the clouds and start to put limits on so much relaxation, take stock of the situation to make the right decisions regarding their obligations.

It seemed that the addition of the Garos, who had always been there, but had not been seen, was bringing much needed peace to the youngsters so that they could continue their training with a sound mind. On the other hand, even though it might interfere with the purpose of the mission, withdrawing the Garos might cause them to return to their previous state. Either decision was risky, and they pondered when would be the best time to return the creatures to their state of invisibility.

But the fear that this might cause the young people to lose the fabulous harmony that now balanced them and helped them to better channel their powers through perfect psychic control, was increasing the days and further complicating the decision to separate them.

"The days have passed faster than I expected, and the unexpected progress of my grandchildren is undeniable. They are beginning to glow in a blinding way since spending time with their protectors," Mihara confessed.

"Yes, I noticed that too," Nose commented as he watched James and Sasha show their kindred spirits the powers they were developing with each passing minute. The Garos were helping them control and strengthen them as they played.

"Keeping the Garos exposed like this endangers them and all of us. Right now, we are a perfect target for our enemies. By leaving things as they are we run double the risk, for you know what will happen if they harm their creatures. They may be stable and increasing in strength now, ready to begin their training in Arguan lands, but I worry about speed and greatness due to the new situation.

"You know that keeping things like this could mean their death and that would drive the siblings to insanity or worse, so we would lose everything we have gained so far," the Guardian expounded.

"The Garos, whether they are visible or not, will always be in danger, Rasnar. Precisely because no matter what happens they will protect their respective unions at all costs, and because we Arguans see them in the same way, if we return them to their normal state, they will only be invisible to the human eye. Terrestrials are not the enemy. But if we now take this away from the youngsters, returning their creatures to imperceptibility, the effect it will have on them...

"Rasnar, we could lose not only what we have achieved, but my grandchildren, and we don't have the resources or the time to recover what they have advanced thanks to their spirit beasts," Grandma opined.

"As a Talan Guardian, I would never expose a Garo, but you're right: being with their creatures gives the young ones the strength of mind they need, which we clearly can't give them. And it annoys me to recognize that, even though they have that ability, they don't seem to realize that they can maintain the state they are in without having their Garos materialize. If only we could make them understand that... But it's true, time is running out and I don't think we have any other choice," Rasnar extemporized.

"And what about young Carol?" asked Nose.

"Although I am incredulous, it seems that Sasha has passed on some of her powers, so it is clear that the potential of this promising youngster exceeds my expectations. I have to say that all three teenagers are extraordinary, and the siblings' abilities are beginning to demonstrate the lineages from which they are descended, though I worry about where their limits will be. I worry that I will not be able to continue teaching them, and I am troubled that the Council of Argua is not prepared for their magnificence, especially if they bring a human as an ally," Rasnar replied.

"Regarding my grandchildren, for now their creatures stabilize them, and I wish it to stay that way. I am not worried that they might be dejected if their Garos die; you know the melancholic after-effects that people suffer when this happens, so they are aware of it should they decide to show their creatures to the world without being under the protection of the mansion.

"I am proud to see that they take responsibility for their actions, that they accept with dignity the sacrifices to which they must adhere in relation to the consequences of their decisions, in addition to the adversities of this mission. But I have to admit that it alarms me to recognize what I have seen; what they are capable of... Until now I saw them as humans; hence they have Garos, but it is impossible not to recognize that they are descendants of Zotrak, considering the energetic level they have reached with their current powerful and diverse abilities.

"In reality, we do not know what effects the loss of the linked ones might have on them and the collateral damage that would entail. Such an injury could unbalance them, and they would want to vent their anger on our worlds and the beings that inhabit them; a situation in which I consider that we would not have even a small chance of salvation.

"We began this task thinking that we were taking my grand-children to the right place, that we were consecrating them as liberators and even martyrs, but we did not take into account the terrible drifts we would face if we failed in the attempt. I never thought their course would be so highly unstable. Its force is so powerful that it is out of control, beyond the reach of any of us. Even the Twelve.

"As far as young Carol is concerned, she seems to hold her own well for a human. She's a strong, disciplined, brave and very intelligent girl, so I don't mind her staying if it's on her own responsibility, but how do you hide her Garo, so they don't find out she's here?" Grandma asked with interested.

"We know about the conditions of these creatures because their essence is captured in the petals of the bud from which they emerged and were cared for in the garden of Talos. But the secession of powers received by Sasha has altered the human's genes and has also affected her beast, something that will surely be reflected in the remains of the flower. There is a danger that it will be discovered and, consequently, Talan soldiers will be sent to investigate the cause," said the Guardian.

"What would happen if we destroyed her Garo plant?" Nose queried, looking at Rasnar, who was completely silent, as if the oxygen had been cut off from his brain.

It was the first time that something so extreme had been proposed to him. In fact, such an idea had never crossed his mind in his entire life, not even as a mere thought or a silly joke. He had dedicated his whole life to protect his traditions with immense respect, taking his obligations to both the garden and his Garos with colossal seriousness; never once having even considered the concept of desecrating the rules of his land, so he had no idea what would happen if they were to cut the great trunk of one of those flowers from which the creature had already emerged.

"How dare you ask such a question to me, to the Supreme Guardian of Talos himself; to kill, to assassinate one of my lozenges... That is something that goes totally against my principles, my values, and my morality. Something like that could unleash chaos," the Talan criticized.

"Forgive me, Rasnar, I didn't want to offend you, but given the circumstances in which we find ourselves, we have all made sacrifices for the greater good, and although I agree with you in what you say, and although it may be something very risky, since even you don't know what the consequences could be, I don't think we have any other choice," replied the pawn.

"The question is that I do not know the effects of doing what you ask me to do. I have only heard legends of ancient Argua about the death of some flower by natural causes, but not by the hand of a Talan, nor by the hand of any other being, until..."

The Guardian was blocked.

"Until what? Go on, Rasnar," Mihara encouraged, completely intrigued.

"Long before the clandestine meeting with the council, the one that I captured in the fire, in which Zotrak intervened by inserting a Zork into Ashima's body, I had a vision," the Guardian confessed.

"You mean you had a premonition about the state of planet Earth and how it would affect the solar system? Because you already mentioned that to us; otherwise, you would not have convened the assembly," replied the Shawá, encouraging him to advance the information.

"Did you gather the council just because of a premonition?" Mihara asked, surprised, and rather perplexed.

"It was not exactly like that; I mean, yes and no."

Sasha approached the tutors' table on the back of her extraordinary Garo, which moved with great elegance levitating on its arched legs. Despite its coral-covered body, Sasha didn't seem to mind those reef fragments scattered across the creature's torso, even if they did leave chafing on her legs.

"James, Carol and I wanted to make you a proposal," said the girl.

"Is it about your Garos?" asked Mihara.

"I know it's risky, but it's clear to us, and I mean all six of us are willing to take the risk."

At that instant, Sasha raised her arm and three cups and a teapot full of tea appeared from the door, which she directed to the table as she encouraged her brother and her friend to join in and continue with the small meeting she had arranged.

"After seeing that you have learned to make tea without being in the kitchen and bring it here without even moving or holding the pieces, I can't help but see how positive it has been for you to have your creatures. But just because you don't see them doesn't mean they are gone. We must return them to their natural state, for your protection and that of the creature. I want you to continue working on the powers and balancing your inner self; I just wish you knew how to progress in this way without having to expose the Garos in this way," Rasnar clarified.

"One of the principles of Argua, which we are forgetting, is the teaching of coexistence with other beings, learning from them and their kingdoms," said the peon.

"That's true. It seems that having served so long in silence under your people's regime has made you more observant and intelligent than the rest, Nose." Grandmother put her hand on Rasnar's big paw. "My friend, we have done, and do every day, the best we can within our limitations. It is no easy task to fight against you-know-who. And you understand as well as I do, they will never be prepared for what they are about to face. No one can be. The only thing we can continue to do is to give them every possible advantage so that when that day comes, they will give the best of themselves.

"For now, we have not failed them. We should be proud of our work and see this new step as a blessing, because the Garos have given them what we could not. It was an incident that just came about, so I think we should let ourselves be carried along by circumstances and trust our intuitions, even if there is always going to be something beyond our control.

"The only obvious reality of progress is that these creatures strengthen their inner selves and increase their powers, and that is something that only their Garos can give them, something that will make them thrive both to improve their staying power, overcome the dilemmas of the present and the harsh future that awaits them," commented Grandma.

"We are very fortunate, Rasnar, and we owe it to you, for having protected our Garos, for having preserved them for so long in secret and with such passion.

"Thanks to this you have saved our lives, they have made us stronger, so much so that we have been able to fight our own demons to discover who we are."

Carol appeared behind the Guardian with her Garo raised over her shoulder. She had her tail curled gently around the girl's neck. To her astonishment, Rasnar stood up and gave up his seat to the young girl, as Sasha was on the back of his extravagant steed and James lay seated on his Garo's lap, with two of the animal's four arms wrapped around him like a monkey. The Garo mimicked the boy drinking tea with the remaining limbs.

"Relax, Rasnar. I'm fine here. In fact, I'm so fine that I wish I could stay and be reconciled with my soul," Carol said.

"Your soul?" they asked.

"That's what I call her... That's how I feel her because she fills me up without needing anything or anyone. She understands me. Since you made her appear in my life, I don't feel lonely, and I have been mortified by loneliness all my life. So, I want to be clear: I am not going anywhere, because I don't plan to give her up. I will give my life for your cause so as not to lose her. The peace and happiness I have found at last are worth any sacrifice to which I must submit."

Mihara got up and hugged her. Then the young girl burst into tears from the intoxicating affection, something she was not used to. Sasha jumped off her Garo and joined in the warm embrace. Immediately, James gave his cup to the peculiar monster he was attached to, to join the loving circle. But this hunk of an animal couldn't even hold what looked like a toy mug compared to his enormous fingers. The beast became engrossed in analyzing the ceramic object he had just been given and tilted his head almost one hundred and eighty degrees observing it curiously.

"Okay, guys, okay. Let go or I won't be able to stop whimpering and my reputation for toughness will go down the drain," said Carol.

Nose looked at Rasnar with concern.

"If the young human is going to stay, it must be at her own risk. Even so, we are committed to resolving the loose ends involved in supporting that decision."

Immediately, the young woman raised her voice to make it clear that in a few months she would be eighteen years old, so she would be of age to do whatever she wanted. She stated that as far as she was concerned, it would be her own responsibility.

"That is a human law that is of little use to us in the Arguan world. But, well, you may be of much use to us. I must confess that I haven't told you everything about why I came to this world; at least, not in enough detail."

Then Rasnar began to move his ears from side to side.

"Is everything all right?" Nose asked.

But the Guardian kept his ears alert and remained silent. Instantly, everyone could hear something metallic clattering on the floor.

"What is that?" Nose was startled, looking at the Talan.

"It's coming from the house, it is possible..." Quickly, the Guardian flew towards the interior of the mansion. The others chased after him on the Garos, trying to catch up with him. They reached the abandoned room, where they saw that the hole in the chimney was open. Without hesitation, they jumped into the passageway and walked to the pool room. Once there, they noticed that Rasnar had created an energy bubble that contained inside it the box where Carol had kept the book, although the chest was now badly damaged.

"What happened?" Sasha inquired.

"The book has been trying to get out," replied the Guardian.

"But how is that possible?" James asked.

"Do you think we should open it?" asked Mihara.

"My lady, if we do, it must be inside the sphere I have formed to contain it," Rasnar explained.

"Sasha, you were able to make tea without even touching the stove. Do you think you can by telekinesis, or however you do it, use your powers to get the tome out of the box?" Carol wondered aloud, looking for a solution to the mystery.

"I can try, but you should be prepared in case it goes wrong. It could be a trap."

Nose and Mihara got into position, with James at her back and Carol next to him, while Sasha stood to one side of the sphere, from where she watched the object with utmost concentration until it opened. The book shot out from inside, eager to escape, and bounced off the walls of the active energy globe that contained it.

"Sasha, contain it!"

A black divider appeared from between its pages and opened the volume at the page where it was located. To everyone's surprise, what looked like a string began to lengthen to show a tail.

"What the hell is that?" Carol gasped.

"Close the book, Sasha!"

But the young woman did not react in time. A portal had opened through which the creature contained in the book emerged, and half of its body was already out of the tome. So, no matter how hard she tried to close it, the beast was more in this world than in that evil vade mecum.

Rasnar increased the size of the sphere to wax it, but the whole of its body was already outside the pages that had imprisoned it and it was perfectly clear what it was.

"Is it a drakon?" James asked.

"It seems so, but... Could it be a baby? It's so small that it seems harmless," said Sasha, but she received no answer, as everyone was analyzing the situation while watching the creature scratch the protective barrier with its claws. Several hours later, now tired, she curled up next to the now closed book on the side of the box.

"What do we do now? Do we open the sphere and catch the drakon while it is asleep?"

Mihara approached the bubble and observed the dozing specimen which looked harmless. She placed her hand on the sphere and instantly the creature opened its eyes and approached her. It then let out a light purr as it rubbed its head against her palm.

"Rasnar, open the barrier to let it out and freeze the book inside the box with a protective spell."

The kids were stunned.

"Are you sure you want to take the risk of releasing the beast, my lady?" the Guardian wanted to reaffirm, dumbfounded.

"I don't know if it's Riyah's gem or mere intuition, but I have a hunch."

Rasnar did as he was told and the drakon fell into Mihara's arms. To everyone's astonishment, it did not attack her; rather it seemed frightened, so Grandma held it while stroking it to reassure it. The creature responded by curling up with even closer against her chest.

"How the hell did this happen?" James asked.

"I don't know if I'm more concerned about where he came from than how he got here," Sasha said.

"Well, I'm more concerned about why it's here," said the peon, who was suspicious of the little beast.

"How are you going to hide a drakon now? What if it grows to the normal size for its species?" Carol asked, approaching in fascination. It was the first time she had seen such a beautiful and exceptional creature.

Rasnar left the sphere protecting the box with the tome inside on a pillar as a decorative chandelier. Then he approached the beast. But when it sensed his presence, it hid under its wing. It was then that, taking advantage of the fact that it was hiding its face, Nose approached and touched it, but immediately pulled his hand away in dismay.

"What have you seen, my friend?" Mihara asked.

"It's Rombar's memories, but he's dead, so it can only be a reflection. How can it be flesh and blood? It's... It's black magic. We must lock him up right now, now!" Nose answered.

"If she were evil, don't you think she would have attacked us by now?" replied the human.

"What's your explanation for this? She could be a spy!"

The creature looked at Nose and craned its neck back. Then it blew and covered the peon's face with smoke.

"Ohhh, loook. He likes you," James said sarcastically.

"The truth is, for a fan of the legendary Rombar, you got off on the wrong foot with his offspring," Sasha pointed out.

"Every precaution is too little in these times, and this smells bad to me," Nose defended himself, looking at the animal as it growled at him.

Carol, bewitched by that fictional figure of flesh and blood, approached until she was face to face with the mythological beast. It brushed its face against hers as a sign of respect. But when the girl went to caress the little drakon, the animal, frightened, bit her and left her hand was marked with its sharp teeth. After that it moaned, leaving a small trail of black smoke in the air.

"Are you all right, my dear?" Mihara asked, inspecting the young woman's wound, where the drakon's four teeth had left their mark.

But Carol fainted before she could answer. Luckily, James caught her in time before she hit the floor and Rasnar quickly lifted her into his arms to carry her up to her room. There he laid her down to try to figure out what the hell had happened. They were extremely worried.

"We should not have taken the beast out of the sphere. We can't afford mistakes like this, my lady," said Nose in distress, for he had warned that it was not a good idea.

"What's done is done. We will learn from our mistakes, but now we must save the girl. How is she?"

Nose ran his hands over Carol without detecting anything. Her Garo dozed beside her head and showed the consequences of the bond between them. Sasha held her friend's hand and asked her to wake up, but the young woman did not react.

"I will stay here with the girls. The rest of you should go to another room to discuss what we should do. It is not advisable to discuss anything with the young lady in this state. They could be using her to spy on us, so do something before our position comes to light or they detect the human girl's Garo. For not only is there clear evidence that she evolved with the powers that Sasha passed on to Carol, but she is now facing whatever the human is fighting, as the Garo looks as sick as she is."

"Whatever this magic is, it's going to raise suspicions among the Talans, if you haven't figured it out already," the peon asserted.

"Nose is right; go now," said Sasha, forcing Rasnar, Mihara and James out of the room.

Nose lit the fire to heat the room so as not to have to cover the girl. They had to see if her body suffered any alteration. Sasha kept a careful and anxious eye on her companion and the bonded one, who was lying close to her in a fetal position. But when the young woman reached out to comfort the creature, the animal moved away from her in annoyance. Then it opened its eyes and gave her a violent look.

"I don't know, have you seen it?"

The peon approached to examine the Garo in question. A green glow emanated from it, and the Shawá immediately laid his hands on the creature. Then the creature's face changed.

"Sasha, your friend is no longer human. Her Garo is still bound, but not in the traditional way; something inside her is no longer what it was. On the one hand, this puts us out of danger from the threat of being discovered, or at least I think so, but... I don't know if we should now fear what we imagined," he said with extreme caution.

"You mean Carol..." she hinted.

"We must be alert. I will go and report the facts to the others. Stay vigilant until I return and be very careful. We don't know if there is anything left of your friend in her system."

Sasha stood alone in the room, watching her friend's slow breathing, sobbing as she studied her Garo, which now seemed to be possessed by something invading her insides, which was showing through a beam of green light that now shone in the gaze of the intoxicated soul. Sasha felt guilty for bringing her friend into the blissful adventure, seeing the repercussions, the after-effects that could have damaged her forever, before they'd even begun the journey they were to take. She thought that the suffering was going to be constant and would get worse. She even contemplated the possibility of losing her.

Then she came to the conclusion that they were clearly not ready to go to war, not even on a mission, as they were too trusting, inexperienced, and compassionate. How could one operate against evil by being good? Were they to change and become dastardly in order to eradicate evil from the worlds, to attack them with their own medicine? Sasha was really confused; how could she fight without the advantage of not having a conscience? And if they adapted, what guarantee was there that they would not join the evil? Even if they managed to eradicate it, how could they go back to who they were before without becoming a new evil?

The sound of crackling embers in the fireplace, in the dim light of the room, lulled Sasha to sleep. When she awoke, her hand was still clutching her friend's, who was still sound asleep, but something had changed. It seemed that the room had a little more light. She looked towards the window and discovered large tears in the curtains. She immediately sat up and noticed that the floor was littered with pieces of cloth and foam from a cushion which were scattered on the shredded carpet along with paper shavings from torn books. There was no trace of Carol's Garo.

At that instant something touched her head and a ball of light brown fur, like the fur of a rabbit, fell across her face and slid down her cheek as it descended from the ceiling.

"Don't move a muscle, Sasha," Rasnar whispered to her, appearing in the room. Despite being frightened, the young woman began to slowly move her head upward. "Hold still. Don't make any sudden movements or speak loudly," the Guardian ordered, pointing to the being hanging above her. A drakon three times the size of the small creature that had gushed from the tome was anchored to the ceiling plaster with its claws, its fangs biting into the wooden beams. Its hair was falling out as if it were shedding its skin. It immediately dawned on Sasha that this creature was Carol's bonded one, or at least it was, since she had no idea what it had transformed into.

"If she's like this, what will become of Carol when she wakes up?"

The beast stopped gnawing greedily at the beam and fixed its gaze on the girl. Then it dropped onto the bed and curled up close to the sleeping girl's face, piercing the pillow with the tips of its claws as it went. Then it covered Carol with the shadow of its wings while it analyzed with its nose something it must have sensed in her.

"Rasnar, what do we do?" whispered Sasha.

"If we attack the creature, we could harm your friend's spirit, so all we can do is stand still and watch what happens," the Talan replied.

"But what if it hurts her?" she hesitated.

"We'll have to take the risk. Let's stay calm. If the worst should happen, I'll try to overcome the drakon before it can harm Carol."

At that moment Nose came through the door with James at his side and the beast reacted with a sharp movement of its neck, followed by a frightening scream that woke the sleeping young woman. Carol opened her eyes to what was once her Garo, and it immediately tilted its head towards her face. Carol slowly raised her hand to the animal's snout and stroked it. To everyone's relief, the drakon, now calm, rested at her side, and let the young woman continue to pamper it.

Everyone present was stunned, not understanding absolutely nothing of what had happened, nor of what was happening. They could only wait for Carol to give them some kind of explanation.

"Carol, are you alright?" Sasha asked.

"Better than ever. Thank you," she replied, looking at her drakon with tears of joy.

"Please leave us alone."

Rasnar was perplexed at the request but grabbed the siblings and they walked out the door respecting the young woman's decision.

The Burrow

Carol spent practically the whole day in the bedroom while the rest of the "family" waited anxiously for her to come down to the kitchen, where they waited worriedly debating possible theories about what had happened and what to do about it. Then Rasnar sensed something twitching his ears as usual. He opened the kitchen door leading to the garden and the others came out after him to see what was happening. Then they looked up into the sky and there was Carol, on the back of that kind of drakon that seemed to have grown in size and which had bald spots on its body, because its hair was still falling out, but also a certain resemblance to the Garo it once was.

As soon as it set its radiant green eyes upon them, the creature began to descend until it landed in front of Sasha.

"I am sorry to have kept you waiting. We had a lot to talk about and understand about each other. I guess... Well, I know I'm not the same," said the young woman getting off the beast.

"Do you think you could explain how you feel?" asked her friend.

"I think whatever bit me wasn't bad, but it's possible I survived because of the powers you passed on to me, Sasha, so in a way you saved my life. I just remember dreaming of a world that wasn't this one. Maybe it was Argua, but not as you described it to me, but I don't know... A darker one.

"It was a very intense dream and when I woke up, I wasn't clear where I was, but together we were able to deduce more or less what happened to us," Carol clarified with that kind of mutant drakon following her closely. The animal was sticking its wings through the ground like a bat.

Although the girl appeared to be fine, everyone discovered in her gaze a second pair of membranes protruding from the sides of her eyeball, with which she blinked as she spoke to them, changing her eye color to a deep emerald.

"I see things now; it's like I can communicate with someone or something, but I can't quite make it out. The situation is pretty confusing right now. I guess in time I'll get a better understanding of what's going on with me and... what I am," Carol said.

"We're going to help you," said Grandma.

"I don't want to go back to the way I was before. I feel stronger now, in all aspects. I think I have acquired new powers, powers very different from the ones Sasha gave me. I don't know how to explain it, but now my mind works with Ksuma's, in a different way than when she was my Garo," said the girl.

"I'm sorry, who?" James asked.

"Her name is Ksuma," she said.

"Did you name it?" the young man was surprised.

"No, she told me."

At once the family looked at the creature, who was sniffing the environment curiously checking the surroundings, analyzing the place as if it was its first time there, until it suddenly stopped, inhaled sharply, and expelled through its nostrils two long turquoise flares that left a trail of beautiful smoke of the same color. Then she stretched her neck out to Rasnar and, after sniffing his face, sat down in front of him, staring at him with her wings relaxed.

"It is an honor to meet you, Guardian."

The Talan seemed stunned, as if something suddenly whipped through his mind, not having noticed before what now seemed obvious to him.

"You are a born-again Garo. But that... that is impossible. The procedure for one of you to be able to speak is only achieved by death and resurrection and that is not your case, so please explain yourself, Ksuma," Rasnar demanded.

"I know the procedure that a Garo undergoes to reach the level of a reborn, and no, it is not my case, since I have evolved without the need to have died first. Surprised? No wonder, even I couldn't understand what was happening to me. After the bite I felt prey to the animal that was taking over me, without being able to control well the instinct that was driving me crazy inside. In the end, it won me over. But after that, I was still alive, and I had not failed Carol. She is still connected to me, but with more strength, as if we were one, but not as before, because our current link is incomparable and individual.

"It must be what happens to those who are reborn from the ashes, but with the difference that we have achieved it while being totally detached from Talos, and also from what it symbolizes to be a Garo. Our sprout will no longer be in your garden and our destiny will no longer be to perish for each other. I feel that has changed, for better or for worse," the drakoness replied.

"How do we know we can trust you?" Nose hesitated, sensing as he did the appearance of Rombar's reflection emerging from the book.

"With time, which you don't have, so whatever you decide, if we stay, you can only give us a vote of confidence, and if you set us free, we will stay away from society for safety. Unlike a reborn, I can be seen. And I have not yet discovered all my qualities to know if I still have the power of invisibility to the human eye," the creature confessed.

"Decide what you want, but I will not separate from Ksuma. She is a part of me, just as I am a part of her. When I woke up, I was as lost as she was. I felt her suffering in my dreams, inside me... But she gave me strength and I gave her the stability to find the balance we needed to understand what was happening to us.

"Everything is different now. Not only do I feel her, but she feels me too. For this reason, if you separate us, we will be lost, and if you take us away from you...."

Rasnar put his hand on the beast's head.

"I can sense in you that, like the reborn Garos, you have disassociated yourself from Talos, but with greater strength, so that we are no longer in danger of being discovered by one of the Thirteen Kingdoms. But that does not mean that we are not in danger or under a spell, since we do not know the source of the evil that came from the book," explained the Talan.

"Carol and Ksuma, it would help us a lot if you could tell us what you have seen and perceived in those visions you mentioned, as well as the new things you feel, apart from the obvious. The outward change is clear," commented Mihara.

"It is strange. I remember a forest, a very dark one, where I practically could not walk, since its bushes were full of thorns, and they stuck me all over my body. Each spike penetrated my skin, injecting venom that ran through my veins, and this plunged me into a trance during which I glimpsed something in that dark place," explained the young woman.

"It could have been the delusions of the mutation you were suffering in your sleep, effects of the bite poison," James replied.

"I thought so too, until..." The girl lifted the sleeves of her shirt and showed them her arms, belly and legs torn as if she had been walking among thorn bushes.

"That could have been done when she left home. We saw her arrive on Ksuma's back; she didn't leave, and we don't know where she was," Nose replied perceptively.

"I remember feeling trapped in that place. I screamed, but no one seemed to hear me, until suddenly someone grabbed my ankle. I was so frightened that I cried out even louder, but that arm pulled me so hard that I fell to the ground. Then it dragged me through the brambles to a hole, from where another hand emerged, covering my mouth, and pulling me into the burrow. I was terrified, but I didn't want to fail you."

The young woman ran to Sasha and, trembling, hugged her tightly. Her friend reacted trying to appease her anguish, with many doubts about what she had heard. She distrusted the one she considered her sister. This confusion made her uneasy; something had changed in her. The previously innocent and trusting Sasha no longer existed and, in her eyes, everyone was a suspect. So, no matter how much affection and intimacy there had been between her friend and her, and even with her family, she didn't care, because she no longer trusted anyone.

"What happened once you got there? Did you see who dragged you in?" she asked.

"I only remember darkness, as if I was blindfolded, my mouth gagged and dragging invisible chains, as I could not move. I think I was paralyzed with panic. I only remember someone repeating over and over again that they had made a mistake, that I was not Miha, that he had failed and that he should return the human to her land," Carol said.

"Did they ask you anything? Did you tell them anything about us?" asked Nose.

"Never! Sasha is my sister! You are my family now! Please believe me when I tell you that I would never betray you! Even though I was completely terrified, I would never betray you," the young woman replied, fearing that she would be rejected.

"You mean they sent you here, safe and sound, back to earth, as if nothing had happened? Without explanation or interrogation? I don't believe it! You're lying!" shouted the peon.

"From what I could hear, it was just one person. I think he was talking to himself; possibly a man... No, possibly not, I'm sure. He apologized for killing me; from his tone he sounded desperate, angry with himself. He kept repeating aloud to himself that he had failed. I suppose he must have thought that being human, I would not survive my spiritual return to Earth, so he didn't care if I heard him. And then he threw me back here; he didn't even give me time to speak to ask. Anyway, I felt like I had my mouth covered. I think he did it to stop me from screaming," Carol said.

"Do you think it is related to the images we saw in the volume?" Nose wanted to know.

"It's possible it was sent to gain access to Mihara, but how did it get here, and who could have thrown it at Sasha?" asked James.

"If all this is true, the target was Grandma, and as far as I know, she held the creature in her arms and did not bite her or try to harass her but was gentle with her. It only attacked Carol. None of this makes any sense," Sasha reflected, about to explode.

"That's true, but maybe the plan went wrong and the drakon wraith got carried away by the feelings Rombar once experienced for Riyah. We must remember that they were best friends. And at that precise moment, just like now, Mihara shared her essence with the Shawá gem in question. Maybe that saved her, and the botched spell was truncated when she sensed Riyah; maybe that's why she attacked the human and not Mihara... It was Rombar's attempt to protect his old friend the Shawá Lady," Rasnar explained.

"That makes sense, but it's still just theories. The truth is that none of us here trust Carol as we did before. The addition of Ksuma is somewhat difficult to accept," said Grandma with great concern.

"Carol would never abandon me or give me away. She had the opportunity to do so many times, and she never failed me, so I must vote for her," said Sasha.

"Dear, we can't afford any more failures," her grandmother replied.

"And what other options do we have?" James asked. Well, if Sasha trusts them, so do I, and that's two votes in favor, four counting our Garos, so we're already in the majority," proposed James, standing next to Carol. He then took the opportunity to hold her hand.

Thus, despite their mistrust, the Guardians had no choice but to accept this manifestation of faith or inattentiveness.

The Mission

After several days of adjusting to the new team, confidence with the new Carol and Ksuma began to improve. It even seemed that the mysterious change in the young girl had brought her even closer to Sasha. She shared her unusual powers with the siblings during tutor-led training sessions and became more relaxed around young James. After the trauma suffered from the change from human to mutant, the armor the girl had woven over the years to protect herself seemed to be weakening and she let her guard down out of necessity, choosing to communicate and understand, rather than repress and isolate herself.

It seemed that the Garos were also starting to get along better with Ksuma thanks to the bond that united the youngsters, but well, whatever it was, the team was moving forward at an unprecedented speed, and they considered starting new challenges and even launching a mission together.

Carol had demonstrated that her skills, both individually and on the back of her creature, were very useful for the group and she proved it with demonstrations, since she had to face them alone, in the middle of the combat field, an aim connived by the siblings themselves. Sometimes they were badly wounded despite being under the supervision of the teachers, who were always concerned about protecting the lives of the siblings in case they exceeded certain limits, but this served to prepare them for any adversity and gain confidence, which improved their creativity and initiative as warriors and brought out the special abilities of each one of them. These abilities were discovered as time went by amidst the traps and constant challenges that were unexpectedly presented to them in the training sessions planned by the tutors and among themselves. Without mercy, they began to participate as attackers, alone and in groups, but ended up becoming obsessed with the training, which they were already practicing alone. They were aware that the time had come to prepare for the battles, which were sure to begin very soon.

After an arduous workout, one day like any other, Rasnar decided to gather the whole team without having discussed it before with Nose or Mihara. He intended to announce something really important. Surprised, the trainers and the youngsters were dissatisfied as they were not pleased with the interruption of their routine. They were fully committed to it; eager to continue with the exercises; so, they reacted somewhat sparingly to the Guardian's intrusion, although they had reluctantly accepted the break, he asked them to take, because Rasnar had again promised them answers. So, they obeyed his orders and finished their tasks. Then they went to their rooms to take a good bath to wash off the mud that covered them from head to toe and to present themselves clean for dinner.

They had assumed it would be another session in front of the fire, like the previous ones, a place where they solved riddles as a family. Sasha and Carol debated about it while taking a relaxing bath in the secret room's pool, with young Sasha's Garo reproducing the bubbles of a jacuzzi thanks to the movement of its flexible, convex legs. Ksuma, meanwhile, heated the water using her ability to emanate fire, which left the friends in glory.

James had to settle for a far from pleasant shower, struggling to clean himself while trying to wash the madman in his Garo with soap, for although the bonded ones could not be seen by the rest of the humans, they could smell them. And the young man's creature stank. Its fur barely touched the water, unlike Sasha's Garo, which practically spent its days stuck in the lake.

For the first time, James had a responsibility to take care of for life. They were inseparable for both good and bad. The young man had to adapt to the ways and size of the beast in a slippery shower. His big friend was behaving as if it was a game and trying to escape from his bondage by sliding around the house with a naked James chasing him in desperation. Definitely a very different situation from that of the girls, who were almost asleep from how relaxed they were in that hot tub they had set up, enjoying a calmness that uncovered a surprising aspect of Sasha's Garo.

Relieved of the burden he bore from the strain his linked one had hitherto endured, the Garo stopped creating bubbles and left the water alone, thus exposing the coral parts of his wet body, which revealed a hypnotic glow of unparalleled colors. Carol and Ksuma stood rapt, deeply stunned under the effect of that skillful gift of Preciosas, proving that even in moments of pleasure and rest one could learn new skills to consider.

Meanwhile, the adults dispersed. Mihara took some time for herself. She needed to reflect in her private bathtub, which was surrounded by plants and had glass walls and vault through which she could see outside: a wonderful starry sky. Inspired, she raised some water as a panel in front of her and on it painted images of memories of the periods she had lived together with Aztrak; remembrances of her childhood, of her mother....

As for Nose, he continued to enjoy his daily showers, something he loved; sitting on the floor, he let the water fall as if it were rain. The synesthesia of sound and bodily sensation amazed him as he played with the element. It was his most intimate moment; he could be himself and forget about his position as a peon. Rasnar, on the other hand, hated bathing, but no one knew why. Despite being somewhat feline, he didn't lick himself too much to clean himself. James encouraged him every day, trying to provoke the beast without getting under his skin. Luckily, the keeper had a special method, a unique trick that kept him from being dirty or smelly. Without anyone seeing him, he would hide in the forest and shed his fur, shedding his dead cells. He managed to sow new plants with every hair that touched the ground, which, in turn, germinated quickly. Then the same flora cleansed his body and gave him an intoxicating aroma.

Shortly afterwards they were all ready for the meeting. To everyone's surprise, this time there would be no home-cooked dinner, as Rasnar had brought pizzas for everyone, probably posing as Bill. This meant the announcement was possibly about a very important matter, so the youths sat by the fire, impatiently waiting for the warden to project a film over the flames, while they devoured the food.

"Do you remember why I came here? The reason I used as a cover to come and train you?" the Talan began.

"Yes, to change the conditions of planet Earth in order to save the Sun and keep the solar system alive. In this way, you protect Argua, don't you?" replied the young man.

"Wow, James, you surprise me more and more every day," Mihara complimented him with a grin from ear to ear.

"Well, that was no excuse, much less a bluff. That's why the Thirteenth Kingdom let me come here, but what they don't know is what it takes to change the course of events," Rasnar commented.

"That is, they let you come because they understood the danger we were in, but they didn't know the resources Argua or the Universe itself needed to save us all, did they?" reasoned the boy.

"You're on fire, James, or rather, you'll be on fire," Carol laughed as she noticed the young man's hand dangerously close to the flames.

"Exactly, and I think the time has come to explain your mission," Rasnar announced.

"But what do we have to do with the planet? Not only do we have to save Argua, but we also have this responsibility? Is this a joke? The situation of our planet is the responsibility of all the beings that inhabit it," answered James, fanning his hand over an ember.

"It is not your task to save the world. Well yes, but mostly within the plan that has been drawn up with you as a team. Let me finish and you will understand," replied the beast.

"Then explain carefully, please, because I want to make sure I understand everything once and for all," Sasha insisted.

"Well, I will try to be as explicit and concise as I can to simplify the matter. What I am about to reveal to you will be your first task since you have already reached the level of training necessary to face the test. But it will not be in Argua, but on planet Earth. What better place to examine you and in a discreet manner, with dangers as real as those you will encounter once we enter the other world and the different battles we have to face there." The siblings looked at each other with great excitement and fear of the unknown, since what they were hearing was not only going to be the first step to a new adventure, but it would be the experience that would prove if they were prepared in the eyes of their masters. I already explained to you that there are exceptional humans who surpass the limits of the impossible, either because of the adversities this world puts them through or because they are born simply different. These people take their bodies to such a level of effort that, when they reach the point of self-improvement, they abandon their bodies and minds and let their Garo die, but not in vain.

"As you know, the death of the linked being puts an end to the strength of the terrestrial being. They fight hard battles with themselves after losing it. Most of them give up or settle in limbo and fall into a mental cycle from which they cannot get out, which eventually emaciate their physical appearance and lose their spiritual essence. But there are a few who, thanks to their persistence, are able to endure the most agonizing mental tortures, fighting against any kind of mental illness and without needing to take anything to ease their pain. Fighting with themselves on a daily basis, enduring this extreme suffering with great discipline, working against it alone twenty-four hours a day as their only daily routine. This process can last for years and torments them in silence under the gaze of incomprehension.

"What they don't know is that this makes them much stronger, both in terms of their organism and their intellect, and gives them an unprecedented endurance and strength, as well as an understanding of the world and the energy that surrounds them that is far superior to any ordinary human being. These people, who manage to overcome this tough and personal challenge in such an extraordinary way are reborn as new beings. With that, the wonderful miracle of the rebirth of their Garo arises. But this does not make these humans invincible. Far from it, since most of them relapse, some are lost forever and others continue with this struggle in the intimacy of a bubble of constant suffering, in which they appear to be stoic in the eyes of those who do not understand their situation, since they do not see the war in which they are fighting for their life.

"From among these beings appear the most powerful of the reborn. Those can be count on the fingers of our hands. Truly extraordinary beings that rise from the ashes in such a way that they acquire not only more emotional and rational intelligence than any existential individual, but they acquire supernatural powers by Talan decree or, better said, as a reward for their enormous resistance to such an arduous and grim life of drowning in a world that is not prepared for them. Their Garos are detached from Talos, so we completely lose track of them. Their flowers are transformed and are different from the others. They grow on the sacred Mount Tali, a place inaccessible because of the energy surrounding this hill, which nullifies our powers to fly over it. This issue determines that the reach to the buds is enormously difficult and dangerous. Adversities that not only can kill us Talans, but sometimes even destroy the very stem of the reborn Garo, forcing them to repeat their battle, if they are able to do so, a very unfair aspect for their related humans.

"More than once we tried to reach these flowers to save them, but we lost many of our best warriors on these missions. I myself was badly wounded. So, we decided the risk wasn't worth it when we didn't even know if we could transplant them to another, less powerful terrain. As finding them is a hard work of tracking and exploration among the aggressive flora and when night comes their light can be seen from a distance, we decided to leave them there. For this reason, your first mission will be to find these beings. As you will not be able to see their Garos on this planet, the main task will be to find the humans to whom they are linked," Rasnar explained.

"But that would be like looking for a needle in a haystack; it's impossible, we wouldn't even know where to start," Sasha replied.

"For that reason, you must first study the provenance of your targets, the eight primordial elements of the universe, for they are the only hope left to our solar system, to your planet and to Argua.

"If we can find them all and convince them to join us, we will gain more strength to fight the danger that stalks our worlds and their peoples. Soon, under the consent of Zotrak, the Five Sages and the Council of Argua will launch the eight rays that will become the seven principles of nature. The sparks will implant themselves within these extraordinary human beings and turn them into the original essences from which all things are made. That is, the eight fundamental aspects of universal reality in the cosmos and in any being," Rasnar declared.

"Eight beams for nine elements?" she asked, puzzled.

"Well, Sasha, I see you are attentive. Go to sleep, now. Tomorrow we will make an unforgettable trip to the library of Kundalini Kabiri, an old hermit friend whom I haven't visited for a long time," informed the Guardian.

"And where does this old friend of yours live?" asked the young woman, thinking about how to pack her suitcase.

But Rasnar just smiled. Then he got up from his chair and closed the meeting.

"In Gangkhar Puensum," he said, walking out the door.

The Library

The next morning, James was the first to wake up. To his surprise, he had Carol's face in front of his. The boy was gawking at her, thinking that for some inexplicable reason the young woman had gone to sleep in his room that night. The girl opened her eyes and stared at James, who was petrified. At that instant the magical moment was broken. She let out a shriek and pushed the boy away. Behind her, Sasha's head popped up, completely disoriented.

"But what are you doing in my bed, shouting like this?" Sasha exclaimed.

"You mean what are we all doing sleeping together?" James replied, trying to justify the tension of the moment with Carol.

"Your brother's a stalker. He was watching me sleep!" she replied.

"That's not true! I woke up next to you, just like my sister, I swear I'm as surprised as you are!" he insisted.

"Guys, look," said Sasha, interrupting the couple's discussion.

They were in a room full of books and papyrus curled all over the walls, with strange artifacts displayed along the corridor, arranged in several rows of shelves with long stairs to access them. There were numerous wooden floors that seemed to be embedded in a non-uniform stone to which that unusual building was anchored. This had the effect of creating an extravagant asymmetry, as well as establishing a rather eerie icy atmosphere.

"What is this place?" Carol asked.

"Good morning, young promises. You are in the library of Gangkhar Puensum, the white peak of the three godbrothers. What a coincidence, isn't it?" said an unfamiliar voice.

"Is he saying that because we make three?" Carol quietly asked the siblings.

"There's no such thing as coincidence," James said, looking at the scrawny man.

"I see that someone has been watching the cosmos," replied the old man.

"Excuse me, but who are you?" asked Sasha.

"I am Kundalini Kabiri, the only monk who guards this library, unknown to the earthly world until today. Welcome to what I call the terrestrial avernus."

Despite looking like an old man, the monk was very well preserved, as signaled by his physical and mental agility. His movements were quick, and his mind seemed to be brilliant, based on how he spoke, while he drew the curtains of an open window, trying to stop the gusts of icy wind that entered the room.

The siblings stepped forward to the outside and looked at the cracks in the stringpiece floor that creaked with every step and gave them little confidence in the stability of the place. The clouds trying to move into the room. When the clouds cleared the area, they discovered through the cracks in the floor of that cracking balcony the great height at which they were situated in that decrepit building, anchored in some unheard-of way to one of the cliff walls of a rocky and icy mountain.

"We are at 24836 feet above sea level. So far, no human has ever managed to get here. It is the safest and most sacred place you will find on the face of the earth," said the monk.

"How long have you been alone here?" Sasha asked intrigued.

"After 1879 years I lost count, and very rare are the visits that one receives in this place. I only notice the passage of time with the changes in the outside world that are reflected in the illustrations and writings that the library receives. In them I can appreciate the clothing, the appearance, the slang, etc. of the beings of each of the corners of the world that surrounds us. Through the new books that are appearing on the shelves, I see how the events unfold after each occurrence, and the cycle of life from the beginning of the Big Bang until now; this very hour and this very minute; information that makes one realize that, despite the clear evolutionary changes in our history, everything comes and goes. The same mistakes are made through the repetition of identical patterns and the population is always convinced that it is something new. It is the great thinkers, those that investigate to satiety so as to avert the sin of being uneducated and ignorant, who are the only ones capable of seeing that society lives subjugated to a banal and absurd cycle, which goes from beginning to beginning, or from end to end. Like a spiral coil, returning to the transcendental point, of which humans do not seem to be aware as they stumble with astonishment on the same facts and the same fashions, although they show it using a different scenography to camouflage it as something unheard of.

"Thus, rarely does anything surprising come up that catches my attention. However, my work here, at this point, is not something completely routine, as I am in charge of studying, reviewing, ordering, and preserving the documents that arrive; a tremendously important and responsible task for which one must be physically and mentally prepared," explained the old man, imitating the posture of a flamingo with his palms together pointing to the sky. His beaks protruded above the clouds as he balanced on a slender wooden bar that peeked out from the delicate vertiginous vantage point where the girls were miraculously standing.

"A hermit librarian, a millenarian, and a daredevil to boot. Great," said the boy.

"Kundalini's task is revered for its great difficulty, young James. Do not judge him by his appearance, for he has the mental power to spend years in solitude without losing his mind. He spends his time knowing more than anyone else in this world, both in theory and in practice, and is physically trained to defend this sacred place from any kind of external threat," Rasnar commented, stepping out onto the deck as the monk sprang up into the air, bending the one knee on which he stood thousands of feet above the ground, not in the least affected by altitude sickness or vertigo. He supported himself on the deck over the immense void in that complicated posture, leaning his weight only on one leg.

"Seeing the man in such postures on the flimsy structure, knowing how long he had been living there alone, James felt useless and embarrassed. An icy gust of wind, which made the hut creak like a schooner about to sink, made his hair stand on end. He wanted to get the hell out of there.

"My friend Rasnar! What a joy to see you again. We didn't have time to talk last night, but what the prophecy said, you have fulfilled. We'll have time to catch up. I can see it must not have been easy to train these youths, but you have done a great job, from what I have read," the peculiar monk congratulated his friend.

"Anyone who comes here can learn of our existence and discover our plans or those of anyone in this world. We are surrounded by information; that is to say, by dangerous power," commented the eldest of the youngsters.

"Well, the young lady is smart," said the old man.

"Kunda, this is Sasha, descendant of Aztrak, son of Zotrak, and the Shawá Lady Mihara, the daughter of one of the Five Sages, who allied herself with human blood. The boy is her brother, James. And the other young woman is an earthly friend of the siblings, whom…"

"Friend, please," he interrupted the Talan, "what do you take me for? I know everything. You don't need to explain anything to me."

Rasnar bowed his ears.

"You've been alone here too long, Kunda. I think you could use the company, if you don't drive them all crazy first, of course," the beast blurted out.

"You will ask where your creatures are. Only you are allowed to stay here, so you will join the others when you have understood your purpose. Until that time, you will be under my guardianship, and Rasnar' and no one else's," Kundalini informed the three kids.

"I didn't know Garos could be separated from their bonds," Carol replied.

"Humans?" asked the monk.

"Well, part human? Sorry. Does this mean we can separate from them?" the young woman reiterated.

"It seems that you have an advantage, since you have a weapon with which you can train, as well as entrust with separate missions. Someone who will always, no matter what, protect you; a true friend and ally, full of purity and infinite loyalty to her respective bond.

"Now that you know of their existence, you must protect your Garos more than ever. They are the best thing you have and ever will have," Kunda warned.

490

"I love him so much. I miss him already," said the only boy in the group.

"James, please don't spread your energy by making us weak or you'll make us sensitive. You're not the only one who feels this way. We have a job to do, and this kind of remark only makes it harder for us," Carol complained.

"You are my goddess..." said James gawking at her with numb eyes.

"Yuck," Carol replied just as the old man appeared holding a tray with three bowls filled with what appeared to be milk.

"How did you do that? A second ago you were... and now you appear from the inside?" Sasha was surprised.

"Come with me," said the millenarian, walking barefoot on the icy floor that kept creaking as he led them to the last section of the library, like the rest, with a balcony on one side and walls of books around it. But the only difference was that in this one there was a triangle carved into the wood of the floor, full of engravings inscribed on the inside and outside of the geometric shape. Each of you take a bowl and sit one at each corner of the triangle." The youths obeyed and Rasnar sat on the balcony, behind the curtains that were being gently lifted to let in the icy breeze from outside. The wings of the huge guardian, drooping on either side of his body, stood out against the beautiful background behind him. Kunda settled himself in the center of the triangle in the same pose he was meditating on the wood, the one that looked like it was about to fall into the abyss. On one leg, with the other bent over it in the lotus posture, he pressed his palms together and closed his eyes. This milk is not yak milk, as would be expected from the region we are in and the customs of the people. Because of the ritual we are about to perform, it is a more exquisite concoction, a difficult one to obtain, but knowing that you were coming, I made a special request in return for a favor owed me and obtained this elixir for you from the depths of the Himalayan ice peaks," the monk explained proudly.

"It's great!" exclaimed the boy.

"No, no, young James. You must wait; the three of you must take it together when the delta state is closed and thus enter a trance, in tune with your sisters," the old man explained.

"Sisters?" repeated the boy.

"It is the milk of the Snow Venus, the most ancient of the yetis," said the monk.

"I'm sorry, what?"

Kunda smiled and opened his eyes. He had distracted the boy by telling him the truth about the drink they were going to have. Then they could focus on what they needed to do.

He began to recite a few words looking James in the eyes, petrified in the same posture, until with a jump he changed legs simulating the previous posture. This was accompanied by a strong breeze that entered through the gates where Rasnar was standing. The epigraphs surrounding the outside of the triangle rose from the ground. Kunda dropped to the ground in the meditation posture, eyes closed, palms pressed together. Then the letters engraved on the planks inside the figure began to glow.

The man opened his eyelids and the girls heard "drink" in their minds. Without question, the three of them began to gulp the milk from the bowls as Kunda spread his hands apart and extended them toward them until they rested in front of the girls' faces, with the bowls still in their mouths. Suddenly, an eye popped out of each palm, magic that stunned the teenagers. Milk stained their legs as they dropped the bowls. Time seemed to stand still, holding everything physical at a standstill. Meanwhile, the minds were still as active as ever, watching the ocelli emerging from the old man's limbs, elongating, and approaching James and Sasha's faces.

Carol watched the scene with tremendous stupor, immobilized, noticing that those organs were slithering through the air like snakes as they stealthily made their way towards the faces of the siblings. In slow motion, unable to look away from the unpleasant image. At that moment a third eye appeared without further ado between Kunda's eyebrows, and he locked his gaze on Carol's as he approached her. The young woman watched in horror as the librarian's three eyeballs shot out of his body and darted towards them. These then penetrated their skulls, causing eerie anguish that brought them to the brink of a heart attack. He then induced a coma with the conscious fear that it might be irreversible.

The Vision

Dazzled by the flash of several cameras, James looked straight ahead. Several paparazzi were waiting behind glass doors. He glanced behind him in case there were any celebrities but found no one else. Those people were focusing their devices on him, but they were not calling his name, but that of a certain Yóio. At that moment, a burly man came out of nowhere, grabbed him by the arm and pulled him into an elevator. There he stood in front of him, with his back turned, protecting him.

The elevator music was somewhat annoying. His only view was the huge back of the gorilla, which blocked his field of vision. Puzzled, he felt around the back-to-front closet in an attempt to break the ice and ask the bodyguard if he understood anything of what was going on, but when he looked at his own hand, the boy was astonished. It was decorated with rings, bracelets, and even false nails. He noticed that she was also carrying a small purse hanging from her forearm. The young man reacted by letting out a small uncontrolled moan, which came from inside him with the voice of a female, which immediately upset the henchman in front of him.

"What's going on, Yóio?" asked the security officer, analyzing the situation.

"Yóio?" James repeated.

"You must be exhausted from today, so many interviews and the hustle and bustle of the press, plus the masses of fans that have been chasing you down the street. I promise it won't happen again. Someone must have tipped them off about your schedule, but we'll find him or her, so don't worry." The elevator stopped with a pleasant ding and the doors opened directly into a huge and impressive penthouse. You're home. Would you like me to stay, or would you prefer to be alone for a better rest?" James stood silently gawking at the place. It was everything he could have wished for and more. "Miss?"

From somewhere in the house appeared an elegant butler who, with a jerk of his glove, made the escort turn and leave. Instantly, with a clap of his hands, the butler called the staff bearing a splendid cocktail on shining trays. Two maids put their hands to work and gave him a seated massage in front of the incredible views of what looked like a metropolis, given the variety of lights from the skyscrapers. Then James closed his eyes, absorbed by the pleasure of that luxury, and an aroma of incense covered his sense of smell, urging him to open them again. Before his eyes was a new vision quite contrary to the previous one.

Startled, he looked around in amazement. He looked for his maids and the wonderful apartment he swore he had been in, but he was surrounded by candles and flowers arranged over a huge river of brown water. A series of intoxicating chants enveloped him in an area filled with filth and poverty. As attire, he wore a yellow tunic that crossed his torso and covered his lower body.

He wore heavy dreadlocks that hung down to his waist and his limbs were very thin from lack of food, but his stomach seemed satisfied.

The boy watched those filthy waters for a while. He saw candles adorned with chrysanthemums floating on the opaque element inches from where he sat cross-legged on the edge of the shore. Intoxicated by a mixture of burnt wood, olibanum, and spice fragrances, he closed his eyes and entered a Zen state he had never experienced before. When he regained consciousness, he was in a different setting, so he let himself be carried away by this new soul, like an observer trapped in a body and an environment that was not his own.

In this new vision, he decided to learn about the perception of the world by caressing the warm, white sand on which he rested. He looked at the sky. The leaves of the palm trees covered him from the sun, without completely blocking its beautiful rays. He inspected the surroundings and discovered in front of him crystal clear water with perfect waves that called him to intertwine with them, so he got up, took a board that he had at his side and paddled into that incredible sea, watching the shapes drawn by the light on the sand as it moved away from the shore. He passed over an exquisite reef where a varied number of colorful little fish could be seen.

Suddenly, a big wave formed and, as if he had been surfing all his life, he sank the board, dodging the big mountain of white foam that rushed over his body. He emerged unscathed on the opposite side and discovered new breakers approaching. But without fear, he paddled on with excitement until he quickly turned the board into a position where the nose of the board was aligned perpendicular to the shore, and pulled out, joining the magnificent wave with a perfect take off, starting from a right bottom turn. Then he put his back to the crystalline wall and entered an incredible and masterful water tube. He slid his fingers along that translucent wall while listening to the captivating sound of that natural conduit, until he came out with a reentry and climbed up to the crest to come back down again with momentum. He ended up in a beautiful aerial with it flying over the top of the wave. Here James dropped the body with complete confidence, sinking into the sea, circling inside those foamy ripples, letting himself be carried by the subterranean tide, flowing in its waters as part of its current.

The boy felt different, calmer, but, at the same time, ecstatic; a combination that kept him in balance with himself and the world, full of positive energy, with a calm peace, as if he had recharged the batteries of a lifetime. He let the body float to the shore, where someone waved to him from a distance.

"What an amazing session today, Vic," the stranger said as he reached her side.

Then, dismayed, he took her by the hand and made a remark about a wound that was bleeding and staining her shell anklet. But the cut caused by rubbing against the reef did not matter to her. He realized that the body he now inhabited was that of a young woman with a golden tan and long, wild hair.

"I didn't even know I knew how to surf."

The boy looked at her quizzically and asked if she was all right, but the vision degenerated and an eyeball appeared floating in front of him, studying him with incredible attention through a huge pupil. This caused him to retch.

"Welcome, boy," said Kunda as he took his eye away from the young man's face and returned it back to the palm of his hand. Now meditate quietly on what you have seen while your sisters return to us.

Instantly, Carol awoke from her unconscious state with a scream and covered her head with her hands.

"He needs help!" She exclaimed, looking at James.

"It's okay. Easy, it was just a vision, Carol."

At once, Sasha began to breathe rapidly and gasp, sweating heavily despite the coldness of the room.

"Take her out of his vision, Kunda," the boy demanded.

"I cannot alter the course of her path, James," the monk replied.

"She's getting worse, what if something happens to her? Sasha, can you hear me? Wake up, Sasha!"

And with a jerk, the young woman opened her eyes with the old man's eye still tucked inside her head, attached to it by a cord of human flesh, as the ocular nerve ran from the young woman's forehead to the librarian's palm.

"Get it off me, James, get it off my head!" the girl looked at it in anguish.

"Calm down, otherwise you'll block the exit of my eye!" said Kunda, bringing his hand close to the girl's face. Then he placed it on her forehead and left her silent from the blow. He separated the back of the young girl, and everything returned to normal, with no organs coming out or going in from anyone.

"Self-control is not your virtue," said the monk, looking at them doubtfully and crossing his arms.

"What have you shown us?" asked Sasha.

"It was not I who made you see. It is your destiny that shows you what to perceive. I am only the channel that has helped you to discover it in a faster way, but, unfortunately, I have not been able to share your visions, so you must do it as soon as possible so as not to forget a single detail. This information can be very useful," commented Kundalini.

"Our destiny?" James questioned, exalted.

"What do these visions have to do with our mission?" his sister wanted to know.

"Tell me first what you have seen," ordered the old man.

"Answer him!" commanded the Guardian, re-entering the room in an altered state and blocking the doors with open wings.

Carol got up and moved away from the triangle carved into the floor, where the siblings and Kunda were standing. She stood by the walls of books and curled up, covering her head with her hood. Then she remained silent. In an attempt to calm the situation, James shared his visions as he had experienced them, from beginning to end, with great passion and motivation. Then her friend uncovered her head angrily, tears streaming down her cheeks.

"Why have you had such beautiful visions and mine have been horrible? What does it all mean?" Carol demanded.

"I promise that we will explain in due course, but you must tell us what you have seen and felt, in detail now that it is fresh in your mind. It is extremely important to keep as much information as possible, no matter how insignificant it may seem."

Sasha looked at Rasnar and Kunda and communicated through telepathy that it would be only fair if they could all experience what they had seen, sharing everyone's with everyone, to take away the bad feeling that had stayed in both her and Carol's bodies. Immediately, the monk got up from the floor and gave his seat to Carol. He then explained to her that they were going to transfer their visions from one to the other and that to do so each of the young folk should stand on an angle of the triangle. The old man, placed in the center of the geometric shape, would join them through contact.

Carol only had to place her hand on the back of the man's neck, while the siblings would take him by the hands to create a triskelion between the four of them. Then they would pass the visions to Rasnar by means of an energetic sphere that he himself would create on the triskelion. He would remain outside the triangle.

"I was a boy, there was music, but it wasn't Western... I've never heard anything like it, I'm not even sure if it was from this time or before. They didn't speak our language; we seemed to be working for other people, very wealthy people who spoke another language, a different language from the boy I had become.

"I think we were a family of musicians, in Indian-like garb, but with certain differences. That's when I looked into a saucer-shaped metal mirror. I saw that I had a darker complexion than ours, long black hair, and was quite handsome. From my appearance, it was possible that I was a mixture of the two castes, as most of those I felt close to had darker skin than mine.

"I had the feeling that I, the boy, was making the deals for the musicians, that is, for my community. It all happened very fast, but I think we were nomads, as that was not our home. We were somehow entrusted to be there for the enjoyment of a certain sahib. We were in a courtyard; I could hear the crowd mentioning something like "Atash Behrams". I don't know, it seemed like something important, because not only were they talking about it, but they were singing about it sitting on the ground while eating and drinking, feasting in exquisitely embroidered garments.

"They had an incredible pond in the center surrounded by walls adorned with colorful tiles embedded in white marble. Then someone came up to me and told me that he knew what I really was. At that instant, I came out of that vision. I woke up right when... when I killed a man. I remember jumping off a rock, hitting him in the shoulder with a paddle I called a patu... After dislocating his arm with my attack, I took away any chance of him being able to defend himself and took the opportunity to hit him again, this time in the temple. I killed him instantly.

"Every move was on purpose, knowing exactly what I was doing and its consequences, as if I was prepared for that moment and felt strong, alive, so much so... I took the head of my enemy, the man I had defeated, back to my village, where people cheered me and bestowed me the honor of etching new tattoos on my body and face.

"I don't know why I thought I was so much older, so I was in shock when I saw my face as I cooled off in the river. I was just a kid. Then, I lost consciousness and went from a horrible moment to a worse one. I woke up in a huge forest, all alone. In the distance I saw a beautiful mountain. Then I heard a noise and, as I turned around, a huge bear came out of the undergrowth, pouncing on me with its claws and huge teeth. I can still hear the frightening roar of that beast in my head."

Carol separated her hand from Kundalini's skin, thus cutting off the flow of images to the siblings.

"Wow, now I understand why you were so upset when you woke up and your reaction to hearing my visions. I wish I could have had yours and given you mine, Carol. I mean that from the bottom of my heart. It wasn't fair," James sympathized, deeply distressed.

"The visions cannot be chosen; they have been entrusted to each of you for a purpose, so jumping to conclusions is a mistake. Everything you experience, both in the past and present, and whatever comes in the future, are lessons you must learn about yourself and who you are in the world around you," Rasnar explained.

"I'm sorry I don't have much more information about my last vision. I think, from the scream I let out when I saw the bear, I must have been a girl, but I couldn't swear to it," said the young woman.

"What about you, Sasha?" James asked.

"Carol, change places with Sasha. Now it's her turn to share her visions with you."

The girls changed places on the triangle on the floor and, with the same procedure as before, Sasha began to talk with her hand on the old man's head.

"I woke up walking in a street full of people, with illuminated signs everywhere. From the symbols they contained, I would say it was Japan. I could not see myself in any mirror, but I remember going with a girl into a booth, where we took pictures that we could retouch from the same machine through a screen, with effects and drawings, before printing them. That's when I discovered my face. I looked sad or, rather, indifferent; on the other hand, the other girl was smiling, gesticulating with her hands, cheerful. But even standing next to her, I had an exorbitant feeling of emptiness inside me.

"I said goodbye to her and, as soon as I turned the corner, I ran in the direction of a motorcycle. I got on and rode like a maniac until I reached a huge mansion with sliding doors. From the way I was moving I would say that I was hiding from someone, since I was walking very stealthily, barefoot and with the lights off so I wouldn't get caught. I reached a room where there was a cutlass and, behind it, a samurai-like armor placed on a kind of altar at the back of the huge room. I remember looking at the sheathed sword for a while, but when I went to draw it, someone mentioned my name and I moved on to the next vision.

"In it I was digging a small hole. This time it's clear to me that it was a girl, even though I couldn't see my face. I know because I wasn't wearing a T-shirt or anything to cover me from above. From the hole I drew water that I drank eagerly, as if I had been walking for a long time under that scorching sun. Then I used the scarf I was wearing on my head and tied it around my chest to cover it. I remember my hair falling over my face; it was a fluffy blonde curl.

"I continued my labor by walking for insatiable hours, watching the arid ground so as not to leave footprints. My feet were wrapped in cloth so as not to leave a trace. I think I was not only running away, but I was tracking something or someone... Well, at some point I heard a river in the distance and ran towards it, but my ears detected another sound and, instinctively, I threw a boomerang, which I had tucked in my pants, in that direction. Then some white men with an aborigine appeared and were coming towards me.

"I remember that feeling very vividly. They didn't seem to see me as their equal, I think because my hair and skin were not as dark as theirs, but I'm not sure. But I do know that I was frightened at the sight of them, so much so that I went into the water of that stream to hide. I held my breath while holding on to a rock to keep myself submerged. I did not use a rod to breathe because the native would notice and discover me. At that instant I discovered before me a huge crocodile. The intensity of the moment forced me to surface, but the image paralyzed my body.

"Then I felt the men approach the shore to observe the reptile, pointing their guns at it. The animal turned toward me, upsetting the men with its sudden movement, who quickly fired at the crocodile and seriously wounded it. I took advantage of the moment to put the sling in its mouth before it exposed its body to the drift. Upon seeing me, the white men made the aborigine enter the muddy waters where I was submerged to make a check on the dead animal. They forced him to risk his life for a piece of cloth.

"As soon as he had it in his hands and showed it to those men, they assumed it had been swallowed by the animal and turned away. Desperate, with my feet anchored on that rock, I peeked my lips over the surface in tremendous anguish, trying to inhale oxygen, as I had to continue to keep silent so they would not hear me, but there were more crocodiles approaching the area, attracted by the blood of the downed reptile. And without further ado, from there I moved on to my last vision, in which I remember feeling cold on the back of a horse.

"I was riding with a bow that I carried in the hand that held the reins of the saddle and a large bird of prey clutched to the forearm of my other limb. I remember that I was putting the bird's hood on properly, when I noticed what looked like a pickup truck coming toward me at high speed over the plateau where I was standing. Alarmed, my instinct made me gallop in the opposite direction to the vehicle. At some point I released the hawk and guided it with a series of shouts and whistles that I used to give it instructions about our escape as it flew over me. I looked back and..." Sasha removed her hand from Kunda's head, "I came back here, with you," she said aloud, not projecting any more images into the minds of her companions.

"The visions have nothing to do with each other; not even each other's visions have anything in common," Carol commented.

"It's true. It's disjointed, nothing makes sense," James said, looking at the floor.

"To begin with, you should tell us why we had to experience these delusional visions and then explain to us what each of them means. It would be the least you could do after bringing us to the top of the world to subject us to more psychological torture," Sasha stated, looking at Rasnar.

Chapter X
Elements

Meanwhile, in the mansion, Mihara and Nose were dealing with the teenagers' Garos, which were taking over the house, because they were possessed by the anxiety of not being next to the humans to whom they were linked, whose emotions of uneasiness and confusion they could feel. Without understanding where these whirlwinds of feelings were coming from, because they could not see what was happening to those they were attached to, it was only to be expected that the reaction of the beasts was getting out of control.

Following the orders given under the command of the Guardian, who had the power to mislead the creatures while taking the youngsters to the only place on the face of the earth undetectable to the Garos, his fellow tutors had to fight the poor animals that were blinded with frustration, destroying everything they found on their way through the manor, and even facing each other in combat, destroying areas of the forest and crumbling the properties on the Courdeil family estate. Mihara, in a somewhat desperate act, asked Nose to try to use his powers to calm them down, since even he was suffering from the tail whips and the constant flames of Carol's drakon, besides enduring the lifts and throws, and also the endless hugs with which they were trapped or, rather, almost suffocated by the countless flexible limbs of James' monster, which made them roll around until they vomited from the dizziness caused by such antics.

By far the worst of all was Sasha's Garo, which disappeared under the waters of the lake. Terrified, they had to go into the lake and battle against the speed with which it moved and violently attacked them. Overwhelmed by the ferocious and indomitable animal that they tried to tame, always trying not to harm it, as this would affect Sasha, the poor masters would end up dejected and fall asleep anywhere from exhaustion. Then they would wake up in the most hidden places or hanging from anywhere, something that amused the Garos. Thus, in order to rest, they would lock themselves in closets or pantries that would block the animals and remain unnoticed until they woke up. Then they would discover that the creatures they were supposed to protect had once again destroyed the house, leaving obvious evidence of their presence, such as hair, scales and corals detached from the bodies and embedded in the walls, ceilings and, unfortunately, the inside of the refrigerator and pantry. Not to mention the fact that they were left without provisions.

While the peon managed to control the chaos, Grandma tried to contact Rasnar to find out how things were going on the other side of the world, hoping that they would return soon or, at least, offer a solution to the dramatic situation. But detecting the telepathic signal around the library was impossible, since the sacred place was protected from any magic or external technology, as if it did not exist in this world. Therefore, all they could do was wait and be patient.

After the failed attempt to communicate with the Talan, Mihara went in search of Nose to tell him the bad news. He found him inside the house. Sasha's Garo about to ram him with its antlers. Mihara ran towards them, and, with a leap, she jumped over the fountain and put her hand on the animal's forehead, thus avoiding the tip of the antlers. With her other hand she gripped the antler tightly, thus managing to calm the beast's confused instincts thanks to the genes in common with her granddaughter. Then, without releasing her hands, she mounted the back with great care so as not to separate the palm from the head and not to injure herself with the pieces of reef that came out of the creature's body. Once this task was accomplished, she guided it to a huge room that neither Nose nor anyone else had seen yet, as its doors were unnoticed as they blended with the wall. Mihara whispered several words and doors with large locks of worn gold opened to give way to a room designed with a dome and walls reminiscent of glass with white translucent stone resembling alabaster. It contained a formidable cistern that was surrounded by succulent vegetation, wildly scattered throughout the enclosure.

The humidity of the atmosphere was so intense that at first it was suffocating, as it was like breathing the dense vaporized air of a hamam, but after a while it calmed them in such a way that it took them to a kind of trance in which they harmonized mind and body. The animal finally calmed down.

"What is this place?" Nose asked, approaching the plants, and stroking the heron that was grazing on them.

"It is the room where we keep the exquisite flora that my late husband brought back from his extravagant explorations around the world, on which of course I accompanied him. Unheard of plants that we discovered thanks to the little essence I had left as a Shawá at the time; a quality that I used to my advantage to perceive and find them for their peculiar properties. My Charles was so fascinated by this ability that, after our first explorations, he began to plan more and more trips, taking the risk of entering hidden and dangerous places. He loved to see me happily locating new magical species, as he called them, although he then shared them with the Freemasons to which he belonged, he said, for medicinal purposes.

"I remember him bringing samples of each of these plants to his meetings, always keeping this place a secret because of his love for me. I, on the other hand, devoted my time to recreating in this room a fantastic world where I could feel safe, my private comfort zone," she explained.

"Is that why I feel this way?" asked the peon with some seaweed from the pool hanging out of his mouth.

"Well, that's because some of these plants tend to emanate properties with somewhat special effects, both when ingested and when inhaling the scented mist from the environment. But don't worry; for us Shawá s they are not harmful, but if a human were exposed to them on a daily basis, they could kill him," she said with a chuckle, noticing that the peon was gobbling leaves of all kinds.

"It is for that reason that I have the room sealed. I didn't want to poison any of my servants or guests, but now that we are alone, we can enjoy the ecstasy of this place. It will be our secret... Why didn't I do this before with you? Ah, yes, for the children and... Rasssnarrrr," she commented, showing signs of tipsiness.

"We should have come earlier! And me starving to death with this incredible pantry right under my nose."

Neither of them noticed that the toxic effluents emanating from the leaves and flowers of that extraordinary vegetation were spreading outside, because they had left the door of the lair open, and they reached the muzzle of James' and Carol's Garos. Both animals ended up inside the room.

"Hello, friends! Come on in, come on in!" exclaimed Mihara with great enthusiasm, waving to the creatures as she waved across the sargassum pond lying on one of its huge leaves, with

Nose floating beside her, lying on a fabulous flower. The scene stunned the newly arrived Garos.

Meanwhile, Kunda and the three youngsters meditated on the peak of one of the icy mountains, surrounded by snow-capped peaks above blankets of white clouds. The siblings were learning to channel their energy through mental control over the cold they were subjected to, the effect of the frightening altitude, and having to endure the strong gusts of wind that whipped them and covered them with frost. All the while recalling the visions. At one point the three of them put their minds together and at once nine bright points appeared in the distance like stars in the sky. The monk opened his eyes and, from a kind of sack hanging on his back, took out a monocle.

"Observe!" the old man directed, passing the old eyeglass to the three of them. "Tell me what you see."

All three agreed that the triangle they saw in the distance was composed of nine smaller ones, each positioned in a different place on the earth. But unlike Kundalini, the youngsters could only distinguish three of those nine elements. Moreover, in a different color, which meant that the signs appearing in the firmament did not coincide with each other in either hue or location.

"The cosmos has decided your destiny. Each of you will go alone to seek the three forces assigned to you out of the nine you are to find. Now fix your eyes upon the purposes manifested to you and turn the lens of the monocular as soon as you have them in view. In this way you will discover the position of your targets, which will be recorded in the memory of the apparatus, and this will cause both its coordinates and the elements in question to be associated with the eye you use to examine them.

The team did as they were told and three small equilateral triangles were etched on their faces, near where they had placed the magic eyepiece on their skin.

"Well, let's get going. We need to be back at the library in time to show you something important before you leave."

Exhausted, they followed the orders of the old man, who was descending the impossible mountain range covered with ice and virgin snow with the agility of an irbis, when, without warning, Kunda stopped suddenly.

"Do you want to feel what it's like to be God?" The man stretched out his arms and adopted the position of the cross, forcing the siblings to imitate him. "When I tell you, we'll clap our hands in unison, okay?"

The youngsters looked at each other in amazement, as the old man seemed a bit crazy, but the genius knew very well what he was doing, so, despite their doubts about what he was planning, they obeyed. Their applause echoed across the horizon, unleashing an unstoppable echo that shook the ground. The teenagers clung to the stony edge of that summit, unlike the monk, who stood with his arms outstretched before his handiwork, observing the enormous layer of snow that was falling from the mountain slopes, with large blocks of ice that swept everything away as they advanced. The brutal sonority lashed the adjacent mountain ranges, causing the adjacent hills to decline, which gave rise to an unstoppable concert. A visual spectacle of uncontrolled nature, which shook the place with aggressive avalanches that resounded in their ears with their thunderous roar; with waves of snow that smashed them with force.

When the sinister spectacle was over, the teenagers struggled to their feet, perplexed by what they had caused. They had emerged unscathed from a natural catastrophe and felt more alive than ever, powerful, and unstoppable. It was such a gratifying feeling that it made Sasha let out huge laughs, as the young girl was rarely seen smiling and shouted to the horizon with outstretched hands. The old man, surprised, took the others by the hand to feel the same energy. Together they raised their fists as they howled at the whitish landscape, sharing that act of liberation as they felt the earth shudder beneath their feet and the merciless whip of the blizzard. It was the most intense experience of their lives.

Back at the hut, the evening sun slowly dimmed its light like a nuanced watercolors dressing the monotonous expanse of white clouds that traversed the outskirts of the balcony of the library with a rosy haze of pale wine stripes filled with lilac rivers and blue drifts.

"What you are about to witness in heaven are signs sent only to the three of you."

And out of that sea of soft blushes, an emerald aurora borealis began to spread across the firmament, branching out in three paths for each of the young folk.

"Don't you think it's kind of eye-catching? I mean, a lot of people might see it and investigate it," James commented.

"Humans will always be searching in the everlasting quest for what they crave most in this life: answers. But the truth is, they will never get them. In this case, for example, they will only see the twilight as a brushstroke of the same hue, which they will admire for the duration, as a phenomenon to be recorded in history. But for you, both the vision and the meaning of this aurora will be very different. The cosmos will continue to mark the sky with them and show you the way until you find the elements that have been entrusted to you. Each bifurcation is presented with a different color. The hue you perceive will be the manifestation in the firmament that will signal the course of the journey, which you will undertake individually; one that only you will be able to see," the old man explained.

"Kunda, it is time," said Rasnar from the library, drawing the attention of the monk, who immediately covered his head with a thin cloak around his shoulders.

The man entered and walked through the corridors of the dilapidated building. He led the girls and the boy to a rock wall where there was a small altar containing a fuchsia powder with which he impregnated his finger, with which he made a mark of on his forehead. Next, he crossed his arms over his shoulder blades and, leaning the stained area of his forehead against the wall, he recited a few words. Then he separated from the wall and covered his face with his hands. He then uncovered his head and magically stepped through the rocky panel.

Stunned, the youngsters advanced until they noticed the tunnel, something they could only perceive when they tried to touch the wall. They noticed that their hands were sinking into the rock, but they could not see what fate had in store for them once they passed through the mirage and crossed to the other side.

Rasnar gave no room for doubt and pushed the three of them with his huge claws as he went down the passage with them until they reached a room with a huge carving on the floor. A completely illegible outline, full of symbols and words in different languages, encrypted with strange hieroglyphs linked with lines. But that was not the most unusual thing. After a while, after trying to decipher it, the drawing seemed to have a life of its own, making it clear to the eyes of those present that it was alive: its figures moved.

"Welcome to the ancestral chart of the primordial elements that keep alive the soul of this planet and, with it, that of the universe. These unify the akasha, the wu xing, the bhutas, the yin and yang, the feng shui, among many others that I will not mention because we do not have time. In short, the world rests on each of the components that you have in front of you and the way in which they are connected is exposed here. In front of you there is what would be a cosmic x-ray of the planet. This is the importance of the responsibility that falls on my shoulders; hence my dedication to the millenary study of the cosmos and its elements, for without it, the chiromantic interpretation of the engravings could prove fatal to the destiny of all.

"What you see is the Earth speaking to us live, telling us of its past, shouting its present, and warning us of the future that lies ahead, and children, it doesn't look good," Kunda expounded.

"Every sign you saw in the sky, the ones marked in your eyes, are the three elements you have been entrusted to find," Rasnar clarified, breaking the silence.

"That's right, and to locate your elements, you must first know what they are and understand what they are. After that, you just have to follow the trail of the aurora borealis you saw, which will show you the way.

"The color that you distinguished in the celestial tracing is the reflection created in your pupil by these marks. But this sign is not enough to guide you; hence the memories of the visions are so important. Remember that time is running out. Although you have a pathway in the atmosphere that will guide your search, you set the pace. No matter how many obstacles, distractions, and impediments you encounter, you must overcome them by moving forward with alacrity, for your priority from now on will be to find these beings as soon as possible and protect them until they are safe here with us, in order to save the Earth. They are our only hope, the last hope left for our solar system, if we are not too late," said the monk.

"Wait, you want us to go find some strangers, tell them that they are the key elements that will save the Earth, convince them that we are not crazy, and then kidnap them? Clearly, you're all out of your minds. Bringing three people each back here to the frozen nothingness? How? Climbing with our colleagues in a huge sack on our backs?" said Sasha.

"Wow, you took it out of my mouth," her friend commented.

"I don't care how you do it. The tactics and strategies are up to you. I only care that it gets done," Rasnar said.

"So, we take orders now?" James asked.

"No. Rather, you have been asked. You should not be defensive, but proud to have been chosen by the cosmos to save the beings of the universe. It is a privilege. Their lives and our survival are in your hands.

"I know it's a lot of pressure, but, as James said earlier, coincidences don't exist, and everyone's destiny is written in many directions. We are the ones who decide which branch of the tree to hold on to and which to let go of," the Guardian informed them.

"If they have chosen us, entrusting us with different natures, it will be because we are the most able to convince them or, at least, to reach them and make ourselves heard, right?" Sasha checked.

"They may feel as we have felt all our lives, lost and empty, waiting for someone to come along to make some sense of their torments or to find their place in the world," said James.

"I know what it's like to feel different, to expect something without knowing what, so...I'm in," Carol affirmed.

"Well, then, to begin with, you must find out what are the elements that have been bestowed on each of you. They are weakening, for they have deviated from their astral line, which gives them their universal balance. Observing the schematic plan of the soul of the earth engraved on this ground, we will be able to perceive the components that are out of their harmonic orbit, breaking the Tetraktys, source and root of the eternal environment. As it is obvious at first sight, it is formed by the nine primordials that hold the pillars of the energy that flows through the veins of this planet and maintains the balance in all its states, beings, and objects."

After listening to Kunda's words, they looked at the impressions that were so obvious to the monk but could not distinguish anything. Until Sasha noticed three figures that gave off a small flash of the same color as the triangles in the sky. When she mentioned it, the librarian asked her to point them out. He then referred to them as shabda, wood and metal. Instantly, the three triangles marked by the lens appeared around Sasha's left eye; symbols that were tattooed on the central edge of the upper eyelid, the lower eyelid, and the third one on the skin opposite the tear duct. Together they formed a triangle that could be seen when opening the eye, like a screen that projected her gaze towards the sky or towards the emblems that had been assigned to her.

Carol and James experienced the same pattern as the young woman minutes later. Some of those signs carved into the rock seemed to draw their attention on purpose. And unlike Sasha, under her friend's right eye the symbols prithvi, vayu and agni were tattooed: two of them on each vertex and the third on the lower part of one of these. James, on the other hand, showed the shapes of apas, lokasa and alokasa: one located practically on the upper lash line and the other, in the same position of the lower contour, which when closing the eye made the two elements collided and became one. The third unit appeared on the skin at the corner of the eye, in the area opposite the tear duct.

"What is this? Why is my brother having two of his figures merged into one symbol?" asked Sasha.

"It means that these two signs, lokasa and alokasa, form the akasha, the primordial substance from which the physical world originates. In the terrestrial realm they are referred to as sutras or suttas, discourses of the Buddha," explained Kundalini.

"Teachings and precepts concerning the different ways of knowledge to reach the complete spiritual enlightenment of the human being. Aaaaahh! How do I know all this?" said James, surprised at himself.

"Because its wisdom is already part of you, of you, but you will discover it little by little," said Rasnar.

"Lokasa is the material world and alokasa is the unknowable space, which is totally empty. And apas is the soul of the world, emotion, and passion. It's water, isn't it? I think I know what they are. I'm sorry... Excuse me."

James came out of that sort of cave, rubbing his head as if he was having trouble thinking.

"How is it possible that, having wood and metal, which are the easiest to deduce, I cannot assign them to my visions? Nothing I saw in them can be associated with the elements that have touched me. Besides, I am very confused that, when I think of wood, everything is summed up in my head to spring and outward movement.

"On the contrary, when I try to concentrate on the metal, I feel like it's autumn and the movement is inward. I sound like a crazy person rambling," Sasha alluded.

"Have faith. Your intuition and perseverance will help you discover the connection between the visions and the elements that have touched you. The path is already laid out for you; you just have to follow it, guided by your instinct while remaining alert.

"Relax, you'll figure it all out and understand everything one way or another. Everyone learns in their own way. Don't focus on what's blocking you because obsession doesn't move you forward. It is a stone in the road that you must avoid, or it will grow into a rock so big that it will impede your progress. You must look at the space around the boulder, before it becomes a mountain, and see beyond what you think is in front of you. Listen to me: I am not only wise, but I also have a lot of experience, shabda Sasha," said the monk.

"The buzzing... Shabda is also known as the sound, right? That noise, the one that the girl kept in her mind as she tracked her way to... She wanted to go home, which echoed constantly in her mind, and that gave her the strength to continue on her way, because she knew where to continue advancing safely through the middle of nowhere. I think... I guess I'm beginning to understand," said the young woman.

"Then go with your brother and share your intuitive guesses as a team. The perspective of several improves the work, increases its efficiency, and makes it more fruitful," Rasnar said, escorting Sasha out of the room.

Carol was left alone with the librarian. He slowly approached her. The young woman was intently analyzing the letter inscribed on the surface of the stone. Using her mind for unproductive purposes, Carol doubted both herself and her place in the group, as she was the only human with powers that were not really hers, which made her feel like a fraud. Kunda placed her feet on the agni symbol and, with a wave of his arms, caused a river of fire to emanate from it, forming the sign of the element in front of her.

"It represents the conscious intention to create. A northern compound of which the fraction is pure spirit, ascending energy." The old man jumped again, this time stomping on the prithvi symbol, and, with another wave of his hands, a tube of earth emerged from the ground and passed through the agni sign made of fire, extinguishing it until the drawing of the earth element floated before the young woman. "Circular motion, the changes of the cycle. The Mahayana differentiates ten bhumi earths; each one corresponds to a clairvoyance.

"Learning about perception can benefit us. The elements have not been assigned to you by chance, for everything in this life is a warning, a lesson, an apprenticeship, and a destiny." Swiftly, he waved his limbs over the vayu sign, which emerged from the ground like a whirlwind of wind and earth, unraveling the prithvi sign, then surrounding her and turning her into the epicenter of a rather sonorous tornado of sorts. Suddenly, the whirlwind stopped in front of her, making the air contain the earth particles, which moved inside her and created the figure of this element. "Vayu represents the mind, freedom. The vital creative breath, the word. The wind of the storm, which would be the creation. Space as movement and production of vital processes. Light, flight, lightness, perfume, smell."

"Or as they say in China, the ki or breath for the permanence of the being. In the Bible, Yahweh breathed on the man of clay to give him a soul, a spirit... Amon, god of the wind, the hidden, the mysterious, the invisible wind that stirs the primordial water, created life.

Carol approached the effigy levitating before her and obstructed the earth that was moving inside it, making the materialized conjecture disappear. Tiny particles of grain remained in her hand.

"Immaculate earth morality and immaculate earth patience. Now I see, I understand why I was assigned these elements: for my virtues and for what I have yet to learn and understand, for both my body and my mind suffer shortages. Who am I now, Kunda? I don't even recognize myself in the mirror anymore, and when I speak, I am not the same as I was, not even in my own thoughts," Carol articulated.

"Do you remember when you longed for your parents' love and didn't fill that void until Sasha appeared in your life?" The young woman looked at the monk dumbfounded, pondering how it was possible that he knew something so intimate about her, something that no one could know. "Love is just a word, until someone gives it meaning. Until now, you had not given meaning to much in this life, but as it was written, your path, like everyone else's, is hindered by the lessons you have left pending for yourself. It is up to you to see them, to learn from them to reach your destiny, your mission in this life. Or, failing that, you can keep repeating the main pattern of your faults over and over again, slowing down your journey and your inner growth. You will be left behind in time forever.

"Do not fall into a repetitive vortex, living in your own reality, one created solely by your ramblings, in which you are distanced from other people. Remember that it is a path in solitude, for the world ends up sacrificing those who choose to voluntarily blind themselves in the darkness." The young woman's eyes clouded with sadness. "You are not alone, girl. You are much stronger than you imagine."

Kunda hugged her by the shoulders and together they walked out of there with their breath brimming with energy in search of the rest of the team.

"Carol, come out here. You have to see this," Sasha exclaimed enthusiastically from the balcony.

As it was covered with a blanket, the young woman peeked her head through the thin curtains and gazed at the Gangkhar Puensum, the icy mountains with their full expanse of peaks to the depths of the abyss. Without light pollution and clear of clouds, the sky was overflowing with stars, with great constellations falcate at the top of the firmament; some of them, released like fireflies shooting out all over the celestial vault. And in the middle of it all, the beautiful great aurora borealis, branching out in three protruding paths from a large constellation in the shape of an equilateral triangle, composed of stars that shone much more brightly than the others.

"That is the Triangulum Australis, just below the forelegs of the horse of the constellation of the Centaur and the Compass, is the astral triangle that marks your presence, as the three vertices of the cycle of the triangle that you have created in the cosmos and that will mark the path that you are going to undertake.

"The star closest to the horse's hoof marked the beginning of James' passage. Remember he pointed out this particular star as being the same color as his path in the aurora. Carol remarked that the aerolite indicating her path was the one closest to the points of the Compass constellation, while Sasha pointed to the brightest star of all, the one closest to the Peacock constellation."

"These three stars will tell me how you are and where you are going. Everything will be reflected and simplified on this parchment when we observe the position of the ornaments of the firmament in conjunction with the aurora."

Kundalini took a thin piece of paper out from his clothes and stretched out his arms towards the horizon opening the sheet with the four cardinal points marked on it. Instantly, the image of the celestial court was reflected on the sheet like a photograph. After this, all that was printed there disappeared, leaving only the equilateral triangle stamping the constellations of the youths, with their different paths coming out as lines from each of its vertices and splitting the three by a single stripe right at the beginning. They were divided into separate paths with different shapes extending across the entire sheet.

Sasha stretched out her finger to the papyrus and pointed to its grooves while commenting on where they seemed to point on the world map. When she touched them, both the dot designating their star and their bifurcations were marked in gold. James and Carol looked up at the sky and quickly indicated theirs on the paper, as did Sasha.

"Take a look. According to this, we start our journey on the same trajectory, heading southeast, but then James and I go west, while Sasha will head east, and from there northeast," Carol pointed out.

"Hopefully, we'll coincide on some points," said Sasha.

Kunda folded the sheet and tucked it into his robes. He looked at the youngsters and raised his arms with outstretched palms to give them his blessing. Then he entered the library, disappearing behind the fabrics that hung like curtains. Rasnar was leaning against the window frame of that little balcony, dangling three backpacks from his huge paw.

"It's time," said the beast.

The Triangle

"At the top of the great triangle is the number one, the divine number, the beginning of everything, representing the being not yet manifested. At the lower level of this, at the vertices at the foot of this first equilateral, is the number two, the origin of manifestation. Dear students, before us is duality; the feminine and the masculine; the light and the darkness; Adam and Eve; the yin and the yang; the sun and the moon. Under this we find an equilateral triangle divided into three triangles that form the central section between dualities. They symbolize the three main worlds: the celestial world, the earthly world, and the infernal world.

"Positioned on the level below this one, at the base of the great equilateral triangle, are the five triangles that allude to the fundamental elements that form the world and matter: earth, air, water, fire, wood and metal. Together they complete the nine equilateral triangles that make up the great triangle," explained the professor.

"Professor, I have a question: does the position of the triangles that make up the large triangle as a whole also have to do with the symbolism of the female and male sexes? I mean, if the equilateral triangle with the base on the ground were the male and the triangle whose vertex points down were the figuration referring to the female gender, what gender would the third triangle be?" asked Carol.

"Excuse me, miss, are you one of my students?" answered the professor.

"You don't know the answer, do you? You know, I don't think you've asked yourself the right questions so far, because almost all the theories you've put forward about the importance of the triangle are quite limited. But you must understand that they started from a rigid and archaic mentality, what we call... you know, a simplistic mind," elaborated the young woman.

"Well, symbology is also perception. The more agility we have to see different points of view about something, the more we will understand the world around us," said the tutor just before the chimes of the university chapel sounded to mark the end of classes.

The student body rose from their seats as the teacher reminded them of their homework. The students walked out the classroom door leaving Carol alone with the professor.

"On the dollar bill, the base of the pyramid, with its thirteen stories, is drawn three dimensionally, forming the whole dual world around us: height, breadth, and depth. But when we look at the eye that crowns the top, it has only two dimensions, height, and width, embodying something that is out of this world and that is watched over from the fourteenth level. This number was of great importance for the Egyptians because Osiris was cut into fourteen pieces. Of these, only thirteen were recovered. Get it?" said Carol, leaving the professor stunned. "I see you are speechless. I can't believe the trail led me to you. I don't get it. There's nothing special about you. But well, if it has to be you, so be it. Do you want to know more about those who are watching us?" said the young woman.

"I don't know who you are or what your intentions are, but you must know that everything that is said, or thought are mere theories. There is nothing certain that proves that those of whom you speak physically exist," said the professor.

"Does it make you uncomfortable to talk about women's history or other genders than your own? It seems to be a common thing among professors on this planet, apparently... Well, going back to the previous topic, how would you feel if I proved to you otherwise? Would you change your mind? Or would you rather stay here rambling on about your theories for the rest of your life, instead of going out there and seeing it with your own eyes?"

The professor was silent for a while; he seemed to be processing what was coming out of Carol's mouth.

"Young lady, are you aware that there were some enlightened people who were convinced that they could lead the rest of the population and thought they were superior to everyone else? They became so obsessed with the triangle that they thought they were situated at its upper vertex and therefore assumed they had the right to control the state from the top. They watched over everything, dominated with iron-fisted measures, manipulated, and crushed the rest of the world at will, and committed two of the worst sins that can exist: arrogance and oppression. I think you suffer from the former," he said, breaking the silence.

"Professor Graham, you are talking about the syndrome that narcissists, sociopaths, and psychopaths suffer from. Not me. Remember that just because a woman disagrees with you, tries to have a dialogue with good arguments and knows more than you do, you don't have to get nervous and call her a witch. What's the matter, professor, are you afraid to open your mind because you don't like change? Or do you feel the need to annul my sex for fear that we will take away male privileges and end up turning the tables?" she defended herself.

"From ancient Siberia and the Egyptians to the caste system in India, the pyramidal system of classifying a society has created the motto "Divide and Rule," but all human beings are equally vulnerable when we are born. Education and upbringing are what make us different, make us a better or a worse person," he countered.

"Do you really think we're all the same, Professor Graham? Because I think you speak from the position of a privileged white man in a patriarchal system. Tell me, is that a theory, a reality, or is it an ideal that you preach to others for appearance's sake?" Carol replied.

"Don't you think we should be tolerant and open to all beings in the universe, rejoice in the successes of others regardless of sex or background, and appreciate both the outer and inner beauty of every individual, without being driven by jealousy, greed, repression and selfishness?" he challenged.

"I completely agree, but in the proper context, since your hallucination that the world is fine and full of good people or, more accurately, good men, is expecting too much from human beings. Being a woman, I can tell you from experience that we cannot confidently go through life under that pretense or naivety, let alone handing out goodness to those who do not deserve it, as we are educated not to recognize these individuals.

"Your history, your theories, your system, your education and your privilege are like lenses that block your light and keep you in the dark," she continued.

"But it is the fault of the ignorance and lack of emotional intelligence of other individuals. This causes many people to live in a bubble of delusions outside of reality; they evade the real world, the healthy one, and end up in one full of darkness that poisons the mind and heart, turning them into soulless beings," he acknowledged, excusing himself as all men do: blaming others, since none is able to recognize in himself what for us is so easy to perceive, accustomed as we are to normalize the faults they commit against our sex. For some, it is wholly unaware since they have seen or learned little else in their lives. For this reason, they chose to limit themselves to freeing themselves, even paying the consequences of living without being a first class and independent citizen. But Carol always knew how to see and watched the professor speak like so many others. She tried to conceal it so as not to dismiss him, since, for some reason, she needed that individual for her mission.

"You excuse yourself by accusing others, like everyone else... That doesn't make you special; it makes you a coward or a fool. Let's be honest, your approaches have the logic of an ignoramus who only thinks, sees, and opines from your perspective, that is from an advantaged position. Consciously or unconsciously, you follow the pattern of a vital sign without activity, a continuous line fostered by patriarchy, with history manipulated by and for men for more than six thousand years. Your mind is not capable of seeing beyond what has been instilled in you because you are afraid of losing power and that emotional stability that relies on the abuse of others."

The teacher knew that what Carol was saying was true, but he kept it to himself and chose to live in denial. The response of society in general would have been to tell the young woman that she was conflicted, complicated, hysterical, bitter, or to accuse her of having mental problems, an accusation that, in another era not so long ago, would have landed her in an insane asylum. Just like that.

But that girl was perfectly sane. Her opinions were wise and well-argued, with no hint of delusion. She debated her theories with reasonable analyses drawn from a purpose and reality that were undeniable to any intelligent person. Still, the man wondered how she had got into his classroom without him noticing, since he knew all his students. He even wondered if it might have been a joke in bad taste.

But he was also intrigued. This girl was the first and only person who had really captivated him with her guts, with the confidence with which she spoke about the stigmatized issue in question, without any of the typical groping after possibilities and ideas about new theories of symbologies common among the populace. No, the young woman was clear, and made it clear, which is why it was impossible to refute her evidence. They implied new routes to new clues to the truth. Only a man with an IQ high enough to keep an open mind could go deeper into the conversation.

"What do you know about the three conjoined triangles, Professor?" asked Carol.

"They can mean many things. The mineral kingdom, the vegetable kingdom, and the animal kingdom. They can also be the three phases of spiritual evolution and life processes: separatio, fermentatio and putrefacto," he replied.

"The ternary, which represents the angle of the triangle, holds the secrets of creation, the beginning of all things within our universe," she said. "Lao Tse... The Tao begot unity, which begot duality, which produced the triad, which gave life to all things."

The professor was fascinated by the fact that such a young girl had so much knowledge, intelligence, and a need to know. He sensed that she was on the lookout for some kind of answer that, maybe, he wasn't up to answering.

"The Greeks and Romans, following the Platonic school, who drew a thick veil over their most native appetites, considered the triangle as the first of the figures. Do you think that's a coincidence?"

"Well, the union of the three triangles, in Viking mythology, referred to the valknut. Its nine angles represent the nine worlds of Norse cosmology, so, you see, the triangle has always been a symbol of... other worlds," Carol continued.

"But well... These are just theories," said the man, wiping the strange sweat he felt dripping down his forehead.

"You do know, there are five triangles, not four. If your theory is correct, where do the four seasons fit in?" she challenged him.

But the professor could not pay attention. As he wiped his face, he noticed that his perspiration looked a bit slimy. He looked at his hand and, dumbfounded, hurriedly took out the cloth handkerchief he always carried in his pocket.

"I would change places if I were you. I don't think that rag will be enough for you; at least if you are going to continue standing under my friend."

The man looked at the ceiling, towards where the girl was pointing, but he could not distinguish anything but the typical white strip lights that they use in the classrooms, which are so horrible and disturbing; those fluorescent tubes which are used to torture the eyes of the students. Seconds later one of them began to flicker and at once a drop of something liquid hit the teacher's forehead. There was no sign of moisture or seepage in the area of the canopy under which it was located.

After this, he cautiously inspected the girl, who wore a thin chain hanging from her neck with a triangle-shaped pendant approximately two centimeters long on each of its sides, all in a bronze color. The young woman grasped the pendant tightly as she noticed the man's curious gaze on her necklace, thus protecting it from the professor and any deductions he might draw from the ornament.

"How many Native American languages would you say you know fluently, professor? And don't tell me you have a level if it's not true. Let's avoid this waste of time and humiliation for you," the young woman continued.

"This is absurd. Look, I have more classes to teach and I'm sure you should be attending some, so, if you don't mind," he replied, pointing the way to the exit door.

"I need someone who speaks those languages so I can understand the Hidatsa, Mandan, Sioux, Osage, Ioway, Omaha, Otoe, Missouria, Quapaw and Kanza tribes," she explained.

"That's easy, you just need someone who knows Sioux," replied the professor.

"Also, the Blackfoot, Arapaho, Cheyenne, Atsina, Wichita, Pawnee, Arikarau and Sarsi. I need to find an expert who can contact these tribes, so that they will open up to me with the confidence to find something I am looking for and that they are keeping secret," Carol said.

"So, you're planning to go into the Great Plains in search of something that must be sacred to them. Are you crazy? Those lands occupy the central parts of the United States and pass through southern and southeastern Canada. You could travel from North Dakota to South Dakota, as well as Nebraska, Kansas, Iowa, Montana, Oklahoma, and part of Texas without finding whatever it is you're looking for.

"Young lady, you don't know what you're saying. I don't know what you're after, but to get to know all those settlements, or what's left of them, would take months, or even years, and I don't have that kind of time. Besides, even if you managed to traverse the thousands of miles of protected wilderness full of animals and natural anomalies, which pose a danger to everyone, you would have to gain the trust of their people; one that white people like you and me took away from them.

"If what you need is secret and under their protection, it is unlikely that they will show it you for fear of losing even more of their roots. If what you are looking for is so valuable to them, they will see it as their duty to follow inviolable rules to keep it hidden away from today's world out of reverence for their ancient cultural traditions. They have only achieved this by hiding it from us, who knows where, for hundreds of years. Do you really think that a young white girl, who does not know their language or customs, will be able to get any information from anyone on their reservations, or even know where to start?

"If they have kept what you seek secret for so many generations, it is because they have put it above their lives, which means that, today, those people will be considered a sacred caste. You must understand that we almost caused the extinction of their culture when we came to America. If any of these tribes are still intact it is because of the sacrifices of many over the centuries to protect their people from the white man, shielding them from the outside world so that no one will ever know about them. I doubt they would want to hear from you or anyone who is not part of their cabal.

"Do you really think they are going to discard all the effort and sacrifice they have had to make, throughout the history of their race, to keep alive something so pure, just because you ask them to?" queried the professor.

"I am looking for someone, not something. So, I will tell them that I must find that person to tell her that she is not alone, that there is another world that is made for her, a world that will understand her, where she can feel the complete being she is, one hundred percent, and she can grow and shine without needing to hide anymore," Carol replied.

"Who is this person? Why is she so important to them and to you? If they have hidden her for so long, maybe she is no longer alive. Are you looking for someone they revere?" Professor Graham asked.

"Well, leaving traditions, religions, and beliefs aside, no one, no matter how stubborn and entrenched they may be with their way of seeing the world, will be able to doubt what I am going to show you... at least not enough to not let me enter the tribe to dialogue with them. Stay still, professor, don't move, no matter what happens."

The young woman got up from her desk and walked toward the man until she stood behind him. Then she lifted the pendant to place it over the eye of the incredulous teacher, so that he could see through the geometric shape. After this gesture, she placed his hand on the pendant to block his view for a second. He turned and stared at the girl, confused, but she pointed to the ceiling of the room, as she had done before. Then looking up he saw above him the enormous head of a drakon. He swallowed with difficulty.

"Did you drug me? I'm going to call the police," he said.

"Go ahead, call the police. It will be a scandal. You in a classroom alone with a minor alleging that she drugged you." Then Carol's drakon dropped down in front of him and brought its snout full of sharp teeth close to the teacher's body. He pushed the animal while keeping his arms raised trying to avoid it. His shirt showed large sweat stains. You look tense, professor. She won't do anything to you, don't worry."

The man plucked up his courage and reluctantly put his hand on the beast's head, which, to his surprise, began to purr.

"This... is not possible," he uttered, "I'm hallucinating."

"If you want, we can go for a tox screen. But to be honest, we don't have much time. Look, you are fluent in the Sioux, Algonquin, Caddo, and Na-Dene languages. I also read that you know as much about their ancestral customs as you do their current ones. You were taken in by them when you lost your family on that excursion, weren't you? That's the only explanation for your survival for so many years missing. You lived with them in a secret reserve, didn't you? That makes you part of them. I know what that means to you when you're alone."

"I would never ask you to do anything that would shatter that bond you have with them or ruin something that has taken so much effort and dedication to keep secret. What you are seeing is real. Ksuma's drool fell on you, and you noticed that before I approached you to place my amulet in front of your retina," the young woman alluded.

"Where did you get that pendant?" Professor Graham asked.

"Are you going to help me?" she asked.

"How do I know this is real? That I haven't lost my mind because I want to believe in something beyond the pure reality that surrounds me and that I see in my daily life. Maybe I want so passionately to conceptualize my theories that it has gotten out of hand," he commented.

"They have the Beinecke library of rare books and manuscripts here, don't they?" Carol reminded him.

"Everyone knows that; we're at Yale University," the professor replied.

"What would you think if I told you I knew someone who knew the secret to deciphering the Voynich manuscript?" said Carol.

"That's impossible," he replied quickly, touching the beast in fear.

"Are you really going to remain that skeptical while petting a drakon?" The young woman turned around and gestured to the animal. "Let's go, Ksuma. Someone who doesn't want to see will never be able to see even if he had the truth punching his nose. These types of people remain in denial for life, reasoning with lies and delusions of a reality that is immovable in their understanding."

The drakon followed Carol after giving the man one last look. The professor was left alone. After several hesitant minutes, he ran out of the university in search of the young woman, realizing that there was no one left on the premises but him. Repentant, he was walking to his car when a huge drool fell on his shoulder and slowly slid down the sleeve of his jacket. Disgusted, the professor wiped the goo off. Then he realized he was not alone.

"If I go, you must promise me two things under a consensual contract. The first is that once your mysterious mission is over, you will show me how to decipher the Voynich, and the second is that you will tell your drakon, Ksuma, not to spit on my body and clothes ever again, since where we are going, we can only carry one backpack and I won't have many changes of clothes."

Carol appeared mounted on the drakon. As she was in disembodied mode, it seemed as if the girl was levitating in the air. "Is she invisible now?" he was surprised.

"The effect of the pendant is not permanent, but if it is more comfortable to see Ksuma during the trip, maybe we can find a way to make its effect last longer. About the drooling, that was my idea. She doesn't usually behave like that; in fact, this is the first time I've seen her salivate like that. She prefers spitting fire," she replied.

"Well, as long as you don't throw flames at me, we have a deal," he replied.

"Well, then mount up, we have no time to lose," she ordered, offering him her hand.

"Climb onto the drakon? This excursion should be planned and go step by step, asking questions and informing us of what you are looking for in order to get closer to it. That way, we will waste less time than rushing to the first place where we find a tribe. That will only make us end up moving in circles," replied the professor.

"I had a vision, so I know where I want to go, but I don't know the exact spot, so we're going straight to Yellowstone. Apparently, the flight to Montana is only ten hours away, so we should leave as soon as possible."

Disoriented, the man climbed on top of Ksuma and sat down behind the young woman. Then he held tightly to the part of skin that protruded in the area of the animal's spine, but which he could not see. And he let himself be carried away by the madness of the adventure. He had the sensation of floating above the ground due to the transparency of the beast's body.

As it ascended, the distressed professor tightened his grip; he reached a point where he could no longer feel his hands. He tried to keep his eyes fixed on one point and his mind absent so as not to think about the distance to the ground, so as not to suffer the terrifying vertigo that this would produce.

"You should know that going to Yellowstone is not the best idea. Only four of the great Native American tribes lived there, and they were not located where the national park we know today is. To them, the whole area of the geysers and warm springs was evil spirit territory that they didn't want to upset. That and the strip was difficult to access, so there was better hunting in the lower valleys; that is, they only went there when they were being chased and sought refuge to save their lives. In fact, the name they used for Yellowstone was Mountains on Fire," he reported, trying to distract himself from the instability of the flight.

"Then it's the perfect place to hide something valuable," said Carol.

"How could a tribe sitting in the middle of the park go unnoticed when the park receives some 922,018 visitors during the month of July alone?" Professor Graham pointed out.

"What people can't see at first glance doesn't mean they don't exist or aren't there, and if you're still in doubt, go back and keep an eye on Ksuma, a drakon you can't see, but hold on to tightly to keep yourself safe and alive."

After almost nine hours of flying, the professor asked Carol to see the animal again, so she took the pendant and placed it over his eye. But in doing so, he not only discovered the drakon, but also noticed a bronze-colored mist around it.

"It is possible that the imaginary lens of this triangle is dirty or that we are in an area where the air is quite polluted."

Carol brought the animal down, making the professor aware of the track that indicated that tan trail, which looked like an aurora borealis, under which they were flying.

"Does this amulet show you the way to find the person you are looking for?" he asked, dumbfounded.

"Not for me. I can see it without looking through the triangle, but it helps you to understand why I'm so clear about where I'm headed."

The man watched this marvel as the animal flew over a vast wilderness, practically straight into the Burning Mountains. Then it landed next to a geyser.

"There doesn't seem to be anyone to ask about this area. It must be closed to the public at this hour, so all that's left are the black bears, grizzlies, wolves, probably some mountain lions, elk, huge bison, herds of pronghorn, Rocky Mountain rams, a variety of birds, many raptors, including bald eagles, and us. Which of these do you want to start your questioning with?" he pronounced as he practically kissed the ground.

"I repeat, just because I don't see them doesn't mean they're not there," she challenged.

"Do you mean the animals or the tribes of your imagination?" replied the professor sarcastically.

"Could you shout something in their language so they can welcome us properly," the young woman asked.

"How can I speak in the tribal dialect if I don't know which one is in question?"

Carol gestured to Ksuma, and she raised her wings, dug her claws hard into the ground and stretched out her neck. Instantly, she let out a thunderous roar that seemed to come from its gut, followed by a puff of fire that shot up into the sky, signaling her position.

"I guess that will do it." After several hours of waiting, with an empty stomach and extreme thirst, the professor began to get restless and wanted to return, excusing himself that he had carelessly left his things in the classroom and that this would draw the attention of his students and classmates, which would imply a kidnapping that would worry people. "What is it, professor?"

The professor turned and distinguished in the distance what appeared to be a man on a spotted horse. He watched them from a distance with his bare chest decorated with necklaces that descended to the level of his shiny black mane. He carried on it a series of hooked feathers. After several minutes, the rider raised his arm revealing a rifle and slowly approached.

"Is this an optical illusion created by the triangle or am I imagining it?" asked the startled professor, incredulous at what his eyes were seeing.

"Can you still see Ksuma?" Carol replied.

"No."

"Then the triangle had nothing to do with it."

"Apsaróka? Apsálooke?" The professor shouted for the man to hear him. But the native continued to approach silently, riding with dignity on his horse and with his weapon firmly in his hand.

"What did you say?" the young woman asked.

"If I've got his language right, it means, they say, people of the crows. I'm asking him if he's from that tribe, so I know what language to speak to him in, but he doesn't seem to recognize the dialect, either that or he's deliberately ignoring me. Which wouldn't surprise me either, considering that the Crow tribe was one of the most feared, both by the white man and by the other tribes," explained the professor.

"Asaksiwa," the rider greeted with the gun pointed at Professor Graham's head.

"He is speaking in an agglutinative language: words are formed by joining independent monemes. It could be Siksiká or Kainai or Aapáthosipikani, but looking closely at his moccasins now, they seem to be painted with black decorations, possibly self-made drawings, which would indicate that this man is of the Blackfoot tribe, " the professor revealed.

"What does asaksiwa mean?" asked Carol.

"It means 'leave'; he's telling us to leave," the professor replied.

The Amerindian moved the gun in Carol's direction. Suddenly his nag began to get nervous to the point that he lost control of the animal, forcing the rider to drop the gun in an attempt to calm the horse. Without a second's hesitation, the young woman ran to pick up the rifle from the ground and pointed it at the native.

"Girl, put the gun down," shouted the professor, frightened by the tension of the moment.

"We didn't come here in a state of war, you understand? I need to find someone."

The Native American then pulled a machete from his pants and threatened the young woman as he tried to subdue the mount. Calmly, Carol removed the cartridges from the weapon and handed it to Ksuma, who folded the metal as if it were a piece of chewing gum. The warrior watched in astonishment as the young woman left the weapon in the air and then shattered it with some kind of magic.

"Ainihkiwa Aakíí(wa)," said the native, putting the machete away.

"What did he say, professor?" she asked.

"I said sing, woman. Are you a sorceress?" said the native.

"Do you speak my language?" Carol was surprised and regretted having taken the professor with her.

"I am in charge of tracking, finding and showing the way out to every tourist lost in certain areas of Yellowstone, although it is not always necessary to use the language to make myself understood," he replied mischievously.

"If I may ask, to which tribe do you belong?" asked the professor.

"First the woman must sing."

Carol took a step forward and the rider's horse reared back.

"If I may, I need you to look at something," she said.

"Animals sense things we can't see. There's something about you that makes him uneasy. Why should I trust you?"

Carol took off her necklace and passed it to the professor, who very cautiously approached the man, getting the pony to be calm in his presence. The young woman kept some distance from the animal. And holding the pendant with the chain falling towards the ground, he approached the native, who checked that there was no danger touching the chain, so he proceeded to take the triangle confidently.

"The necklace is not a gift; my gift is what it can do for you. The reason I'm here is that I'm looking for someone, a person of great importance who I know is here, hidden somewhere. I think it's a woman, but I'm not entirely sure. If you would be so kind as to look through the pendant, you will understand why your horse is so agitated and know how I learned of your tribe's whereabouts. Sometimes, we are not able to see what is in front of us by ourselves."

The man hesitated; even so, he recklessly brought the costume jewelry close to his eye. But when the triangle touched his skin, he threw the necklace to the ground and galloped over the equine with shouts in the wind. He headed into a lush forest where he disappeared.

"Mental note, never to pass my precious and necessary jewel to anyone ever again," said Carol picking up the pendant from the ground and hanging it around her neck.

"He will come back. He will bring them. He will come with his best warriors, and they will kill us," said the professor.

"That would be very stupid, professor. First, because we have a drakon as a weapon and second, because we have a fucking drakon with us, which, in case you haven't noticed, made your colleague run away. Just because he has seen Ksuma doesn't mean that the others will also be able to see her, so without my amulet, the guy will look like a madman," the girl concluded.

"And there they are. Stay still and control your dinosaur; I'll take care of it," said the professor.

A group of five Native Americans, each dressed differently, came riding up to them on their horses until they stopped in front of Carol, who was pleased to see a woman among them; a dazzling horsewoman who was listening attentively to the man with whom they had spoken earlier. He was explaining to his companions what he had seen and experienced earlier. Then, to the astonishment of the professor and the teenage girl, the group accompanying the warrior began to laugh at him.

"They didn't believe him," the professor acknowledged with a big smile.

The woman got off the mare and approached Carol. Then she picked up the pendant to look through it. Instantly, she released the triangle by dropping it on the young woman's chest. After a few moments in silence, she turned to her own and had them try it as well.

"This doesn't make sense. The women oversaw tanning the skins and making clothes, shoes, and fabric for the tepees. They also set up the tents, kept track of the water and firewood reserves, collected wild plants, took care of the little ones... But they never led a group or acted as chiefs," said the professor.

"The men wrote history the way they wanted to. I don't know why women don't rewrite it the way they want to. You know, we were here before the rest of you arrived, but you tell our history without being part of it, even with images of us riding horses before the Spanish brought them to America. Living hidden from your society does not make us fools or old-fashioned," the woman replied, looking at the professor.

"Why do you bring your magic to our tribe? asked the rider who had appeared alone.

"The universe has led me to you," replied the young woman, pointing to the sky so that the natives could observe the aurora. The Indians took this as a divine sign and forced the intruders to mount one of their nags. Then they tied them together blindfolded to take them somewhere.

"Before we get there, young lady, you might want to know something about some of the commandments of these tribes. The first one is that the earth is our mother, and we should take care of it. The second one is very interesting, as it mentions honoring your relationships. The third one says to open your heart and soul to the great spirit, and it indicates that life is sacred, so all beings are to be treated with respect. It wouldn't hurt to apply it right now when all is said and done.

"The fifth commandment charges us to take from the earth only what is necessary and no more, to do what must be done for the good of all, and to be grateful to the great spirit for each new day. It psyches us up to speak truthfully, but only for the good of others. The world would be very different if we had learned something from this culture. Its contribution to the citizens and the world would have been very beneficial to all.

"Well, as I was pointing out, another of their commandments states that we follow the rhythms of nature, rising and retiring with the sun. And finally, it proclaims that we enjoy the journey of life, but leave no footprints," said the professor.

"Aohkí(yi)," said the woman, bringing a leather canteen to the hostages.

"She's giving us water, Carol. Drink as much as you can; we don't know when they'll offer us more," the professor advised.

After a few hours on the backs of the nags, they finally made them get off. Then they forced them to walk for a while before removing the blindfold that covered their eyes. Then they left them alone in a valley where a young girl was sitting on a rock a few feet away from them. Upon noticing their presence, the girl covered her eyes, making a visor with her hand, to see them better. At that moment, Ksuma grunted, letting Carol know that the girl could see the drakon perfectly well.

The Amerindian smiled and struck the rock on which she was sitting, accompanying this action with a chant that seemed to attract something from among the trees that surrounded the plain. Almost instantly, an imposing bear appeared, running with ferocity towards Ksuma; it showed its enormous fangs between terrifying growls and its face reflected that it was going to be a merciless fight. Seeing this, the professor panicked, but Carol didn't even flinch. She grabbed the pendant and headed for the girl, while he ran off in the opposite direction disappearing into the trees.

In the meantime, the huge bear, which was now aggressively lunging at Carol, trying to stop the teenager's attack on the girl, who remained seated on the boulder, was being held by the tail by Ksuma. As she ran towards her target, Carol removed the necklace from her neck and flipped the pendant chain in the air as she gathered momentum to leap towards the end of her mission.

Then, holding tightly onto the amulet, which was still clinging to her finger, she tossed the chain and managed to reach the other female's neck before she escaped. With a quick flick of the wrist, the pendant lit up and the element disappeared, causing the giant mammal to finally stop fighting. It then bolted into the forest in bewilderment.

Exhausted, Ksuma went to Carol and brushed her with her muzzle as a sign of relief, since they had finally completed their task. The young girl, still in disbelief, looked up at the sky and noticed that the aurora that had accompanied them for so long had finally disappeared.

"I'm going to miss her too."

From the firmament came a murmur emerging from a small hole that was surrounded by a cluster of clouds that made it look like any other storm to terrestrial eyes.

"It looks like we're back to square one, Ksuma. It's been a long time, but we've made it. Do you think they'll recognize me?" Then she climbed onto the back of her drakon and took a last glance back to look at the mounted horsewoman and her warriors. "Come on, Ksuma, let's go back to the family."

And with a flap of her wings, the great animal lifted her body skyward, in the direction of that mysterious opening.

Caucasian

The young woman woke up lying on the grass and somewhat disoriented. She remembered having shot out after crossing the atmospheric orifice that was assumed to be the end of the mission, but when she looked around her everything indicated that this was not the case. The threshold was part of another plan, and worst of all, she had lost sight of Ksuma.

"Carol! Carol!!!!"

The young woman turned around and, to her surprise, a smile lit up her face as she saw her favorite pair of siblings running towards her as they raised their arms excitedly. She eagerly responded by waving hers effusively.

"Carol, Run! Run! Run!"

All the happiness she had experienced was cut short as she realized she had misread the situation. A dozen wild animals were galloping in a stampede after the siblings, or rather, chasing them for some unknown reason. Without a second's hesitation, Carol turned to make a run for it, but her face collided with a thick, furry pelt that instantly began to coil around her body like a huge brown snake. Then small black eyes in a huge head appeared before her. Suddenly, Ksuma roared with fiery rage and frightened the beast, which immediately released her, dropping the young woman on the grass. There she discovered a majestic mammoth facing the drakon with both front legs raised.

The supposedly extinct mammal was being tamed by the whitest woman she had ever seen, whose eyelashes and eyebrows were almost nonexistent. She wore a tattoo of an inverted triangle on her lower forehead. At that instant the albino jumped, darting in the direction of Ksuma's head. She held a necklace of bones, teeth, and seeds tightly which she rattled as she babbled something and faced the thousands of sharp fangs that made up the mouth of the enraged drakon. The animal immediately closed its jaws and let the stranger land on its snout, then gently pulled her to dry land, where the woman ran towards the stampede that was coming towards them.

Shortly before they charged them, the young woman managed to restrain both the beasts and the siblings' Garos by simply placing the bead on the surface of each and muttering an unknown language. She also showed the animals her teeth, engraved with a triangle on each fang.

"Who is that?" the siblings asked Carol when they reached her.

"I don't know, but she seems to be able to control all creatures, including ours, so let's let her do the talking for now."

The albino rose from the ground after bowing to the wildlife lined up in front of her and then walked in the direction of the three young people.

"We knew this day would come soon. Please join us inside the house," the woman invited, climbing back onto the trunk of the huge prehistoric elephant.

Perceiving that the Garos did not feel that the unknown female was a threat, the girls and James decided to follow her across the huge concourse, marching after the cyclopedic quadruped very cautiously, as they could not yet verify whether the situation was good, or bad.

"We have to be careful; we don't know if she's cast a spell on our Garos so she can control us," commented James suspiciously.

"The mere fact that she sees them and interacts with them could be a problem for us," said Sasha in consternation, for if she had bewitched their Garos, they should have sensed it and even been affected as well, but none of them showed any signs of submission.

"What were you doing here? And why were all those beasts chasing you?" asked Carol.

"What about you?" said James.

"I asked first, and I don't remember how I got here. I had just woken up when I saw you running towards me, so you got here first. The last thing I remember is a tunnel in the sky. I went into it thinking it was a quick way back to the library.

"Apparently, I no longer know the difference between which magic is good and which is bad. I'm sorry for letting my guard down and getting carried away. I'd completed my part and was just looking forward to seeing you guys. What about you" Carol insisted.

"The same thing happened to me. I had also completed my task: I captured the three elements assigned to me, but now I have doubts as to whether they reached Gangkhar Puensum.

"Why do you think we're here? Are we still on planet Earth?" Sasha wanted to know.

"This doesn't seem to be part of the plan. No one mentioned anything about this chick with powers, and even though she looks human, with those African features mixed in with her albino complexion, she could very well be from another planet," James mused.

"Well, it's not the only exceptional creature around. It seems to thrive in an environment where its rarity is normalized. The animal we're following is a mammoth. It should be extinct, just like that bird over there, which is clearly a dodo, another animal that disappeared at the hands of man," said his sister.

"Sasha, look."

Before them, a beautiful black stone castle with engravings of ethnic faces on the facade, which was covered with climbing plants, was surrounded by a considerably dissimilar fauna and flora, recreating an environment more or less suited to the needs of each of the animals present there. Curiously, prey lived peacefully side by side with predatory beasts. It was fascinating to see that they lay peacefully, and even walking without fear, free and respectful under the same sky, without barriers that separated their natural instincts, which now seemed muted and nonexistent.

"Brother, that's a Tasmanian tiger and this cutie playing with your creature is a woolly rhino. Look at our sister, she gets along well with the quagga. They seem to have found similarities in their oddities, although I must admit that my biggest intrigue is to decipher why Ksuma and the black emu have been staring into each other's eyes for so long," the woman said in a strange accent.

"I'm sorry, who are you to take the liberty of talking to us as if you were family?" asked Carol.

"I am the one who was waiting for you. I have something for you inside the house. Don't worry, your companions will be fine with mine. Nobody hurts anyone here, despite their differences," said the mysterious girl.

"But they're not animals," James disagreed.

"Brother, we all are," replied the stranger.

"Brother? As far as I know I only have one sister," replied the boy.

"Hi, I'm Sasha. Sorry if we seem a bit suspicious, but we don't know anything about you or this place, and the truth is that we should leave as soon as possible because we have important things to do," she interrupted.

"I know, I'm here to help you," the albino replied.

A Javanese tiger, sitting at the entrance gates of the fortress, greeted the woman with a hug. She then let the teens inside, where they could see impressive wooden decoration filled with exquisite artifacts scattered around the room like a museum of antiques.

"Who is the white man like an explorer with the three-day beard who is in all these pictures, surrounded by natives from all over the world?" the boy asked.

"He also knows celebrities. Look, this is Michael Rockefeller. It must have been done before he disappeared," Carol replied.

"The man who raised me died. Now only I am left to care for and protect his legacy. He left me this for you. The Courdeils," said the snowy one as she passed them a photograph.

"It's... mom and dad, James."

A thrill of surprise and sadness shrank the siblings' hearts and moistened their eyes as they tried to contain their emotions.

"What's your stepfather doing with them? Guys, isn't that Bill? What the hell?" Carol exclaimed.

James mentally connected with his sister to discuss doubts about their parents, in case they might have known that Bill was really Rasnar or if they only knew the burly, stocky, tanned man of color they were dealing with as a human.

"What does this picture mean?" Sasha asked.

"This portrait is not the only thing I was to give you. The next thing I am going to give you I must give to only one Courdeil and there are two of you. I was given clear instructions, so which one of you should I give it to?" the albino wanted to know while a tabby beast approached her.

"This is a Thylacinus cynocephalus. He has guarded your treasure and carried it with him today as a precaution. I could smell in the air that something special was going to happen and I didn't want humans or other beings to look in the obvious place: the safe where my father kept it," she commented, caressing the beautiful animal while extracting a white gem from its marsupial pouch.

"It looks like Grandma's paperweight," said the young man.

"Sasha, James, I'm worried that our Garos are not with us. We don't know this woman or the terrain we're in," Carol hesitated, turning her back to the girl.

"My name is Deesa. It is the name given to me by the white man in the hat in the photograph, the one who raised me after rescuing me from my own people," she said.

"Do you have any information about the relationship between your stepfather and the Courdeils? Or at least why they're in this picture together, along with Bill and another man we don't recognize," Carol probed.

"I only know that you were united for the greater good, something to which both you and I belong, body and soul. Unlike your friend and the man who raised me. They chose to be a part of it of their own free will, appropriating the powers of others," Deesa replied, looking at the siblings.

Carol felt those words pierce her chest. Ksuma, who was trying to stick her head in through the door of the mansion, also felt it and had come in search of her. As she could not, she had to reduce her size to be able to enter. But Deesa stepped in and touched the beast's snout to convey something that instantly calmed it down.

"You need my help to continue your mission. The one who was like a father to me did not save me on a whim; he found me because it was his destiny. It was his life's project to devote himself to my education and training, and he used the same devotion he had for the secret society. He prepared me for this day right up to the moment of his death. So, it can be said that I have been waiting for you practically all my life.

Sasha noticed the woman's teeth, marked with triangles. It wasn't a matter of aesthetics, any more than the symbols worn as pendants by her brother, her friend or herself. And for some intuitive reason, she looked at the photo again, this time taking a closer look.

"They all wear a triangle as an accessory, just like us," said James sensing his sister's thoughts.

"You need me as a source of information and as a helper, and time is against you with every passing minute. Do you think that if I wished any evil for this planet, I would have waited for you to finish your work with the nine elements before bringing you here?"

Deesa left the house and went to clean the gem in a pond in the garden. Animals flocked to it like a magnet, even the fish in the small marsh.

"I learned that I could communicate with animals at a very early age. In Africa, my flesh was highly prized, so as soon as I was born, they began to put a price on every part of my body. I could have been just another girl, sold by my father in exchange for some goats to help the family, since being born female in this world of degenerates has no more value than being sold as a sexual object.

"But it turned out that I was not just any baby, but an albino hatchling, a symbol of fortune to my parents. My pallor was going to bring them a lot of money if they sold me for parts, so, overcome by a disconcerting situation, they secretly hid me until I reached adulthood so that my limbs would be longer, and they could cut me into more fragments. The purpose was to get more economic benefits at the cost of their daughter's life: little pieces of my being would be sold at a high price for the luck, welfare, and fortune of our neighbors, of the people of our village and of the villages near ours, and even beyond. That is why they never gave me a name, so as not to be emotionally attached to me. Despite being a human being, they found it easier to treat me as if I was just one of their cattle.

"Since I knew nothing more than that, I thought it was normal, so I simply learned to be chained on the ground in silence, sleeping on my excrement, waiting for the leftovers to be thrown to me to eat before the animals and insects overtook me. I spent every day of my life like this until some lionesses attacked the cattle in the village and I was left alone at the mercy of one of those beasts. But instead of attacking me, it began to lick my face. It was the first time I received a mother's affection. But my tribe returned with fire and spears and killed the ferocious creature that was desperately trying to defend me from them.

"My biological parents tried to stop the mob that rushed at me, for I was their most precious commodity: not a daughter, but a business. It was then that the fear of the child I never had a chance to know came out of my being with cries of anguish and despair; a shudder that reached the ears of an elephant that had long experienced hatred for humans. An anger they had earned when they killed members of their herd to get the ivory for the tusks, leaving the poor animal without family or friends.

"That giant saved my life by pulling down the mud wall and breaking the chain that tied me to that tribe. He managed to pull it loose from the post. But my parents arrived in time to grab the loose end of the tether and pulled on it until my wrists were scarred for life. A bitter memory I will have to deal with until I die.

"That was the trigger that made the best and the worst of me come together that night to discover how different I am from the rest. For some reason, the animals understood me, they loved me and, aware of that, I didn't want someone else to die because of me. Surely, I endured that horrible situation for so long, alive and without losing my mind, because without being aware of it, I communicated with the cattle. I knew nothing else, for, like them, I too had been caged. I had more in common with those creatures than with men of my own species. Talking to the animals comforted me, it was part of my life. Often, I asked for their help and collaboration so as not to die of hunger, cold or madness. But that day my world changed when I discovered how powerful I was and how insignificant humans were.

"I looked at their actions and not at the words with which they had manipulated me to convince me that I was scum. That night I could see in the faces of those present the truth flowing like waterfalls from their eyes and an angry feeling clouded my mind with a call to war. I communicated with animals so large that I began to bleed from my nose until I lost consciousness. I ended up hanging from the trunk of the majestic mammal. The next morning the animal was still standing. It had walked all night with me on its back in order to get away from the despicable humans, but that peace was short-lived, for it was not long before I discovered that man never ceases to seek, hunt, and extinguish.

"Still, I was very lucky. My four-footed hero was accompanied by other species of animals. They moved as if in a caravan, like a large herd. That very day I knew that not only did I have the power to communicate with them, but that I could achieve peace by creating a new community and building my own family.

"We marched on until we came upon a sort of natural fort of huge rocks with a cave inside that would protect me from the sun. So, we settled there. The wildlife I was living with was bringing me fresh cattle meat and fruits. I had never eaten so well in my life. I enjoyed sharing those delicacies with my brothers and sisters; I could not ask for more, until one day I discovered what had happened when I lost consciousness. The fateful night I was released my parents were eaten by hyenas after being trampled by a rhino. I remember thinking that I could never be as happy as I was at that very moment," she said as the animals crowded around her."

Deesa threw the gem towards the siblings, but before they could catch it, it was snatched away by a bird of prey.

"I'm so sorry you had to go through something like that. I can't even imagine what you must have felt and suffered, but I have to ask you something. Do you know how your tutor got that stone?" Sasha asked.

"It was given to him by a creature from another world."

Sasha was petrified. She remembered the night when she first learned about magic, relived the scene when she woke up alone in that little room and immortalized the moment when she and James peeked through the large window of the mansion looking for her grandmother. Then they discovered terrifying eyes watching them from outside the big house. They terrorized their little souls with a huge claw, which he hid when he saw the young, hooded lady approaching him. If so, Grandma must have known something, but why didn't she mention it? Could it have been Mihara and Rasnar who sent the gem?

"Time is running out, my sister and brother, to which of the two of you should I give the stone, the girl, the boy? In the animal kingdom, he who deserves leadership must prove it by exposing his power in a fight to the death," proposed the albino.

"Don't listen to her. She's crazy because of a childhood trauma. We should leave the gem here and go as soon as possible. Neither Rasnar nor Kundalini mentioned any of this; we only have three pendants for three paths in heaven. We must complete our mission by returning home without distractions. You can always tell them what happened and come back here for the stone, if necessary," Carol commented.

"But what about the picture? That picture is proof of the relationship between this woman and our family," James replied.

"Well, let Deesa come with us, so we can clarify everything together with Mihara and Rasnar, to have better answers, okay?" replied her friend.

"Carol, she can dominate the Garos, which makes her a risk. I am willing, this may be the ultimate test that will lead us to where we should be," said the boy eager to know more about his parents.

"James, remember that we carry the darkness in us, and I let myself be carried away by it once." Sasha lowered her head. She was still holding the photograph in her hands. Then she noticed the effigy that so clearly showed the union of several people under the apparent secret society to which they were linked, without knowing why they were associated. "Nor do I know what the purpose of the existence of Freemasonry was. Are we its leaders or are we under someone's command? It seems obvious from the portrait that most of the members have disappeared, and it doesn't look like that coincidence was mere coincidence. How did they come to create it or join it? And against what?" Sasha wondered aloud, desperate for answers.

"The truth will appear when you make a decision."

Now they not only had to save planet Earth and Argua, but they had to unravel the truth that the ghosts of his past had confronted, even if it might cost her life or that of her brother. The question was whether she could bear the burden of her own brother's non-existence better than her own death.

"Why does this have to happen to us?" Sasha muttered.

"It is never easy to be yourself."

Hearing Deesa utter these words, something stirred inside the young girl, who recovered a moment of history she had forgotten, one in which her beloved parents were arguing with a man in a hat in one of the mansion's rooms. It happened the morning of their disappearance. Those same exact words came out of that stranger's mouth. She had forgotten it until that precise moment when the albino unintentionally unearthed the scene in her memory. She herself unintentionally burst into that room, cutting the tension of the instant. Then the hatted gentleman she had never seen before approached her with an open book in his hand and showed little Sasha an ink-impregnated page that formed the figure of a dark-souled monster confronting a girl like her. How could she see so clearly now something she had completely forgotten; with the image of the ring the individual wore on one of his fingers and the engraving of a triangle. Her father indignantly closed that tome and handed it back to the man while shouting at him to go away.

The girl looked again at the photo showing her parents and recognized the man in question.

"The one who was your guardian visited my parents the morning of their passing," Sasha said.

"I don't know, I wasn't there," Deesa answered the young woman.

"That's your answer to everything, isn't it? What you were taught to say when in doubt," James replied.

"That book, the drawing I saw, the ink marks... That's the same book that was thrown at me, isn't it?" Sasha asked.

"I don't know what you're talking about," the albino defended herself.

"Of course not," said the boy.

"The book shows what we want to see, what we want or expect to happen, right? That's why, when I was in the rain, I only saw an ink stain, because that's what I wanted to see. I wanted to be right and decipher the riddle of its cover. Carol and I saw ourselves reflected in its pages because what we really longed for that stormy night in the library was not to get caught. James saw a cross because he wanted to see more," said Sasha.

"And I probably saw Aztrack tied up underwater because what I wanted most of all was to see Grandma happy. She still loves him even though he's gone. You played with her feelings by using her hopes," James pointed out.

"And the book showed a girl overthrowing evil because that's what your father wanted. That's why he wet one of the pages of the book, to intentionally show my parents what was going to be my future or yours, right? But my father refused, and they made him disappear along with my mother, for he had witnessed that scene. And now he sends his adopted daughter, the one who rescues animals from extinction to finish exterminating my lineage by poisoning my best friend and trying to get her to murder my own brother," said Sasha angrily.

"What have you done to us, witch?" asked Carol, facing Deesa.

"You are wrong. The book was not my adoptive father's, but your grandfather's, an acquisition for which he paid millions to feel a little closer to your grandmother, the one with the waterpowers. And it was your father who showed that magical tome to mine. It was your father who dipped one of the leaves, giving himself away. My guardian only went to talk to the Courdeils about his discovery, but when he told his supposed friend, his little girl came through the door and your father's worst fears were put on paper. Thus, my savior realized the similarity between the offspring of his comrade and the figure in the drawing, deciphering the enigma of the mysterious manuscript with the exposure of the precious secret that your dear parents, aware of how special you were, were trying to hide.

"If I hadn't sent one of these precious creatures to throw the tome at you, you would never have awakened from your pitiful bubble or made the slightest effort to defend who you are. You had to open your eyes and see the truth, or you would have spent the rest of your miserable life hiding in the shadows," Deesa snapped.

"The drakon you sent with the book bit me and made me change, both me and Ksuma. I almost lost my Garo because of you. You almost turned it into a beast unable to recognize its soulmate or any of us," Carol exclaimed.

"You are a human who, fortunately or unfortunately, has become a member of the team, but you are the weakest of the family and, therefore, the one who can die from any attack, which puts the others at risk.

"When one link falls off, the chain loses strength and evil gets free rein, understand?" replied the albino.

"I could have died and Ksuma with me. She could have turned into a mad creature, killing us all; he could have even killed many other innocents because of your great stupidity," Carol protested.

"But it wasn't like that, was it? You're still yourselves, but in an improved version, so you're welcome.

"Besides, creatures don't kill people; humans kill them," said Deesa positioning herself millimeters from the drakon's snout.

"How can we trust you?" James asked.

"Our parents belonged to one of the most powerful Freemasons in the world. The triangle they wore was their way of showing that they belonged to this cabal in question, one that continues to function today, hidden, and silent, waiting for Sasha's awakening. Always keeping a watchful eye on every little step taken by the girl of prophecy, the female who will give us hope when the prediction of our catastrophic future comes true, for she is haunting both this world and the world of your beloved beasts and beyond.

"For centuries the cult has revered power, but power does not exist without wisdom, a quality that comes from experiences in other cultures, as well as a deep study of the history that precedes us all, the history that has not been tampered with. But the man who found me, as I told you, did not do it by chance. He raised me as a daughter, but his purpose was the result of his absolute obsession: to find the pieces of a puzzle that would save us all from massive destruction.

"This gave way to the analysis of extraordinary cases in which human persons like me were discovered and exposed by the media for the fact that they had managed to do something considered miraculous; an event for which there was no scientific explanation. Then my father observed a common pattern among certain humans who had lived in misery for most of their existence, trapped in a mental prison from a very early age, when they were children of an extraordinarily strong nature. They suffered from one day to the next a brutal change of both personality and attitude. Thus, they spent the rest of their childhood, adolescence and even adulthood immersed in agonizing bitterness, living in silence in a heartbreaking way, without any understanding from their loved ones or their social environment.

"Overnight and without knowing how or why, these beings had digested a radical change and showed the world something extraordinary, even though they had everything and everyone against them, without receiving any help regarding their situation or the disease that plunged them into infinite sadness. In these cases, the victims coincided in one detail: they had come to see spirits, creatures from another world, strange things that had tormented them and against which they had had to fight throughout their lives. Until, naturally, one day these beings extirpated all resistance, leading them to surrender, thus accepting abandonment, adopting the resilience that gave them that impenetrable strength that preceded them, but no one was able to appreciate.

"After the process of acceptance, these people became capable of creating and doing incredible things never seen before and achieving inner peace with the approval of the whole world. Their success was only appreciated when they proved their worth and the same people who abandoned them in their worst moments were the ones who applauded them. Thanks to their triumph they were able to be free, to be themselves, and they walked away from everything and everyone, without remorse or sorrow. Although they were unable to forget or forgive for obvious reasons.

"Freemasonry interpreted it as cases of abduction and invested time and money in the study of what appeared to be the transition of the afterlife. It discovered the existence of other lives outside of this planet, coexisting in the same universe. But my father discovered something that others failed to see: these beings were not parasites from another galaxy using the body to hoard worshippers and provoke a war against humanity. And this made the secret society put him in the spotlight, labeling him a spy and an ally of the aliens.

"My tutor was the only one to realize that it was not a threat, but an enriching fact in the history of our planet. It showed that we ourselves are part galactic and that as we sharpened our senses, we were able to embrace that part of us that we have blocked, the part that prevents us from having powers. He announced that, if we continued in this way, we would end up annulling that gift completely, until there would be no trace of our power or sixth sense left, eradicating our true self. And this event could seriously affect the Earth.

"This idea was corroborated with the discovery of the Garos, something he managed to perceive after the exhaustive study of each individual case, with the historical reading of past experiences and ancient accounts of other cultures, until he believed in them so much that they became his only reality. He spent his days meditating and exposing himself to all kinds of experiences, some of them extremely dangerous, putting his theories before his life in order to find his inner self, his spirit or, as he called it, his reborn from beyond.

"My father came to your house because he trusted your parents. He wanted to communicate to them his discovery and the fears that were haunting his conscience with the acts committed by the guild and the direction he was taking in this regard. When your father took out the book in order to give him an explanation about the magic of the world he did not know, to try to decipher the relationship between us and those beings through the water, you came through the door and your father's worries were reflected on the page of the blank manuscript he had just moistened. On it was sketched a girl facing a fearsome darkness, which my father took as a prophetic sign that you would save us all. But when the Courdeils suffered that fatal accident, that same day and without their bodies being found, he went into a cycle of paranoia. He said that the organization was after him and that was why he had to contact those beings as soon as possible. He had to accept his inner self in its totality to form a single being that would reach the ears of the two worlds and prevent the disappearance of the cosmos.

"I found my father drowned in the pond of this house. He had left a letter hidden for me with indications of the steps I should take from that moment on in case he did not make contact with the other world around us. But the news only spoke of a case of suicide, an invention of powerful people making us believe a lie, knowing that the reality was that he sacrificed himself for all of us.

"It wasn't his fault your parents disappeared. He protected you, Sasha. He saw to it that we were both safe. He knew we were special, and he hid us from the evil that scatters the ignorance that overflows the people of this world. He offered us the chance to live and shine by being who we really are, in a world cruelly designed to make us all the same, that classifies us by gender and despises those of us who are unique with disgust and envy," Deesa challenged.

"You forget that I had no powers back then. I did absolutely nothing unique, nothing other than marginalize myself from society, becoming a misfit," Sasha explained.

"That's what you think. When we were kids, we didn't value our potential, because it seems normal and every day to us; something so natural that everyone should see it. My father did enough research to discover the true identity of your grandmother Mihara and forged an alliance with her and others to fight against evil to save the universe.

"He provoked a division of ideals from within Freemasonry, managing to split it into two parties of completely opposite values. Some went too far manipulating the media, committing atrocious acts, rambling irrational, and inhuman barbarities from public and powerful positions, giving a deplorable example to the entire universe, and establishing erroneous values in our society and in future generations. The other division was forced to create a clandestine Freemasonry. Your grandmother was one of the founders. She had the support and participation of many other beings of extreme power and generosity, but they act from the shadows.

"Do not blame Mihara. We are all part of an entity greater than ourselves, and this implies assuming its conditions, directly and indirectly, to one day be able to take control. Something to be prepared for," said Deesa.

"I thought we were in an advanced society. We should be able to coexist with opposing ideas; it is the definition of democracy since everyone has the right to express themselves. But if we must fight to do so, stooping to their level, so that our freedom of speech, our true selves and our rights are not taken away, then so be it," Carol replied.

"Yes, we can, and we will prove it by example, so I will not fight against my sister, but with her. I need not override the opposite but work together with her for the good of both of us, as equals, regardless of race, gender, or species. We will polish our unique qualities, highlighting the differences as virtues," James offered, taking Sasha's hand.

"You are right. May you achieve your purpose without losing such valuable principles. The world will be a better place for everyone," commented Deesa, offering them the gem on the palm of her hand.

"Don't let go, James, and let's grab it together."

Holding hands, they joined the other so that Deesa dropped the stone on the joint. Instantly, an explosion of light blinded them, leaving the siblings lying on the ground, each with a piece of the gemstone embedded in their forehead. For an instant, the youngsters stopped having complexes, shame, prejudices, limitations, fears, sadness, anger, and those emotions that had prevented them from being better people and enjoying every second of their lives. Those limitations became nothing; they disappeared without a trace, even from memory.

It turns out that the only certain thing in this life is death; no one and nothing can escape it. The clock is ticking, but not in our favor, unless we accept our destiny, living and letting live. Nothing is more important than amortizing the present - the only true thing - until the day it is our turn to leave. It might be today, tomorrow, in a month, or in a few years. But when it happens, there will be no turning back.

www.ingramcontent.com/pod-product-compliance
Lightning Source LLC
Chambersburg PA
CBHW022359110726
47903CB00004B/1053